Malibu had been very ~~~ the place was bursting ~~~

Or maybe *because* it ~~~. There was one vampire who'd definitely made his life more intense and more exciting – Sienna. Being with her made him feel more alive, even though entering her world had nearly made him *dead*. He'd been attacked by a crazed vampire, consumed with bloodlust, and shot with a crossbow by a vampire hunter . . .

And yet in spite of all the near-death experiences, Jason wouldn't have had his life any other way. Sienna was worth it all.

'Stylish, edgy and addictive'
Publishing News

'Outrageously addictive, super cool, and as sharp as a wooden stake right to the heart'
The Bookseller

Also available in this seductive,
supernatural series:

Bloodlust & Initiation:
2 Vampire Beach novels

Ritual & Legacy:
2 Vampire Beach novels

High Stakes & Hunted

ALEX DUVAL

2 Vampire Beach novels

RED FOX

HIGH STAKES & HUNTED: 2 VAMPIRE BEACH NOVELS
A RED FOX BOOK 9781849410007

First published in Great Britain by Red Fox,
an imprint of Random House Children's Books
A Random House Group Company

Copyright © Working Partners Limited, 2009

1 3 5 7 9 10 8 6 4 2

HIGH STAKES
First published in Great Britain by Red Fox, 2008
Copyright © Working Partners Limited, 2008

HUNTED
First published in Great Britain by Red Fox, 2008
Copyright © Working Partners Limited, 2008

The Random House Group Limited supports the Forest Stewardship Council (FSC),
the leading international forest certification organization. All our titles that are printed
on Greenpeace-approved FSC-certified paper carry the FSC logo. Our paper procurement
policy can be found at www.rbooks.co.uk/environment.

Red Fox Books are published by Random House Children's Books,
61–63 Uxbridge Road, London W5 5SA

www.kidsatrandomhouse.co.uk
www.rbooks.co.uk

Addresses for companies within The Random House Group Limited can be found at:
www.randomhouse.co.uk/offices.htm

THE RANDOM HOUSE GROUP Limited Reg. No. 954009

A CIP catalogue record for this book is available from the British Library.

Printed in the UK by CPI Bookmarque, Croydon, CR0 4TD.

HIGH STAKES

by Alex Duval

To AC, for letting me tag along
on the trips to Malibu

Special thanks to
Laura Burns & Melinda Metz

One

'March in Malibu. Perfection,' Jason Freeman murmured to himself as he stared out over the Pacific. The afternoon sunlight glinted off the surface and caught the rising waves, turning them into a glimmering paradise that just begged to be surfed.

'Jason, stop staring out of the window. I'm desperate!' Smiling, Jason turned to see his girlfriend, Sienna Devereux, gesturing frantically around Mystère. 'I can't find the dress.'

Jason glanced about the tiny boutique. There had to be 500 dresses crammed into the ultra-posh space. 'Um . . .'

'The *red* dress,' Sienna said, a note of exasperation creeping into her throaty voice. 'The one I've been talking about all week.'

'Um . . .' Jason said again. It was true; she'd been talking about a dress all week. But it hadn't occurred to him that he was supposed to be actually listening to the details.

'You're hopeless,' Sienna said, shaking her head, but a smile played along her lips.

'Too bad Belle had therapy today,' Jason said. Usually Sienna's best friend would be the one helping score a fashion find, while Jason would be out riding the waves. As much as he loved Malibu – and as much as he loved Sienna – Jason wasn't entirely comfortable hanging in the pricey boutiques along Cross Creek Road. No matter how hard he tried, he still couldn't tell the difference between a Prada bag or a pleather knock off from Target. When it came time to find clothes for himself, he still preferred to hit the Gap like a normal person. Although ever since he'd started dating Sienna a few months back, 'normal' was a thing of the past.

That was because 'normal' didn't include vampires.

Jason had barely been in Malibu for a month before he was neck-deep in vampire society. Everywhere he turned in DeVere Heights, the exclusive neighborhood where he lived, there was another vampire family. Zach Lafrenière, the coolest guy in his class at school? A vampire. Brad Moreau and Michael Van Dyke, his friends from the swim team? Vampires. And, oh yeah, Sienna Devereux, the girl he'd fallen head over heels for the very first second he laid eyes on her? A vampire.

It had been hard enough adjusting to the fact that

vampires were real. But then Jason had kept getting all caught up in vampire-heavy situations. Like when Luke Archer, a rogue vampire, had been overcome by the Bloodlust and tried to kill him – which was nothing compared to the vampire hunter who'd shot a metal stake into Jason's chest, thinking he was a vampire. The guy had actually killed Belle's boyfriend, leaving Belle in need of therapy to help get over her grief.

And then there was Jason's Aunt Bianca. She'd been a vampire for years and kept it from her family. But now Jason knew, and his younger sister, Danielle, knew. And they also knew that Bianca was slowly going insane as a result of her transformation from human to vampire.

It had been a pretty vampire-filled school year. Every time Jason thought he might be able to relax and just enjoy his time with Sienna, some kind of vampire issue intervened. 'Thank God it's spring break,' he muttered as he looked through another rack of dresses.

'Nothing but fun in the sun for a whole week,' Sienna agreed. 'That's why I wanted the red dress so much. There's bound to be a party or two during spring break, and I look fierce in this dress.'

'You look fierce in everything,' he told her. It was true.

Sienna gave him her slowest, sexiest smile. 'But you

would especially like me in this. Trust me. That's why I wanted it.'

'Then why didn't you buy it last week when you first saw it?' he asked.

'I didn't have enough with me.'

That one stopped Jason in his tracks. '*You* didn't have enough money? Just how much does this dress cost?'

She slapped his arm. 'I had maxed out my credit card paying for our group dinner at Duke's the night before. I figured the dress could wait a few days.'

'I've searched two whole racks,' Jason announced. 'And the only red thing was this. But I think it's a belt.' He held up a long, flimsy scarf-like thing.

'That's a shirt,' Sienna told him.

He frowned at it. 'If you say so.'

'We've looked through every single thing here. Somebody else must have bought it,' Sienna sighed in frustration.

'I'm sorry,' he said, reaching for her hand.

'It was a *killer* dress,' Sienna replied. 'I can't believe it's gone.'

Jason held out his arms. 'You need a hug.'

'I need that dress.' But she laughed and stepped toward him. 'But I'll take a hug, too.' She slipped her slim, tanned arms around his waist and laid her head on his shoulder.

Perfect, Jason thought, as he always did when he held her. It had been a hard road for the two of them. When they had first met, Sienna had still been with her longtime boyfriend, Brad. And after she and Brad had split up, her parents had tried to prevent her from dating Jason. But now, at long last, he and Sienna were together for real.

'Oh, my God!' Sienna exclaimed, and jerked away from him.

'What?' Jason cried, instantly on alert.

She ignored him, her dark eyes fixed on the glass doors of the store. 'I can't believe it,' she murmured. Her hand gripped his arm so tightly it hurt. '*She* shouldn't be here . . .'

'Who?' Jason twisted around to see what Sienna was staring at. Had his Aunt Bianca come back to town? Or was it some other vampire-themed threat to his happiness?

But instead it was just Sienna. Or at least someone who looked almost enough like Sienna to be her clone. The dark-haired girl was walking jauntily across the street, literally stopping traffic as she passed. The cars had a green light, but nobody seemed to mind the fact that a gorgeous girl had stepped out in front of them.

Jason heard some appreciative honks and catcalls as she made her way up onto the sidewalk in front of Mystère. She turned and flashed the cars a peace sign.

'Hmm. Sleek black hair, check. Kickin' bod, check. Gorgeous smile, check,' Jason said. 'But wait, *you're* standing right here. Which means that *she* could only be—'

'Paige!' Sienna cried, racing for the door.

Jason flung the red shirt-scarf thing over a rack and went after her. By the time he caught up, Sienna was out on the sidewalk, her arms tight around the other girl.

'What are you doing here?' Sienna squealed.

'Getting my hair cut,' Paige replied.

Sienna quickly released her and studied the hair for a moment. 'Looks gorgeous.'

'Thanks. You'd think I could find a good salon in Paris, but . . .' The girl's throaty voice trailed off as her eyes traveled over Jason, taking him in from head to toe. 'Wow! Brad's had a lot of plastic surgery,' she cracked.

'This is Jason Freeman,' Sienna announced, grabbing Jason's hand. 'Jason, this is my sister.'

'The famous Paige.' Jason nodded. 'I've heard a lot about you.'

'It's all true, no matter what they say,' Paige

murmured flirtatiously, twirling a lock of dark hair around her finger. 'Especially the naughty stuff!'

'Naughty?' Sienna repeated, raising an eyebrow.

'Too cheesy?' Paige laughed. 'Anyway, nice to finally meet you, Jason. Sienna hasn't bothered to tell me much about you, but I've managed to find out quite a lot all on my own.'

Jason didn't really know what to say to that. He settled for, 'She was probably scared that if she told you how cool I am, you'd fly back from Paris and steal me away.'

'And I might have,' Paige agreed, with a teasing little toss of her head.

'Well, you are older, right?' Jason said.

'And taller,' Paige added.

'See?' Jason teased Sienna. 'I could always trade up.'

'Enough!' Sienna smacked Jason on the arm – a tiny bit too hard. 'Paige, how come you're back from college so early?'

Paige reached out and rubbed Jason's arm where Sienna had hit him. 'That's gonna leave a mark,' she said.

'Probably,' he agreed, shooting Sienna a smile. 'But I don't mind. I dig the "super-strength", as Adam would call it.'

'Who's Adam?' Paige inquired, absently twisting her

hair up into a bun, then letting it go again so that it cascaded down her back.

'Adam Turnball,' Sienna told her. 'Jason's best friend.'

Paige looked blank.

'You know, the sheriff's son,' Sienna prompted.

'Oh!' Paige's full lips curved into a mischievous smile. 'I forgot Sheriff Turnball had a son.'

'Paige had a few brushes with the law when she was at DeVere Heights,' Sienna told Jason. 'She and Sheriff Turnball are old friends.'

'It wasn't my fault. It's just that I had a rule. If a guy wanted to date me, he had to be able to walk out to the end of the jetty at the beach,' Paige said innocently.

'During high tide, in the middle of the night,' Sienna added.

So it helped if he was a vampire with great eyesight, great balance, superhuman strength, and the ability to heal fast if he hurt himself on the rocks, Jason thought.

Paige just shrugged. 'I can do it, so a guy who wants to be with me should be able to do it, too.'

'Adam's father has a thing about that jetty,' Jason said.

'Yeah, because people slip and fall and crack their heads open. Or they get swept off it and drown,' Sienna said. 'The sheriff looks bad when people start dying in his town.'

Paige just shrugged again, a wicked little gleam in her eye. 'Nobody drowned. I was always there to save them.'

'And to get caught by the sheriff so Mom could have a heart attack every time he brought you home in the cop car,' Sienna pointed out.

Jason watched as the two sisters laughed. They looked so much alike that they could pass for twins. But the more he saw them together, the more he noticed their differences. Paige was constantly in motion, playing with her hair, talking with her hands, bouncing on the balls of her feet as she spoke. Sienna was the exact opposite, as calm as still water. It was one of the things Jason loved about her – you could never be sure exactly what was going on beneath the surface.

'You still haven't told me what you're doing here,' Sienna was saying. 'You're supposed to be in school for at least another month. And I thought you were then going backpacking round Europe for the summer.'

'Yeah . . .' Paige hesitated for an instant, then her dark eyes lit up. 'Wait, I forgot! I bought you something.' She flipped through the four shopping bags on her arm and held out one that said 'Mystère'.

'Weren't we just in there?' Jason asked.

'Yes,' Sienna replied, her voice filled with excitement. She grabbed the bag from her sister and pulled out a red dress, its silky skirt spilling over her hands. 'Oh. My. God! You got me the red dress!'

'Isn't it killer?' Paige exclaimed. 'I was in there earlier and the second I saw it, I knew it would look incredible on you.'

Sienna flung her arms around Paige's neck. 'I don't know how I survived without you this year.'

'Neither do I.' Paige laughed. 'Have you ever been to El Corazon?'

'That place on Ellice?' Sienna asked. 'Uh, no. It's a hangout for bikers.'

'Yes. But the salads are to die for. I'm not kidding.' Paige cocked her head to the side. 'You're not afraid of a few guys on bikes, are you, Jason?'

'With you two there to protect me? No way,' Jason replied.

'Good. You're driving.' Paige looped her arm through Sienna's and headed off down the sidewalk.

Jason shook his head and followed the Devereux girls. It had been a wild ride since the moment he met Sienna. And with her sister back in town, he had a feeling it was about to get even wilder . . .

Two

'Freeman!' Adam called out the instant Jason's feet hit the sand at Surfrider beach. 'I hear Paige is back in town.'

Jason gaped at him. 'I literally just dropped Sienna and her sister at home, and we didn't see a single other person from DeVere High the entire time we were at lunch,' he said. 'So how can you possibly know that Paige is back?'

'I'm connected, what can I say?' Adam shrugged and switched his folded beach towel from one arm to the other. 'So what's she doing here? Even in Paris, college goes until May, or so I'm told.'

'I don't know,' Jason admitted. 'Sienna wasn't expecting her, that's for sure. You should've seen her face when she spotted Paige.'

'She's probably just being mysterious,' Adam replied. 'You know, show up when you're least expected. It's a classic *femme fatale* move.'

'No movie talk. It's spring break,' Jason told him.

Adam could barely go for two minutes without referencing one film or another. In fact, he was usually filming everything he saw while he was busy spouting the references. 'Where's your camcorder, anyway?' Jason asked.

'You told me no filming during spring break, and I am nothing if not obedient,' Adam explained.

'I didn't tell you that, Belle did,' Jason pointed out. 'No filming, no movie talk, no dorkiness—'

'*Geek*iness,' Adam corrected him. 'It's a fine distinction. The dork is a social outcast. The geek is merely a connoisseur of a specific—'

'That, right there, is geekiness,' Jason interrupted. 'Stop it.'

'Fine.' Adam looked resigned for about two seconds. Then he brightened. 'Wait, if Belle isn't here to see me being geeky, do I still have to obey her?'

'I can't promise not to rat you out,' Jason said. 'The vampires can always tell when I'm lying, and if she asks me . . .'

'Oh, fine,' Adam grumbled. 'No film talk.'

Jason clapped him on the back, then peered out over the white sand of the beach to the swell of the blue-gray water. Stellar. The sun would be up for another few hours, and there was plenty of time for surfing.

'Incoming!' A volleyball flew through the air and landed at Adam's feet.

'Nice catch, Turnball,' Brad Moreau joked, jogging down the wooden steps from the cliff to the beach.

'I don't do balls,' Adam said. 'Not unless there are *bonita chiquitas* present.'

'Well, the only girl here is Brad,' Michael Van Dyke put in, following Brad down the stairs. 'And he's not very *bonita*.'

'I am, too,' Brad protested. He scooped up the ball. 'Everybody's gonna be here soon. You guys up for a game?'

'Sure,' Jason replied.

'Nope,' Adam said at the same time.

'OK then.' Brad and Van Dyke headed over to put up the volleyball net.

'If you're not gonna play, and you don't have your camera, what are you going to do?' Jason asked.

'Don't you worry about me, I've got a plan. You see, my ignorant friend, where the male of the species gather to show off their hunting and fighting skills' – he nodded toward Van Dyke, who now had Brad in a playful headlock – 'the females will soon follow. And when they arrive, I will be there to study them. Closely.' Adam marched over to a spot just out of volleyball range and unfurled his beach towel with a flourish.

Jason left him to it and headed over to the net. Aaron Harberts and Kyle Priesmeyer from the swim team came jogging up the beach to play. Jason was glad to see them. Sometimes the games got a little *too* crowded with vampires, and it was hard to keep up. Jason was a good athlete, but the vampires were faster, stronger, and more agile than any human – even him! It would be nice to have some other humans in the mix.

'Boys against girls!' somebody yelled behind him. Jason turned to see Maggie Roy waving from the wooden steps. Erin Henry was right behind her.

'There's only two of you,' Brad called back.

'So? We'll kick your butts anyway.' Maggie hurried over to Van Dyke and jumped up to hug him, wrapping her long, tanned legs around his waist and her arms around his neck.

'That makes your threat real convincing,' Erin said wryly.

Maggie grinned. 'Just cause I'm dating him doesn't mean I'm afraid to kick his ass!'

'Please. I rule at volleyball.' Van Dyke put her down and held out his hands for the ball.

'Obviously you two need to be on different teams,' Jason said. 'How about me, Van Dyke, and Brad against the girls. Oh, and Harberts and Priesmeyer.'

Harberts smiled tiredly. 'Nah, I'll sit this one out. That way the teams are even.' He went over and flopped in the sand next to Adam.

Jason peered at him, noticing the dude's pale skin and the bags under his eyes. *I wonder who he went out with last night,* Jason thought. *Erin, maybe?* It was easy to spot the humans who had been recently fed on by a vampire, if you knew what to look for. When a vampire was feeding on you, it felt amazing, like the best make-out session of all time. But afterwards, you felt exhausted. Happy, but exhausted. Harberts seemed to be in the happy place. And he had the whole week of spring break to recover.

'I hear Paige is home,' Brad commented as he served the ball.

Jason glanced at him, surprised. 'Fast grapevine.'

'You know it.' Brad laughed. 'You should be used to that by now – everyone in DeVere Heights knows one another's business.'

The ball came flying at Jason, so he set it up for Van Dyke to spike it. 'She's a trip, huh?'

'Who, Paige? You can't even imagine,' Brad replied. 'She once tricked the entire soccer team into shaving their heads on the same day. And believe me, it wasn't pretty.'

'Not everyone has a head as beautifully shaped

as mine,' the shaven-headed Priesmeyer put in.

'What's she doing back so early, anyway?' Van Dyke asked. 'She flunk out of college?'

'She probably just got bored in Paris. You know Paige,' Brad told him. They both laughed.

Jason opened his mouth to ask what they were talking about. Then Maggie leapt up and slammed the ball straight at him, and Jason forgot all about Sienna's big sister. The game kicked up a notch, and it took all his concentration just to keep up with the fast and furious volleys. By the time the game was over, even the vampires looked beat.

'Attention, attention!' Adam called suddenly. 'As your Surfrider Beach social director, I have an announcement to make. The queen and her court have just arrived.'

'What's he talking about?' Brad asked Jason.

'I'm never really sure,' Jason told him.

'Paige!' Erin shrieked. She and Maggie took off across the sand at a run. Jason turned to see Paige bounding down the steps toward them, with Belle Rémy right on her heels. Sienna followed more slowly, walking with Zach Lafrenière.

'How can I not have my camera for this?' Adam complained, coming up to Jason as the other guys headed over to greet Paige. 'I mean, look at them.

They're like a primetime soap in action. Beautiful girls, strapping guys – all with shiny hair and white teeth.'

Jason nodded, gazing at the group. 'Didn't you tell me Zach went to Paige's prom with her when he was just a freshman?' he asked.

'Thereby cementing his reputation as the single coolest human being on the planet,' Adam agreed. 'Well, not that he's a human. He's a vampire. He's a super-human. Wait, are they human? I never thought about that before. They're not *not* human, right? I mean, they're not a different species, are they? Are they?'

Jason just raised his eyebrows.

'I'm being geeky, huh?' Adam asked. 'Right. I'll take it down a notch.'

Zach stood next to Paige as she hugged all the others. He was actually smiling. *Have I ever seen him smile before?* Jason wondered. 'Do you think he's still into her?' he said.

'Hmm, tough call,' Adam replied. 'He does look suspiciously happy and relaxed. But I'm not sure there was ever anything romantic between them. Their families are such old friends, I kinda figured she took him to prom because he was safe.'

'Paige doesn't strike me as somebody who likes to take the safe option,' Jason said as Harberts wandered back over.

'You got that right,' Harberts told Jason. 'That girl is so hot she's dangerous. Must run in the family.' He dropped down onto Adam's towel and closed his eyes.

'That's my towel,' Adam pointed out.

Harberts was already asleep.

Adam turned back to Jason. 'The thing is, two weeks before her prom, Paige caused a mini-riot during a charity fundraiser,' he went on. 'Apparently she'd agreed to go to the prom with three different guys, and that was the day they all found out. Paige didn't really care, she just wanted to be able to wear three different dresses. She figured she'd go with one for cocktail hour, one for the dance, and one for the after parties.'

'So she wasn't dating any of them?' Jason asked.

'Nope. She always liked to keep her options open. I don't remember ever hearing that she had an actual boyfriend. Do you, Aaron?' He nudged Harberts with his bare foot. Harberts kept sleeping.

'Let me guess. The three guys found out, and they all banded together and refused to go with her?' Jason said.

Adam snorted. 'No, that's what would've happened if it was an old John Hughes movie. Actually, in that version they would've banded together and forced her to pick just one of them. And then she would've picked her geeky-yet-adorable best friend and gone with him instead.'

'Did she have a geeky-yet-adorable best friend?' Jason asked.

'No, I was too young for her to notice back then,' Adam replied.

'OK, focus. What actually did happen?' Jason asked.

'They all got into a really loud fight and ruined Mrs Devereux's silent auction for the International Red Cross. So Paige got grounded for a week, and she was so pissed off that she refused to go to prom with any of them. She took Zach instead.' Adam's eyes grew wide. 'Holy cow, could Zach have been the geeky-yet-adorable best friend?'

Jason glanced over at Zach, who looked like a young Keanu Reeves on a particularly good day.

'I know what you're thinking,' Adam said. 'You're thinking that, if he was, the rest of us might as well just kill ourselves.'

'Actually—'

'But you have to realize that the supernatural types have different definitions of geeky,' Adam went on, glancing at Harberts to make sure he was still asleep. 'In their world, it obviously means incredibly good looking, suave, and rich.'

'Then how come Belle thinks *you're* geeky?' Jason teased.

'Oh, you are cold. Cold!' Adam said, shaking his

head. He glanced down at Harberts. 'I'm never getting my towel back, am I?'

'I don't think Harberts is moving anytime soon,' Jason agreed.

'In that case, let's go say hi to the womenfolk.' Adam started across the hot sand, and Jason followed. But saying hello wasn't easy. Maggie, Erin, Belle, Brad and Van Dyke had Paige surrounded. Sienna was hanging back, letting the other girls have their time with her celebrity sister. But she definitely looked happy and relaxed. It was nice to see.

'But what about the cuffs?' Maggie was asking. 'American *Vogue* said not to cuff jeans anymore.'

'Maybe, but on the streets of Paris people were wearing cuffs,' Paige told her. 'And that's what matters, at least to me. Who cares what *Vogue* says?'

Brad's eyes glazed over. He grabbed Van Dyke's arm and hauled him away. 'I'm maxed out on the fashion talk. Come on, let's play.'

'But—' Van Dyke grumbled.

'So are you,' Brad interrupted pleasantly, dragging him off toward the volleyball net.

Maggie turned back to Paige. 'How about the shoes?'

'Forget the stupid clothes, I want to hear about your love life,' Erin put in. 'French guys? Tell us.'

Paige hesitated, then shook her head. 'I thought it was a little too obvious to date French men in France.' She tossed back her hair and grinned. 'If you really want to make them crazy, you have to date an American while you're there. Or even a Brit. It just baffles them.'

'I'm feeling unwelcome in this conversation,' Adam murmured to Jason. 'I don't think boys are supposed to hear this stuff. Our delicate egos can't handle it.'

'Paige is just teasing,' Zach said, coming over to join them. 'She only says that kind of stuff to get a reaction. Turnball, Freeman, good to see you.'

'What's up, Zach?' Jason replied, since Adam was staring in amazement. 'Big spring break plans?'

'Not yet. But I'm sure something will come up.' He glanced at Paige, then headed after Brad and Van Dyke.

'I'm sorry, but did Zach Lafrenière just greet us in a friendly manner?' Adam asked, still staring after Zach.

'He did,' Jason confirmed.

'Huh,' Adam murmured. 'That's so unlike him.'

It was true. Zach tended to be standoffish in general. Not that he was ever rude or anything, but he didn't usually go out of his way to be friendly.

'I think Paige brings out the best in him,' Jason commented. 'He's just happy she's back. So is Sienna.'

'Yeah, Paige is fun,' Adam said. He nodded toward

the girls, who were still grilling Paige on life in Paris. 'They're all happy she's back. They adore her. It's like watching Yoda with the younglings.'

'I heard that!' Belle called. She gave Adam a mock-stern look.

'Oops.' Adam turned bright red. 'The movie refs, they just come pouring out of me without any warning.'

'Well, admitting you have a problem is the first step,' Jason told him. 'Besides, everybody references *Star Wars*. I don't think that should count.'

'You should take that up with Belle at the next meeting of the Make Adam Cool Club.' Adam sighed. 'I guess I might as well play volleyball. Harberts is hogging my towel, anyway. You coming?'

'Yeah,' Jason said. He shot Sienna a smile, and she smiled back.

'Hold up!' Paige cried as he and Adam turned to go. 'Are you getting a game on?'

Jason nodded.

'Then I'll come with you. I haven't even said the words "beach volleyball" since I left for Paris. I want to play!'

She bounded down the steps and over to the net. 'Boys versus girls!' Paige yelled. She grabbed the ball and executed a perfect serve right into the middle of the boys' side. Zach leapt underneath it, smacking it up just before it hit the sand. Jason swooped in and spiked it over the net . . . and Sienna spiked it right back. This time it hit the ground.

'One-nothing!' Paige called with a wicked grin. She and Sienna slapped each other a high five, and the game was on.

It wasn't until the girls had slaughtered the guys 10–7 that everybody collapsed onto the sand to catch their breath. But even then, Paige seemed full of energy.

'You know what's the weirdest coincidence?' she asked.

'That you and I wear the same shoe size?' Adam joked.

Paige peered at his feet. 'You do have itty-bitty tootsies,' she teased, 'but I was talking about the fact that my parents are off on their cruise to Alaska this week. The very week that I get home. Isn't that weird?'

'I think what you're trying to say is, "isn't that cool?"' Zach told her.

Paige giggled. 'You got me.'

'Are you thinking party?' Maggie asked. 'Please tell me you're having a Paige Party!'

'It's up to Sienna.' Paige slipped her arm around Sienna's slim shoulders. 'What do you say, SiSi? Should we disobey the no-parties-in-the-house rule?'

'You have a no-parties rule?' Jason asked, surprised. 'I didn't know that.'

'It's my fault. I had a Halloween party my senior year that got a little out of control,' Paige admitted.

'It made the news,' Sienna said dryly.

'That's just because we invited those two reality show bimbos and they got into a fight for the cameras,' Paige replied. 'Mom and Dad will never know about this party, I promise. We won't even invite anybody who doesn't live in Malibu.'

Sienna hesitated.

'I'm thinking theme party,' Paige told her in a singsong voice.

'Oh, come on, Sienna,' Erin cried. 'A theme party would be such a perfect way to start off spring break.'

'What's the theme?' Sienna asked.

A big, slow smile spread over Paige's full lips. '1960s cocktail party.'

Sienna's eyes lit up, and Jason knew she was hooked. 'You mean with little hotdogs on sticks and pink drinks served in cool glasses?' she asked.

'And miniskirts and bouffant hairdos and fake eye-lashes,' Paige added. 'And lounge music!'

Suddenly everyone was talking at once, putting in ideas for the party. Jason watched Sienna talking animatedly with her sister. She was psyched about playing hostess, he could see.

But a tiny trickle of worry ran down his spine. The Devereux sisters having a party – that would be one of the biggest things to happen all year. And when big things happened in DeVere Heights, trouble usually followed.

Three

'Do I look OK?' Danielle asked as she and Jason walked toward the front door of Sienna's house the next night.

'Dani, you've asked me that three times now,' Jason told his younger sister. 'You look great. You know you look great. You spent two hours getting ready and making sure every single thing on your entire body looked completely perfect.'

'Yeah, but did it work?' she pressed. 'Do I actually look perfect?'

Jason rolled his eyes. 'Is there some guy here you're trying to impress? Because you're obsessing.'

'No.' Danielle bit her lip. 'I haven't really been in the mood for dating again since . . .' Her voice trailed off, but Jason knew what she was talking about. She'd been in a serious relationship with a vampire, Ryan Patrick, but they'd broken up after Aunt Bianca had talked them into having Ryan transform Dani into a vampire. They hadn't gone through with the transformation, thankfully, but it had been a close call. A blood test

27

had shown that Danielle's DNA was incompatible with the vampire genes. If she'd transformed, she would eventually have gone insane – just like Aunt Bianca. The stress of the whole situation had been too much for the couple to handle, and they'd decided to call it quits.

Still, Dani and Ryan had really been in love. The breakup had hit her hard. Jason nudged her with his shoulder. 'You don't have to date until you're ready,' he told her.

'I know.' She adjusted the strap of her vintage black cocktail dress. 'But I have to look good. I need to impress Paige Devereux.'

'Paige? Why?'

'Jason, are you the most oblivious person in the world? Paige is, like, famous in DeVere Heights,' Danielle said. 'I've been hearing stories about her since the first day of school.'

'Well, yeah, so have I,' he admitted. 'But so what?'

'So what? So she's important, that's what,' Dani said. 'If she likes you, it means you're cool. It's as simple as that.'

'Wow, I didn't realize she was so all-powerful,' Jason joked as he opened the door. Immediately, Frank Sinatra's voice hit his ears. The music filled the entire house.

Dani sucked in a breath. 'Look at this place,' she said reverently.

'It *is* pretty spectacular,' Jason agreed. Usually, Sienna's house was very spare, all beiges and whites on top of one another. But tonight the whole thing was drenched with color. Huge panels of gold lamé hung from the high ceilings all the way to the floor, one on each wall. Every single surface in the room had a tall vase on it, each one a different jewel-tone color. And each vase had an arrangement of gigantic calla lilies exploding from the top. Even the lighting was colorful: glowing patches of pink light pooled on the marble floors and bathed partygoers in a rosy glow.

'Temptation?' Paige purred, stepping up to them.

Jason took in her teased hair, her heavily-lined eyes, and her clingy gold cocktail dress. 'Huh?' he said.

Paige beckoned lazily, and a waiter rushed over with a tray of drinks in martini glasses. The liquid inside was dark red.

Blood red, Jason thought.

'Temptation,' Paige repeated, her voice husky. 'It's our signature cocktail.'

This is feeling like a bad vampire movie, Jason thought. And then Paige laughed.

'It's the theme,' she reminded him. 'Silly Sixties

cocktail party, remember? They always had a signature drink.' She turned to Dani. 'Who's this?'

'I'm, um, Danielle . . .' Dani practically whispered. Her gray eyes were wide. She looked as if she were meeting Nicole Kidman instead of Paige Devereux.

'My sister, Dani,' Jason explained. 'Dani, this is Paige.'

'Sorry, I should've figured out who you were,' Paige said, smiling warmly at Dani. 'Sienna told me Jason's sister was gorgeous. I was just expecting a little blondie like Jason, but your hair is such an incredible red!'

'Thank you,' Dani gasped, putting her hand to her hair. 'I actually teased it for this party. I've never tried that before.'

'It totally worked,' Paige assured her.

Danielle smiled happily.

'Jason, you take a Temptation,' Paige ordered him. 'I think Dani needs a Sweet Tooth.'

'What's that?' Dani asked.

'I'll show you.' Paige grabbed Danielle's hand and pulled her off toward the flower-decked bar in the living room. Jason took a red drink from the tray, feeling grateful. His sister had been so nervous on the way here, but Paige had managed to put her at ease in about ten seconds.

The music switched from Sinatra to some kind of

Dean Martin and Sammy Davis Jr sing-along as Jason moved further into the house.

'Crab cake?' asked a waitress in a sparkly minidress.

'Sure.' Jason took one and put it in his mouth.

'Check it out!' Danielle cried, rushing back over to him. 'Is this the best thing ever, or what?' She held up a lowball glass with some kind of clear drink in it – and an upside-down cherry lollipop. 'The lollipop is the stirrer! Isn't that too cute?' Dani's gaze shifted to something over Jason's shoulder. 'Ooh, there's Kristy and Billy. Later.' She took off, leaving Jason in her wake.

He laughed. She'd certainly got over her nerves. But as he watched her head over to her friends, he noticed someone else watching, too: Ryan Patrick, Dani's vampire ex-boyfriend. The guy's eyes were glued to Jason's sister.

'Poor Ryan. He's still a little lovesick,' a throaty voice murmured in Jason's ear.

Startled, he turned to see Sienna standing next to him. Her black hair was done up in some kind of complicated twist, and long gold earrings dangled almost to her shoulders – which were bare, because the little hot-pink cocktail dress she was wearing was strapless. Jason swallowed hard: sometimes he couldn't even believe how beautiful she was. He slipped his arm around her waist and drew her close for a kiss.

'Is this the new boyfriend?' somebody asked.

Jason drew back from Sienna, and realized that three people he'd never seen before were staring at him.

'Yup,' said Sienna.

'Cute, huh?' Paige put in, rejoining them. 'Jason, meet Tiffany, Jon, and Suze, some of my old DeVere High friends.'

As Jason said hello, he did a quick vampire check and decided that Tiffany and Jon were the fanged type and Suze wasn't. There was an indefinable air about the vampires that he was starting to recognize. He was developing 'Vladar'.

'Where's everybody else?' Sienna asked.

'Paige is the only one who's back from college so far,' Suze said. 'The three of us are all up at Stanford, so it was easy for us to fly in for the weekend, but the rest of our crowd is spread all over the world. And Paige didn't give us much notice that she was having a party.'

'When people get home in May, we'll have another big soirée,' Paige put in. 'This party's for you, SiSi. I think you deserve some fun.'

'I agree.' Jason squeezed Sienna's hand.

Just then, a loud crash reverberated through the house. 'Oh, *snap*!' some guy yelled. 'You totally broke that sculpture!'

Sienna shot Paige a panicked look, but Paige just patted her arm. 'No worries,' she said. 'I've got it.'

She headed across the room, followed by her friends. 'Hey, guys,' Paige called. 'What's going on?'

Stu Obermeyer, a big guy from school, gestured to his friend, who was even bigger. 'He's so drunk that he's walking into things. He broke your statue.'

'I did not,' the other guy growled. 'You pushed me!'

'Oh, that little statue,' Paige said, stepping in between them. 'It's not valuable, don't worry. But maybe you two could help me move it outside before it gets knocked over again? You look strong enough to carry it, even though it's made of stone.'

'Yeah, we can help,' Stu told her. The other guy nodded, and they both picked up the broken sculpture and followed Paige out the front door.

'Jon will get them to leave now,' Sienna said. 'He'll drive them home.'

'What about the sculpture?' Jason asked her.

'It's a statue of a peacock that Paige rented for the party. You don't think we'd be crazy enough to leave real artwork out, do you?' Sienna laughed.

Just then, Paige came back into the room with Tiffany. Paige had a pitcher of cocktails, and began offering refills to anyone who needed them – and some who didn't.

'Your sister is great at the hostess thing,' Jason said. 'Stu and his drunk friend didn't even phase her.'

'Nothing rattles her,' Sienna replied. 'And she was born to party.'

'Then let her handle things, and come dance with me,' Jason said, pulling her out to the patio, where couples were swaying underneath palm trees strung with tiny white lights. Sienna snuggled against him and began to move. Jason closed his eyes and let his hands slide down her back.

'Jason! Help!' Adam's voice broke the moment.

'He can't help you,' Jason heard Belle say sternly. 'Nobody can help you!'

Jason opened his eyes just as Adam ducked behind him. 'I think she might actually hurt me,' Adam said. 'You've got to protect me, man.'

By now Belle had caught up to him. She stood with her hands on her hips, frowning. 'Do you see what he's wearing? Do you?'

Adam sheepishly stepped from behind Jason, revealing his outfit: tight green corduroy pants and a matching double-breasted jacket.

Sienna burst out laughing. 'You look like Austin Powers!'

'It's a Sixties theme party, isn't it?' Adam said. 'I'm dressed appropriately.'

'Adam, you're only supposed to use the theme in ways that make you look *good*,' Belle told him. 'You don't see Jason wearing puke-colored skinny pants!'

'No, mine were at the cleaners,' Jason joked.

'But it's a theme party,' Adam repeated helplessly.

'Which means it's an excuse for girls to wear really great vintage dresses,' Belle replied. 'That's the whole point. Nobody cares what the boys wear — as long as they don't look ridiculous.'

'But that's sexist,' Adam argued. 'Guys should get to have fun, too.'

'A month. I've spent an entire month trying to teach you how to be a chick magnet.' Belle threw up her hands in despair. 'And now you do this. You're hopeless!' She turned and stalked off, the full skirt of her dark red cocktail dress swinging around her legs.

Adam followed. 'But I'm being ironic! I just need to find the kind of girl who appreciates ironic.'

Jason glanced at Sienna, and they both burst out laughing. 'How long before she gives up on him entirely?' Jason asked.

'She won't stop until she finds him a girl,' Sienna said confidently. 'Belle doesn't like to fail at anything.'

'I don't know, Adam can be pretty stubborn. I think he might just be too much for her to handle.'

'Maybe we should bet on it,' Sienna joked.

Jason held out his hand, pinky extended. 'I'll bet you that Belle gives up on Project Find Adam a Girl within the next two weeks.'

'Ooh, I didn't know he was a gambling man,' Paige cut in, making her way across the patio with a now-empty pitcher. 'Careful, SiSi. Jason might be more my type than yours!' She passed them by with a wink.

'Does she flirt with everyone?' Jason asked.

'Yup. Boys, girls, dogs, cats. She flirts with waiters and salespeople and totally random people on the street.' Sienna chuckled. 'It's just who she is, she doesn't even realize she's doing it.'

'That's why it's charming,' Jason decided. 'She makes everyone feel as if she likes them.'

Sienna nodded. 'I think she does like everyone. I always wanted to be more outgoing the way Paige is.'

Jason took her hand. 'Well, don't start tonight. I was thinking we'd go in the opposite direction. Less outgoing, more private?'

'Sounds nice,' Sienna murmured, moving in for another kiss, 'but I don't think I can really skip out on my own party. How about we find a spot on the couches in the game room?'

'There's a game room?'

'Just for tonight,' she explained. 'Old-style board games, Twister and ping pong – stuff like that.'

'As long as I'm sitting on a couch and you're kissing me, I don't even care if people are playing Parcheesi behind us,' Jason quipped.

They found an empty loveseat in the game room, but it was only a few minutes before Belle found them. 'He's got Lisa Folliero interested,' she cried excitedly as she flopped down next to Sienna. 'Look!'

Sure enough, Adam had Lisa – Jason was pretty sure she was a junior – engaged in learning how to best hit a ping pong ball. Nearby, Paige was arranging a couple of rows of lowball glasses on the ping pong table.

Sienna squinted at the table. 'What are they playing?'

'Cocktail pong,' Belle said. 'It was Paige's idea. Beer pong with cocktails.'

'Sweet Tooth versus Kamikazes,' Paige announced. 'Lisa's a Sweet Tooth. I'm a Kamikaze. Who's with me?'

'Wait, if you're on the Kamikaze team, that means you stand on the side with the Kamikaze shots, right?' Adam asked.

'Right. And you try to hit the ball into a glass on the Sweet Tooth side,' Paige told him. 'Then the team on that side tries to hit balls into your Kamikaze glasses.'

'And if a ball lands in the glass on your side, you have to drink it?' Lisa asked.

'You got it,' Paige said. 'So who's with me?'

'I am,' Adam replied immediately. 'I'd much rather

be forced to drink a Kamikaze than a Sweet Tooth. I don't have one. A sweet tooth, I mean.'

'Oh. My. God. He is so clueless,' Belle exploded. She leapt up off the loveseat and practically ran over to Adam. 'No! I'm on the Kamikaze team with Paige,' she told him. 'Adam, you have to be on the Sweet Tooth team with Lisa.'

'But I don't like Sweet—'

'I'm Kamikaze. You're *with Lisa*,' Belle repeated, dropping her voice to a whisper.

'I think she would actually smack him upside the head right now if she didn't think it would drive Lisa away,' Sienna commented. Jason nodded.

'No, if he doesn't like that drink, he doesn't have to play,' Lisa said. 'I'm sure somebody else is willing.'

'I am,' Brad called from a card table in the corner. 'I'll kick your butt, Paige!'

Belle threw up her hands in defeat, but Van Dyke grabbed Brad's arm and yanked him back into his seat. 'We're in the middle of a hand.'

'Oh, all right,' Brad grumbled, turning back to the poker game he was playing with Maggie, Zach, and Van Dyke.

'I think I can handle a few Sweet Tooths,' Adam said quickly, finally getting the point and trying to rescue the situation. 'Or is it Sweet Teeth?'

'You'll have to drink a lot more than a *few*,' Paige teased. She raised her little paddle and swatted the ball over the net. It landed in a lowball glass with a soft *plop!*

Adam stared at the lollipop drink in dismay. 'Allow me,' Lisa said. She grabbed the glass, took out the lollipop, and downed the whole thing in one gulp.

'This is not going to end well for Adam,' Jason said with a laugh.

The doorbell rang, its jangly chime echoing through the house and clashing with the upbeat vintage surf music playing in the game room. Sienna started to get up, but Brad was closer to the door.

'I'll get it,' he called. 'I'm folding anyway.' He tossed his cards on the table and disappeared into the living room.

Paige took another shot with the ping pong ball, landing it neatly in a grape-lollipop Sweet Tooth. Lisa grabbed it before Adam could get to it. She was busy downing it when Brad came back into the room with a huge bouquet of white roses.

'Something beautiful for the beautiful hostess,' he said, presenting the flowers to Paige.

Paige raised an eyebrow. 'You trying to work your way through all the Devereux women, Brad?' she teased.

'No man could be that lucky,' he said, kissing her hand.

Paige laughed. 'What a smoothie.'

'I wish I could take the credit, but a delivery guy brought these,' Brad told her.

'Who are they from?' Belle asked.

'Let's see,' Paige said breathlessly. She pulled out the little red envelope and removed a card. But as she scanned it, the smile vanished from her lips and her face went pale.

'Paige?' Sienna said, standing up. 'You OK?'

Paige raised her dark eyes to Sienna's, and for a fleeting moment Jason thought he saw fear there. Then Paige shoved the flowers and the note into Sienna's arms, ran for the steps and disappeared downstairs.

Jason hurried to Sienna's side. 'Just what does that note say?'

Sienna pulled it out. '"Always thinking of you. Can't wait to see you again",' she read aloud. 'It's signed "M".'

'Well, that seems romantic,' Belle said, confused.

'Who's "M"?' Adam asked. 'Other than the James Bond character.' Belle swatted him on the arm.

'I don't know,' Sienna said slowly.

'Is Paige all right?' Lisa asked.

'Sure,' Sienna replied, forcing a smile. 'She's fine. I think she's just had a little too much to drink.' She turned to put the flowers down on a side table, and her eyes found Jason's.

He could see that she was worried. 'Let's get back to the cocktail pong,' he called cheerfully. 'I'll sub in for Paige.' The sooner he got everyone's mind off Paige's weird behavior, the sooner Sienna could slip away and check on her sister.

As Belle took the paddle and prepared to serve, Sienna mouthed a silent 'thank you' to Jason.

He nodded. He'd done what he could. But he had a feeling that the white roses were only the start. Paige was in some kind of trouble, and he and Sienna both knew it.

Four

'Please, please stop hitting balls into our drinks,' Adam begged about half an hour later. 'If I have to swallow one more Sweet Tooth I may turn into a lollipop.'

'Wuss. I've had twice as much as you,' Lisa told him, giggling.

'I know, but sugar makes me woozy.' Adam fake-collapsed onto the loveseat. Lisa collapsed beside him.

'Looks like it's going well,' Jason whispered to Belle, his cocktail pong team-mate.

Belle frowned at the loveseat. 'Oh, no . . .'

'You guys,' Adam said slowly, 'I think Lisa just passed out.' Jason and Belle rushed over.

'Lisa?' Belle said. 'Hey, Lisa, are you OK?'

Lisa burrowed into the plush cushions of the loveseat and let out a snore.

'How much did she drink?' Jason asked.

'Well, half the Sweet Tooths, thanks to you guys,'

Adam said accusingly. 'Couldn't you have missed just a few?'

Jason grimaced. 'Sorry. I wasn't even thinking about that. I guess I figured Paige had watered the Sweet Tooths down.'

'She did,' Belle said. 'But Lisa was drinking champagne cocktails before we started this game.' She sighed. 'I should have realized she was getting drunk.'

Kyle Priesmeyer came over, pulling on his '60s-style sport coat. 'I'll take her home, you guys. Lisa lives right next door to me.' He took Lisa's hand, and she woke with a start.

'Sweet Tooth!' she cried.

'Time to go, Lee,' Kyle told her, pulling her to her feet. She held on to his arm and they started toward the door.

'Thanks, Kyle,' Jason said.

'I'm driving a group of neighborhood kids home, one more is no problem.' Kyle shrugged. 'You have to be the designated driver sometimes, right?'

'Right.' Jason clapped him on the back.

'I'll help you get her out to the car,' Adam offered, heading off with them.

'She's not even going to remember half of this,' Belle sighed, watching them go. 'Adam's first big flirting victory, wasted.'

'At least you know he can do it,' Jason pointed out.

'Maybe there's hope for him yet,' Belle agreed. 'Where did Sienna go?'

'To check on Paige.'

'And now I'm back,' Sienna put in, appearing at the top of the steps.

'How's your sister?' Jason asked.

'I'm perfect.' Paige bounced up the steps and struck a dramatic pose. 'Obviously.'

Everybody laughed. 'Want to play a few hands?' Van Dyke called to her. 'We're thinking of switching the game to strip poker.'

'Not at my respectable party, Michael,' Paige replied sweetly. 'But that gives me an idea.' She strode over to the poker table and snatched up a deck of cards.

'Strip Twister?' Brad joked.

'Nope.' Paige began shuffling, flipping the cards expertly through the air. 'Better.' She glanced around the room, meeting everyone's eye in turn. Letting the tension build. 'Vegas.'

'Vegas?' Jason repeated.

'Las Vegas, Michigan boy.' Paige flipped a card at him. 'Sin City. The best place in the entire world!'

'What about Vegas?' Sienna asked.

'We go there. Now!' Paige sent the rest of the cards

flying up into the air like a fountain. 'Vegas, baby! It's so much better than boring old Malibu.'

'Boring?' Jason said incredulously.

'I like this idea, Paige,' Van Dyke said. 'I haven't been to Vegas all year.'

'Besides, think about it. It's spring break,' Paige went on. 'All kinds of tourists are going to show up here, hogging our sand and surf. Who wants to deal with that? We should do something different, something exciting.'

'No,' Sienna said.

Paige whirled around, shocked. 'No?'

'We're too tired from the party, and half of us have been drinking too,' Sienna pointed out. 'We can't drive to Vegas tonight.'

Paige opened her mouth to protest, but Sienna beat her to it.

'We'll go tomorrow. First thing in the morning.' That slow, sexy smile Jason loved crept across Sienna's face. 'I have the perfect dress for Vegas.'

Paige flung her arms around Sienna's neck and laughed out loud. 'Vegas, here we come!'

'Shotgun!' Paige called the next morning as Belle pulled her parents' Escalade into the Devereux driveway.

'Fine with me,' Adam mumbled. 'I can sleep better in the back seat. Whose idea was it to leave before the sun was even up?'

'See that fiery yellow ball in the sky? That's the sun,' Jason told him.

'Well, it's not up very high,' Adam grumbled.

'It's a long drive to Las Vegas. We have to get an early start if we want to get there and still have time to play,' Sienna explained.

'Besides, I called Belle and told her to bring us all coffees,' Paige announced. 'Prepare to wake up.'

Van Dyke's Hummer pulled into the driveway behind Belle. The side window slid down, and Maggie waved. 'Everybody psyched?'

'You know it!' Paige called back. She pulled open the passenger door and climbed into the front seat next to Belle, while Jason, Adam, and Sienna took the back.

Zach hopped out of the back of the Hummer and went over to Paige's window. 'Let's make sure we have each other's cell numbers in case the cars get separated,' he said. 'I'm assuming you're not still using the international number.'

'I got a new number the instant I got back to the States,' Paige confirmed.

'Paranoid much?' Brad called from the Hummer.

Erin yawned next to him in the back seat. 'Seriously.

We just drive in a straight line from here to Vegas. How could we possibly lose each other?'

Zach ignored them and checked his phone against Paige's. When they were done, he climbed back into the Hummer, and Van Dyke peeled out.

'Vegas!' Paige cheered as Belle took off after him.

Jason took Sienna's hand and squeezed it. He could hardly wait to see the lights and crowds of the famous city. 'I can't believe my parents are letting me go to Vegas,' he said.

'Why wouldn't they, with me here to chaperone you little kiddies?' Paige joked.

'Oh, that reminds me, nobody tell my father that Paige is with us,' Adam put in. 'He's only letting me come because Jason is going. And, apparently, Jason is a fine upstanding boy.'

'Your father loves me,' Paige said with a dismissive wave.

'He does say you were the most polite juvenile delinquent he's ever known,' Adam agreed. 'And that he thinks you're going to do very well once you get over your youthful high spirits.'

Paige turned in her seat. 'You read my police reports!'

'Every last one,' Adam admitted. 'I was thinking of doing a movie with a hot girl as the main character. She

48

has a wild streak, but really she's just misunderstood. I figured your history might inspire me.'

'Are you kidding? I never even got arrested. Your dad just escorted me home a lot,' Paige said.

'I know, but it was fun reading anyway.' Adam took a long swig of his coffee. 'Hey, Jason, where's your sister? How come she didn't come along?'

'She already had plans for spring break,' Jason replied. 'She and Kristy decided they wanted to hang in Malibu for the week, because, and I quote, "Why go to some strange place to meet hot guys when hot guys from strange places are going to be coming to Malibu for spring break?" '

'I like their thinking,' Adam said. 'It's very efficient. Maybe I should've stayed home and waited for all the hot girls from strange places to descend on me.'

'It's not too late,' Sienna said. 'We aren't even out of Los Angeles yet. We can just drop you off.'

'A tempting offer.' Adam pretended to look thoughtful. 'But there's a *CSI* mega-shoot in the Mojave around Las Vegas this week. I've got to see that. Gil Grissom, in the flesh.'

'He's fictional, you know,' Jason said. 'You'll only get to see the actor.'

'Yes, but I have a vivid imagination. He'll still be Grissom to me.'

'How do you know about this mega-shoot?' Belle asked suspiciously from the driver's seat.

'I saw it on *CSIFiles.com*,' Adam replied. 'Why, is that geeky?'

'That's a rhetorical question,' Sienna told him.

'*CSI* is boring,' Belle commented. 'I like *CSI: Miami* better. At least it has the beach.'

Adam clutched his heart. 'Blasphemy!' he declared.

'You all need lives,' Paige said cheerfully. 'Thank God I got home in time to rescue you from your slavery to the TV schedule.'

Sienna yawned and leant her head on Jason's shoulder. 'Wake me up if anything interesting happens.'

You're snuggling up against me, that's interesting, Jason thought. He leant his head on hers and closed his eyes, letting her warmth lull him to sleep.

'Crap!' Belle's voice startled Jason awake. He sat up quickly, automatically glancing out of the window. Flat desert stretched as far as he could see.

'What's going on?' Sienna mumbled sleepily beside him.

'I can't see Van Dyke,' Belle muttered.

The voices woke Adam, on the other side of Sienna. 'Are we there?' he asked. 'How long was I sleeping?'

'All of you slackers have been asleep for two hours,' Paige told them. She was turned in the passenger seat, peering out the back window. 'Van Dyke's been behind us the whole time.'

'Well, he's not there now,' Belle said. 'And that SUV is totally tailgating me. I don't know when he got behind us. He must've cut in front of Van Dyke.'

Paige dialed Zach on her cell. A second later, Zach's voice came over the speaker. 'Paige.'

'Zach? Where are you guys?' she asked.

'Sorry, we pulled over for a minute. Van Dyke thought we blew a tire, but it must've just been a rock hitting us or something. We're on the way now. Just go slow and we'll soon catch up.'

'OK,' Paige replied, and hung up.

'Going slow is easier said than done,' Belle complained, hitting the brakes. 'This SUV is still right on my butt.'

'You're supposed to slow down when somebody is tailgating,' Paige replied. 'It makes them realize they're behaving badly.'

'OK.' Belle slowed some more.

Jason shook the sleep out of his head and looked around. The highway was only one lane in each direction here, with desert on both sides. Out the back window of the Escalade, he could see a black SUV following closely. But the windows were tinted, so he couldn't see the driver.

Belle slowed to a crawl. 'Why doesn't this guy just pass me already?' she asked. 'There's nobody coming the other way.'

'Hang on.' Paige hit a button on the dashboard, and the sunroof slid open. She unclicked her seatbelt and stood on the seat so that she could stick her head out of the sunroof.

'Paige!' Sienna protested.

'Go ahead and pass!' Paige yelled to the SUV. She waved her arms to encourage them.

After a moment, the SUV pulled into the other lane, sped up, and roared past the Escalade. 'There's Van Dyke,' Belle announced, checking the rear-view mirror.

'Hi, everyone!' Paige yelled to their friends in the other car.

'Paige, sit down,' Sienna begged. 'They can't hear you, anyway.'

Paige plopped back down in her seat and put the seatbelt back on. 'Well, that was exciting,' she joked.

'Not worth waking up for, though,' Adam said, settling back to sleep.

'I guess we should've gotten more coffee,' Belle commented.

'The desert is making us sleepy. It's boring,' Sienna said.

'Not to me. I've never seen it before,' Jason said. 'When we moved from Michigan, we flew over the desert. I think it's cool this close up.' He gazed out of the window, taking in the variations of brown and red in the rocks surrounding them. He'd always assumed that the desert would be sandy, but in fact it was mostly just rocky ground and short, scrubby plants.

And a black SUV with tinted windows.

'Hey!' he exclaimed as they passed the SUV, which was now parked on the roadside. 'Isn't that the car that just passed us?'

'Where?' Belle asked.

'Pulled over on the side,' Jason said.

Belle glanced in the rear-view. 'Could be. I didn't really notice it.'

'Lots of people stop to stretch their legs in the desert,' Paige said. 'It's a long drive with no rest stops.'

Jason frowned. He was positive that it had been the same SUV. Why would it have pulled over so soon after passing them? he wondered. He figured the only reason to pass another car was because you wanted to go fast.

Unless they never wanted to pass us at all, a voice whispered in his mind. *Unless they were following us on purpose, and now they've pulled over to wait for us.*

'Something wrong, Jason?' Sienna asked, studying his face.

'No,' he said quickly. 'Nothing's wrong.'

He hoped it was the truth.

Five

'Michigan Boy's first glimpse of the Strip,' Adam said in a deep narrator voice, his camcorder trained on Jason's face.

'Hey!' Belle cried from the driver's seat. 'I thought I said no filming during spring break!'

Adam dropped the camera and gaped at her. 'That rule can't possibly count now that we're spending spring break in Vegas. There is much to record here, woman!'

'I'm forced to agree with Adam on this one,' Jason put in. 'This place is incredible.' He rolled down the window to get a better view. And there, about six metres away, was a *pyramid*. With a sphinx in front of it. And an obelisk. 'That pyramid is huge!'

'It's a hotel,' Sienna told him. 'Most of the rooms are inside the pyramid, and you have to take an elevator that goes on a slant in order to get to them.'

Jason grinned. 'Cool ride!'

'I like the Eiffel Tower better,' Belle said. 'The whole Paris Hotel is my favorite hangout in Vegas.'

'Ugh, I don't need to see Paris again, even in miniature form,' Paige commented. There was a sour tone in her voice that surprised Jason.

Apparently Sienna caught it, too. 'Why? What was so bad about Paris?' she asked.

Paige turned and shrugged. 'Nothing. I just like New York New York better. It has a replica of the Statue of Liberty out front,' she told Jason. 'And a really fun rollercoaster that goes all around the hotel.'

'A rollercoaster in a hotel?' he asked skeptically.

'Don't knock it till you've tried it,' Adam said.

'This city is insane,' Jason decided. 'There's a little Egypt, a little Paris, a little New York – and they're all just hotels!'

'There's also one that's like Venice and one that's like ancient Rome . . .' Sienna told him.

'Which one are we staying in?' Jason asked.

'The best one of all,' Paige replied. 'Zach made the arrangements – and there's no charge for any of us either.'

'No way,' Adam gasped a minute later, when Belle turned the Escalade into a wide circular driveway. 'The Rouge et Noir?'

'Let's party,' Paige said, giggling. She flung open her door and jumped out even before the black-uniformed valet could help her.

Jason let the guy open his door for him, then he turned to help Sienna out. 'The Rouge et Noir Casino Hotel Resort,' he read, staring at the tall neon sign on the Strip.

'We'll get the bags, sir,' the valet told him. 'You go on in.'

Paige and Belle were already on their way, with Adam ten steps behind, filming them. Jason took Sienna's hand and they followed their friends. Behind the Escalade, he spotted Van Dyke's Hummer with another valet unloading it.

As they stepped in to the hotel, Jason nearly gasped. The place was stunning. Jet-black shiny marble floors stretched as far as he could see. Heavy red drapes hugged the floor-to-ceiling windows, and red brocade ottomans with thick black fringe dotted the lobby. Off to one side, a scalloped entryway led to the casino. Jason caught a glimpse of gaming tables and slot machines. A cocktail waitress wearing a can-can skirt walked by.

'Mr Lafrenière!' called a thin man in a tuxedo. 'Welcome!' The guy rushed out from behind the huge obsidian reception desk, grabbed Zach's hand, and pumped it enthusiastically. 'We're honored to have you back with us.' His eyes traveled over the group. 'And all of your party, of course. I'm Joseph Chalmers, the manager here.'

He shook everybody's hands, then turned back to Zach. 'So. What would you like from me?'

'Just the six rooms we spoke about for now,' Zach said, following Mr Chalmers over to the desk.

Adam came over to Jason. 'Nice place, huh?'

'I think that might be a Van Gogh on the wall,' Jason said. 'A real one.'

'Probably. This is the most expensive resort on the Strip. They can afford the good art.'

'Can I get you anything while you wait?' another can-can waitress asked, appearing from nowhere. 'If you'd like to take a seat in our VIP lounge, I'd be happy to bring in some drinks.'

'That sounds wonderful,' Paige told her. The waitress led the way over to a room hidden by a thick curtain. Inside were a bunch of overstuffed chairs and couches, and a huge window that looked out over the Strip. Paige hurled herself onto a chaise and grinned.

'Are we seriously in a lounge while we wait for five minutes to check in?' Jason asked. 'Really? You need a lounge for that?'

'Sure,' Adam said. 'Maybe you should install a lounge like this in your house. You know, for when you have to wait for your sister to get out of the bathroom in the morning.'

'That takes a lot longer than five minutes,' Jason told him.

The waitress came in and set down a heavy gold tray. On it were tall glasses and sparkling crystal-studded bottles of mineral water.

The others gathered around, grabbing drinks.

'Cool. Bling H_2O,' Brad remarked.

'What else would you expect in Vegas?' Erin laughed.

Jason hung back.

'Having some culture shock?' Adam asked quietly, sitting next to him.

'A little,' Jason admitted. 'I kinda figured we'd be staying at a cheap motel five miles off the Strip. But the way the hotel manager greeted Zach, it was like he's royalty or something. I mean, he's still just a high-school kid.'

'With a seat on the DeVere Heights Vampire Council,' Adam reminded him.

Jason was surprised. 'You think that matters? We're nowhere near Malibu.'

Adam shrugged. 'My guess? Zach's family knows the owners of this hotel. For all I know, they may *be* the owners of this hotel. Look, Paige said he'd sorted out the rooms so there's gotta be some kinda connection. Anyway, our friends are international jet-setters, my man. Enjoy it.'

'I've got our room keys,' Zach announced, stepping through the curtain. 'Paige, you and I have the two penthouse suites. The rest of you are on the 17th floor, just below us. Brad and Van Dyke, you're in 1701. Erin and Maggie, 02. Sienna, are you with Jason or Belle?'

'Belle,' Sienna replied, shooting Jason an apologetic look. She leant forward to whisper in his ear, 'Otherwise it would be Belle and Adam, and Belle's just not up for a male roommate right now.'

Jason nodded.

'But you know I'd rather be in a room with you,' she added, her breath hot on his neck.

Adam cleared his throat loudly. 'So it's me and Freeman. Excellent.'

Sienna pulled away from Jason, smiling. 'What's our room number, Zach?'

'1703.' He handed her a key card, then gave the last one to Adam. 'I say we get settled in and meet in the hotel restaurant for dinner in an hour. Sound good?'

'Sounds perfect,' Paige replied.

'Just so I know, in a hotel where the manager wears a tux, is there a dress code for this restaurant?' Adam asked.

'Of course,' Zach replied. 'Didn't you bring your tux?'

'Uh . . .' Adam looked panicked.

'Just kidding,' Zach told him. 'Whatever you have is fine. They're not going to expect us to play by their rules.'

'This is so much fun,' Paige squealed. She grabbed Zach and kissed him on the cheek. 'Thank you for arranging it.'

'Not a problem.' Zach pulled back the curtain and led them all toward an elevator marked 'Private'. Inside, there was no control panel. Zach just pulled out his key card, waved it over the sensor, and the elevator shot up. 'Brad, your key.'

'Oh.' Brad pulled out his key card and waved that over the sensor, too.

'It knows which floor to stop on based on our keys,' Zach explained. 'You can also use the keys as money while you're in the hotel.'

Everybody nodded, and Jason got the feeling that even the vampires were a little impressed with this place. The elevator glided to a stop on the 17th floor to let people out.

'See you downstairs,' Zach said as the doors shut on him and Paige.

The hallway was done in shades of red and black, just like the lobby. When they got to their rooms, Sienna gave Jason a lingering kiss.

'Just to hold you until dinner,' she murmured.

Adam was already sprawled on one of the two huge beds when Jason got into the room. 'You know, this bed is bigger than my entire room,' he commented.

Jason took a look around. To the right were the beds, each set on a raised dais of pale gray marble, and there was a huge bathroom with two sinks, a shower, and a gigantic tub. To the left was a living area with couches, a wide-screen TV on the wall, and a bar. The entire room bowed out in a big U shape, and the curve of the U was a bank of windows. Jason wandered over to take a look.

'I think I can see every hotel on the Strip from here,' he said.

Adam joined him at the window and let out a soft whistle. 'If this is what the regular rooms are like, I can't wait to see Zach's penthouse suite. Speaking of which, maybe I should iron my T-shirt before dinner. I know Zach said it doesn't matter, but . . .'

'Did you even bring a jacket?' Jason asked, amused.

'I'm not really sure what I brought,' Adam admitted. 'We were at the party late last night, and then we left so early today that I kind of packed in my sleep.' Adam went over to his suitcase, which the bellhops had placed on a stand at the foot of the bed. He opened it up and stared at the contents thoughtfully.

Jason peered over his shoulder. The suitcase

contained a camcorder and all its various accoutrements, right down to a folded tripod. And a bunch of shirts crammed in around the lenses, wires, and other pieces of equipment. 'You used your clothes for packing material,' he said.

'Well, I had to cushion the camera somehow,' Adam said reasonably.

Jason reached in and pulled out a wadded-up cotton shirt. When he shook it out, it turned out to be a perfectly decent button-down, with about a million wrinkles.

'See? Iron required.' Adam began hunting through the closet. 'There has to be an iron, right? Even millionaires get wrinkles, don't they?'

Jason unzipped his own suitcase and pulled out his toiletries bag. 'I'm going to take a shower. Good luck with the clothes.'

By the time he was clean and dressed, Adam had made himself presentable. He'd even scrounged up a tie – although it had a picture of E.T. on it.

'Drink?' Adam asked, checking out the minibar. 'I'm feeling beer-ish. And a bottle only costs ten bucks.'

Before Jason could answer, there was a knock at the door. He went to get it, hoping to see Sienna. Instead, Zach stood in the hallway.

'Are you heading down to dinner already?' Jason asked.

'In a few. I wanted to give you these first.' Zach held out two Nevada drivers' licenses. 'Your ID for the week. Vegas is no fun if you're not legal.'

'Thanks.' Jason took them and studied them as Zach headed off to Brad and Van Dyke's room. 'How'd he get our pictures?' he asked Adam.

'He has his methods,' Adam replied in a fake-mysterious voice. He glanced at his ID, then took a closer look. 'Dude. This is nice work. It looks real!'

'I know. Although it will be weird if we're all exactly twenty-one on our licenses.'

'I'm twenty-two. Ha!' Adam said. 'It's my real birthday, though. I only have to remember the fake year if some bouncer decides to quiz me. That Zach, he thinks of everything!'

Jason pocketed his ID. 'I'm going to go get Sienna.' He went over to her room, and she opened the door just as he was about to knock. She looked incredible, her hair done in loose waves for a change, tumbling down over her shoulders to the most amazing, strappy, clingy red dress Jason had ever seen.

'That *is* a killer dress,' he stammered.

'I told you.' Sienna leant in and brushed her lips against his.

'Hey, Belle!' Adam yelled over Jason's shoulder. 'Are you in there? I can't see you over the lovebirds.'

Sienna rolled her eyes and laughed. 'Geez, we can't even get a single romantic moment? Tough crowd.'

'You two get plenty of romance,' Belle said from inside the room. She grabbed her purse and pulled the door shut behind her. 'Let's go.'

Down in the restaurant, they were ushered to a table in a roped off area of the dining room, separated from the noise and the crowd by a row of tall plants with exotic red flowers in bloom.

Zach and Paige were already there, sitting at the head and foot of the table like a king and queen. Paige took one look at Sienna and squealed with delight.

'I knew that dress was perfect for you! You are the hottest babe in this entire town!'

'I don't know about that,' Sienna said, but she smiled with delight.

Brad and Van Dyke showed up a minute later, and finally Maggie and Erin came in, giggling. 'Erin just lost twenty dollars in a minute and a half,' Maggie announced.

'Serves me right for playing five dollar slots,' Erin said.

'I don't play slots,' Brad put in from across the table. 'Roulette is my game.'

'You have a *game*?' Sienna teased.

'I do now,' Brad replied. 'I've decided to focus on one thing for the whole week. You know, see if I can figure out a system.'

'You can't ever beat the house,' Van Dyke said scornfully. 'Everybody knows that.'

'It's still fun to try,' Paige replied. 'It's always fun to see if you can find your way around the rules.'

A waiter in a black tux showed up with the wine list. While Zach was reading it, Paige beckoned him over. 'What's your name?' she asked.

'Max.' The waiter looked her up and down and smiled.

'Mmmmax,' Paige murmured, her voice dropping an octave. 'I love that name.'

Max smiled a little wider.

'Tell you what, Max. Even if these unadventurous types just go for soft drinks or wine, I want something more exciting,' Paige said. She put her hand lightly on his arm. 'Can you take care of me?'

'Sure. Yes. I'd be happy to,' Max said. 'I know just the thing.' He practically ran toward the bar.

Erin chuckled. 'Paige, you're such a flirt.'

'What? I would've said the same thing to a waitress,' Paige replied with an innocent look. Then she burst out laughing.

'You're certainly in an outrageous mood tonight,' Sienna commented. 'Did you hit the bar before dinner?'

'Nope, I hit the bubble bath whirlpool tub in my amazing penthouse suite,' Paige replied. 'Though I have to admit, I took the complimentary bottle of Bollinger into the tub with me.'

'Bubbly in the bubble bath,' Van Dyke said. 'Sweet.'

'It is. I'm jealous,' Maggie put in. 'We have the big bathtub, too, but we didn't get any champagne.'

'Neither did we,' Belle said.

'You didn't?' Paige's smile faltered.

'Nope. It must be something they only do for the penthouse suites,' Sienna said. 'You lucky girl.'

Paige's dark eyes went straight to Zach. 'Did you have a bottle in your suite?'

Zach shook his head. 'I wish.'

'So it was just me?' Paige asked, her voice worried. 'That's weird.'

'Hey, don't question it,' Brad advised her. 'It's not like they can take it back.'

'Zach, is the steak here any good?' Erin asked. 'I'm in the mood for a nice, juicy ribeye.'

'I'd go with the *filet*, actually,' Zach replied. 'Is everyone having steak? Shall I order up some drinks too? Still or sparkling? And maybe a bottle of wine . . .?'

Everyone started talking at once, figuring out what to order, but Jason's gaze stayed on Paige. She was staring off into space, her brow furrowed. Even when Max returned with some kind of green, fizzy drink, she only managed a wan smile.

Something's worrying her, Jason thought.

'Paige? What are you getting?' Sienna asked.

'Hmm?' Paige snapped out of her reverie and smiled at her sister. 'Um, the risotto with truffle sauce. You know I can't resist a good truffle.'

She was back to normal, Jason could see. But it was an act. There was something brittle about Paige's smile, and he found himself thinking of her reaction to the white roses the night before. She'd acted weird then, and she was acting weird now. When the waiter reached over to take her menu, Paige jumped in surprise, shooting him a fast, suspicious look.

I'm wrong, Jason realized, watching her. *It's not that something is worrying Paige, it's that something is scaring her!*

But in a hotel like this, where every single person seemed to be treating Paige like a queen, what could there possibly be for her to fear?

Six

'Where should we go first?' Paige asked as Jason polished off his last bite of cheesecake. 'Clubbing or gambling?'

'Maybe we should find Zach,' Erin suggested. 'It seems kind of rude not to hang out with him after he paid for this incredible dinner.' Zach had shot off right after his steak, heading for a poker game at which he'd arranged a seat.

'Oh, don't worry about him,' Brad replied. 'Anyone who leaves before dessert doesn't deserve friends.'

'Yeah, even if it *is* dessert that he paid for,' Van Dyke joked.

'I heard there's an amazing DJ at the club in Paris,' Maggie put in.

'Paige is sick of Paris,' Jason said.

Sienna's sister turned to him, eyebrow raised. 'That's right,' she said. 'I am. I vote for that new place. What's it called?'

'Intervention,' Brad said.

Paige nodded, and as the others kept on talking, Sienna leant in to whisper in Jason's ear. 'Thanks for stepping in. I don't know what Paige's deal is with Paris, but she's pretty down on it. Even in hotel form.'

Suddenly Adam stood up. 'Everybody excuse me, if you would. I'm not going clubbing or gambling, so I'll say goodnight.'

'Oh, no,' Belle protested. 'You did not come to Vegas to go to bed early.'

'Who said I was going to bed? I'm getting my camera and going out,' Adam told her. 'I feel the need to shoot some footage. Sin City beckons.'

'Yes, and it beckons us to Intervention,' Paige told him. 'Believe me, there will be plenty of footage there.'

'Yeah, but it will just look like some expensive movie, with all kinds of beautiful people,' Adam complained. 'I want reality. I mean, *my* reality, not *your* reality which is basically the expensive movie reality.'

'So what's your reality?' Jason asked.

'I want to shoot the seedy underbelly of the neon beast that is Las Vegas,' Adam said.

They all stared at him for a moment.

'That is so *not* your reality,' Van Dyke said.

'I know, but it will make a great movie.' Adam loosened his E.T. tie. 'And I'm never going to see the seedy underbelly hanging out with you guys.'

'But Adam, I was going to find you an actual show-girl to hook up with,' Belle said. 'That's my mission for this week.'

'It will just have to wait. Art before romance.' He gave her a wink and headed out.

'All right, no more deserters,' Paige said. 'We're going to Intervention. Now.' She stood up and strode out of the restaurant, and Jason and his friends followed her like baby ducklings.

Paige led them through the center of the Rouge et Noir Casino, and Jason couldn't help noticing how many heads turned as she passed. Well, as she and Sienna passed. Each Devereux girl alone was enough to grab attention, but together, they were heart-stopping.

Paige held up her hand. 'Detour,' she called, veering off the main artery through the casino and winding her way through the poker tables. 'Let's tell our darling dinner host where we're going.'

Zach sat at one of the tables, intent on the game in front of him. As they watched, he slid a stack of chips forward to place his bet.

'He just bet 3,000 dollars!' Maggie gasped.

'That's hard core,' Van Dyke said.

Erin gazed at Zach. 'We better not distract him,' she said. 'If he's on a streak, we should leave him to it.'

'You're right,' Paige agreed. 'You have to respect a streak!'

Intervention was in the next hotel over, and they were able to take the monorail system right there. Within five minutes, Jason found himself standing in line outside a darkened door, watching as two humongous bouncers let in a few people now and then, and told most of the others to leave. The word 'Intervention' was written in hot pink neon on the wall over their heads, casting a rosy glow over everything.

'This is so cool,' Belle said, standing on the tips of her toes. 'This place has only been open for a month, and already it's in all the gossip magazines.'

'Is that a good thing?' Jason asked.

'Sure, it means all the prettiest girls in town will be here hoping to get their picture taken,' Brad replied. 'That's always a good thing.'

'Yeah, same goes for the hottest guys,' Erin agreed.

Jason glanced at the line and then at the bouncers. 'This place is packed. Even with our fake IDs I don't think we're getting in,' he murmured to Sienna.

Sienna smiled. 'Don't worry. Paige is here,' she said.

When they got to the front of the line, Paige gave the bouncers her flirtiest smile. 'Hi, boys. Long night?'

One of them took a moment to check her out, and Jason noticed that Paige was suddenly about twice as beautiful as she usually looked. *She tones it down in her everyday life*, he thought. *This is what she* really *looks like.* Jason knew that all of the vampires were incredibly beautiful, supernaturally beautiful, in fact, and that to fit in with regular people they adjusted their appearances slightly. But with no adjustments, they were stunning, and right now, Paige was practically glowing.

The other bouncer didn't seem as impressed. 'The club's pretty full. We have to be choosy.'

'But you'll let *me* in, won't you?' Paige asked, letting her full lips pout a tiny bit. She grabbed Sienna's hand and pulled her up to the bouncers. 'And my baby sister.'

The bouncers gazed at Sienna in her red dress. At the two Devereux girls together.

'She has her heart set on hearing DJ Wink,' Paige continued. 'I know you're not going to disappoint her.'

The bouncers exchanged a glance. 'Wink isn't spinning here tonight,' the first one said.

Paige raised her eyebrows. 'That's not what I heard. He told me he was going to be here at midnight. He doesn't lie.'

'You're a friend of his?' the other bouncer asked.

Paige winked. 'Well, he likes to think so, but I keep him guessing.'

The bouncers chuckled. 'How many people did you bring?' the first one asked.

'These eight.' She waved toward Jason and his friends.

'OK.' The bouncer stepped back and held the door open for her. 'If you're a friend of Wink's, you're welcome. VIP area is straight back and to the right.'

'Aren't they going to card us?' Jason asked.

'Shh,' Sienna ordered. 'Just come with me.' She grabbed his hand and pulled him right past the two big guys. They didn't even glance at him.

'Sisters. Jeez,' the first bouncer was saying. 'Think they're single?'

'Man, we're not in their league,' the other one replied. 'Hell, we're not even playing the same sport!'

Jason hid a smile as he left them behind. If only Adam had been here to catch that line on film.

'How did you know DJ Wink was planning to be here?' Brad asked Paige. 'Do you really know him?'

'Nope. I tipped the concierge at the hotel to let me know the word on the street.' Paige grinned.

The VIP area was a group of couches separated from the rest of the club on three sides by a curving waterfall. Jason and Sienna settled onto one of the couches with their backs to the water, and looked out over the club. There had to be a hundred people writhing about on the huge industrial dance floor, and a hundred more waiting in line at the neon-pink bar.

'That's cool,' Jason commented. 'There's actually neon inside the bar.'

'Look around, there's neon everywhere,' Sienna replied.

She was right. Lines of multi-colored neon snaked through the walls, across the ceiling, and under their feet. The whole place looked as if it was constructed of some kind of heavy, clear plastic, and the neon was embedded within. Now that Jason took a closer look, he could see lines of blue and purple neon peeking through the water of the waterfall, and a rim of green neon along the floor all around the VIP area.

'Drinks?' asked a waiter wearing black leather pants – and nothing else.

'Champagne,' Paige replied immediately. 'Your best.' She reached out and tucked a fifty dollar bill into his waistband.

The waiter grinned and moved off.

'Paige! He's not a stripper!' Maggie exclaimed, scandalized.

'Even if he's dressed like one. Kind of,' Van Dyke added.

Paige shrugged. 'The important thing is that he'll totally take care of us.' She leapt up. 'I'm going to dance.' Without another word, she was gone. A minute later, she appeared on the dance floor, shaking her booty with abandon.

'That looks fun,' Brad said. 'I'm going with her.'

'I feel like a soda so I'm hitting the bar,' Erin announced. 'Wanna come, Belle?'

'Sure.' The two girls headed off, winding their way through the crowd.

By the time the waiter showed up with the champagne, Jason and Sienna were the only ones there to enjoy it. Van Dyke and Maggie had joined a game of 'I Never' with a group of wealthy fraternity brothers taking up another table in the VIP section.

Jason poured a flute of champagne for Sienna and one for himself. 'To spring break,' he said. 'May everyone have a great time and forget their worries.'

'I'll drink to that.' Sienna clinked her glass against his and took a sip. 'Want to dance?'

'No,' Jason said. 'I finally have you alone. I want to make the most of it.' He pulled her to him for a kiss. She tasted like champagne and smelled like flowers. He lost himself in Sienna, and lost track of time.

After a while, Paige came back to the table and ordered another bottle of bubbly along with a trayful of sodas. Brad brought a few girls into the VIP section and settled himself on a couch with them. Jason had a feeling Brad was going to feed, but he didn't pay much attention. He was pretty buzzed on champagne and Sienna.

Maggie and Van Dyke were making out on another couch, and Erin and Belle were out on the dance floor. Paige joined the 'I Never' game with the frat brothers, one of whom was quickly drinking himself into a stupor. Jason was vaguely aware of the big bouncers coming to drag the dude out and put him in a cab.

'I wonder where Adam is,' he heard Belle say a while later.

Reluctantly, Jason pulled himself away from Sienna and turned to see that Belle and Erin had finished dancing and were back in the VIP area.

'What time is it?' Jason asked.

'Almost two,' Belle told him.

'Not that you two care,' Erin teased. 'You should've just spent the night in the hotel!'

'Sorry,' Sienna said sheepishly. 'I guess maybe we could go dance now.'

A roar of laughter came from the other table. 'That's two!' Paige cried, throwing her arms up in triumph as one of the frat guys fell to the floor with a smile on his face. Paige snapped her fingers. 'Waiter boy! Can you get the bouncers to send my friend here home?'

'What are you doing, Paige?' Jason called.

'Drinking these guys under the table,' Paige called

back. 'They bet me I couldn't keep up because I'm a girl.' She grinned at the three brothers still sitting with her. 'But it's two down, three to go!'

'She's a vampire,' Jason murmured to Sienna. 'Doesn't that mean she can handle a lot more alcohol than those guys?'

'Mm-hmm. But they don't know that,' Sienna said.

Jason glanced at Paige. She was laughing and there was a wild look in her dark eyes. She was obviously having fun, but there was an edge to her mood that made Jason uneasy and she was drinking far too much. *She reminds me of Tyler*, he realized. His best friend from Michigan had been involved with drugs and it had really changed his behavior. Whenever they'd gone out, Tyler had seemed like the life of the party, but Jason knew that there was desperation underneath. The kind of desperation that had led Tyler to steal a valuable chalice from Zach's house, and almost get himself killed by the DeVere Heights Vampire Council as a result.

There's something strange going on with Paige, he thought. *Maybe Sienna can figure it out.* 'Sienna . . .' Jason began, turning to his girlfriend.

'Do I want to dance with you?' she finished for him. 'You bet I do!' She stood up, took his hand, and pulled him after her toward the dance floor. This late at night, the music had turned to slow grooves, and the mood on the floor was sultry.

'I wanted to ask you about Paige,' Jason said.

'Hmm?' Sienna gestured to the speaker nearby. 'I didn't hear that.' She was already moving to the music, her hips swaying, the red dress clinging to every curve of her body.

'Never mind,' Jason said, moving in close. He slid his hands along her hips and pulled her against him. He'd worry about Paige later.

They stayed on the dance floor until last call, then made their way back over to their friends. Paige had just finished helping the last frat brother out to a cab. She waved to the rest of them from the door of the club. 'Hey, guys, the bouncers are holding cabs for us!'

Sienna grabbed her bag from the VIP table, and they all made their way out to the waiting taxis. By the time they got back to the Rouge et Noir, it was after three o'clock.

Belle yawned as they made their way into the lobby. 'I am beat.'

'Me too,' Erin said.

'Not me. I'm ready to gamble,' Brad replied. 'Wanna hit the tables for a bit, Van Dyke?'

'You know it,' Van Dyke replied. He turned to Maggie. 'Coming?'

'Nope. I want to get up early tomorrow and do some shopping,' she said. 'Vegas has the best boutiques ever.'

'Ooh, count me in,' Belle told her.

'And me,' Erin added. 'So I'm going to get some sleep. What about the rest of you?'

Paige was staring off into the casino. 'There's a little crowd over there,' she said. 'And where there's a crowd, there's fun. I'm going to check it out.'

'We'll go with you,' Jason offered. He had a feeling Paige's idea of fun might lead to trouble tonight.

'OK. See you in the morning,' Belle said. She, Maggie and Erin headed for the elevator.

Paige stopped a cocktail waitress who was making her way out of the casino. 'What's going on over there?'

'Oh, it's a big money table. Texas Hold 'Em,' the waitress said. 'It's a real showdown.'

'Poker, no can do,' Brad said. 'My game is roulette.' With a wave, he and Van Dyke headed off to the roulette tables.

'Let's check out the big game,' Paige giggled. She headed over to the table and worked her way right to the front of the crowd, Sienna on her heels. Jason followed. He noticed that the other spectators glared at him for cutting in front of them, but everyone just smiled at the Devereux sisters. When he got to the front, he caught his breath; there were two players at the table, and one of them was Zach!

'He's in a big money game?' Jason whispered to Sienna.

'I'll say. Look at that stack of chips in front of him.' Sienna laughed. 'How can he even see over them?'

Zach did have a pretty big pile of chips. But so did the player across from him – an older, Japanese man, in a suit that obviously cost a couple of thousand, at least. The guy was flanked by two huge bodyguards, both of them staring at Zach as if he were a bug they'd like to squash.

Zach paid no attention to them. He kept his eyes fixed on the Japanese man.

Slowly, the man pushed his chips in for a bet. His expression was deadly serious, but that didn't stop all the spectators from gasping and laughing in excitement.

'The bet is eleven thousand, that's all in for Mr Yakamoto,' the dealer announced. Jason checked out the cards on the table. Five face up: the king of hearts, the five of diamonds, the seven of diamonds, the king of spades, and the four of diamonds.

Zach matched Mr Yakamoto's bet.

The dealer turned to the Japanese man. 'Mr Yakamoto?' she said.

He put down the two cards in his hand: the other

two kings. 'Four kings,' he announced proudly. Everybody gasped, and a few people applauded.

'Uh-oh,' Paige murmured.

'Yup. It doesn't look good for Zach,' Jason agreed.

But Zach seemed unruffled. He waited for all the talking to die down, still holding his two cards. Mr Yakamoto stared at him.

'Mr Lafrenière?' the dealer invited.

Zach put his cards on the table: the three of diamonds and the six of diamonds. 'Straight flush,' he announced.

The place went wild. People gasped in shock, and then burst into clapping and whooping.

'Straight flush beats four of a kind. All to Mr Lafrenière,' the dealer announced, pushing Yakamoto's chips over to Zach's pile.

Finally, Zach allowed himself a smile, which only made the onlookers cheer louder. Mr Yakamoto angrily shoved his chair back from the table and stalked out, followed by his bodyguards.

'Any other takers?' the dealer asked. 'Another hand, Mr Lafrenière?'

'No thanks,' Zach replied. 'Can you cash in the chips for me?'

'Of course, sir.' The dealer shot him an appraising look. 'You know, there's a tournament this week over at the Bonheur: the Ultimate High Stakes Invitational. You've got what it takes.'

'Think so?' Zach asked.

She nodded. 'It's 250,000 dollars to buy in, but you never know. You could make yourself a millionaire in just one night.'

Jason waited for Zach to laugh at the outrageously expensive buy-in, but Zach just nodded. 'I'll keep it in mind.'

A quarter of a million dollars? Jason thought, stupefied. *He'll keep that in mind?* Jason glanced around at the swanky hotel, at his supermodel-gorgeous girlfriend, at their high-school friend who could apparently afford a poker game that held the title of 'Ultimate High Stakes'. 'I think maybe I fell asleep in the Escalade and I'm still dreaming,' he said.

Sienna ran her fingers lightly over the back of his neck. 'No dream,' she murmured. 'Let's go to your room. Maybe Adam is still out and we can be alone.'

Jason's pulse quickened at the idea of Sienna alone in his hotel room. 'What about your sister?' he asked.

'She's busy.' Sienna nodded toward Paige, who had run over to give Zach a congratulatory hug. 'She won't miss us.'

'Then what are we waiting for? Let's go,' he said, pulling her away from the crowd. He kept his hand on the small of her back as they walked back toward the lobby.

'I've been wanting to get you alone all night,' Sienna told him. 'And the VIP lounge didn't count.'

Jason opened his mouth to answer – just as his cell phone gave off a loud beep. He and Sienna both looked at it in dismay. With a sigh, Jason flipped it open and glanced at the screen. 'It's a text.'

'From who?'

'Adam.' Jason frowned at the message. 'It just says In trouble. Red Lake.'

'What does that mean?' Sienna asked anxiously. 'What kind of trouble?'

'I don't know.' Jason quickly dialed Adam's number. Before it even rang, the call went straight to voicemail. Jason hung up and dialed again, a worried feeling growing in the pit of his stomach. He got voicemail again. 'Dammit, he's not answering!' he cried.

A few people nearby looked over, and he realized he was yelling. 'What does Red Lake mean?' he asked Sienna desperately, trying to quiet down.

'Jason? What's going on?' Paige came rushing over, followed by Zach. 'You sound upset.'

'It's Adam,' Sienna answered for him. 'He sent a text that says he's in trouble.'

'What trouble?' Paige asked. 'Wasn't he just off filming?'

'It just says trouble and Red Lake,' Jason told her. 'And I think his phone is turned off now. He won't answer.'

'Red Lake?' Zach's voice was grim. 'There's a bar called the Red Lake.'

Jason didn't like his tone. 'Where is it?'

'Off the Strip, in the seedy part of town,' Zach replied. 'It's a dive bar. If Adam is in trouble there, he could be in *real* trouble.'

Jason met his eye. 'Let's go.'

Seven

'What the hell was he thinking?' Zach asked as the cab turned down yet another dark and deserted street.

'He wanted to film the seedy underbelly,' Jason explained.

Zach raised an eyebrow.

Jason sighed. 'I didn't really think he'd *find* the seedy underbelly. I mean, it's Adam.'

'Exactly.' Zach shook his head. 'Adam at the Red Lake. That's the kind of place even I wouldn't visit alone.' He let the "and I have superhuman strength and can jump thirty feet in the air and fight like Jackie Chan" part go unsaid, which Jason appreciated. In fact, he was appreciating Zach a lot right now. What with paying for them to stay in the amazing hotel, arranging the incredible dinner, and now helping bail Adam out of trouble, Zach was starting to seem like the greatest guy ever.

'This place is nowhere near the Strip. How did Adam end up here?' Jason wondered aloud.

'Hopefully he'll still be here, so he can tell us himself. Try his cell again.'

Jason dialed. Voicemail picked up. 'It's still not working.'

The driver pulled over in front of a dingy one-story building with a single yellowish light bulb hanging outside. 'Ten dollars, fifty,' he said.

Jason shoved some money into his hand. 'Can you wait for us?'

The driver snorted. 'Not for ten dollars, fifty.'

'Fifty dollars for you to wait,' Zach told him. 'Fifty more to take us back to the hotel when we're done here.'

The driver sized him up. 'It's your money, kid. But I think you're crazy going in that place.'

Zach just handed him a fifty and climbed out of the car.

Jason followed. 'Fifty bucks?' he queried.

'We're not going to find a cab in this neighborhood, and we may need to leave in a hurry,' Zach told him. 'It's worth the money.'

They walked over to the metal door and pulled it open. A fat guy in a faded Metallica T-shirt sat on a stool inside. He took one look at them and laughed.

'Our friend is inside,' Jason told him.

'No, he's not,' the bouncer replied. 'You boys just get

back in your taxi and go drink on the Strip like you're supposed to.'

'We'd rather drink here,' Zach told him, walking inside.

The guy stuck out a beefy arm that hit Zach across the chest. 'This is a local place. You two are tourists. *Stupid* tourists,' he said. 'You think you're gonna slum it in here, get a taste of the real Las Vegas?'

'We just want to get our friend,' Jason explained.

'No.'

'And who's going to stop us?' Zach asked. Something in his voice made Jason look over at him, and he saw that Zach had changed. His face looked sharper, his neck thicker. His whole body just looked *bigger* some-how. And Jason could swear that his dark brown eyes had become flat-out black.

He's changing his appearance, Jason realized. The vampires could alter the way they looked to do more than simply tone down their supernatural beauty when they wanted to. He'd learnt that back when he was fighting Luke Archer, the bloodlusting vampire who'd made himself look like an entirely different person when he was on the hunt.

The bouncer stared at Zach, too, obviously thrown.

'We're going in,' Zach told him.

The guy dropped his arm. 'Fine. But if you get into

trouble, it's on your head. I told you, you don't belong here.'

He's right about that, Jason thought as they walked in. The Red Lake was dark, but that didn't disguise how filthy the floors were. The air smelled like stale cigarettes and stale beer. And the clientele consisted entirely of big, mean-looking guys. Jason suddenly felt like an idiot in his polo shirt and sport coat. At least Zach could make himself look large and nasty.

'Freeman.' Zach nodded toward the back of the room. There was a table under a hanging light, and a bunch of guys were gathered around it playing poker.

Adam sat in the corner, surrounded by dangerous-looking dudes. He held a few tattered cards in his hands, and a stack of money was piled on the table in front of him.

Jason stared in surprise. 'I thought he said he was in trouble.'

'Doesn't look like trouble,' Zach replied. 'I'd say he's at least ten grand up. Maybe more.'

Jason headed over to the table, trying to ignore the stares of the other patrons. When Adam spotted him, a huge smile spread over his face. 'Jason!' And then he saw Zach, and his smile got even bigger. 'My friends are here, guys. Deal me out.'

The four nasty-looking guys at the table turned to check out Jason and Zach. The one dealing the cards grunted and started to shuffle. Adam took his money and started to get up.

'Not so fast,' The dude closest to Jason said standing up. He was at least six foot five, and had a tattoo of the Grim Reaper on the back of his shaved skull. 'You have my money.'

Adam froze. 'I won the money. You all saw me.'

One of the other guys, a skinny dude with black, greasy hair, laughed. 'He won the money, all right.'

'Let's go, Turnball,' Zach said, stepping forward.

But the Grim Reaper was still standing between Adam and the door. More importantly, he was standing between Adam and his friends. 'Sit your ass down and play,' he ordered Adam. 'You can leave when I've won my money back.'

'He has to go now,' Zach said evenly. 'We're not waiting.'

'If he tries to leave with my money, I'll break his arm,' the Grim Reaper replied, his eyes never leaving Adam.

Adam's face paled and he sank back down into the chair.

'That's not very sportsmanlike,' Zach said softly.

The skinny dude laughed again. 'You want in,

pretty boy? You can play, too. Teach us all to be sportsmanlike.'

'We're leaving now. Adam, get up,' Zach said flatly.

Adam glanced at Jason. Jason nodded. Slowly, Adam stood up. He shoved the money into his backpack and started inching his way around the table. When he reached the Grim Reaper, the guy pounced.

Zach hit him before Jason even realized he'd pulled back his arm. The big guy's head snapped to the side, and he stumbled backwards.

Instantly, all the lowlifes jumped to their feet. Jason heard a hollow thudding sound, as if something heavy had fallen to the ground. He caught a glimpse of something black and metallic under the table. *A gun?* he thought frantically. And then the skinny guy was rushing him.

Jason instinctively ducked the blow. He wrapped his arms around the guy's waist and tackled him to the floor, landing with his weight on the dude's chest.

'Oof!' The skinny guy struggled for breath, trying to wriggle out from under Jason. Jason punched him in the jaw, then punched him again. The guy stopped struggling.

As he climbed to his feet, Jason could see Zach moving – fast. The Grim Reaper was down, his chair was knocked over, and another guy's fist was flying toward Zach's head. Then somehow Zach wasn't there anymore. The guy's punch went wide. Zach grabbed him in a chokehold from behind and spun quickly, using his momentum to throw the guy into one of his friends. They both hit the ground, hard.

Where's the gun? Jason wondered, scanning the floor around the poker table. Zach could win in a fight, but if he got shot, he'd still be in bad shape. The floor was covered with the shattered glass of beer bottles knocked over in the fight, and cards were everywhere. But there was no gun.

'Break it up!' the bartender shouted. Jason saw the big bouncer heading toward them, and Adam scooping up his backpack again. As the bouncer rushed Zach, Jason slipped in behind him and jabbed the guy in the small of his back. The bouncer gave a grunt of pain, and his momentum carried him forward, right onto his face.

Zach was moving so fast it was hard to see what he was doing, but, in another second, he had the last of the poker players pinned against the wall.

'Adam, let's go,' Jason commanded.

'That's fine, you can go,' gasped the guy Zach had pinned.

'Thanks.' Zach let him go, then turned and nodded at Jason. Jason shoved Adam in front of him all the way to the door. Everybody watched them go, but nobody dared to interfere.

Outside, the cab was waiting. Jason jerked open the door, waited for Adam and Zach to get in, then jumped in behind them. 'Let's get out of here!' he cried.

The driver peeled out, racing down the deserted street and around two more corners before slowing down. He glanced over his shoulder at them. 'I don't know what happened in there, but you boys are crazy,' he said. He grabbed the little door in the plastic divider between the front and back seats and slammed it closed.

Jason and his friends stared at it for a moment. Then they all laughed.

'So thanks for saving my butt and everything,' Adam said. 'I wish I could've filmed you in action, Zach, but I was too busy being terrified.'

'What were you doing in that place?' Jason asked.

'Well, I started out in a bar just off the Strip. You know, so I could see how the real people party in Las Vegas.'

Zach snorted.

'That wasn't bad. It was this excellent little Hawaiian-themed place with surfboards on the wall.'

'Three metres away from the Strip isn't exactly the mean streets of Vegas,' Zach told him.

'Yeah, I don't think theme bars really attract the downtrodden locals,' Jason agreed.

'I know. So I asked the waitress there where I could go to find real Vegas types. And she sent me to another place a few blocks further away. I think it was called McAllen's or something like that. I got some great footage of these guys playing poker. They had all kinds of good, cinematic tats.'

'Like the Grim Reaper?' Jason guessed.

'Yeah,' Adam said sheepishly. 'Anyway, they noticed me filming them and they asked me to join them. So I did. And I won, like, a thousand dollars!'

'Let me guess. Once you were winning, they asked you to leave the nice Irish pub and go with them to the Red Lake,' Zach said.

'Right. Wait, how did you know that?' Adam asked.

'It's a standard con artist move. Get the mark to feel all self-confident, then start the real con job,' Zach explained. 'They made you think you could win some real money, then they took you to a place where they could rough you up if you decided to bail on them.'

'You think they were con artists?' Adam gasped. 'I thought they were just mean guys.'

'Who knows?' Jason put in. 'But they thought you were a naïve rich kid, and they figured they could bleed you for all your money.'

'I guess. Except I'm not rich,' Adam said. 'So instead they bled me for everything else. They took all my money, then when I ran out they took my watch. Then my camera. That's when I sent you the text.'

Jason nodded.

'They saw me do that, so they took my phone,' Adam said. 'I figured they were gonna make me keep playing until they had the shirt off my back! But it's your shirt, Jason, so I didn't care too much.'

'What?' Jason examined Adam's button-down white shirt. 'That *is* my shirt!'

'Yeah, I can't believe you really thought I was willing to *iron*,' Adam said. 'Anyway, then the skinny guy joined in the game, and I think he threw the others off, because I started winning again.' He grinned. 'I won it all back, and then some.'

He dug through his backpack, doing a quick count of the money as the cab turned back on to the Strip.

'How much?' Jason asked.

'I'd say 15, maybe 18,000 dollars.' Adam did a little dance in his seat.

'Sweet,' Zach commented with a nod. 'Too bad it's counterfeit.'

Eight

Adam stared at Zach in open-mouthed horror. 'Say what?'

'It's counterfeit.' Zach took a twenty from Adam's hand and held it up to the lights of the Strip. 'Look. The watermark is wrong. Check it against one of mine if you want.' He dug out a twenty and handed it over.

As Adam frantically held the two bills up to the window, Zach went on. 'And I'll bet you every dollar I won at the Rouge et Noir tonight that the serial numbers on those bills are sequential. It's not the kind of thing you would've noticed in the middle of a poker game, but I bet you could line them up in order.'

'Don't take that bet, Adam. Zach won a ton of money tonight.'

'Yeah, *real* money,' Adam agreed, slumping back against the seat. 'And here I thought I had suddenly turned into a poker god.'

'I think the skinny guy wanted you to win so that he

could funnel the fake money to you. Then you'd go spend it around town,' Zach said.

'But the Grim Reaper wasn't in on the plan,' Jason guessed. 'He was just trying to take you for as much as he could get.'

'So you're saying I got taken in by two different con men with two different agendas, all in the space of one poker game?' Adam asked. 'Damn! I should've been filming that.'

'Even you couldn't film and play at the same time,' Jason consoled him.

Adam was rifling through ten and 20 dollar bills as they talked. 'I can already see four sequential numbers,' he moaned. 'Zach is totally right. It's fake. Oh, my God!'

'Don't freak out,' Zach said, glancing through the divider at the driver.

'Why not?' Adam cried. 'I'm trafficking in counterfeit money!'

'You are not,' Jason said. 'Trafficking means spending it. All you're doing is carrying it in your backpack.'

'That's still illegal,' Adam argued. 'What if I get caught? My father will kill me!'

'You're not going to get caught,' Zach said. 'You haven't done anything wrong.'

'But the cops won't believe that. I'm sitting here

with thousands of fake dollars!' Adam clutched his head. 'I can see the headlines now. *Sheriff's Son in Funny Money Ring Bust*. I'm a dead man.'

The cab pulled up in front of the hotel, and Zach handed over another fifty. The driver just snatched it and peeled out.

'I don't think he liked us,' Jason commented, watching him go.

'He was just worried those guys from the Red Lake were going to come after us,' Zach said. He yawned. 'I seriously need to sleep.'

'Sleep? We can't sleep,' Adam said. 'You have to help me figure out what to do with this cash.'

'Keep it in your bag and don't spend it,' Jason told him, leading the way across the empty lobby to the elevator. 'The cops aren't going to randomly ask to search your bag.'

'What if they do, though?' Adam insisted.

'Then they would be breaking the law and doing an illegal search,' Zach replied. The elevator whooshed up to the 17th floor. 'You, of all people, should know that, Turnball.'

'No. I have to get rid of it,' Adam was saying as the doors opened. He stepped out into the hallway with Jason, still talking. 'But how? That's the hard part. Maybe I can just throw it away?'

'Goodnight, guys.' Zach let the doors close before Adam could stop him. Jason headed to their door and swiped the key card to open it.

'I don't think that will work, though,' Adam went on as they stepped inside the room. 'It's hard not to notice someone throwing away thousands of dollars.'

Jason flopped face down onto his bed. 'It's almost five in the morning, Adam. Goodnight.'

Adam ignored him. 'Maybe I could just put a few bills into trash cans all over Vegas. I guess that would take a long time, though. Or maybe I could just bury it in the desert . . .'

Jason pulled the pillow over his head and went to sleep.

The morning sun streaming through the hotel windows woke Jason at about ten o'clock. Yawning, he sat up and looked around.

Adam was gone.

'Oh, my God, he actually went to bury his counterfeit money in the desert,' Jason said aloud. He dragged himself out of bed and trudged over to the bar, where Adam had left a note propped up on the coffee maker. Jason rubbed the sleep out of his eyes and read it: '*CSI* shoot today. Meeting Grissom. Woohoo.'

There was a knock at the door. When he opened it,

he found Brad, Van Dyke, and the Devereux girls standing in the hallway.

'Did you just wake up? Lame,' Van Dyke greeted him. 'Got any mini muffins in your bar? I ate all of ours.' He pushed his way past Jason and went to search the bar.

'What's going on?' Jason asked as the rest of them trooped in. Sienna stopped to give him a kiss.

'Maggie, Erin, and Belle are off shopping, and Zach is MIA,' Paige told him. 'We figured we'd wake you guys up before finalizing plans.'

'Where's Adam?' Sienna asked. 'You did find him last night, didn't you?'

'Yeah, he's fine. He's at the *CSI* shoot,' Jason said. 'But we didn't get home until five. Maybe Zach's still asleep.'

'Whatever. He can take care of himself,' Paige said with a dismissive wave. 'The question is, what are *you* going to do?'

'Huh?'

'Will you be having a manly day with Brad and Van Dyke, or will you be getting pampered in the hotel's world-class spa with Sienna and me?' Paige gave him a mischievous grin.

'That's a trick question,' Brad said. 'If you choose the spa, we'll all think you're a loser. Men don't do spas.'

Jason thought about that. Sienna in a little spa towel and not much else? That sounded like a good deal to him. 'What does the manly day consist of?'

'Van Dyke wants to go down to the MGM Grand Arena. Apparently there's a press conference for the big title fight this weekend,' Brad said.

'Hey! Sometimes the fighters get into it at those press conferences,' Van Dyke said with his mouth full of muffins. 'That would be a really cool thing to see.'

'And afterwards, we can do a little rock climbing out in the desert,' Brad went on. 'Work up a sweat after all that partying last night.'

Jason nodded. Rock climbing definitely sounded fun. 'What happens at the spa?'

'Um, salt rubs and chemical peels,' Sienna admitted.

'That sounds painful,' Jason said.

'Yeah, but afterwards there are massages and manicures.'

That settled it. 'Manly day it is,' he told Brad. 'See you girls at dinner.'

'Let's meet in the VIP lounge in the lobby,' Paige said. 'Eight o'clock. Last one there has to buy me a sinful chocolate dessert!'

Sienna came over and gave him a long kiss. 'I'll be all freshly scrubbed and massaged,' she murmured. 'Can't wait.'

'Me neither,' Jason agreed, watching her leave with her sister. No matter what the day was like, tonight promised to be amazing.

'Wow!' Van Dyke said just after eight o'clock that night. 'She looks incredible.' He clapped Jason on the back. 'You're a lucky man, Freeman.'

I definitely am, Jason thought, watching Sienna walk across the lobby toward the VIP lounge where they'd waited while Zach checked in. Either she was letting her true face show, or the spa treatments were every bit as good as she claimed. Her skin was glowing, her black hair shone like obsidian, and her luscious lips were as red as ripe cherries. He had to kiss her. Right now.

Jason walked over to meet her and pulled her into his arms. 'Let's blow off everyone else and have a romantic dinner by ourselves,' he suggested, planting kisses up her neck to her ear.

Sienna smiled delightedly. 'Now that would be an evening to remember,' she said. 'Unfortunately, our friends would never let us get away with it.' She gestured over his shoulder, and Jason turned to see Erin, Belle, and Van Dyke all watching them with amusement.

'Stop being so mushy, Freeman,' Van Dyke called. 'You're making me look bad with Maggie. Now I'm going to have to be all gooey and romantic when she shows up.'

'Why did we come with them again?' Jason asked jokingly. He pulled away, but kept hold of Sienna's hand. 'You look nice and relaxed.'

'The spa was great,' she said. 'And it was nice to spend some one-on-one time with Paige. She hasn't been herself since she got back from Paris.'

Jason nodded. He'd had a feeling that was true. 'Well, I can't say rock climbing was very relaxing,' he told her. 'It was about a hundred degrees out there. But the views were killer.'

The private elevator opened across the lobby, and Brad and Maggie appeared. 'Zach called,' Brad told the others when he reached them. 'He said he's busy tonight.'

'Doing what?' Belle asked.

Brad shrugged. 'Who knows? It's typical Zach.'

'He does enjoy being mysterious,' Jason agreed.

'Where's Adam?' Maggie asked. 'And Paige?'

'Adam isn't back from the shoot yet,' Jason said. 'I'm sure he's going to stay there until every single actor, cameraman, and grip has packed up and gone home.'

'Where's your sister?' Erin asked Sienna. 'Isn't she late?'

'I guess.' Sienna checked her watch. 'Wow. It's almost eight thirty.'

'Paige is never late,' Brad said, an edge of worry creeping into his voice.

'I know.' Sienna frowned. 'She was just planning to take a shower and get dressed for dinner. I don't know why it would be taking so long.'

'Maybe she fell asleep,' Jason suggested. 'She has been partying pretty hard, even since before we came to Vegas.'

'Yeah, but so has everyone else.' Sienna pulled out her cell phone. 'I'm going to call her.' She dialed, and gave Jason a smile as she waited for Paige to pick up.

Suddenly the blood drained from Sienna's face.

'What?' Jason asked, concerned. 'Sienna? What's wrong?'

'Paige's phone . . .' she said. 'The message says that it's been disconnected. But she's been using that phone all week.' Sienna's eyes clouded with fear. 'Something's wrong!'

Jason nodded. 'Let's go check on her.' He grabbed Sienna's hand, and they jogged back over to the elevator. Moments later, they were knocking on the door of Paige's penthouse suite.

There was no answer.

'Paige?' Sienna called through the door. 'Paige! Are you in there?'

Still nothing.

Jason banged on the door.

'Who . . . who's there?' Paige's voice called from the other side.

Jason felt a rush of relief. Paige had probably just slept through all their knocking. She was there and she was fine. But then again . . . Her voice sounded frightened. More than frightened. Terrified.

'Who is that?' Paige demanded again.

'It's me, Sienna. And Jason,' Sienna called back. 'Let us in.'

After a moment, the door swung open. Sienna went right in, so Jason followed. Paige looked awful: pale and drawn, with sunken cheeks. She wore only a bathrobe, and her long dark hair was wet and clearly hadn't been combed. She didn't even say anything, just closed the door behind them and sat down on her bed.

Jason noticed that her hands were trembling. 'Paige, are you sick?' he asked gently. 'You don't look so good.'

Sienna went over and felt her sister's head to see if she was feverish, but Paige shook her off. 'The bath-room,' she said. She drew her legs up underneath her and didn't say anything else.

Jason strode over to the bathroom and glanced around. Everything looked perfectly normal.

Sienna came up behind him. 'What's going on?' she murmured.

'I have no idea.' He turned back to Paige. 'There's nothing here, Paige. What's wrong?'

Paige leapt to her feet with an energy that surprised Jason, rushed over to the bathroom, flipped on all the lights, and turned the hot faucet in the sink all the way on. Then she stalked over to the shower and turned that on full blast, too, spinning the handle all the way to 'Hot'. Steam poured out of the open shower door.

'Paige, I don't understand,' Sienna said. 'What's this all about?'

Paige didn't answer. Instead, she pointed at the mirror that took up the entire wall behind the sink. It was already steamed up from all the heat.

And then Jason saw it: words, written on the mirror in the condensation that the steam had created . . . 'See you soon'.

Nine

Sienna gasped.

'Someone was here,' Paige whispered, frightened, as she walked back to her bed. 'Somebody was inside my hotel room!'

Jason nodded grimly as Sienna rushed over to the bed and threw her arms around her sister.

'Oh, Paige, no wonder you're all freaked out!' Sienna exclaimed.

'"See you soon",' Jason read aloud. He turned to Paige. 'What does that mean?'

Paige bit her lip and looked down at her hands.

'Is it a threat?' Jason asked gently. He had a feeling Paige knew more about this than she was letting on.

Slowly, almost imperceptibly, Paige nodded. 'It's . . . it's kind of a threat.'

'From who?' Sienna demanded. 'Who's threatening you?'

Paige took a deep breath. 'In Paris, there was this

guy. I met him almost as soon as I got there for college, and we started dating.'

Sienna nodded.

'And it got pretty serious pretty fast,' Paige went on.

Jason noticed Sienna's surprised expression. He remembered Adam's story about the three prom dates, and how Paige never dated anyone seriously. Somehow he got the feeling that Paige hadn't meant the situation in Paris to get serious, either. Even now, she looked a little confused as she talked about it. *In Malibu, Paige was always in control of her relationships*, Jason thought. *But it was different in Paris.*

'Who was this guy?' Sienna asked.

Paige looked her in the eye. 'His name is Marc. Marc Lessard.'

Sienna gasped.

'Who's he?' Jason asked.

'Lessard,' Sienna said. 'As in, *the* Lessards?'

'Yes,' Paige whispered. 'His father is Pierre Lessard.'

'Who are the Lessards?' Jason demanded.

'They're one of the Thirteen Families,' Sienna told him. 'See, back when the vampire clans first decided to organize, there were thirteen particularly powerful families who got together and formed the first High Council. It was hundreds of years ago, in Paris.'

'And these Lessards are still around?' Jason asked.

Paige nodded. 'Yes. Most of the original families died out over the years; there are only four left—'

'Three,' Sienna corrected her. She looked at Jason. 'Your Aunt Bianca's husband was a member of the fourth family. He was the last of his bloodline.'

'And he didn't have any kids,' Jason said. He'd always known that, but all of a sudden some other things began to fall into place. 'He didn't leave an heir, except Bianca. That's why she was so obsessed with turning Dani and me into vampires, to make sure that her late husband's family didn't die out!'

Sienna nodded. 'You have to understand, Jason. There are a lot of vampire families. But the Thirteen Families were the most powerful. They had the *most* powerful vampire abilities, so their word became law. Anyone descended from those families is, well, special.'

He looked from Sienna to her sister and back. 'You're descended from them,' he guessed. How could they not be?

'We are,' Paige confirmed. 'So are the Lafrenières. So are most of the vampire families in DeVere Heights. But our families are descendants of other branches of the Thirteen Families, branches that married other vampires who weren't of the Thirteen. None of us are pure. Not compared to Marc Lessard.'

'The Lessards are one of the original Thirteen

Families,' Sienna explained, '*and* they've only ever married women from the Thirteen Families. They're one of the most revered clans among us.' Sienna explained.

'Marc's father, Pierre, is a really high-ranking French diplomat,' Paige said. 'He has more connections than anybody else in the vampire community.'

'Wow!' Jason thought about the kind of connections the Devereux family possessed, and about the major pull Zach's family had. It was hard to imagine an even more powerful and connected family.

'Paige, to be dating Marc Lessard . . . that's a pretty big deal,' Sienna said. 'It's like going out with Prince William or something.'

'That's what I thought, at first.' Paige laughed bitterly. 'But it didn't turn out to be so romantic and great. He was a complete psycho.'

'What?' Sienna cried.

'Not at first, I guess. I don't know.' Paige pushed her wet hair back from her face. 'He was really into me, always sending flowers, buying me things, calling all the time. And he was a Lessard! He took me to state dinners, and his father introduced me to all kinds of famous people. It was like living in a movie or something. But after a while, I felt a little smothered. You know I like my space.'

'Sure,' Sienna said.

'Well, Marc wasn't so happy about that. He thought I should be with him all the time. He even wanted me to drop out of school because it was taking up too much of my attention.'

'Is this why you didn't come home for Christmas?' Sienna asked.

Paige nodded. 'He couldn't bear to be away from me, he said. And he was incredibly jealous. Once Zach sent me a text message on my phone and Marc found it. He totally lost it. He threw my phone into the Seine!'

'But you've known Zach since we were babies,' Sienna said, frowning.

'Exactly, but Marc didn't want me talking to any other guys,' Paige sighed. She got up and began pacing nervously about the room. 'Anyway, I finally dumped him.'

'Good,' Jason said. 'He sounds like an overbearing jerk. I don't care if he is the vampire Prince William.'

'Yeah. But he wouldn't accept it,' Paige said.

'What do you mean?' Sienna asked.

'He just refused to let me break up with him. He acted as if it had never happened. He kept showing up at my apartment, leaving me voicemails, sending me flowers, like I'd never said it was over.'

'Freaky!' Sienna exclaimed, glancing at Jason.

He nodded. 'Did you try to break up with him again?' he asked Paige.

'Of course I did! Every single time he contacted me, I told him it was over. After a while, I stopped even trying to be nice about it. But he just kept telling me he loved me. I changed my phone number, I refused to see him . . . It didn't stop him.'

'But if you wouldn't take his calls, and you wouldn't see him . . .' Jason began.

'He followed me. I'd be at a café, and suddenly Marc would show up and sit down with me. Or I'd be out clubbing with my friends, and he'd be there. I know he was following me – or having me followed. How else could he have found me so often?'

Sienna chewed on her lip thoughtfully. 'He does sound pretty intense, but do you really think he was stalking you? Maybe it was just coincidence. You obviously hung out in the same crowd in Paris—'

'I'm not exaggerating, SiSi!' Paige cut in. 'You don't understand. He . . . he killed my boyfriend.'

Jason and Sienna both stared at her.

'The guy I started dating after Marc,' Paige went on, picking up her hairbrush and putting it down again, agitated. 'His name was Rob. He was from San Francisco and he was there for college, like me. He was really laid back, the total opposite of Marc. And I was so sick of Marc shadowing me! So when Rob asked me out, I said yes. We only went on a couple of dates, and then Marc found out.'

'What happened?' Jason asked.

Paige let out a little sob.

Sienna took her hands. 'Calm down, Paige. Just tell us what happened.'

'Marc showed up in the street outside my apartment and started yelling up at me that I belonged to him and I should know better than to be with another guy. I called the police, but that didn't matter. As soon as they saw who he was, they left him alone.'

'And Rob?' Jason prompted.

'Rob's car hit a tree the very next day,' Paige said, tears streaming down her cheeks. 'His brakes went out while he was driving downhill, he lost control and the car slammed right into the tree. The police said it was an accident, but I know it was Marc. I know it! He must have got someone to cut the brakes.' She dissolved into sobs and collapsed onto the bed. Sienna held her and rocked her back and forth. Jason met her gaze over Paige's head. He didn't like this story one bit. This Marc Lessard was clearly powerful, but he sounded kind of nuts. And that wasn't a good combination. Jason found himself thinking about Aunt Bianca, who was also a powerful vampire, and who was also pretty unstable.

His aunt had caused him and his friends a lot of trouble. Was Marc going to do the same?

Suddenly Paige sat up and wiped her eyes with the back of her hand. 'Enough. Anyway, that was the last straw. I threw my things into a bag and got on a plane home the next morning.'

That's one mystery solved, Jason thought. Nobody had known why Paige was back early, but now it all made sense.

'So it's over,' Sienna said. 'Good. It will all be OK now that you're back here with your old friends, with your family.'

'No it won't. Don't you see?' Paige jumped up and began pacing again.

Jason felt the hairs on the back of his neck stand up. 'The flowers?' he guessed. 'Those roses at the Sixties party?'

Paige nodded. 'Exactly. He's here. He followed me to Malibu. He's the one who sent me those stupid roses.'

'Are you sure?' Sienna cried.

'Yes. I recognized his handwriting on the card. He always put a little curl at the end of his "y". That's why I wanted to come to Vegas, to get away from him – at least until Mom and Dad get home.'

Jason's gaze shifted to the mirror in the bathroom.

'See you soon,' he read. There was a curl at the bottom of the 'y'.

'Oh, my God. You think he's here, in Vegas!' Sienna exclaimed.

'He must've followed me again.' Paige stopped pacing and sank to the ground. 'I bet he's the one who put that Bollinger in my suite last night, too. It's just like the things he was doing in Paris.'

'That car on the road,' Jason said, remembering. 'The SUV with the tinted windows. We told it to pass us, remember? And then I saw it on the side of the road later, like it was waiting for us.'

'You think that was Marc?' Sienna asked.

Jason nodded grimly.

There was a loud knock on the door, and all three of them jumped.

'Hey!' Van Dyke's voice bellowed. 'Who's in there?'

Sienna let out a nervous giggle of relief, and Jason went to open the door. Brad, Maggie, Erin, and Belle stood behind Van Dyke.

'What's going on?' Van Dyke demanded. 'You two have been gone forever.' He stepped into the room and began looking around. 'Hey, Paige, sweet suite.'

The others followed him in. Brad glanced at Paige and immediately frowned. 'What's wrong?' he asked.

Paige just threw up her hands and disappeared into

the bathroom. Sienna quickly filled them all in on what had happened in Paris.

'I can't believe Marc Lessard is some kind of stalker,' Erin said. 'I met him once, when I was in France with my parents. He seemed so charming.'

'Apparently he is, until you try to dump him,' Brad said. 'What are we going to do about this?'

'Nothing,' Paige said from the door of the bathroom. She'd brushed her hair and put on some makeup, and she looked like her usual, take-charge self. 'I'm not going to let Marc ruin everyone's trip.'

'Nobody cares about spring break, Paige,' Sienna assured her. 'It's much more important to keep you safe.'

The others all nodded agreement.

'We should all be on our guard,' Jason said. 'Now that we know he's here, we can keep an eye out for the guy.'

'Yeah. Nothing bad can happen to Paige while we're watching her,' Maggie put in.

'I know – we'll all take shifts standing guard tonight,' Brad suggested. 'Two person teams, or maybe three person. This suite is huge, we can all stay in here overnight. Each team keeps watch for four hours while the others sleep. Then we switch.'

'No,' Paige protested. 'That's crazy.'

'I think it's a great idea,' Belle said. 'I already lost one person I love this year. I don't care what it takes, I don't want to lose another one, Paige.'

Brad put his arm around Paige's shoulders and gave her a squeeze. 'Don't you worry. If Marc tries anything, he'll have to go through all of us first.'

'Besides, it'll be fun,' Erin said. 'You can sleep and the on-guard team can watch movies on your giant plasma TV.'

They all laughed, but Jason could tell the laughter was forced. *They're nervous*, he realized. *They're all vampires, they're all super strong. And they're worried.*

And if the vampires were nervous, that could only mean one thing: the situation was very, very bad.

Ten

'This is the plan,' Zach said. 'I have a friend who runs a wine bar in a hotel right down the Strip. We're all heading over there. It's very friendly.'

As in vampire-friendly, Jason assumed.

Zach turned to Paige. 'It's a place where you'll be perfectly safe, and all of us can relax for a while.'

Everyone in Paige's suite was already more relaxed. It had happened the moment Zach arrived – which was about ten minutes after Brad had put in a call to him. Zach could be aloof some – make that most – of the time, but the guy came through when you really needed him.

'After that, we'll head over to *Spamalot*,' Zach continued.

'Oooh, I love all that old Monty Python stuff. I love you, Zach!' Paige gave an excited bounce on the suite's white leather sofa, eyes gleaming. She really did remind him of Tyler sometimes. Like Tyler on drugs. But Jason was pretty sure this was the natural Paige or, at least, the stressed-out natural Paige.

'*Spamalot?* Really?' Erin asked. 'I thought it was sold out for, like, ever.'

'Not a problem,' Zach answered.

Jason was starting to suspect there wasn't anything that was a problem for Zach. He pulled out his phone and quickly texted Adam the plan. 'Wanna come?' he concluded.

He shook his head when he read Adam's reply. '*CSI* SHOOTG ALL NITE. SEE U AM.' His friend was such a geek. And that was a good thing, he thought. Adam didn't need to get all tangled up in this new vampire crisis. He was human. He'd be a lot safer amid all the fake blood and murder, far away from any chance of encountering the real thing.

Of course, Jason was human, too . . .

Sienna reached over and squeezed his hand. Yes, Jason was human, too, but his situation was completely different. He squeezed Sienna's hand back. Completely, amazingly different.

'What are you all waiting around for?' Zach asked. 'Go get ready. I'm not taking you anywhere unless you clean up a little.'

Paige hopped up. 'I'm going to wear my new Lanvin. The one with the ruffles.' She fluttered her hands from her shoulders down to her midriff, indicating, Jason assumed, where all the ruffles were.

Jason laughed. He didn't get how she could be so *thrilled* about wearing a dress or going to some play, when less than half an hour ago, she'd been borderline hysterical with fear.

But Paige managed to hold onto her giddy excitement throughout the night. As they walked into the bar, which was all black, white, and metal, her enthusiasm for the party – hell, for life – shone so brightly that she soon had people from several tables around them making toasts to her.

At *Spamalot*, she laughed so hard one of the knights made a joke about her from the stage. It was clear he was a little smitten by the Lady Paige.

In a way, Paige was a lot like Zach. Not in personality, but in charisma. They could both control the mood of the group. Every single one of them had fun that night, despite the underlying tension, and it was mostly because of Paige.

It wasn't until they were in their hotel, heading toward the elevator that the earlier unease started to come back strongly. Maybe it was being back in the hotel, a place everyone knew Marc had been able to infiltrate.

Paige pulled a lipstick out of her purse and slid a fresh coating over her lips. Jason didn't get why, since they were already home. He guessed she just needed something to do with her hands.

'Jason and I will take the first shift watching Paige's room,' Zach announced as the elevator door opened with a *ping*. 'You and Van Dyke relieve us at four,' he told Brad as they all boarded.

'I'll get a wake-up call,' Brad answered. 'I may also have to pour water over Van Dyke's head. You know he sleeps like a coma patient.'

'Hey, untrue!' Van Dyke protested.

'Whatever it takes,' Zach told Brad with a grin.

'Do you want me to stay with you, Paige?' Sienna asked.

'We all could,' Belle added quickly. 'Slumber party!'

'I'm actually kind of tired,' Paige admitted.

Physically tired? Or just tired of pretending that she was having fun, fun, fun? Jason wondered. Maybe both.

'And you know I like to hog the whole bed,' she added.

'Well, call if you need anything,' Maggie said. 'Or if the boys get in over their heads. You know we can kick butt a lot harder than they can.'

'Zach just wants us well-rested in case some truly bad meanies show up,' Erin agreed.

'You figured me out,' Zach told them

The elevator opened on the 17th floor. Maggie, Erin, Belle, Brad, and Van Dyke stepped off. 'You coming, Sienna?' Belle asked.

Sienna held the door open with one hand. 'Maybe I'll wait for you in your room,' she told Jason. 'Adam's out for the night, right?'

'Right. I'll let you in.' He stepped out of the elevator and headed along the corridor with the others as the elevator doors slid closed behind him.

Jason let Sienna into his room with his key card. 'I'll be back as soon as Brad and Van Dyke come to take over,' he promised. Then he leant closer. 'Don't worry, I won't let anything happen to your sister.'

'I know.' Sienna kissed his cheek. 'See you soon.' She closed the door and Jason ran up the stairs to the 18th floor.

Zach let Jason into Paige's suite. She was getting settled in the bedroom, so Zach and Jason got settled in the living room. Jason picked up the remote and started flipping through the channels.

'Anything grab you?' he asked Zach.

'Whatever,' Zach answered.

Jason stopped on *300*. That movie would definitely put the plasma through its paces. He kept the sound really low; he wanted to be able to hear anything out of the ordinary.

It was kind of amazing to think about how much activity was going on in the casino below them, and in all the casinos, bars and clubs around. Up in the suite, it could have been another planet. The only sound came from the TV. Jason figured Paige had to have fallen asleep pretty much right away.

'I'm going to get a soda, want one?' Jason asked after about an hour. He felt like he was losing his edge. Not that he was about to fall asleep, just that he wasn't alert for any suspicious sound the way he had been at the beginning of the shift.

Zach shook his head. Jason grabbed a Coke from the bar and took a swig as he walked back to his chair. The carbonation bubbles felt good, popping against his dry throat.

'So what's the deal with the Thirteen Families?' he asked as he sat down again. 'Paige said the Lessards were one of them.'

Zach looked at him for a long moment. Was it not OK that Jason had asked a question about the vampires? After everything he already knew? He'd been shot by a vampire hunter for chrissakes!

'The first Vampire High Council was set up by the Thirteen Families during the Renaissance in France,' Zach finally replied. 'For some reason, the vampires from the Thirteen Families were particularly gifted in their vampire abilities. They were that bit faster, stronger, *more powerful* than "ordinary" vampires. For that reason, they became powerful politically.

They were the most prestigious of all vampires.

'Paige, Sienna, Brad, myself – most of the DeVere Heights vampires – have an ancestor from one of those Thirteen Families. But in each case, the ancestor married outside of the Thirteen – thus their bloodline, and their unusually potent vampire abilities, were diluted slightly.

'However, of those Thirteen Families, there are still three in existence today who had an ancestor on that first Council and who have had a member on every High Council since. They've always married other vampires from the Thirteen Families – so no dilution of their blood with "ordinary" vampires and no dilution of their powers. The Lessards are one of those families. They're rich, prestigious and unbelievably powerful,' Zach said flatly. 'That's all there is to know.'

Jason nodded thoughtfully as he and Zach turned back to the movie. He knew just how powerful the DeVere Heights vampires were. He could hardly imagine what the vampires of the Thirteen Families must be like.

'Whoa!' Jason couldn't stop himself exclaiming as an elephant went flying off a cliff.

'Yeah,' Zach agreed.

* * *

127

'Did you hear that?' Jason asked Zach several hours – and some extreme ass-kicking by the Spartans – later.

'Brad and Van Dyke,' Zach told him.

'You sure?'

Zach checked his watch. 'It's four.' He got up, checked the peep hole, then swung the door open. Brad and Van Dyke walked in. Brad looked a little bleary-eyed. Van Dyke looked a little wet.

'Anything?' Brad asked.

Zach shook his head.

'See you guys later,' Jason said as headed for the door. He couldn't wait to see Sienna. 'You're staying?' he asked Zach, who'd returned to his chair.

'Yes,' Zach answered.

Hmm, *could* there be some romantic interest there on Zach's part? Jason wondered. Maybe going to the prom with Paige meant something different to him than Sienna thought. Or maybe it was just Zach's extreme sense of duty kicking in. He was on the DeVere Heights Vampire Council. And even before that, he'd seemed to feel responsible for every vampire in the Heights, at least the ones in high school.

Jason felt a little weird leaving now, but he really wanted to see Sienna. And three vampires made for some pretty heavy-duty bodyguards. 'See you,' he said again and closed the door. He headed toward the elevator at a brisk walk, not allowing himself to break into a jog. He realized it had only been a little more than four hours since he'd seen his girlfriend. But she was waiting for him. In a fancy hotel room. Alone.

During the short elevator ride, he pulled out his key card, so he had it ready. He bolted down the hall, slid the key card through the lock, then opened the door and stepped into the room. All he heard was the soft hum of the air conditioner. No TV or radio or anything.

He quietly walked forward without turning on the lights, expecting to see Sienna asleep on his bed.

But it was empty.

So was Adam's.

She hadn't crashed on one of the sofas in the living room, either.

'Sienna?' Jason called. He backtracked to the bathroom and knocked. The door swung open. The room was empty.

She decided to go to her own room. She probably didn't like being alone after what happened to Paige, he told himself.

He'd just go next door, tell her that the first shift had gone by with no problems. It was late, but Sienna would want to know. He hurried to her room and gave a quiet knock.

No answer.

All the saliva in Jason's mouth evaporated. He knocked again, trying to swallow. 'Just a second,' Belle called.

OK. OK, OK. They'd been asleep. Duh. It was four in the morning.

Belle swung open the door. 'Is Paige OK?' she asked.

'Yeah, fine,' Jason said. 'I know it's late, but could I talk to Sienna for a minute?'

Belle smiled. 'Did you forget? She's waiting for you in your room, lucky boy.'

Jason's stomach did a slow, sickening roll. He shook his head. 'No, I just came from my room,' he told Belle. 'She's not there.'

Eleven

'Maybe Sienna popped over to Maggie and Erin's room,' Belle suggested. 'When Mags and Erin get together, sleep isn't something that usually happens. If the three of them found something fun to do without me, I'm not going to be happy.' Belle's words were playful, but her eyes were anxious. 'Let's get over there and see what's what.'

Jason led the way, trying not to freak out. He wasn't going to freak out before he had all the facts. OK, he was already freaking out a little, but he wasn't going to let Belle see that. When he reached Erin and Maggie's room, he gave three sharp knocks. The door swung open almost immediately. Seemed like Belle was right about Maggie and Erin and the not sleeping.

'Is something up with Paige?' Erin asked.

'Yeah did the psycho show?' Maggie added, crowding into the doorway next to Erin.

'She's fine,' Jason told them. 'And there's been no sign of Marc. Is Sienna in there with you?' he asked, forcing himself to keep his voice low and calm.

'Sienna? No. Last time we saw her was right after we got back from the show,' Maggie answered.

Jason's body went cold. 'She was supposed to be hanging out in my room, waiting for me, but she's not there.'

'And she wasn't with me in our room either,' Belle put in.

'I guess she could have gone down to the casino . . .' Erin suggested half-heartedly.

'By herself?' Belle snapped. 'Please.'

Jason agreed. The odds on that were worse than winning a million on the dollar slot machine.

'I'm going back to Paige's suite,' Jason told them. 'Maybe Sienna went to check on her and the two of us just missed each other somehow.' His brain hardly believed it. His gut didn't believe it at all.

'I'm going with you,' Belle said.

'Us too,' Maggie added. 'Give us half a minute to throw on some clothes.'

One minute later, Brad opened the door to the suite, eyes wary. Van Dyke was stretched out on the sofa, but Jason could see his muscles were tense. Zach stood leaning against Paige's bedroom door, one booted foot crossed over the other. His posture looked much more relaxed than the other guys' did, but Jason could tell his eyes were taking in every detail. He was on high alert.

'Did Sienna go in to see Paige?' Jason asked.

'Since you left?' Brad queried.

Jason nodded.

'Nobody's been in there but Paige. It's been completely quiet. Why?' Zach's voice was low and calm, with just a thread of steel running through it.

'Because she's not anywhere!' Belle exclaimed. 'She was supposed to be in Jason's room, but she's not there. And she's not in my room either, nor Erin and Maggie's. Something's very wrong!' Belle seemed an inch away from completely losing it. Why wouldn't she be? It hadn't been so long since her boyfriend had been murdered by a vampire hunter. The world still had to feel like a seriously dangerous place to her.

Zach stepped smoothly away from Paige's door as it swung open.

'What's going on? What's wrong?' Paige demanded.

'Sienna's missing!' Belle cried.

'At least, we don't know where she is right at this moment,' Jason added. He agreed with Belle. He thought something was very wrong too. But the way to help Sienna was for him – for everyone – to stay as calm and focused as possible.

Paige's fingers flicked up to her mouth, then to her throat. 'Oh, God, what was I thinking? She shouldn't have been alone even for a minute. Sienna should have had guards on her, too. Marc's abducted her. I know it!' Her voice caught. 'This is all my fault!'

'Let's all sit down,' Zach told her firmly. Everybody sat down in the huge living room. Dawn was just beginning to break, and the earliest beams of sunlight were competing with the crazy neon colors of the Strip.

Paige began to pace. 'Marc knows how much I love SiSi. I talked about her to him all the time. So he's going to use her to make me do what he wants,' Paige cried.

'Sit down!' Zach ordered, pointing at one of the overstuffed armchairs.

Paige obeyed. Zach was younger, but there was something about him that commanded respect.

'Marc's already killed one person to try to force me to go back to him. Now he has Sienna. What if he . . . ?' Again her fingers fluttered to her lips, like she couldn't stand to let the next words escape from her mouth.

Zach walked over to the bar, took out a bottle of Evian, and handed it to her. 'Have some water,' he said.

The room was silent except for the click of the screw-top cap as Paige twisted it off, then the soft sounds of her swallowing the water. Jason, Brad, Belle, Van Dyke, Maggie, and Erin all stared at her, trying not to look like they were staring. Zach didn't bother to hide his gaze. He kept his eyes on her face.

'*Whooo are you? Who? Who? Who? Who?*' Adam bellowed, as he strolled into the room, shattering the silence. '*CSI* has to have one of the most kickass theme songs of all time.' He flopped down on the floor, yanked off his shoes, and opened the bar fridge with his toes. 'So what's up?' he asked as he tried to extract a Vault with his feet. 'Did I miss anything? Not that I could have missed anything more cool than the *CSI* set. I got the big G.G.'s autograph, and Lady Heather's. You people with questionable taste probably think of her as Julie Cooper from *The O.C.*, but she'll always be Lady Heather to me—'

'Adam!' Jason finally managed to cut in. 'Sienna's missing.'

Adam straightened up fast. 'For how long? Who saw her last?' He suddenly sounded a lot more like the son of a sheriff than a fan with a geek-on.

'About one o'clock. She told me she was going to head back to our room to wait for me to finish my shift guarding Paige,' Jason told him.

'OK, back it up further,' Adam said.

'My old boyfriend followed me here from France,' Paige answered, spinning the bottle of water back and forth between her palms. 'He wants me back, and I know he snatched Sienna as a way to' – she gave a harsh bark of laugher – 'as a way to get my attention.'

'The guy is psycho,' Brad added. 'He killed the guy Paige started going out with after she stopped seeing him.'

'And is he, you know, well-endowed dentally?' Adam inquired.

'Yes, he's one of us,' Belle replied. 'He's from one of the Thirteen Families. That means he's practically royalty.'

'Big ears, weak chin, got it,' Adam said. Belle glared at him. 'Sorry. I sometimes use inappropriate humor to get through serious situations.' He looked over at Paige. 'Don't worry, we're going to get her back.'

'We are *absolutely* going to get her back,' Jason seconded. And he meant it. No matter what it took. No matter what big vampire family Marc was from, or how criminally crazy he might be.

'What about hotel security tapes?' Erin asked. 'They have cameras all over the place. Would they show us anything?'

'They could confirm that Sienna really did get snatched by Marc,' Van Dyke said.

'I already know she did,' Paige insisted. 'What else could have happened to her? Sienna wouldn't just wander off, not when she was afraid Marc might be coming after me.'

'Confirmation is good,' Zach said firmly. He nodded at Van Dyke, who was instantly on his feet. 'There's no reason for any outsiders to know what's happened,' he added, as Van Dyke headed for the door.

'Got that,' Van Dyke said as he left the suite.

'Let's just assume we get confirmation that Marc took Sienna,' Jason said. 'Then what?' He turned to Paige. 'Any ideas where he'd take her?'

'Not around here,' Paige answered. 'We never even talked about Vegas.'

'What about friends of his?' Maggie suggested. 'You must have met some of them when you two were going out. Would any of them have any ideas?'

'No one's going to go against Marc, don't you get that?' Paige demanded. She squeezed her water bottle until it cracked and water ran over her hands and down onto the carpet. She didn't even seem to notice. 'I got close to some of his friends, yeah. And maybe some of them even liked me more than they liked Marc. But that doesn't mean they'd help me if it meant crossing him.'

'So it doesn't sound like he's royalty. It sounds more like he's mafia,' Adam commented.

'That's a good way to think of it,' Paige told him.

'The Thirteen Families are not *exactly* like the mafia,' Zach corrected.

'In terms of power, they are. In terms of intimidation and control over the rest of us,' Paige insisted. She raised the water bottle to her lips. Her brow furrowed as if she had no idea how the cracks had appeared all over it.

'We could at least call around the other big hotels and try to find out where he's staying,' Erin suggested. 'There are only a few places that would be up to Lessard standards.'

'Except that Marc sometimes finds sleazy attractive,' Paige put in. 'He could have decided to stay at a grotty motel for a laugh.'

'It can't hurt to try and track him down,' Brad told her. He looked over at Erin. 'Let's grab the phone book and call some of the most likely places.' They headed over to the desk.

'So what else?' Jason asked. He needed to be doing something – anything that had a chance of getting him to Sienna.

Silence filled the room like some kind of noxious fog. 'On the way back here, I stopped at the Elvis chapel,' Adam said, rapid fire. 'There were two dudes dressed as Elvis, getting married by Elvis. Elvis was even playing the organ. It was awesome. Really. I mean it. Awesome – like that scene in *Magnolia* where it starts raining frogs.' He glanced around. 'OK, none of you know what I'm talking about, because the movie didn't come out last week. But it was unexpected, and strange, and beautiful. So I just kind of stood there, transfixed for a minute. Then I realized I was intruding on something private, so I turned around and started out, and I passed by this collection plate. And it hit me: a collection plate would be a great place to get rid of all that funny money! I reached for my backpack, but I couldn't do it . . . Anyway, that's not the point. In the chapel—'

'Is all this leading to an idea you had about finding Sienna?' Belle demanded sharply.

'Yeah,' Adam admitted. 'Sorry. Staying up all night does not lead to thoughts coming out of my mouth in a logical order. The thing is, even though *I* didn't want to intrude, there were a lot of tourists watching the wedding like it was just another show on the Strip. And thinking about that got me thinking about how many freakin' tourists there are in this burg. And that means we have a huge pool of potential witnesses.' Jason frowned. 'I don't follow. Marc and Sienna aren't getting married in an Elvis chapel. At least, they better not be. Why would tourists especially notice them?'

'Adam's onto something. I've seen pictures of Marc in *Paris Match*,' Maggie said. 'He's pretty delectable, right?' she asked Paige.

'Yeah. Until you get to know him,' Paige agreed.

'And Sienna, Sienna's gorgeous!' Maggie went on. 'The two of them together, they'd be hard to miss – even if they were just doing something ordinary. Maybe a valet saw them getting into a car. If so, we could find out what kind of vehicle they're in.'

'Good idea,' Brad called from the desk.

'Yes, but, I'm sorry, my mind keeps sticking on one thing . . .' Belle said.

'What?' Jason asked.

She looked over at Adam. 'You totally made me lose focus. Now I keep wondering, *why* couldn't you just leave the counterfeit money in the collection plate? That seems like the perfect place to get rid of it.'

Jason let out a groan. He couldn't believe they were talking about this now.

'I know. It should have been perfect,' Adam agreed. 'But I couldn't do it to the big guy.'

'God?' Belle asked.

'Elvis,' Adam replied.

'Enough!' Jason burst out. 'I think that's a good point about Sienna and Marc. Unless he altered his appearance and made Sienna change hers, there's a real chance somebody noticed what kind of car they got into. It's probably the SUV I saw following us on the way down here, but we should—'

He was interrupted by the sound of Paige's cell. She whipped it out of her purse. 'It's Sienna,' she said as she checked the screen.

For the first time since he'd walked into his room and found it empty, Jason was able to take in a full, deep breath.

'SiSi? Where are you?' Paige said into the phone.

As Jason watched, all the animation drained out of her face. She listened in silence for a moment, then said, 'I'll be there. Don't do anything stupid, Marc. I'll be there as soon as I can.'

'What did he say?' Zach asked the moment Paige hung up.

'He has her. I knew he did. He gave me coordinates in the desert. He said . . .' Paige blinked back tears. 'He said if I want to see my sister alive, I'll meet him there so he and I can talk.'

'He's not trustworthy, you know that,' Brad pointed out, hurrying back over to the group.

'It doesn't matter!' Paige cried. 'He has my sister!' Her hands curled into fists, and Jason could almost see her fear turning to fury. 'And I am *not* going to let that evil piece of slime hurt her. I'm not!'

Paige leapt to her feet. Belle grabbed her by the arm.

'You're not going alone. There's no possible way,' Belle said.

'No, she isn't,' Zach said calmly. 'I'm going with her.'

'So am I,' Jason added.

'What exactly do you think you'll be able to do?' Zach asked.

'I'm pretty good in a fight. I saved your butt once, remember?' Jason told him. 'Anyway, it's not your decision. Sienna's in danger. I'm there.'

Twelve

Zach smoothly maneuvered the Escalade off the high-way onto the Mojave Road. Road was pushing it, in Jason's opinion. He thought it should be called the Mojave Dirt Track. Or the Mojave Sort Of Cleared Stretch of Sand and Gravel.

'Marc *would* want to meet out in the middle of the desert,' Paige said, staring out at the miles and miles of scrubby brush, broken by the ruins of an old corral and part of an adobe farm house. 'He has a well-developed sense of the dramatic. He thinks of his life like it's a movie. He's the star. Everybody else is just a disposable extra.'

'Everybody but you,' Jason muttered.

'Yeah,' Paige answered, her fingers tightening on the dash. Jason knew it wasn't Zach's driving she was worried about. It was her sister.

'I hope he brought water for Sienna.' Paige hit the CD-changer. Hit it again. 'That guy at the gas station told me there's no place for supplies inside the whole

Mojave preserve. You could tell he thought we were crazy to be driving in here without caravanning it in case there was an emergency.'

Paige reached for the CD-changer again. Zach reached out and caught her hand. 'Trust me. I can handle this guy.'

'It's just that he doesn't think like a regular person,' Paige said. 'He takes risks no one else would take. He—'

'Trust me,' Zach repeated.

Paige sighed. 'Are we getting close to the coordinates Marc gave me?'

'I'm assuming that's him up there,' Zach answered.

Jason leant forward. 'Where?' All he saw was desert and more desert. Wait. He squinted. There was a little spot of black out there.

'Faster. Go faster,' Paige pleaded.

Zach took the Escalade up to 105. Jason could feel the sand sucking on the tires. He kept his eyes locked on the spot of darker color among the tans and yellow-greens. Yeah, that was an SUV parked up there. Jason hardly blinked as they sped forward, bouncing and jerking over the ruts in the trail. Not only was it an SUV, he realized. It was *the* SUV. The one that had been tailing them on the way into Vegas.

'There he is!' Paige exclaimed. 'I don't believe this.

He's sitting there drinking a beer, like he's at a damn tailgate party.'

'More like a costume party,' Jason commented. Marc was wearing tight cords, suede boots, an untucked tuxedo shirt, an unbuttoned tan vest, a floppy felt hat and shades. 'Is there a new store I don't know about? Cowboy Rockstar Wannabe?' Jason asked, going for a joke that wasn't even Adam-worthy.

'Takahiro Miyashita,' Paige told him, tossing out the name of a designer Dani *adored*.

'Let me handle things when we—' Zach began, but he didn't get a chance to finish. As he pulled over toward Marc's SUV, Paige scrambled out of the Escalade before it was even parked.

Zach cursed softly under his breath as he came to a stop. Jason ignored him. He was on the ground in seconds, right behind Paige. Zach followed them both.

'Where is my sister?' Paige snapped into Marc's face.

'We'll get to that,' Marc told her. Jason noticed that he had just the faintest of French accents. 'Want a beer? I also have a thermos of mojitos. Very refreshing in the desert.' He acted like Jason and Zach weren't even there. Jason peered into the darkness inside the SUV. He didn't see Sienna. Was she tied up in the front seat? Had Marc even brought her?

Marc reached into the cooler behind him and pulled

out a silver thermos and a cocktail glass. Paige slapped the glass out of his hand. 'Where's Sienna?'

Zach took a step forward. 'I'm—'

'I know who you are, Lafrenière,' Marc interrupted. 'And I'm sure I don't need to introduce myself. But this is none of your business. Or that human's, whoever he is. This isn't a council meeting. This is between me and my girlfriend.'

'It's not quite that simple when you've kidnapped the daughter of a DeVere Heights—'

' "Kidnapped" is such an ugly word,' Marc broke in. 'Little Sienna is perfectly safe – a long way from here, with plenty of air conditioning.'

So she wasn't in the SUV. Jason knew he'd been stupid to even hope for that.

'And she'll stay that way as long as Paige sits down and has a conversation with me,' Marc continued. He patted the spot on the tailgate next to him. 'A conversation *à deux*,' he added.

'Fine. I know how you are when you don't get your way,' Paige said, sitting down next to Marc and waving Zach and Jason back.

'You usually enjoy it when I get my way,' Marc said flirtatiously, as if he was just trying to patch up some little fight the two of them had had.

'Let's give them a few minutes to see how this plays

out,' Zach said under his breath as he and Jason backed up a few steps. Jason nodded. But he was going to listen in to every word. Anything Marc said could lead them to Sienna.

Marc took a long pull on his beer. 'You sure you don't want something? It's hot out here.'

'You wanted to talk. I'm ready to talk.' Jason heard Paige snap. He could hear the strain in her voice as she struggled to keep calm.

'You look beautiful,' Marc said. He ran one finger down Paige's cheek. 'Did you wear that shirt for me? You know it's my favorite.' He moved his finger down her throat and traced the V of the shirt's neckline.

Paige shivered.

Marc grinned. '*You* might say you don't want to be with me, but your body says different.'

'That was revulsion,' Paige shot back.

Jason could almost feel an electric charge arcing between them. Paige had an energy – a wildness about her – that Jason had seen when she partied. And it seemed like she'd found her counterpart in Marc. Right now, it felt as if at any moment the power they both generated would go nuclear, destroying them – and whoever else happened to be around.

Marc laughed. 'You keep on telling yourself that, baby girl.'

Paige jumped to the ground and faced Marc. 'You're delusional, you know that? You sent me flowers. You sent me champagne. They didn't work. That's when a *sane* guy moves on. But you won't accept that there is any girl anywhere who doesn't want to be with you. That just couldn't happen to Marc Lessard!'

Don't piss him off, Jason thought. *Be careful, Paige. Keep him calm, please.* Had Paige forgotten that Marc had already murdered one person she cared about? Anything she said could push Marc over the edge. Sienna could be the next person to end up dead.

'But think about it,' Paige went on, her voice sharp as mirror shards. 'You had to put my sister in danger to get me to speak to you. Doesn't that prove that I don't want anything to do with you? It's over, Marc. It's been over for a long time. Just tell me where Sienna is so we can both move on.'

Jason studied Marc's face. Was he going to tell Paige to go to hell? That she could forget about ever seeing Sienna again?

To Jason's surprise, Marc laughed. 'It's never going to be over between us, Paige, when are you going to realize that? Sometimes you might hate me. Sometimes I might even hate you. But that's because there's a deep connection between us. You're the most important person in my life. And I'm the most important person in yours. Come back to Paris with me – now, today. We belong together.'

'And Sienna?' Jason couldn't keep himself from bursting out.

'If you come home with me on the next flight, I'll let Sienna go,' Marc promised Paige.

'You got away with arranging Rob's "accident", but he wasn't one of us. Do you honestly believe that you – even you – can kill another vampire without bringing disgrace down on your entire family? And that would be just the beginning. The councils would demand justice, and—'

'You underestimate my father,' Marc said flatly. 'It would be simple for him to cover up any . . . mishap. You don't realize how deep the loyalty to him runs, or how many secrets he knows about all the families, secrets they would do almost anything to protect.'

Paige lowered her head and stared at the ground. Jason could almost feel her trying to come up with another solution, anything that didn't mean she had to leave with Marc.

'Come with me. You know you want to. We can be dancing at Batofar tonight,' Marc coaxed.

He really is delusional, Jason thought. *He thinks all she wants is some sweet-talking, a few more flower deliveries.*

'It's true, what you said,' Paige murmured, her voice so low that Jason had trouble hearing her. 'There is something between us. I think about you all the time, even though mostly when I think about you now, it's about how much I hate you, how much you've hurt me.'

Marc laughed again. 'That's a start.'

Paige raised her head, and when she did, the beginnings of a smile were on her lips. 'But wouldn't you rather have me go back to Paris with you because I *want* to, not because you found a way to force me?'

'Of course,' Marc replied. 'It's just that I know once you're back there, you won't believe you ever wanted to be anyplace else.'

'Wanna bet?' Paige asked, her little smile stretching into a grin, her eyes glittering feverishly.

She's come up with some kind of plan, Jason thought, uncertain whether that was a good thing or a bad thing. Jason couldn't guess what the plan was – or if it had a chance in hell of working – but he knew she'd concocted something.

Marc took off his sunglasses. 'What did you have in mind?'

'A game. A gamble. You still like to gamble, don't you?'

'Always,' Marc answered with a smile.

'Paige, I don't think this is—' Jason began.

She waved her hand at him impatiently, cutting him off. 'You win, and I go to Paris with you. Willingly, I promise, *if* Sienna goes free.' She tossed his hat on the ground and ran her fingers through his tousled blond hair.

'And if I lose?' Marc asked. 'Not that I ever lose.'

'You go back to Paris alone. Sienna goes free. It's a winner takes all proposition,' Paige explained. 'Are you in?' She was in full-on flirt mode, and Jason could see that she had Marc, hook, line and sinker.

'Don't I even get to know what we're playing?' Marc asked.

'Does it matter, since you never lose?' Paige taunted, moving a step nearer to him.

'It does not matter. We will play any game you say.' Marc closed the distance between them and kissed her. 'To seal the deal.'

Paige kissed him back, a longer, deeper kiss. 'Just so you'll remember what you're playing for.'

Was she as insane as Marc? Jason wondered. Did she even remember that her sister's life was what they were *really* playing for?

'The Ultimate High Stakes Invitational is tonight at the Bonheur. A Texas Hold 'Em tournament for very high rollers. You and Zach will enter. Whoever loses their money first loses the private gamble as well.' Paige glanced from Zach to Marc. 'Acceptable?'

Jason noticed Zach's eyes narrow slightly, and realized that he had been caught a little off guard – something that rarely happened. Nonetheless, Zach gave an almost imperceptible nod.

'Marc?' Paige asked.

'I'm in,' he told her. 'I'm looking forward to it.'

'Swear on your family name that you'll honor the terms,' Paige demanded, her face suddenly serious.

'Couldn't we just kiss on it again?' Marc asked.

'If you win, you can have all the kisses you want,' Paige told him. 'Now, swear!'

'I swear on the Lessard family name,' Marc answered gravely.

'Until tonight then,' Paige said softly, giving him a little wave as she, Zach, and Jason started back to the Escalade.

'I'm going to be collecting on all those kisses,' Marc called after her.

'I'm going to be getting my sister back,' Paige answered, too quietly for him to hear.

Jason glanced at Zach. He had the feeling Zach wasn't too happy about the way this meeting had gone down. Jason definitely wasn't.

Thirteen

'Am I absolutely brilliant? Or am I absolutely brilliant?' Paige demanded as Zach got the Escalade turned around. 'I played him like a violin!' She gave a trill of laugher, high and long, and bordering on the hysterical.

'Yeah, brilliant,' Jason answered sarcastically. 'Now whether Sienna lives or dies is going to be decided on a couple of hands of Texas Hold 'Em.' Not that he'd ever actually let it come to that.

'You left out the part that it's a couple of hands of Texas Hold 'Em *played by Zach*,' Paige countered. '*You* think I'm brilliant, don't you, Zach?' She reminded Jason of a three-year-old hitting the peak of a sugar high.

'I think only an idiot would have baited him the way you did,' Zach said abruptly, concentrating on the narrow road.

Marc tore by in the SUV, passing on the left so he could blow Paige a big, juicy kiss. She pressed her lips against the side window in response, leaving a dark cherry lip print. The sight of it made her laugh again.

'It worked, didn't it?' Paige asked. 'I said what I needed to say to get him to agree to the gamble. That's what I wanted to do, and that's what I did, because I'm – everybody say it . . .'

Nobody cooperated.

'. . . brilliant,' Paige finished alone, clearly frustrated that Jason and Zach weren't in celebration mode.

It's probably relief more than anything making her act like this, Jason thought, deciding to cut Paige some slack. It had to be nerve-twitching getting face to face with Marc, flirting with him, *kissing* him, even though she knew he was a murderer and that he was holding her sister hostage. She probably had a gallon of extra adrenalin running through her veins right now.

'So we have a few things to figure out,' Jason began. 'Things like Zach might, just possibly, lose. Then what? You can't seriously be thinking of going to Paris with that sociopath.'

'I've seen Zach play poker. I'm not that worried,' Paige said.

'How's he even going to get in the game? Or Marc?' Jason protested. 'It's invitational, as in *you have to be invited.*'

'I can make a few calls,' Zach said, with a grim smile.

'And Marc will have no problem. But let's assume for a minute that I *do* win. Do you really think Marc's just going to release Sienna and leave you alone forever?' he asked Paige.

'He swore on his family name,' Paige reminded him. 'That means something to us.'

'To *most* of us,' Zach corrected. 'Are you actually going to trust the word of a guy who kills to get his own way?'

'Good point. *Excellent* point, in fact,' Jason put in. 'Plus the game has a quarter mill buy-in. Zach can't even sit down at the table for less than that. How are we supposed to come up with that kind of cash?'

'I'll handle that part,' Zach answered, without elaboration.

For Jason, coming up with $250,000 would require a lot of elaboration, but, whatever.

'So, we're back to having to trust the word of a deranged killer,' Jason said.

'Marc's father is completely obsessed with what it means to be one of the Thirteen. He's all about family honor, and so is Marc. He'll keep his promise,' Paige insisted. 'And even if he doesn't, which he will, the whole point of the deal was to buy us some time. If we work fast, Zach won't even have to enter the tournament tonight. We'll find Sienna before the game even starts.' She flicked Zach in the arm. 'Right?' she asked. She flicked Jason. 'Right?'

'Right,' Jason said.

Zach gave one of his trademark nods.

Paige nibbled her lower lip. 'Worst case scenario, we don't find her before the tournament, Zach kicks Marc's butt at poker, and Marc hands Sienna over.'

No, Jason thought. *Worst case scenario, we don't find Sienna before the tournament. Marc kicks Zach's butt at poker, and the only way to get Marc to hand Sienna over is for Paige to go to Paris with the guy – who happens to be about a half a minute away from beginning to foam at the mouth.*

Not an acceptable scenario.

He checked his watch: eight-thirty a.m. The tournament started in less than twelve hours. That's all the time they had to find Sienna.

'So, we have less than eleven hours to find her,' Jason said, wrapping up his recap of the meeting with Marc. 'Any ideas?' He glanced around the group gathered in Paige's suite.

'I'd say follow him,' Zach suggested. 'But we have no idea where to start looking.'

'Yes we do. Brad and I found out where Marc is staying,' Erin volunteered. 'The Bonheur.'

'Happiness,' Jason translated aloud, remembering the French Sienna had managed to inject into his brain.

'You'd think he'd get enough French atmosphere at home,' Adam commented. 'Why didn't he go for the hotel with the sphinx out front, or Circus, Circus? Although circuses always seem sort of French to me. I don't know why. There's something about the red coat the ringmaster wears, and some of the clowns are mimes, so—'

'He's probably not staying there for the atmosphere,' Brad interrupted. 'He's probably staying there because it's free.'

'His daddy owns the place,' Erin explained.

'Unbelievable!' Jason burst out. 'We challenged him to a poker tournament being held in the casino his father owns. Why didn't we just say Zach would play blindfolded and make it even easier for Marc to cheat?'

'He's not going to cheat,' Paige insisted. 'Family honor is a huge deal to Marc. And his father. His dad would never allow a crooked game in his casino.'

'Besides, there's always a director at a tournament to oversee the game, someone unaffiliated with the casino,' Zach explained. 'So there will be an outsider to enforce all the rules.'

'We need to get over to the Bonheur and see if we can spot Marc before the game.' Van Dyke stood up. 'Then we stay on him.'

'He probably has at least a couple of his boys with him,' Paige said. 'Marc doesn't like to travel without an entourage. They're probably taking turns watching Sienna. Somebody should follow them too. Anybody have a laptop? I can find pictures of the key players.'

'I'll get mine. I brought it so I could edit my seedy underbelly footage,' Adam answered. He hurried out of the room.

'Do you think Marc could be holding Sienna at the Bonheur?' Maggie asked. 'Since his dad owns it and everything?'

'Unlikely,' Brad said. 'Too many people. It would be hard to whisk Sienna past all the hotel guests and the gamblers down in the casino. She wouldn't be going willingly, and if they'd drugged her—'

Jason heard Paige suck in a sharp breath.

'It isn't likely that they did,' Brad added quickly. 'Because that would make it even harder to transport her into the hotel unnoticed.'

'Laptop,' Adam announced as he came back into the room. He set it down on the coffee table and opened it. Paige went online and quickly found some pictures of Marc. It seemed like he was Paris's Paris Hilton – if

Paris Hilton was a guy and wasn't arrested so often.

'Here's one with Olivier, Marc's cousin and chief lapdog,' Paige said, tapping the screen. 'And here's one of Didier, who is basically a hunk of muscle that does Marc's dirty work.'

'A yummy hunk of muscle,' Erin commented.

Paige continued. 'Both of those guys should be with Marc. He takes them everywhere.' She brought up another picture from a gossip site. 'This weasely looking creature might be with him too. His name's Gilles. Half the time Marc's pissed off at him for something. The rest of the time, he's one of the regulars.'

'Brad and Van Dyke, I want you to take Marc,' Zach instructed. 'He might decide to check in on Sienna personally.'

'If he does, I want to be there,' Jason protested.

Zach shook his head. 'From what Paige said, Marc isn't likely to be alone. The meet in the desert was an exception. I want two of our kind on him and whoever he has as back-up. Besides, he got a good look at you in the desert.'

'I'm not just sitting on my butt while Sienna's being held hostage,' Jason said. 'I'll follow Didier.'

'Fine,' Zach agreed. 'Take Adam and Belle with you.'

Jason nodded.

'Maggie and Erin, you're on Olivier,' Zach continued.

'Let's not worry about Gilles unless one of us sees something to indicate we should. It doesn't sound like Marc would trust Gilles enough to deal with Sienna by himself anyway.'

'Doubtful,' Paige agreed. 'But why don't I follow him?'

'I don't want you out of this room,' Zach answered. 'If Marc or one of his guys spots you, they could drag you straight to the airport. You could be on your way back to Paris before any of us even knows what happened.'

Paige shot Zach a who-are-you-to-be-giving-orders look. 'And what are you going to be doing?' she demanded.

'I'm going to check with a few contacts I have in town to see if the Lessards own any other property in Vegas,' Zach explained. 'Then I'm coming right back here to baby-sit you. If anyone needs back-up, call my cell, and I'm there.'

Jason didn't think he'd ever heard Zach talk so much at one time, but there was no time to dwell on that. 'Is my team ready to go?' Jason asked. He wanted to get out of there. He needed to be doing something, anything, to get Sienna back.

'*Your* team?' Adam repeated. 'How did it get to be your team? Did I miss the vote for captain?'

'Don't be an ass,' Belle told him as she gently pushed him out the door. 'It's his team because he loves Sienna.'

It was true. And the thought of being without her was like teetering on the edge of a bottomless pit.

'The Bonheur is only a few hotels down on the Strip. Should we walk it?' Belle asked as they headed for the elevators.

'Let's take the Escalade and valet park it. I want to be able to get to it quick if we spot Didier leaving the hotel,' Jason answered.

'Where are you? Di-dier? Where? Where?' Adam sang under his breath to the tune of the *CSI* theme song as they waited for the elevator to arrive. He was still singing it when they walked up to the Bonheur casino.

'Just something to think about: singing the name of the guy we're supposed to be tailing might give us away,' Jason told him.

'Oh, right.' Adam switched over to humming. "Hmmmm-hmm-hmm. Hmm. Hmm." He had his camcorder perched on his shoulder. Jason thought that that, at least, had been a good call. Adam had pointed out that the zoom lens would come in handy – they couldn't very well walk around with binoculars.

'Should we split up?' Belle asked.

'I don't think we'll need to,' Adam said.

'Why not? This place is huge,' she protested.

It was. Huge and crowded and noisy. Slots spinning, dice rolling, roulette wheels turning. Jason was having trouble focusing his eyes on individual faces; his attention kept getting jerked to a new sound or motion.

'Check out the viewfinder,' Adam replied, moving closer so Jason and Belle could see the little screen. 'I think I've found our boy.' He zoomed in on a twenty-something guy playing video poker.

Belle nodded. 'He's gotten blond tips – not such a great style decision – but that's definitely Didier. How about if I take that empty machine that backs up to his? I can keep him in sight, but he won't be looking at me. He'll be watching his poker hands.' She looked to Jason for an answer.

'Great, go,' he told her. 'And, Adam, just keep doing your filmhead thing.' Jason scanned the area. 'I'll head over to that bar over there. The way the mirror's positioned I'll be able to watch Didier without even facing in his direction. He's not going to be able to blink without one of us seeing.'

Jason drank five Sprites as he watched Didier. He was starting to realize why cops on stakeouts brought bottles to pee in. *That's why there are three of you*, he told himself. He stood up, left some cash on the bar, and wandered over to Adam. 'I'm hitting the bathroom. Be right back.'

'You should have gone before we left home,' Adam joked as Jason walked away.

The men's room was empty when Jason walked in. He figured a lot of gamblers had to be on hot streaks they were afraid to interrupt.

He emptied the five sodas out of his bladder and headed for the sink.

Just then, the door opened with a slam. Jason jerked his head toward the sound and saw Adam rushing in.

'The red junglefowl is in flight!' Adam burst out.

'What?' Jason demanded, drying his hands on his jeans.

'Didier's heading for the main exit,' Adam explained.

'Why didn't you say so?' Jason asked as they rushed out of the bathroom.

'It was code. The red junglefowl is the national bird of France, so that's Didier. And "in flight", well that's obviously code for leaving. *Didier is leaving,*' Adam answered in a rush. Then he went on thoughtfully. 'Actually I think it's only called a red junglefowl when it's wild. There's another name for the domesticated one.'

'How do you even know this crap?' Jason asked as they careened through the casino, trying not to crash into anyone.

'Saw it—'

'In a movie,' Jason finished for his friend.

'There's Belle!' Adam exclaimed. 'I told her to watch and see which way he went.'

'He headed down the Strip, going north,' Belle told them breathlessly when they reached her. 'He's walking. Should I get the Escalade?'

'No, if he's walking, we should be walking too,' Jason said. He led the way outside. 'Do you see him?' Jason didn't. At least not yet. He put on his sunglasses.

'Across the street,' Adam answered. 'About half a block ahead of us.'

'Don't speed up,' Jason warned. 'And try and look tourist-ish – like we're just out to have fun.'

Belle immediately pasted a bright smile on her face. 'That's the Venetian up there. Have you guys ever been in?' She didn't wait for them to answer. 'It has a real canal. Well, a real fake canal. It's so cheesy, but Sienna actually loves it. She made me ride around in a gondola for almost three hours last time we were here. It was an all-girl weekend.'

She blinked rapidly and Jason realized thinking about Sienna had brought tears to her eyes. 'You two can take a gondola ride tonight,' he promised. 'I'll even— Wait!' Jason interrupted himself. 'The red junglefowl is making a left turn. Did I get the code right?' he asked Adam.

'The red junglefowl is *flying west,*' Adam corrected. He looked over at Belle. 'Don't worry, he'll get it down.'

They turned down Flamingo and kept pace half a block behind Didier.

Adam came to an abrupt stop as Didier disappeared into a place called the Treasure Chest. 'Er, Belle can't go in there,' he said awkwardly.

'Yes, I can. I have fake ID too,' Belle reminded him.

'That's not what I mean. It's a . . . It's a . . .' Adam shook his head, at a loss for words.

'Spit it out,' Belle sighed. 'The red junglefowl has come to roost in a topless club.' She grinned and rolled her eyes. 'I've probably seen more topless girls than you have, Turnball.'

'I can't believe this place is even open. It's barely noon,' Jason commented as they walked toward the club.

Belle laughed. 'You didn't think breasts were only visible at night, did you?' She opened the door to the Treasure Chest. 'After you,' she told Jason and Adam.

'That's what I like to see,' Adam said. 'They have a

buffet.' He practically ran toward it.

Belle snorted. 'Do you think he's a little embarrassed to be here with me?'

'I'm not.' Jason took a seat on a lip-shaped padded bench, one that was as far away from the stage as possible. Didier had gotten himself a seat way up front. It didn't look like he was planning on going anywhere anytime soon.

'I hope she's OK,' Belle said. Jason had a hard time hearing her over the techno music.

'Try not to worry too much,' he told her – like he could take that advice. 'Sienna's pretty good at taking care of herself.'

'True. My girl's a fighter.' Belle smiled at him. 'I mean, *our* girl.'

They sat in silence – silence except for the pulse-changing bass beat of the music – until Adam came back over.

'I had an idea for you,' Belle told him. 'For getting rid of your . . . excess money.'

'Lay it on me,' he said.

'Go sit next to the fowl and feed the g-strings,' Belle suggested, jerking her chin at the stage.

Adam blushed. Yes, actually blushed. Jason was going to be reminding him of this moment for a very long time to come – once Sienna was safe again.

'I couldn't do that,' he finally answered. 'Those girls, they work hard for their money. And they're all so pretty. They deserve better than the funny stuff.'

Jason couldn't take the waiting around anymore. He shoved himself to his feet.

Adam raised his eyebrows. '*You're* not going to do some tipping, are you?'

'No, I'm going to do some butt kicking,' Jason replied. 'It's ridiculous sitting around waiting for the fowl to decide to fly off again. I'm going to take him outside and punch on him until he decides to squawk about where Sienna is.' He started toward Didier.

Adam circled around in front of Jason, blocking his way. 'You're going to have to go through me to get to him,' he said.

Jason could tell Adam was serious, but he was serious too. 'Get out of my way.' He glanced around Adam to make sure Didier hadn't started paying attention to them. He hadn't. Nobody had. It wasn't the kind of place where people got curious.

'The guy is probably, you know, *special*,' Adam warned. 'You could get yourself mangled. Sienna wouldn't like that.'

Jason sucked in a long breath, giving himself time to absorb Adam's logic. 'Fine. We'll keep watching,' he snapped. He returned to Belle and sat back down, but all he could think about was Sienna.

'If anyone has hurt her. I mean, if she's so much as broken a nail, I'm going to make Marc pay. And I don't care how "special" he is.' He looked over at Adam. 'No one is going to stop me.'

Fourteen

'I don't believe this guy,' Belle complained. 'I mean, yes, breasts are very nice, but does anyone really want to just sit and stare at them for hours?'

Adam shot Jason a guilty I-kind-of-do look, and Belle caught him.

She laughed. 'I guess Didier isn't the only one who would give that question a big "yes".'

Jason's cell rang and he picked it up fast. He saw Zach's name on the screen. 'Anybody make a move?' he asked.

'Not as far as I know. I assume you have nothing to report,' Zach replied.

'No. Our guy's been sitting front-row at a strip club for the last three hours,' Jason told him.

'Adam is almost up to his chin in his own drool,' Belle added loudly.

'Were you able to find out if the Lessards own any more property in Vegas?' Jason asked.

'They own five, besides the hotel,' Zach replied.

Jason made writing gestures at Belle and Adam. Belle handed him a purple Flair and Adam passed him a couple of cocktail napkins.

'Give 'em to me,' Jason said. He jotted down the info as Zach listed them off.

'I'm going to check in with the others,' Zach told him. 'I'll let you know if anything's happened.'

Jason hung up. 'You think you two can cover Didier without me for a while?'

'Why? What do you have planned?' Adam asked.

'A little recon. One of the places the Lessards own is an antiques warehouse at the edge of the city. Sounds like the perfect place to hold a hostage,' Jason explained.

'Take the Escalade.' Belle held out the keys and the valet parking ticket. 'Didier got here on foot, so we probably won't need wheels to follow him – if he ever leaves. And, if we do, there are a ton of cabs around.'

'Thanks,' Jason said.

'Call if you need back-up,' Adam instructed. 'My heroic chin and I are available to come to your rescue if you get into any trouble.'

'I'll keep you posted.' Jason left the club and retrieved the Escalade. With the help of the Streetpilot GPS system in the dash, he was able to pull up just down the block from the warehouse in less than twenty minutes. He didn't want to park right in front. He needed to suss out what kind of surveillance was in place.

Trying to look casual – although it wasn't exactly the kind of street anyone would pick for a stroll – Jason walked by the warehouse. He didn't spot anyone guarding the outside, so he crossed the empty parking lot that backed up to the loading dock. Nobody called out, demanding to know what he was doing there, so he continued around the building. The only sounds were his own breathing and his own footsteps. The place felt deserted. But that didn't mean Sienna – Sienna and, possibly, guards – wasn't inside.

Unfortunately, the windows were positioned too high for Jason to get a look inside. He retraced his steps. Hadn't he seen a— Yep, there it was, a Dumpster right around the corner.

Jason climbed up on top of it, grimacing at the noise his feet made on the hollow metal box. He froze for a moment, listening. When it didn't seem as if he'd alerted anyone, he took a cautious peek in through the nearest window.

The thin coat of grime on the glass and the dim light inside the warehouse made it hard to see, but there were rows and rows of wooden crates.

Jason's eyes flicked up and down each row of crates,

on alert for the smallest movement. Nothing. It really didn't look like Sienna was down there. But there was another whole floor. And there was a fire escape with a ladder that could take him up there.

He sidestepped his way over to the edge of the Dumpster, and reached up for the bottom rung of the ladder. A twinge of pain from his old crossbow bolt wound radiated through his chest. Damn, was he ever going to be able to forget that he'd been shot by a vampire hunter who'd mistaken him for a friend of Dracula? Or was that spot on his chest always going to hurt when he moved a few degrees in the wrong direction?

It's not like it's something you'd ever actually be able to forget anyway, he told himself. A crossbow bolt in the chest – that was a memory that stayed with a guy pretty much forever, twinge or no twinge.

Jason jerked down on the ladder with both hands. It gave a squeal of protest and lowered about an inch. He gave it a yank. Nothing. The thing was completely jammed. Well, if the ladder wouldn't come down to him, he'd have to go up to it.

Jason adjusted his grip on the bottom rung of the jammed fire escape ladder – the only rung within his reach – and swung himself up to climb the ladder.

Halfway up, he felt a strong hand – an inhumanly strong hand – grab his shoulder. *On the upside,* he told himself, *a vampire guard means I'm probably very close to Sienna.* He looked over his shoulder, and his mouth fell open.

Paige stood behind him on the metal ladder.

'How'd you get up here?' he asked.

She laughed. 'It helped that I'm not a clumsy human boy,' she replied.

'OK, forget about how, *why* are you up here?' Jason demanded. 'You're supposed to be hiding out so you don't get snatched by Marc or one of his goons.'

'It's my fault Sienna got kidnapped,' Paige answered. 'When I heard Zach on the phone telling you all the places the Lessards owned, I figured this was the most likely spot for Sienna to be stashed. So when Zach went to the bathroom, I decided to come over and check it out.' She raised one eyebrow at him. 'I didn't hear Zach tell you to search the warehouse. You're rogue too, aren't you?'

Jason gave a reluctant snort of laughter. 'Rogue! Yeah, that's me.'

'So, are you going to keep climbing? Or do you want me to go first, since I'm the one with the preternatural powers?' Paige asked.

Jason answered by continuing to climb.

'You have a cute butt,' Paige commented from below him.

Jason didn't know exactly how he was supposed to answer that kind of compliment, especially from his girlfriend's sister, so he pretended he hadn't heard and kept climbing until he reached the top of the fire escape.

He and Paige crouched down and peered through the window that led to the metal platform they stood on.

'Just more boxes,' Paige murmured.

'Let's go inside, just to be sure,' Jason said. He tried to open the window. 'Locked,' he told Paige. He wrapped the bottom of his shirt around his fist and punched it through the glass.

'You should have let me do that,' Paige told him. 'I heal like it's nothing.'

'All I was thinking about was getting in there,' Jason admitted. He plucked a fragment of glass out of his forearm, then carefully reached through the hole in the window and flipped the latch.

'You really love my sister, don't you?' Paige asked, her voice serious.

'Yeah.' Jason shoved the window up and climbed into the warehouse.

'SiSi has very good taste,' Paige said as she followed him.

It felt just as deserted inside the place as it had out. *She's not here*, Jason thought, but he didn't say it aloud. He didn't know for sure; why not let Paige hope for a little while?

Quietly, they wove through the corridors of boxes. There was no Sienna, and nothing to indicate that Sienna had ever been there. It was the same with the small office, the rows of boxes downstairs, the bathroom, and the larger office.

'I really thought I'd find her,' Paige said. 'When I heard Zach say "warehouse", I thought for sure . . .'

'Me, too,' Jason answered. 'But we're all working on it. Maybe someone else is about to find her right now.'

'So we all got nada, zip, an endless void of nothing, a—'

'Thanks for that recap,' Jason said, interrupting Adam before someone – possibly Jason himself – felt the need to kill him.

Belle gave Adam an affectionate pat on the knee. 'I thought it was very creative,' she told him.

Brad used his fingers to scrub his face. 'All we can do now is get Zach over to the tournament.'

'And be there as back-up if something nasty goes down,' Van Dyke agreed.

'Then we need to go get ready,' Maggie said. 'None

of us could walk into a big money invitational game looking the way we do.

True, Jason thought, taking in the little rips at the bottom of his shirt. And the streak of blood.

'Is the invitational part going to be a problem?' Erin asked. 'We didn't think about that.'

'Actually, we did,' Zach said, 'and I'm expected, so let's meet downstairs in the lobby at seven forty-five p.m.'

'Less than an hour to make myself gorgeous,' Adam said, shaking his head. 'I don't know if I can do it.'

'I don't know if you could do it even with *unlimited* amounts of time,' Van Dyke joked, herding everyone but Zach out of the suite.

'Hey. You holding up OK?' Adam asked when he and Jason split off from the others at their room.

'Sienna can take care of herself. I have to keep reminding myself of that,' Jason answered. He slid the key card through the reader and opened the door.

'She could definitely kick my butt,' Adam agreed. 'And the butt of my dad, who is, as you know, a sheriff with years of training.'

Jason headed over to the closet and pulled out the suit Sienna had insisted he buy a few weeks ago. He changed his clothes as quickly as possible, then grabbed his new shoes. Sienna had insisted that he buy a pair of loafers to go with the suit. She called them light green with a 'world-weary patina', whatever that meant. He called them gray. They'd mock argued about it all the way home in the car. And then they'd made up for the mock fight with some real kissing.

'Those just slide on, in case you're wondering,' Adam said. 'There's no Velcro or laces or anything. It's kind of freaky, I know.'

Jason realized that he'd been staring at the loafers for an embarrassing amount of time. 'Thanks. Because that *is* actually what I was wondering.'

'You're looking very shiny,' Adam told him.

'It's from the Roberto Cavalli Spring collection. And I believe the term you're looking for is "high-sheen",' Jason corrected, straightening his jacket but totally failing to carry off the fashion-conscious image with conviction. They both knew only Sienna knew that kind of stuff.

'And what about me?' Adam flung out his arms theatrically, giving Jason a good look at the intricate lines and dots covering his shirt. 'Don't I look pretty?'

'Am I supposed to be seeing a dinosaur pop out of your chest or what?' Jason joked. 'It looks like you're wearing one of those optical illusion posters. I used to have one in my bedroom when I was a kid. When you stared at it just the right way, with your eyes almost crossed—'

'I think what you're trying to say is that this op-art print captures the mood of the Seventies with skill and wit,' Adam interrupted. 'At least that's what Belle said. She bought it for me. I'm supposed to pay her back after I sell my first movie or marry an heiress thanks to her coaching.'

'You'd better hope she's willing to keep coaching you, then, because—' Jason broke off. 'How can we even be talking about this stuff? Why are we even bothering to change clothes? It's insane. Sienna is being held hostage somewhere, and we're . . .' He shook his head.

'What we're doing is dressing in the appropriate way for the next stage of the plan to get Sienna back,' Adam told him. 'We need to look like we belong in a private room at the Bonheur, because that's where we have to be right now.'

Jason nodded. 'All right. You're right. We just have to hope that Zach wins and that the honor of his family name actually *means* something to that scuzball, Marc,' Jason said. 'Let's get downstairs.'

Van Dyke and Maggie were already in the lobby when Jason and Adam showed up.

'A cravat, Van Dyke?' Adam asked. 'Really?'

'Clearly I need to get you a subscription to *GQ*,' Van Dyke told him. 'For so many reasons.'

'I think he actually looks cute,' Belle said as she, Erin, and Brad joined them. 'Lounge lizard-esque, in a good way.' She reached across Adam and unbuttoned one more button on Jason's high-sheen shirt. 'Sienna did a good job when she took you shopping. You clean up real nice.'

Jason shot a nervous look at Maggie. 'Are you sure? It seems like Maggie and I are wearing almost the same thing.'

'It looks a lot better on her,' Van Dyke laughed.

The three-piece suit did look hot on Maggie. She looked every bit as sexy as Belle did in her short, sparkly rhinestone-covered dress.

'The name's Lafrenière. Zach Lafrenière,' Brad murmured as Zach headed toward them.

No kidding. Zach was wearing a tux. Black with satin lapels. White handkerchief in the pocket. He hadn't bothered with a tie, and his white shirt was open at the neck. He hadn't tried to comb down the spikes in his short black hair, and he had a little stubble going, just a little. He definitely looked like a guy who'd walk away from a card table a winner.

'Let's roll,' Zach said calmly, and walked out of the hotel lobby.

'Do you have the, uh, what the rat pack would call the "do-ray-mi" *on* you?' Adam asked as they made their way down the Strip toward the Bonheur. 'Because that's a lot of music to be walking around with.'

'I arranged for the 250,000 dollars to be transferred to the casino. I'll receive it in chips when we arrive,' Zach told him.

Adam shot Jason a raised-eyebrow, do-you-believe-this-guy look. Jason shrugged.

'So, do you have any tips for negotiating a better allowance?' Belle teased. 'I wanna be a high roller too.'

Zach smiled at her. 'My parents are generous. But I've managed to make a few lucky investments in the past few years.'

'Lucky investments? How lucky are we talking?' Van Dyke burst out.

'Lucky enough,' Zach said, clearly ending that particular line of questioning.

'I don't get the whole 250,000 dollars thing exactly,' Maggie admitted. 'They can tell you how much to bet?'

'Maggie, if you didn't spend more time in the water than out, you'd pick up some of this basic life information,' Erin told her. 'Most tables have minimum bets. But at tournaments like the one tonight, with the high rollers, they have a buy-in. Tonight's is 250,000 dollars. Everyone is committed to play for that amount and starts out with that many chips.'

'So the winner will get . . . ?' Maggie asked.

'There are six players in the tournament,' Van Dyke said. 'That means there's one and a half million in the pot. Most of that will go to the winner. Pretty much everyone else at the table will be walking home with empty pockets.'

'That's not going to be me.' Zach stopped in front of the Bonheur and opened the nearest door, waving the group inside. Then he led the way deep into the casino, down a steep flight of stairs, and over to a room with a green brocade door. There was a man in a tuxedo clearly standing guard. Zach told the guy his name, only his name, and the guard whisked the door open. Zach's phone calls had obviously gone well.

Jason's eyes immediately went to the wall on the left. It was almost entirely covered by an enormous built-in aquarium, alive with fish. Then he saw Marc, already seated at the sleek cherry-wood table in the center of the room.

'He sure wears that Fendi well,' Erin murmured.

Jason took a closer look at the guy. He had on a very classy gray suit – Fendi, according to Erin – with a white shirt and tie underneath.

Mr Yakamoto – the older Japanese man that Zach

had won from the other night – sat to his left. Zach strolled over to the table and took a seat some distance from Marc. Yakamoto didn't seem very happy to see him, but Marc sure did.

'Let's grab seats,' Brad said, leading the way up a short flight of stairs to a raised gallery set well back from the game table. Tables and chairs stretched down its length. As soon as they sat down, a waitress glided up and asked for their drink orders. Jason noticed that the players were being offered complimentary beverages. It looked like Zach had gone for water with a slice of lemon. Smart choice.

They had a good view of Zach, who was sitting facing toward them, but they could only see the back of Marc's head. 'Hey, isn't that that sexy actress?' Van Dyke asked. 'The one who was in that movie where she was a lesbian?'

'*Bound*,' Brad said. He shot a look at Adam. 'See, we do know some old movies.'

'You mean you have an encyclopedic knowledge of anything that involves girl-on-girl action,' Maggie said, laughing.

'That's definitely her,' Adam confirmed. 'Sitting down right next to our Zach.'

'Most definitely,' Brad agreed.

A middle-aged guy with way too much bling for

a) the room and b) his age, came in and plopped down between the actress and Mr Yakamoto. He was followed by a short man who, like Zach, was dressed in a tux. When he took his seat, on the other side of Zach from the actress, the tournament's six players were all in place.

'OK, I'm going to need some commentary,' Maggie said. 'I've only played poker about twice, both times at a party.'

Van Dyke wrapped his arm around her. 'Not a problem.'

A tall woman with wildly curling strawberry blond hair entered the room. She had to be a vampire. With her flawless ivory skin and glowing pale blue eyes, she couldn't possibly be human. The neck of her ankle-length black gown was high, and the sleeves were long, but as she passed by on her way to the main table, Jason could see that the back of the dress was cut so low there was no way any underwear was going on.

'She's the dealer,' Van Dyke said.

Several extremely clean-cut twenty-something guys followed her, carrying trays of chips. They distributed them to the players in silence.

'Hard to believe those pieces of plastic represent more than a million bucks,' Adam commented.

Another woman walked to the head of the table. She

had light brown hair in a sleek bob. 'Good evening, players and guests. My name is Hilary Mayer and I am the manager of the Bonheur. If there is anything my staff can do to make you more comfortable tonight, please don't hesitate to ask.' She smiled. 'I know none of you have come here to listen to me. You all know the rules, and Mr Barstow, your director for the night, will be on hand if there are disputes of any kind.' She nodded to the angular man standing several feet away from the table. He nodded back. 'So, again, welcome, and good luck,' Hilary concluded, then took a seat in the gallery.

The dealer placed a silver disc in front of Marc, who sat to her left. 'That's called the button,' Van Dyke told Maggie. 'It shows who the dealer is.'

'I thought you just said that that woman is the dealer,' Maggie answered.

'She is,' Adam put in. 'In tournaments, there's always a professional dealer. But usually each player takes a turn dealing, and that's important in the rules. So, in terms of the rules, the person with the button counts as the dealer, even though they're not actually dealing. Got it?'

'Got it. It seems stupid, but I've got it,' Maggie replied.

Yakamoto and Too Much Bling pushed chips in

front of them. 'The two players to the left of the dealer have to put in what's called the "small blind" and the "big blind". It's a mandatory bet,' Jason explained, doing his part of the commentary for Maggie. 'It looks like the small is 1,000 bucks, and the big is 2,000. Those amounts will go up as the game goes on. It's to keep the play aggressive. Bigger blinds mean players will risk more on less than great hands.'

'The game is No-limit Texas Hold 'Em,' the dealer announced in a throaty voice that easily carried to the gallery. A hush descended on the room as she began dealing two cards face down to each of the players.

Sexy Actress quickly checked her cards. 'Raise 2,000 dollars.' She slid the chips out in front of her. A monitor mounted in the center of Jason's table showed a close-up as the dealer confirmed the bet.

'Ooh,' Adam observed. 'She could have just called and put in the amount of the big blind – 2,000 dollars – but she chose to take it up a notch.'

'Fold,' Zach said.

'That means he's out for the rest of this hand,' Van Dyke explained. 'He can't have any good cards; he didn't even wait for the flop.'

'I understood the "fold" part without the translation,' Maggie said. 'But "flop"? I'm lost again.'

'The betting for this round is going to continue

until everyone has either folded, gone all in – that means bet all their chips – or matched the highest bid,' Van Dyke told her. 'Then the dealer will turn over three cards. They're called the "flop" and they are community cards. The players will use them with the two cards they already have – "hole" cards, they're called – to come up with their poker hands. After the flop, there's another round of betting.'

'Right. So if you're holding a pathetic little three and a six in your hole cards, but then two more sixes come up in the flop, suddenly you're holding three of a kind!' Belle added. 'Not a fabulous hand, but a lot better than what you started with.'

'So why did Zach fold without waiting for the flop?' Maggie asked. 'He can't really know how good his hand is until he sees the three cards, right? Or am I missing something?'

'It's true that the flop can change your hand,' Erin told her, 'but there's a round of betting before the flop. If Zach's got really bad cards, and the betting gets high in that round, then he'd probably choose to fold instead of matching the bet.'

'Yeah, he's probably just playing a tight game, being cautious,' Brad put in. 'Don't worry. I'm not even going to admit how much money Zach has taken off me playing Hold 'Em.'

Zach folded before the flop on the next hand too. A hand that Marc won. Jason's gut clenched. 'I hope he has a good enough hand to stay in – at least until the turn – soon,' he murmured uneasily. Before Maggie could ask, he explained. 'After the flop, there's another round of betting. Then the dealer turns up one more card – that's called the "turn". Then there's more betting. Another card goes face up – that's the "river". Those two cards are community cards too. The last round of betting comes after that.'

'So then you can use any of the five cards on the table with either of your two hole cards for your hand?' Maggie queried.

'Yes, either or both,' Adam clarified. 'But Zach's pulled out way before that point.'

Jason leant forward, all his attention on Zach as more hands were played. Zach folded often – and lost almost as frequently. He didn't win a single hand.

In contrast, Marc played loose, betting on hands when the odds would have told a more cautious gambler to fold – and it was paying off.

About an hour into the tournament, Jason and Adam exchanged a what-in-the-freaking-hell look. Zach still hadn't won a hand. Was it possible that their friend was simply outclassed?

Fifteen

'He folded again. Unbelievable!' a man at one of the other tables of observers said loudly enough for Jason – and probably Zach – to hear.

Adam covered his eyes with both hands. 'That's a lot of hands where Zach's folded. And when he hasn't folded, he's lost!'

'Thanks for the update,' Brad snapped irritably.

Adam spread his fingers and peered at him. 'Sorry. It's just . . . I guess the pressure's getting to me.'

Brad nodded. 'To all of us.'

Jason tried to keep his impatience from getting totally out of control as the hand played out.

'At least Marc didn't win that last hand,' Erin commented.

'True,' Maggie said, 'but he already has about 43,000 dollars more than he started with.'

'And Zach has 20,000 less,' Van Dyke added.

'That isn't nearly as much as Yakamoto's lost, though,' Erin commented.

'At least Yakamoto's in the game. Zach, he's . . . Well, it's almost as if Zach doesn't want to play,' Jason said, frowning.

'Look, Zach's a great player, I'm telling you,' Brad insisted.

'I've played with him, too,' Van Dyke put in. 'And he whips my butt. Not playing like this, though. I've never seen Zach playing like this.'

Is Zach so freaked out about Sienna that he can't concentrate? Jason wondered. But that just didn't seem like Zach. Jason had seen him under extreme pressure before, and Zach was the ice man.

The dealer was shuffling the cards. A new hand was about to begin.

'Zach has to have a plan,' Paige said. It was the first time she'd spoken since they'd entered the private room. It was like she thought that if she poured every ounce of concentration she possessed into watching the game, she could somehow make it turn out the way it had to in order to save her and Sienna.

The bidding started around the table. When it got to Zach, he said, 'Raise 10,000 dollars.' Jason heard Paige draw in a sharp breath.

'Oh, yeah!' Adam yelped loudly. Not exactly good tournament etiquette, but Jason was pretty sure everyone in the Malibu group was feeling the same way; Zach had finally made a decisive move.

'He was just hanging back,' Brad said, clearly relieved. 'He probably has everyone's tell nailed.'

'OK, I thought I had all the vocabulary down. But "tell"?' Maggie asked.

'It's something a player does, without realizing it, that tells what kind of hand he's got going,' Van Dyke explained. 'Like an unconscious tick.'

'John Malkovich had an awesome tell in *Rounders*,' Adam joined in. 'When he had a great hand, he'd pick up an Oreo cookie and twist it open right next to his ear, then eat each half.'

'Never saw it,' Van Dyke said.

'No girls making out, I guess,' Maggie teased.

'Shut up, you guys. I want to watch Zach!' Paige exclaimed.

The other players all called Zach's bet.

'If they "call", it means they're agreeing to match the highest bet of that round,' Van Dyke whispered to Maggie. 'At the end of the round of betting, they all have to have either called or folded.'

The dealer turned over the flop cards: queen of hearts, queen of clubs, eight of spades.

The pot was at $72,000 as the next round of bidding started. Marc bet $15,000. He must have liked what he saw in the flop. Yakamoto folded, as did Too Much Bling.

191

Sexy Actress called. Zach raised $15,000 without a moment's hesitation, his eyes on Marc. Other Tuxedo Guy folded, but Marc saw Zach's $15,000 raise, and raised another $15,000, answering Zach's challenge.

'Gotta say this for Marc, he has *cojones*,' Van Dyke muttered.

Sexy Actress folded. Zach called.

'Zach has *cojones* too. I've seen them,' Paige answered. Now that Zach was clearly in the game, she'd gotten a little of her old sparkle back.

'You're bad,' Erin told her.

Paige winked at her. Yeah, Paige was definitely feeling a little more hopeful.

When the round of betting ended, Zach, and Marc were the only ones still in. The pot was up to about $177,000.

The dealer flipped the turn card: jack of hearts.

'A queen and a jack in the hole wouldn't be bad,' Brad observed.

Did Marc have those? Jason wondered, as he watched Marc bet 30 grand.

Zach, face expressionless, voice flat – the way they'd been the whole game – called. Marc looked surprised. Jason could tell he was trying to read Zach and failing.

The dealer flipped the river card: three of diamonds.

Marc eyeballed Zach, 'Check.'

'What's he doing?' Maggie asked.

'He's trying to figure out what Zach has, so he's passed the betting to him,' Van Dyke explained. 'He still has the right to bet – or fold – after Zach bets.'

'Raise 100,000 dollars,' Zach said calmly. The crowd gasped.

'That brings the pot up to about 337,000 dollars,' Adam whispered. 'They each have something like 90 grand of their own money on the line. That's going to be a big bite for the loser.'

Now everything rested with Marc. Jason knew that Marc must be holding good cards to have played this far, but what did Zach have? And what would Marc do?

Marc watched Zach for a long time, but Zach's face was expressionless. 'Call,' Marc said at last.

' "Call" means matching the highest bet,' Maggie muttered to herself, trying to keep all the info that had been thrown at her straight.

'Since Marc called, Zach has to show his hand,' Van Dyke told Maggie.

Zach flipped his cards face up on the table: eight of diamonds, eight of hearts.

'Full house,' Adam breathed happily. 'Beat that, you freak.'

Marc shoved his cards into the center of the table without showing them, indicating that Zach had won.

He'd just won a pot of – Jason did some quick math – something like $437,000. And Marc had just lost more than $180,000. He'd won a decent percentage of the earlier hands, but it still wasn't going to be easy for Marc to recover from that.

'Somebody get me some popcorn; I'm starting to enjoy the show,' Adam said, when Zach won the next hand.

Jason started to feel like he was sucking in helium instead of air as the next two hands went to Zach too. He felt happy when Sexy Actress took one. Even Too Much Bling taking a pot felt kind of good. Money they got was money Marc didn't have. They were helping to escort Marc right out of the game. Then he could take them to Sienna, and the Vegas trip would be back on track.

'I know him,' Paige mock bragged to the people sitting at the next table when Zach won another hand. 'He took me to the prom. I'm serious.'

'What's Marc down to, anybody know?' Brad asked. 'He's gotten a lot more cautious these last few rounds.'

'He's only got around 80,000 dollars left to play with,' Erin answered.

'Poor, poverty-stricken baby,' Adam muttered as the dealer began to shuffle the cards.

'It's actually true,' Jason said. 'The bidding has been

getting steep the last few hands. Marc could be out of the game soon.'

'Ooh, then after we get Sienna back, can we go to the Star Trek Experience?' Adam asked. 'The Final Frontier Desserts at Quark's Restaurant are supposed to be awesome.'

'I'm sure Zach will be happy to take you there with his winnings,' Jason answered, smiling at the image of Zach Lafrenière in the middle of that cheese-fest of a place. 'You two could get your picture taken with a Klingon, or whatever.' He returned his attention to the game, just in time to see Zach raise $15,000 in the round of bidding after the river. Marc went all in.

' "All in"? Why can't people just use regular language?' Maggie complained.

'That means he's betting everything he's got,' Van Dyke said gleefully. 'Now, if he loses this hand, he's out of the game.'

'Call,' Too Much Bling said. He was the only one left in the hand besides Zach and Marc.

'Call,' Zach said too.

Too Much Bling flipped his cards: two of hearts, six of clubs.

The guy had been bluffing. A two and a six was an 'always fold 'em' hand in Texas Hold 'Em. It lost 90 per cent of the time, even with only four players. The community cards: six of hearts, eight of clubs, king of hearts, four of diamonds, jack of spades, had only given Too Much Bling a pair.

Zach flipped his cards next: king of diamonds, queen of hearts.

'Do I see a king kong?' Adam cried. 'Yes, I see two kings for Zach. With a nice queen kicker if things get ugly.'

Maggie sighed. ' "Kicker"?'

'If Zach and Marc tie – like, in this case, if they both have a pair of kings – the winner's decided by who has the higher card unused in their hand. That card's called the "kicker". Zach has a queen as his kicker,' Jason told her.

Marc flipped his cards.

'I am *not* seeing this,' Brad groaned.

Marc had the king of clubs – with the ace of spades as a kicker. Aces high. He didn't have nearly as many chips as Zach, but he'd just got himself back in the game.

'Crap,' muttered Van Dyke.

Paige nibbled nervously at one of her cuticles.

Jason glanced at his watch. Sienna had been gone more than 17 hours. Where was she? How was she being treated by Marc's goons? It was killing him to sit here, sipping on a beer, not knowing what was happening to her, but it was all he could do. For now.

He forced his thoughts away from Sienna and back to the game – where he watched Marc take another pot.

'I guess this would be the definition of a hot streak,' Maggie said a half an hour later. Zach and Marc had reversed positions. Now Zach was down to about his last $70,000, and Marc was up to over $500,000.

Marc had been winning a staggering amount of hands, and when he hadn't won, he'd got himself out early, so he hadn't lost much.

'I feel like I've somehow been transported to Htrae,' Adam said.

'What?' Jason asked, without looking away from the game.

'Htrae. You know, Bizarro world. It's "Earth" spelled backward. Backwards versions of the superheroes live there, like Batzarro, the World's Worst Detective,' Adam explained.

'Never, ever mention the word Bizarro or Batzarro or that Hhht thing again unless you want to die a virgin,' Belle told him.

'Marc just won again.' Erin rubbed at the monitor with a cocktail napkin, as if there had to be something wrong with the screen. Even without the close-up from the monitor, it was easy to see the large stacks of chips piling up in front of Marc.

'This is wrong,' Brad burst out. 'Streak, or no streak, Lessard's winning too many hands.'

Jason's gut agreed that something was wrong.

As the dealer began to shuffle, Zach lifted his head briefly toward the gallery and raised his eyebrows.

'Did you see that?' Van Dyke asked. 'Zach clearly thinks there's something wrong, too.'

'Could Marc have found a way to cheat?' Belle asked.

'The big and small blinds are going up,' the dealer announced. 'The big blind is now 10,000 dollars. The small blind is 5,000 dollars.'

'Why don't we double that?' Marc suggested suddenly. 'Let's really get this game moving. I have a plane to catch.' He looked up at the gallery too – and winked at Paige.

'He's cheating. Look at his face. He's so sure he's going to have me on that plane!' Paige exclaimed. 'I actually thought family honor meant something to him. I knew nothing else did, but I was sure that . . .' Paige shook her head, her eyes wide with shock and disbelief. 'Obviously, he'll do whatever he has to to get what he wants.'

I knew this would happen, Jason thought. *I knew Marc Lessard couldn't be trusted*. He didn't say it aloud. Paige was already hurting so much, he didn't want to torture her.

Adam nudged Jason in the ribs. 'Daddy has really good security in this place, don't you think?' he asked softly, nodding toward one of the many security cameras, this one mounted in the perfect position to view Zach's cards.

'Yeah,' Jason answered. 'I'm interested in the rest of Daddy's security system. Let's take a little field trip, see if we can find anything the director hasn't caught.' He and Adam stood up.

'We'll be back,' Jason told the rest of the group. Then he had an idea. He turned to Erin. 'Hey, Erin, would you come with us for a minute?'

She nodded, and the three of them quietly left the private room. 'What's up?' she asked.

'We think Marc might be using the casino security system to cheat,' Jason explained. 'We need to find a way into the surveillance center.'

'And I'm here because . . . ?'

Jason hesitated. His idea didn't seem quite as great right now as it had inside the private room. 'We're not just going to be able to walk into the security area. We're going to need a door code, or something . . .' He hesitated again. 'And, uh, sometimes a girl can have an easier time convincing someone to give out that kind of info.'

'Totally,' Adam jumped in. 'Especially a hot girl.

199

Agent Sydney Bristow wasn't ashamed to use her hotness. She was genius smart and could handle any weapon, but, sometimes, what the mission needed was a short skirt and a pink wig.'

'I left my pink wig in my other purse,' Erin joked. 'And my dress? Long, not short.'

'You don't need a wig; your hair is perfect,' Adam told her. 'And the dress is smokin''

'I'm not really a flirty kind of girl. Let me go get Belle. She excels at "persuasion"'. Erin took a step back toward the private room.

Jason stopped her. 'We don't have time. Zach's hemorrhaging money. He's not going to be able to stay in the game much longer.'

'Hey, hey! Portly security type heading toward a staff-only door at three o'clock,' Adam cut in. 'Go, Agent Erin.'

Erin fluffed her hair. 'Fine. But I still say you should have asked Belle.'

Jason and Adam pretended to be deep in conversation as they watched her head toward the security guy. She turned around and headed back to them less than a minute later.

'OK, you didn't need Belle. The code is' – she held out her hand and read it off her palm – '060681. He gave it to me so I can visit him later.'

'Cool,' Jason said. 'Now, will you go back in and tell the others that Adam and I are going to try and figure out how Marc's cheating?'

'Are you sure you don't want me as your partner instead?' Erin asked. 'You saw how fast I got that code. I think I might actually be good at this "agent" thing.'

'Adam's feelings will be hurt if he doesn't get to play, too,' Jason told her.

'OK. Be careful, you guys,' she answered, getting serious.

'Let's do this,' Adam said as Erin walked away.

Jason did a quick check of the hall. All clear. 'OK, try and look staff-like,' he said as they made their way toward the staff only door.

'In these clothes I guess we'll have to be managerial type staff,' Adam commented.

Jason punched the numbers Erin had given him into the keypad next to the door. The lock opened with a *click*.

'If we get caught back here, that's pretty much it,' Adam remarked as they entered the secure area and the door shut behind them. 'It's pretty much "go to jail, go directly to jail, do not pass go, do not collect 200 dollars".'

Sixteen

'We're past the point of no return, that's what I'm saying,' Adam said, when they were deep into their exploration of the employee-only area. He paused at the end of the hallway, near the bathrooms. 'Left or right?'

'Which seems to have less potential for doom in your always optimistic opinion?' Jason asked.

'Left is lucky, I always say,' Adam answered.

Jason turned right. 'Come on.'

'Why did you even ask?' Adam complained. He cracked the first door they passed. 'Another bean counter office.' There'd been a whole row of them in the last hallway they'd gone down. 'Guess there are a lot of beans to be counted in a casino.'

Jason opened the door on the opposite side. 'Oh, sorry,' he said, when a woman in a severe suit snapped her head toward him. 'I was just looking for Bob. All these doors look the same.' He shut the door quickly.

'Bob?' Adam mouthed at him as they continued hurriedly down the hall.

'Every place has a "Bob",' Jason explained.

They did more door checks, and found more offices – all empty.

'You still have the left-is-lucky feeling?' Jason asked when the hall branched again.

'Yeah,' Adam replied, starting to turn right.

'Let's try it your way this time,' Jason said, turning left. They found a couple of small conference rooms, a big conference room, a little kitchen, and – after a few more twists and turns in the staff-only maze – the security hub. It had to be. Behind the wall of shaded glass windows, Jason could see dozens of TV screens. He couldn't make out the images, but they had to be feeds from all over the hotel and casino.

'The door's over here,' Adam whispered. 'And it's locked. We need a key card to swipe it open.'

'Remember the bathroom we saw, about two turns back, the one with the mop and bucket outside?' Jason asked. Adam nodded. 'Somebody was in the middle of cleaning back there – the mop would have been in a supply closet otherwise. I'm thinking whoever does the cleaning here probably has access to all the offices.'

'So smart *and* so good looking. It just isn't fair,' Adam joked as they trotted back the way they'd come.

The mop and bucket were still outside the bathroom door.

Jason led the way into the men's room. A sloshing sound inside one of the stalls gave away the location of the cleaning person. And – score! – a maroon Bonheur blazer lay on the padded bench next to the sinks. This was almost too easy. He hurried over to the blazer, praying there was a key card in one of the pockets.

Before he could check even one, the stall door swung open.

Adam leapt into action. 'Do you have any of that Vamoose stuff?' he asked the cleaning guy, using his body to block Jason from view. 'You know, that powder that you sprinkle on puke when it gets on the carpet.'

'Why do you need that?' the guy asked, not sounding happy.

Jason fingered the pockets of the blazer as fast as he could. He felt something thin and hard. It was a key card. He jammed it into his own pocket. 'We don't need it right *now*,' he told the cleaning guy, stepping up next to Adam. 'It's just that he has a nervous stomach, and it's his first week on the job. He's just a little worried there might be an incident.'

'Don't worry about it if you don't have any. I'll bring some from home. I buy in bulk,' Adam said over his shoulder as he and Jason hurried out of the bathroom.

They did a dorky high five as soon as the door was shut behind them, because the situation demanded it, then they tore back to the hub.

'So, our plan is just to walk on in there?' Adam asked.

'You left out a crucial part,' Jason told him. 'Our plan is just to *stealthily* walk on in there.' He slid the key card through the lock and held his finger to his lips as he stepped inside, holding the door open for Adam.

They quickly moved to the cover – the not-quite-enough-cover – of a nearby pillar. Jason scanned the room. The banks of TV monitors he'd spotted from outside seemed to form a big hexagon in the center. Jason could see three work stations on each of the sides visible to him from this angle. But each of the stations was empty. Weird. What was going on?

Well, Marc's father does own the place, Jason reminded himself. Maybe Marc arranged to have most of the security force out of the way for a while. It's not like he'd necessarily want tons of staff in on the fact that he was cheating in the poker tournament – if Jason and Adam were right about what was going on.

As quietly as he could – fortunately loafers were good for stealth – Jason moved toward the nearest workstation. He snagged a heavy flashlight, just because he felt a little better with something weapon-like in his hand, as he circled around the hub. The flickering images on the screens kept tugging at his attention, making him feel like someone was moving up alongside him.

He froze as he heard a murmuring voice. None of the monitors he'd passed had had the sound on. Jason listened hard. The voice was coming from around the next corner.

'He has a seven of hearts and a jack of diamonds. You're fine,' it said. The speaker had an accent. A *French* accent.

Got him, Jason thought. The speaker had to be Marc's partner.

In one fast move, Jason snapped his body around the corner. A beefy man wearing a headset with a small microphone leapt to his feet, but before he could get out a word of warning into the mic, Jason slammed the flashlight down on his head.

The man slumped back into his chair, chin resting on his chest. Jason pulled the guy's headset off and held it up so Adam could see it. Adam pointed to a monitor near the center of the bank. It showed Zach's arm – Jason recognized the onyx cufflinks – and his cards. Right now, they were flat against the table, but as soon as he raised them slightly to take a look, the camera would show his hand.

Jason clicked off the headset. He checked the one side of the hub he hadn't seen. 'He's the only one in here,' Jason told Adam.

'I wish I'd brought the counterfeit cash,' Adam said. 'I could have stuffed it in our French friend's pockets. I think he deserves a nice, long jail sentence.'

'Oh, man. Look at Marc squirm.' Jason pointed to a monitor filled with Marc's face. The close-up was so tight, he could see the tiny droplets of perspiration that had begun to form on Marc's forehead.

'Is he wearing eyeliner?' Adam demanded.

'The right beauty products aren't going to be able to save him now,' Jason answered. 'Zach just won the hand.' He and Adam high-fived again. Because, again, it was essential.

'Hey, what's wrong?' Adam asked, letting his hand fall to his side. 'You look like you remembered there's no Santa or something. You did already know that, right, about Santa? I didn't spoil anything?'

'What I just remembered is that Marc is scum,' Jason said. 'What I just remembered is that he's a cheating piece of crap.'

'OK, I'm with you. That's why we're here. That's why you just went all Joe-Pesci-in-*Goodfellas* on his accomplice over there,' Adam answered.

'But what was the point?' Jason burst out. 'Marc's

lying, cheating scum. That means even if Zach beats him – which he will now that we've evened the odds again – Marc's not going to just walk away from Paige. And he's not going to release Sienna as long as he thinks that keeping her hostage will make Paige do what he wants.'

'Not a problem,' Adam said, a grin spreading over his face.

'Were you listening?' Jason demanded.

'Uh-huh. But I was also watching a little TV. I'm a good multi-tasker,' Adam answered. 'Check out what's on over here.' He tapped the monitor three to the left of the one showing Marc's big head.

Jason sighed – he didn't have time for Adam's goofiness right now – but he turned to look at the screen, and took a deep breath for what felt like the first time all day, because there was Sienna. She was sitting in the casino vault, picking at her nail polish. She looked bored out of her skull, but completely unharmed.

'You found her! We can go break her out!' Jason cried. Then he stopped, realizing that there was a problem. 'Yeah, let's go break her out . . . of the vault of one of the biggest casinos in Las Vegas!'

Adam raised his eyebrows. 'Yeah. We're about' – he did some quick counting on his fingers – 'two short.'

'Huh?' Jason said.

'It takes eleven to break into a casino vault. Maybe more since they had George Clooney *and* Brad Pitt,' Adam explained. 'Of course, we have vampires, so maybe eleven would do it. Except you and I aren't vampires. Although, as you might remember, I do have the very heroic chin, and you have managed some minor feats of heroism in your time as well.'

'The only way Sienna's getting out is if Marc lets her out,' Jason said thoughtfully, as he stared at the monitor showing his girlfriend. 'And he's definitely not going to do that if he loses, which we've just pretty much guaranteed he will.'

'Yeah, he just lost another hand,' Adam agreed. 'He's hurting without his inside man.'

Jason knew that if Marc lost, he'd need Sienna as a bargaining chip more than ever. He racked his brains, trying to find a way to outwit Marc. He felt like a hamster on a wheel. No more options. No place to turn.

'Wait,' Jason said, an idea hitting him. 'Wait. What if Marc wins?'

'Isn't that what we're in here trying to *stop*?' Adam asked.

'Yeah, but right now, I think our only shot is for Zach to throw the game and *lose*,' Jason told him. 'If

Marc wins, he'll let Sienna out. That's the only way he *will* let Sienna out. Then we just have to come up with a plan to keep Paige from having to fly off to Paris with him.'

'You mean, a plan to keep Paige from having to fly off to Paris with the *psycho murderer who travels with a pack of bodyguards*?' Adam asked meaningfully.

'Yeah,' Jason agreed. 'So we need to work fast.'

Seventeen

'Looks like Marc just called for a break. At least I figure it was him. He must badly want a break right now, and all the players are getting up from the table,' Adam commented. 'Is this a good thing or a bad thing in our must-work-fast plan? By the way, I don't actually know what the plan *is*.'

'I don't either, not exactly,' Jason admitted. 'For now, just go tell the others what the deal is. Especially Zach. Tell him that when the game starts back up, he needs to start losing.'

'Got it. What are you going to do?' Adam asked.

'Stay here and try to think up the next part of the plan,' Jason said.

Adam gave Jason a salute and hurried out of the security hub. Jason locked the door behind him; he didn't need any surprises right now.

But he got one almost right away: Marc's voice coming through one of the speakers. 'Philippe, what the hell? I told you not to take the headset off for anything!'

Jason shot a glance at the unconscious guy – Philippe, obviously. Still out. Good. He put on the headset, switched it on and mumbled, 'Tech glitch, sorry,' trying for a French accent. He hoped the mumble, the brief message, and the accent would keep Marc from realizing that someone new was on headset duty.

'It had better not happen again!' Marc snapped. 'We're on a fifteen minute break. We, not you. The headset stays on.'

Jason grunted in response, which seemed to satisfy Marc. He checked the monitors and found one that showed Adam talking to Zach and the rest of the group up at their table in the gallery. Zach nodded his head, like he was agreeing to the plan. All good, so far.

But Paige . . . Paige looked like she was approaching meltdown. Why wouldn't she be? The thought of being on an airplane with Marc in a few hours—

Wait. Airplane. Airplane meant airport. That was it! He'd just come up with the second part of the plan. At least, there was a possibility it could work, which was better than what they had now, which was nothing.

Jason started for the door, then hesitated. He'd given Philippe a good whack with the flashlight, but the guy wasn't going to stay out forever. *Duct tape*, he decided. *A place like this should have duct tape around. Every place should. It's an essential item.*

He started to search the workstations, and noticed some cables had been duct-taped together. He was right. There had to be a roll of duct tape someplace. He found it in the bottom drawer of a filing cabinet, and used nearly all of it in binding Philippe's hands together behind him, and taping his feet to the legs of the chair. That would slow him down.

Jason hesitated again. He'd done a decent job with the restraints, but . . . He pulled off Philippe's tie. Good thing all the Bonheur employees dressed so nice, and that Philippe was trying to blend. He wrapped it round Philippe's head, covering over his mouth.

'Could have been worse, guy,' he said to the still-unconscious Philippe. 'I could have used one of your socks.'

He patted his jacket pocket to make sure he still had the key card for the security room, then hurried out and back through the maze of corridors that led to the public part of the casino. He almost ran into the cleaning guy. 'Night, Charles,' he said, remembering his name from the tag on his jacket.

'Night . . . sir,' he answered.

Jason rushed directly to the private poker room and up to the gallery. 'Let's go outside a minute. For an update,' he told Zach and the others. He didn't wait for an answer, just turned around and made for the door.

215

'I think I have a plan,' he said when the group was assembled out in the hall.

'We heard the first part of the plan from Adam,' Belle said. 'Make Zach lose a quarter of a million dollars. And let Marc think he can take Paige to Paris.'

Adam winced. 'That's not exactly how I put it.'

'Close enough,' Jason said. He shoved his fingers through his hair. 'I know it sounds stupid. And there probably is a better plan, if we had time to come up with one, but I think it can work. I think it can save Sienna *and* Paige.'

Zach chopped one hand through the air. 'Get to it. What's the rest?'

'I'm going to need Adam's counterfeit money.' Jason looked at his friend.

'It's yours. It's a lot to ask, yes. But I will sacrifice the phony money – that could get me thrown in jail or disowned – to your plan,' Adam answered solemnly.

'We also need Marc's suitcases. I'm sure he has them packed and ready to go to the airport,' Jason went on. 'Any bright ideas on how to get them?'

'I've got one,' Belle announced. At least the voice was Belle's. Her short blond hair had darkened and lengthened. Her face and body had grown rounder. Her nose tilted up a little, and her lips were a bit thinner. She smiled. 'I'm sure that I, Ms High-powered

Hotel Manager, can get into any room I wish.'

'Genius!' Erin told her. 'You look just like her.'

'Of course, I don't carry bags. I'm much too important for that. I'll need bell boys,' Belle declared. She pointed to Brad and Van Dyke.

'You can just snap your fingers at any bellboy,' Van Dyke protested.

'I look a lot like Ms Mayer, but I'm not an exact match,' Belle told him. 'I don't want anyone who really knows her to get too good a look. Besides, I want to see you two in those cute little bell boy suits. Hey, Belle and the Bell Boys. Keep the suits and we'll start a band.'

'I'd pay to see *that* group,' Maggie said, giving Van Dyke's butt a pinch. 'The pants on those uniforms are tight.'

'Mmm-hmmm,' Erin agreed.

'This is humiliating,' Brad muttered.

'You love it,' Belle told him. 'You wouldn't spend so much time working on your muscles if you didn't want to get looked at.'

'Now, that's true,' Adam said. 'I don't do the exercise thing, because I'm shy. I know that the ladies would not be able to stop staring at my body if I worked out, and that would make me feel so, so uncomfortable.'

'Do it,' Zach told Brad and Van Dyke.

And that was that. Although Van Dyke did say, 'I

work on my body because athletics are an important part of being a well-rounded, healthy person,' as Belle led him and Brad away in search of uniforms.

Jason strode after them. 'Meet me back in the security hub when you get the suitcases. It's through that door. The code is 060681.' He quickly ran down the turns they'd need to take to reach the hub. 'There are a few people working back there. A couple in offices and a cleaning guy. Be careful,' he added.

'We will,' Belle promised him. 'See you later.'

Jason returned to the group.

'I'm heading back to our hotel to get my bag of dirty cash,' Adam said.

'Meet me back at the hub. I'll be going over there in a few,' Jason replied.

'Adam, out,' Adam said as he moved off.

'So what's my mission this time?' Erin asked.

'I need you and Paige and Maggie to go back to the table in the gallery,' Jason told her. 'Marc will get suspicious if he notices we've all disappeared. And he'll go nuclear if Paige goes missing.'

'Unlike the boys in their uniforms, Marc losing it is not something I want to see,' Maggie said. 'Let's get back inside.'

Paige nodded, looking a little dazed, as the three girls started for the private room.

'I need to get back, too,' Zach said. 'The break's about over.' He didn't move. Just looked at Jason. 'Are you sure you know what you're doing?' he asked finally.

Jason shrugged. 'It's the only thing I can think of,' he admitted.

Zach gave a short bark of laugher. 'At least you've managed to get out of some tight spots before. You have a decent track record.' He nodded at Jason, then disappeared through the brocade door.

Hope my record holds, Jason thought. He reentered the staff area and made it back to the security hub without being sighted. It was a start.

He did a Philippe check. Was he in a slightly different position than when Jason left? His chair seemed to be further to the left. Jason noticed that there were grooves in the carpet.

He snatched up the flashlight and held it over Philippe's head. Philippe's eyes snapped open. *Knew you were faking*, Jason thought.

Philippe shook his head, pleading.

'Sorry, guy,' Jason said, bringing the flashlight down with a *thunk*, 'but I need some privacy here.' He did remove the tie, though. Jason wanted to make sure Philippe could get enough oxygen.

Jason sat down in one of the empty chairs and checked the monitors. The players were returning to the table. He pulled on the headset and made sure the mic was live, then he gave a little cough so Marc would know his cheat system was operational.

He checked Paige. She still wasn't looking great, but Maggie and Erin were clearly doing all they could to get her through.

Jason cracked his neck as the dealer whipped out the hole cards. He'd fooled Marc into believing he was Philippe once, when he'd spoken about three words. Was he going to be able to pull it off again?

'Ten spades, seven hearts for Zach,' he said, with his phony French accent, as he watched Zach check his cards on the monitor. 'Ajax for the woman,' he added, warning Marc of Sexy Actress's ace/jack combo. He'd noticed that some of the screens showed the other players' hands too.

Marc didn't seem to notice anything wrong. He didn't even seem to have noticed that some of the Malibu group had vanished. Paige was probably all he cared about.

On the other hand, Jason thought, Marc was a poker player. His poker face could just be that good.

Jason talked him through winning that hand and avoiding defeat on the next one, then got him started on another hand. Then he decided he had time to check the other monitors to see how the rest of the plan was coming along. Marc wouldn't be expecting more help right away.

Jason walked around the corner to the next bank of monitors, his eyes darting back and forth as he scanned them. OK, yeah, there was Adam coming back into the casino with his backpack of funny money. Perfect.

Through the headset, Jason heard Marc expel a loud breath. Maybe he needed advice faster than Jason had thought he would. Jason circled to the monitors that showed the game.

'The turn gave white suit three of a kind,' he said, then he moved to a different wall of monitors and searched for Belle. He couldn't stop himself from smiling when he spotted her striding through the hotel lobby with Brad and Van Dyke scurrying behind her, loaded down with luggage.

Jason flicked off the headset, pulled out his cell and hit speed dial four.

'Whassup?' Adam responded.

'Belle and her boys have the suitcases. They should be at the staff-only door in two,' Jason told him. 'Wait for them, OK? I gave them directions, but the hallways are confusing. Actually, call me before you go in. It's pretty empty in here still, but the cleaning guy is around, and some executive type is making microwave popcorn in the kitchen.'

'Got it. Adam, out.' He hung up.

Jason flicked the headset back on, and checked the monitors showing the game. Zach and Marc were heading into a showdown for the pot. Zach was about to lose. Excellent. Everything was coming together. For now, anyway.

Other Tuxedo Guy's chips are really getting low, Jason thought as he waited for Marc's inevitable win. *He's not going to last much longer.* Sexy Actress wasn't doing badly, while Yakamoto had turned into some kind of a maniac, making all sorts of wild bets. It wasn't working out entirely badly for him, though. Too Much Bling was looking nervous.

Jason's cell rang. It was Adam. Jason flicked off his mic, then picked up the phone. 'You ready to come in?' he asked.

'If you're ready for us,' Adam replied.

Jason found the TV screens that showed the staff-only section of the Bonheur. 'Right, the exec is making another bag of popcorn. He burned the first one. The woman in the suit is still in her office, door almost closed. And the cleaning guy is in the big conference room. That's everybody.'

As Jason watched, Adam, Belle, Van Dyke, and Brad came through the door. Jason did a quick check of all the other people in the staff area. None of them seemed curious about who was coming in.

The game! Jason remembered suddenly. He put down the phone, flicked on the mic, and moved back around the corner to the bank of monitors showing the private poker room. The hole cards had just been dealt. Yakamoto was flying American Airlines.

'Pair of aces, to your left,' Jason told Marc. It couldn't have made him happy. He was holding the three of clubs and the eight of diamonds. It was a bad opening hand. He didn't need Jason to tell him to fold. He was already doing it.

Zach had a mediocre hand and he'd just shoved what looked like $25,000 worth of chips out in front of him. The guy was good at everything – even losing.

Jason paced around to check out the staff section monitors. *Oh, no!* Where was his cell? He hurried back around and snatched it off the work station next to Philippe, who was still zonked. 'Ad—' He'd forgotten to turn off the mic. Damn. But he hadn't said a whole name or a word or anything. He cut the microphone. 'Adam, go left. Popcorn is coming your way.' He checked the monitor that showed Adam and the others. They'd made the turn down the left hallway just in time. 'You were right. Left is lucky.' He watched the executive enter his office. 'OK. You're good to go. I'm going to open the door for you.'

Jason pulled off the headset. Marc had folded. He definitely didn't need advice right now. He hurried over to the door and opened it just in time to usher Adam, Belle, Van Dyke, Brad, and the luggage inside. He made sure the door was locked behind them.

Belle resumed her regular appearance with a smile. 'That was fun.'

'Real fun, yeah!' Van Dyke said sarcastically, dropping his load of bags to the ground.

'Empty one of the carry-on bags and fill it with the counterfeit cash,' Jason said.

'You only needed one? Why did we carry them all down here then?' Van Dyke whined.

'What is your problem?' Brad asked with a grin. 'Were they too heavy for your little twig arms?'

'If we only needed one, one bell boy would have been enough. And that bell boy would have been you,' Van Dyke told him.

'Put this in there, too,' Adam said, pulling a gun out of the backpack.

Everybody scrambled away from Adam – fast. 'Whoa! Where did you get that?' Jason asked, staring at the gun in his friend's hand.

'It's the one that lowlife pulled on Zach, when you guys had to ride to the rescue,' Adam explained. 'I asked myself, "Is it safer with me or with the lowlife?" and I decided it was safer with me. But now we have a worthy home for it – with another lowlife!'

'You are—' Jason began, but he was interrupted by a loud banging on the door to the security hub.

'Why is this door locked?' a man demanded from outside. 'Open up immediately!'

Eighteen

Jason stared at Adam. Adam stared at the gun in his hand. Belle stared from Jason, to the gun. Brad and Van Dyke stared at each other.

More pounding. 'Who's in there?'

'Dirty money and a gun and breaking and entering. I'm going to be an old, old man when I get out of prison,' Adam whispered, blinking rapidly. 'An old, old virgin man.'

'I'll save you,' Belle whispered back, the words coming out a little garbled as her lips became thinner. Her eyebrows straightened. Her hair lengthened. Her cheeks puffed out. And she was looking a lot like the hotel manager again.

'It's Hilary Mayer,' Belle snapped. She whipped the door open, not waiting for Adam to hide the gun or for Van Dyke and Brad to deal with the counterfeit cash. 'I reserved this time for crisis training for the new team. We're covering a hostage scenario. Do you really need to be in here now?'

The lanky security guard stared at Belle.

'Well, do you?' she repeated.

'I was scheduled—' he began.

'Then it's not your fault,' Belle interrupted, with an impatient wave of her hand. 'I'll speak to your supervisor. Somebody clearly isn't reading their memos in a timely fashion. Go home. You'll be paid for your shift.'

'Thank you, Ms Mayer. S-s-sorry about the inconvenience,' stammered the guard. He turned and rushed away.

Belle laughed as she locked the door behind him. 'I think Ms Mayer kicks butt.'

'I think *you* do,' Adam said. 'That was truly impressive.'

'I have to check on Marc,' Jason told them. He hurried back over to the monitors showing the game and pulled on his headset. The dealer was shuffling the cards.

Jason checked the chips piled in front of all the players. Zach's had gone down significantly. Yakamoto had made a haul with his pair of aces. Marc hadn't lost anything because he'd folded. And Other Tuxedo Guy was absent from the table. He must have gone all in and lost. Sexy Actress was doing OK. Too Much Bling still looked worried, and from the number of chips he was showing, he was right to be.

The hole cards were dealt.

'Zach has a jack of hearts and a three of diamonds,' Jason said into the mic. 'And there's a pair of tens behind the dealer button.'

Belle came over and opened her mouth to speak.

Jason held up one finger until he'd flicked off the mic. 'What?' he asked.

'Marc's bag is all packed,' she said. 'We ended up getting his cases from the luggage storage area. He was already checked out. He's definitely in a hurry to hit the airport. So, now the bell boys should just take everything back, right?'

'Yep,' Jason agreed.

'Zach doing OK?' Belle asked as the dealer showed the flop.

Jason checked out the community cards. No jack. 'I'm pretty sure he's about to lose again,' Jason told her.

'Good,' Belle said.

Jason checked the other monitors. Thanks to the flop, Marc now had a pair of aces – good enough to beat the two tens Too Much Bling was holding. 'You'd better tell Brad and Van Dyke to hurry,' he warned Belle. 'As soon as Zach is out of the game, Marc's going to want to leave for the airport. His bags need to be ready.'

Belle nodded and disappeared around the bank of monitors. Monitors!

Jason hurried after Belle. 'Don't leave yet,' he told Brad and Van Dyke. 'Let's check the monitors first.' He pointed to the ones that showed the staff section where the hub was located. 'The cleaning guy is vacuuming one of the smaller conference rooms now, and the two execs are in their offices. You should be OK,' he told them. 'Go!'

'If you get caught, just use the uniforms,' Belle put in.

'Yeah, we can come up with a work reason to be in here. We *are* staff,' Van Dyke agreed.

'No, I meant use them to flirt your way out, because you guys are so irresistibly cute in them,' Belle answered.

Jason felt a flicker of paranoia – either paranoia or reasonable fear – and decided he needed to do a Philippe check. It looked like the guy was still out. Two head-smashes in such a short time would probably do that to someone, Jason figured.

'Check it. It's happening!' Adam exclaimed, watching the game on the monitors.

'Zach's going all in!' Belle cried.

Jason scanned the monitors, checking the turn card and the river. 'Yup, this is it. He's going to lose. And he'll be bankrupt with this hand.' Jason pulled on the headset; he wanted to hear what was happening.

The dealer confirmed that Marc had won the hand and that Zach was now out of the game.

'I want to cash out,' Marc announced immediately.

'What?' Sexy Actress cried, her voice a squeak.

'You can't do that,' Too Much Bling said flatly.

'I can do whatever I like,' Marc told him.

The director stepped forward. 'In a regular game, you could, of course, cash out whenever you wished,' he said politely. 'But this is a tournament. Each player's buy-in is part of the tournament pot. You are welcome to continue to play and perhaps win the pot, but you cannot take any part of the pot while the tournament is in play.'

'Damn right you can't,' Too Much Bling said, fingering his small pile of chips.

'Fine. Keep the money. I've won something much more valuable,' Marc said calmly. With a silky smile, he rose from the table, climbed the steps to the gallery, and held out his hand to Paige. He was all romance and gallantry, just as if he wasn't insane at all.

Paige put her hand in Marc's, and even on the monitor, Jason could see her fingers were trembling. Together they walked back down the stairs.

Jason took off the headset. 'Let's get out of here. I want to be ready to roll.'

'Marc just said something to Zach,' Belle said. She leant close to one of the monitors. 'I don't know what it was, but Zach and Paige both reacted. I couldn't tell if they were just surprised or . . .'

'Or what?' Jason asked.

'I don't know,' Belle said. 'Paige might have looked scared.'

Jason, Adam, and Belle watched the monitor as Marc led Paige from the room. As soon as they were out of the private room, a man hurried up to Marc.

'That's Didier, the guy we were following today,' Adam pointed out.

Jason grabbed the headset again, but Marc had switched off the receiver. Jason saw Zach nod at something Didier said, then the two of them left the room together.

'What are they doing? What's happening?' Jason ran to the monitor that showed Sienna. She was still in the vault. He grabbed his cell and punched in Zach's number.

'Is everything OK?' Jason burst out as soon as Zach picked up. He knew he sounded panicked, but he couldn't help it. 'Are they doing what they said? Are they letting her go?'

'I'm being taken to her right now,' Zach told him. 'Marc is taking Paige to the airport. Meet me in the lobby.' He hung up without giving Jason a chance to reply.

'We're supposed to meet Zach in the lobby,' Jason told Adam and Belle. 'I'm hoping he'll have Sienna with him.'

They all started for the door. 'Do we need to do anything with our friend back there?' Adam asked, nodding in Philippe's direction.

'He's not gagged. He can call for help when he comes round,' Jason said.

'I'll put on my Ms Mayer, so we won't have any trouble getting out of here,' Belle said, and she quickly did her transformation thing. But they didn't need Ms Mayer and her butt-kicking abilities. Nobody tried to stop them.

They started to run as soon as they hit the 'civilian' hallway, Belle getting her own face and body back on the fly before they hit the crowded casino. They dodged and weaved, trying not to knock anyone down.

'There she is!' Belle shouted. 'With Erin and Maggie and everybody.'

Jason had already spotted Sienna. He *felt* her from all the way across the room. He picked up speed, weaving around slot machines and roulette tables and people, people, people . . . until he had his arms around her. 'Are you OK?' he asked.

'I'm fine. I'm fine.' She reluctantly pulled away. 'We have to get Paige. Why did you give up Paige for me?'

'We didn't. Not really. We have a plan,' Jason promised. 'I'll explain it on the way to the airport. We have to get over there – now!'

Nineteen

Belle managed to cram the Escalade into a parking spot labeled 'compact'. Then she, Sienna, Jason and Adam scrambled out and started to run across the parking garage.

'We left practically right on top of them,' Jason called to Sienna. 'We're going to find them.' He heard footfalls coming up behind him fast. Marc's goons? He shot a look over his shoulder. No, just the rest of the Malibu group.

They burst out of the garage. Jason didn't hesitate. He plunged across the street, ignoring the horns of the cabs, cars, and shuttles. *If they don't like it, they can hit me*, he thought grimly.

The electronic doors leading to the international terminal slid open in front of him, and Jason barreled inside, Sienna on his heels, and everyone else right behind them.

'The arrival/departure info,' Sienna called out. She veered toward the monitors mounted in the wall by the car rental kiosk. Jason followed, and skidded to a stop in front of the screens.

'Any departures to France?' Belle asked from behind him.

'I'm looking.' He scanned the columns.

'I don't see anything!' Sienna said. 'At least, there doesn't seem to be anything in the next few hours.'

'Let's split up and check all the ticket counters,' Brad suggested. 'We don't know what kind of connecting flight they could have got.'

'Good idea. Whoever spots Marc and Paige first, call me on my cell,' Jason answered.

'Van Dyke's car, start this way. Belle's car that way,' Brad instructed. And they were gone.

'One of us should peel off at every ticket counter,' Jason called as he ran with his group. 'Belle, you first. Go!' She darted away.

'I've got the next one,' Adam called, leaping over a pet carrier containing one very yappy little dog.

Jason gave Sienna's hand a squeeze without breaking stride, then broke away, heading toward the Virgin Atlantic counter. The line was snaking out past the ropes leading to the counter. Mounds of suitcases were piled all over the place.

He tried to scan the line. It was impossible to see everyone from all the way back there. He plunged forward, making sure to look at each person he passed. No Marc. No Paige. No Marc. No Paige.

'There's a line here!' an annoyed woman snapped.

'Friend up there, holding my place,' Jason answered without pausing. No Marc. No Paige. No Marc. No Paige. He stumbled over a lawn-size garbage bag that somebody was using as luggage.

'Watch it!' a guy in a USC sweatshirt yelled.

Yeah, I'm very sorry I damaged your Louis Vuitton, Jason thought. No Marc. No Paige. He could see all the way up the line now. No Marc. No Paige. All the way up.

Crap! Jason wheeled around and pushed a hole through the line. Then he ran.

'Sir!' a security guard called. 'You're going to have to slow down.'

Jason forced himself to walk for three steps. He wanted to shout at the man, tell him it was an emergency, but it's not like he could explain that his girlfriend's sister had been kidnapped by a killer – a killer who was also a vampire.

Before he could start to run again, Adam and Sienna hurried over to him.

'We've checked all the counters from here to the end,' Sienna said. 'A bunch of them were empty.'

Jason didn't have to ask if they'd seen Paige or Marc. It was obvious that they hadn't.

'No calls from anybody, right?' Adam asked.

'Not yet,' Jason answered.

'What if Marc chartered a private plane?' Sienna burst out. 'They wouldn't be at any of the ticket counters. He definitely has enough money to do it, too. Would they even have to go through airport security? It would ruin your plan if they didn't.'

Jason had had time to give Sienna a quick version of the plan on the five-mile drive to the airport. 'I think they'd still have to go through security,' he said. He looked over at Adam.

'Everybody does. If they didn't before 9/11, they do now,' Adam confirmed, but he didn't sound completely sure. He sounded like he *wanted* to be completely sure.

'Let's go help search the other half of the terminal,' Jason suggested. They turned around and saw Belle heading toward them. She'd already met up with the rest of the group.

'Paige?' Sienna asked as they rushed to meet their friends.

'Sorry, sweetie,' Erin answered.

'We checked everyplace we could get to without a boarding pass,' Brad added. 'The international terminal's just not that big.'

Jason turned to Zach. If anyone knew the answer to the chartered plane question, it would be him. 'Zach, do you—'

'Oh, my God!' Maggie exclaimed. 'Look back there.'

Jason turned. A small crowd had gathered by the newsstand.

'This is outrageous! I want my lawyer here. Immediately,' he heard a voice yell – a voice with a slight French accent.

'That's Marc,' Sienna said.

The crowd parted enough for Jason to see Paige and Marc flanked by airport security.

'I have to get over there.' Sienna started toward her sister.

'Wait,' Zach said. 'I'll make a call. I have an acquaintance.' He turned and walked away.

'Let Zach do his thing,' Jason advised Sienna as the guards escorted Marc and Paige through a door marked 'AIRPORT SECURITY'.

She nodded, and the group took the row of plastic chairs that had a direct view of the airport security door. Zach returned a few minutes later, and stood next to Sienna, arms crossed.

'Oh, man, you are good,' Adam exclaimed, when Paige walked out of the door – unescorted – ten minutes later. She ran straight over to Sienna and hugged her.

'What happened?' Sienna cried.

'Marc got caught taking counterfeit money and a gun through security! I thought I was going to get arrested, too, but then, suddenly, everyone was saying that there was nothing illegal in *my* bags and that *I* hadn't done anything wrong, and one of the guards actually apologized to me.' Paige shrugged. 'So here I am.'

'You think those guys might be here for our friend?' Van Dyke asked, nodding toward three cops who were walking into the terminal. They strode straight over to airport security.

The smallest smile crossed Zach's face. 'I think it's a good possibility,' he said.

'I'd bet money on it,' Adam agreed. 'The real stuff,' he added. 'Any takers?' There weren't any, so nobody lost any cash when the police came back out with Marc in handcuffs.

Belle pulled out her camera-phone and got a shot. 'For your scrapbook,' she told Paige, with a grin.

Paige stood up. 'Marc!' she called. When he looked her way, she blew him a big, juicy kiss. He did not look too pleased. Belle snapped another picture, and passed her phone around so everyone could see.

'So now what?' Paige asked. 'We still have days to fill with Vegas fun!'

Sienna rolled her eyes. 'I think I speak for everyone when I say the only fun I want to have right now is a nice, quiet ride home.'

She definitely spoke for Jason. It had been close, very close, but Paige and Sienna were both safe. He was definitely ready to go home. The relief flooding through him right now was better than anything Vegas had to offer.

'It's not going to be any fun. The movie is pure chick flick. That was clear from the commercials,' Jason complained as he drove down the PCH. Not that there was anything he'd rather be doing than hanging with Sienna pretty much anywhere. 'There's crying in it. I saw crying.'

Sienna looked over her shoulder at Belle and shook her head.

'And there's the wearing of cute pajamas,' Adam put in. 'That is one of the four horsemen of the chick flick, *Cute Pajamas*. All I can say is somebody better be buying me a large popcorn with a large Dr Pepper, and Goobers. I'm going to need Goobers mixed with the corn to survive this. It offends my film lover sensibilities.'

'I just want explosions,' Jason said. 'And it wasn't that kind of crying I saw. It wasn't crying because there was just an explosion and somebody's leg got blown off. It was I-got-my-feelings-hurt crying. This is the last night of spring break. I shouldn't have to deal with crying.'

Actually watching some crying with Sienna was fine. Going back to school was fine. *Normal* was fine. More than fine – even if it was DeVere Heights normal, which was always a little less than.

'You don't have to go,' Sienna told him as he pulled into the parking lot of the New Malibu. 'Belle and I are happy to watch the chick flick all by ourselves.'

'And we'll enjoy it. Because we are chicks,' Belle added. 'Then we call one or two of the numerous cute boys we know, who will be more than happy to pick us up and take us home.'

'Now that just sounds dangerous,' Adam said. 'And as the son of the sheriff, I should know. I'm going to have to insist that I accompany you.'

'And I'll have to accompany Adam,' Jason said. 'He gets scared in these kinds of movies.'

'Hmm. What do you think, Belle?' Sienna asked as Jason parked.

'I think it might be acceptable. If someone buys me a medium popcorn with a large Diet Sprite.'

'Fine,' Adam muttered.

'My parents got a letter of apology from the Lessards today,' Sienna said as she stepped out of the car. Suddenly, the cool Malibu night felt cold, and the brilliant stars in the clear sky seemed much further away.

'What did it say?' Belle asked.

'It just apologized for Marc's behavior, without going into specifics. It also included a check to cover any "inconvenience" – a check that will exactly cover the money Zach lost,' Sienna said. 'Paige made some acceptable stuff up for my parents. They'd freak if they knew what really happened.'

'Is Paige doing OK?' Belle asked. 'I know that on the trip back she was acting like her usual self, but I wasn't sure if that was real.' None of them moved toward the theater. They needed some privacy for this conversation.

'I don't know if it was real, either,' Sienna admitted. 'But that's still how she's playing it. Although, she's not going back to school in Paris; she's looking at colleges in London.'

'With Marc back in Paris, I don't blame her,' Adam commented.

'He's lucky he has parents who can play the diplomatic immunity card,' Jason said. He still felt a little spurt of anger at the way Marc had got away with everything. True, the fake money and the gun hadn't been his, so he hadn't technically deserved to be arrested. But he'd done so many worse things that he deserved to be punished for.

'You're going to miss Paige, I bet,' Belle said to Sienna.

'I am. For sure,' Sienna sighed. 'But I'm not going to miss the drama. Paige always brings the drama.'

'And the fun,' Belle added.

'Yeah,' Sienna grinned. 'We should get inside,' she said. 'We don't want to miss the beginning.'

'God, no,' Adam cried as they started for the box office.

'I forgot, I'm also going to need Sour Patch Kids to mix with my popcorn,' Belle informed him.

'That is truly disgusting,' Adam replied.

'I *was* going to resign as your dating mentor after you pulled your disappearing act in Vegas,' Belle said. 'But you clearly need me too much. No matter what a girl does or says, you can *never ever* use the word "disgusting" in reference to her.'

Jason and Sienna laughed. Jason wrapped his arm around his girlfriend and pulled her close, taking a second to appreciate the fact that she was there with him. Unhurt.

High Stakes

The two of them always seemed to beat the odds and somehow work things out. All Jason could do was hope things stayed that way. He was certainly willing to take the gamble – to face anything and everything that being in love with a vampire brought his way – as long as he had Sienna by his side.

HUNTED

by Alex Duval

To JN, for all the laughs along the way!

Special thanks to
Laura Burns & Melinda Metz

One

The sound of the waves crashing in. The slap of a football being caught in a pair of hands. Girls talking. Guys laughing. Seagulls cawing. A volleyball net flapping in the breeze coming off the ocean. Jason Freeman grinned as he dug his toes deeper into the sun-warmed sand of Surfrider Beach, his eyes closed behind his new Diesel sunglasses. This strip of beach – just your basic paradise – had become his home away from home since he'd moved to Malibu from Michigan at the beginning of his senior year. If someone dropped him on this spot, blindfolded, he'd know it just by the sounds.

That didn't mean he wouldn't miss the visuals, because he definitely would. Jason shoved his sunglasses onto the top of his head, then rolled onto his side, giving himself the perfect view of his favorite Surfrider Beach sight – his girlfriend, Sienna Devereux, in one of her many bathing suits, this one a black bikini with a top that tied in a bow in front. That bow made Jason's fingers itch.

Sienna slid up on one elbow and pulled her big sunglasses down on her nose. She gave him a playful smile, a smile that made him think she could read his mind about that tie.

'You know exactly what I'm thinking, don't you?' Jason asked.

Sienna glanced over to his surfboard, which was jammed in the sand a few feet away. 'That there are some all-time, classic waves out there and you can't let them pass you by?' she asked, widening her eyes with extreme innocence, putting a little surfer-dude spin on her words.

Jason shot a look at the ocean. There *was* some pretty tempting wave action going on out there. He looked back at Sienna. But that bikini bow . . .

How spoiled am I? he thought. *Sitting here trying to decide between two natural wonders: the Malibu coast and my scorching girlfriend. Answer: so insanely spoiled.* Malibu had been very, very good to him. Even if the place was bursting with vampires.

Or maybe *because* it was. There was one vampire who'd definitely made his life more intense and more exciting – Sienna. Being with her made him feel more alive, even though entering her world had nearly made him dead! He'd been attacked by a crazed vampire consumed with bloodlust, and shot with a crossbow by a vampire hunter. And then there was the Aristocratic French vampire who'd been stalking Sienna's sister.

And yet in spite of all the near-death experiences, Jason wouldn't have had his life any other way. Sienna was worth it all. He'd give his life for what they'd already had together, although, ideally, it wouldn't come to that.

'Go ahead. Surf if you want to,' Sienna sighed, settling back to sunbathe.

Jason grinned. 'No way. I'm not surfing. There are much more exciting things to do right here.' He moved closer to Sienna – then reached across her and grabbed the copy of *Cosmo* sticking out of her beach bag. 'I have a lot of reading to catch up on. I haven't even *started* to study the Body Language Decoder.' He opened the magazine and locked his gaze on the page, like it was mesmerizing.

'Decode this,' Sienna said, plucking the magazine out of his hand and tossing it across the sand.

Jason laughed. Then he kissed her. Teasing Sienna was fun, but kissing her was more fun. Way too soon, she pulled back a little and gazed out across the ocean, her expression thoughtful.

'What?' Jason asked, running his fingers down her cheek.

'Just wondering how many days we'll have like this,

with all of us,' she answered. She turned toward the beach where most of the guys were playing football and some of the girls were getting up a volleyball game. Her eyes skipped from face to face, taking in all their friends, pretty much all of them vampires, scattered over 'their' piece of the beach.

Sienna had just brought up the topic that every senior at DeVere High had been avoiding: life after high school. They were just a breath away from graduation. In the fall, they'd be scattered all over the place at different colleges. Forget fall; they'd start splitting up as soon as high school ended. Everybody had summer plans.

'All of us, not that many more times,' Jason admitted. 'But a lot of us, most of the summer. And the two of us, pretty much constantly. Even in the fall. I'm at CalTech. You're at UCLA. We'll practically be room-mates.'

'And together, we're going to own L.A.!' Sienna agreed with a smile, but her dark eyes didn't have all of their usual sparkle as she looked across at her friends.

'So you noticed it too. I can see it in your eyes,' Belle Rémy commented as she grabbed three beers from a nearby cooler and sat down on the other side of Sienna. 'Do you think we should stage an intervention?'

'What?' Sienna asked, staring at her best friend.

'For Adam,' Belle answered. 'Weren't you watching him about to crash and burn with that girl over there?' She jerked her chin toward where Adam Turnball and a short, curvy girl wearing cut-off jeans, a flowered bikini top, and what Jason always thought of as 'smart-chick glasses' – the ones with the black frames – stood loading fish tacos and chips and salsa onto paper plates.

'Well, she's smiling. She doesn't seem to be attempting to back away,' Sienna commented.

'But I heard him use the words Godard, Truffaut and David Lynch in one sentence,' Belle explained. 'And he was using the intense voice. You know, the voice that's one level down from where there's spittle.'

'It's all good,' said Jason. 'Well, not the spittle part. But that girl – yes, that cutie – is here as Adam's date. He invited her here all by himself. Her name's Brianna Graham and Adam met her at a young filmmakers' convention. That means that Godard, Truffaut and David Lynch are actual total turn-ons for her,' Jason explained.

'Huh. Well, good for my little dating protégé.' Belle gave a small nod of approval. 'Maybe someday he'll be able to flirt with someone who *isn't* a film freak.'

Michael Van Dyke intercepted a pass and ran the

football over to the cooler in time to hear Belle's analysis of Adam's love life. 'No girl who looks like that is a freak,' he told her. 'Except for the *good* kind of freak. Know what I'm saying?'

'Belle, are you going to bring us our beer today or what?' Maggie called. Her shortie wetsuit glistened in the sun as she took a practice serve over the volleyball net.

Brad Moreau, Sienna's ex and, kind of surprisingly, the guy who had ended up being one of Jason's closest friends, trotted up to them, breaking the strained silence that had fallen. 'Van Dyke, we're in the middle of a game here,' he said.

'I've officially called a beer break,' Van Dyke replied, hoisting the cooler onto one shoulder and trotting toward the football players.

'Make a stop over here!' Erin shouted from the other side of the volleyball net. 'Belle's deserted us!' Van Dyke obediently veered in her direction.

'Listen up, you guys,' Brad said to Jason, Sienna and Belle. 'Party tonight at my place.'

Sienna raised one eyebrow. 'I thought you were going to cut your parents a break and let them have one out-of-town trip where you *didn't* throw a party,' she said. 'Especially since the trip's for their anniversary and everything.'

'I was,' Brad answered. 'But there's an epidemic in our town and I feel it's my responsibility to do something about it. If I don't provide an outlet for the rampaging "senioritis", some serious damage could be done.'

'Brad's right,' Belle chimed in. 'I definitely won't be held responsible for my actions if I don't have a party to go to tonight. And nobody's parents should go on a special anniversary Caribbean cruise without expecting the offspring to take a little advantage.'

'Besides, this could be our last chance to party *chez Moreau* before we all go off to different colleges and don't see each other again until our ten-year reunion, where we won't be able to think of anything to say to each other,' Brad added.

'Except to talk about how fat and bald the men have gotten and how all the women still look so fabulous,' Belle agreed.

Sienna laughed. 'Wow, I can't wait.'

'So, you're coming tonight, right?' Brad asked.

Sienna shot a glance at Jason. 'We *might*,' she answered.

'What's this "*might*"?' Brad protested. 'I'm telling you—'

'Brad, get over here!' Van Dyke yelled. 'We're combining football with volleyball and a little Frisbee, and we need a rule consult.'

'OK!' Brad called back.

'I want in,' Belle said, leaping to her feet. 'Flying folleyball is definitely my game.'

'Get yourselves over to my place tonight. No excuses,' Brad said, with a grin over his shoulder to Sienna and Jason, as he and Belle headed off.

'Do you have something else planned for tonight?' Jason asked.

'Well . . .' Sienna gave him one of her slow smiles, the kind that always made his stomach flip-flop in a good kind of way. 'Didn't you say your parents had plans tonight?'

'Yeah. They're off to some business dinner,' Jason replied.

'And there's *no* possibility Dani is going to miss a party at Brad's . . .' Sienna continued.

That was true. Jason's younger sister would not let a juicy party pass her by. It just wasn't possible. He felt a slow smile slide across his own face. 'So, we could be al—'

Jason didn't have time to finish. Adam slid to a stop in front of them, spraying sand in his wake. 'Should I ask her to the party?' he burst out. 'I think she might actually *like* me. But is it too soon? Because the party is tonight. And we're already doing something today. This, I mean. We're here together. So that would be two events in a row. And isn't that uncool? Am I not supposed to be sort of aloof? Vince Vaughn would definitely tell me not to ask. I don't want to be like the guy in *Swingers* who filled up the answering machine – not that I was going to ask on an answering machine. I was going to ask in person. I'm not a raging doofus, but . . .'

Sienna and Jason looked at each other. Sienna unscrambled the Adam-speak first.

'OK . . . did Brad mention the party in front of Brianna?' she asked.

Adam sucked in a deep breath. 'Yeah.'

'Well, then it would be rude not to ask her if she wants to go,' Sienna decreed. 'Tell her that Brad was definitely inviting everyone.'

'Really?' Adam grinned.

'I don't think at this stage in your dating life you should be playing hard to get,' Jason added.

And Adam was off, sending up another shower of sand.

'What was that *Swingers* answering machine thing he was talking about?' Sienna asked.

'I don't know. Some movie thing. And I never ask him to explain his film references anymore. Ask one movie question and you can't get a word in for at least half an hour,' Jason answered. 'So, before the Adam interruption, we were talking about my house – which is going to be empty tonight, which means we could be alone.'

Sienna snuggled up against him. 'That was what I had planned. Is it uncool of me to tell you that?'

Jason grinned, shook his head and wrapped his arm around her.

'Who knows how many chances we'll have to be alone this summer?' Sienna went on. 'Then when we're in college, we'll both have room-mates . . .' She let her sentence trail off.

She's right, Jason thought. Next year in L.A. was probably going to be great. But could it really compare to what he already had? Was that possible?

'Right now, let's not think about anything but today,' Jason suggested. He pulled Sienna tighter against him, trying to absorb every detail of this moment with her, with their friends, trying to lock in the memory of this little stretch of paradise on earth. Because, in Malibu, things had a way of changing quickly.

Two

'I can't believe I let you drag me away from Sienna for this,' Jason complained to Adam. 'She was wearing the black bikini. Not that it isn't a thrill a minute standing around in the drugstore with you.' He checked his watch. 'You do realize we've been here, in this same aisle, for thirty-two minutes.'

'Thanks for the update,' Adam muttered. He picked up a small orangey-red box, one he'd already picked up about twenty times. He put it down again, and picked up a small neon-green box that he'd also picked up about ten times already.

Jason shook his head. 'I'm still opposed to the Night Lights. One, the name is stupid. It sounds like something that should be in a baby's room. Two, do you really want to be illuminated down there on your first try? I mean, if you know you have the moves, then maybe, but . . .'

'But "Caution Wear" sounds like heavy-duty protection,' Adam commented. 'It doesn't exactly sound

11

fun. Or romantic.' He shot a look down the aisle to make sure it was still clear. 'Can you see it? "Hey, Bree, excuse me a minute, while I slip into the Caution Wear".'

'I don't want to see it. I don't want to *think* about it. Do they sell brainwash in here?' Jason groaned, scrubbing his forehead with both hands.

'I heard this is the brand they use in movies,' Adam said, pointing to another one of the little boxes.

'That's all you'll have to tell Brianna,' Jason joked. 'By the way, Van Dyke was pretty impressed that you scored such a babe,' he added.

'I'm totally impressed with myself,' Adam admitted. 'I mean, she's so out of my league, right? She looks like she could be on one of these boxes' – he tapped the nearest row of condoms – 'and I look like, you know, me.'

'You don't exactly look like you've been raised in the cellar or anything,' Jason told him. 'You shower. You brush your teeth. Belle has stopped you wearing all your truly geek-squad clothing.'

Adam shook his head. 'Still, Brianna and I don't match up on the hot scale, I know. But on the, well, the *soul* scale, we are a perfect match. Two minutes after I met her at the conference, she was telling me how *Inland Empire* had made her swear she was going to shoot in digital her whole life. And just a couple of weeks ago, I wrote this whole blog about deciding that I was never going to shoot on film, that it sucked all the spontaneity and lightness out of a piece. And CGI — well, it can be awesome — but now, I see something with CGI and a little part of my head is saying "fake, fake, fake". Brianna agrees totally. She—'

'OK, OK, I get it. You've found the girl who is worthy of the gift of your precious virginity,' Jason interrupted. 'So pick a box, any box, and go pay.'

Adam shot a look at the counter and groaned. 'I can't.'

'Can we just leave then?' Jason asked. 'Clearly, you aren't going to need any condoms tonight. If you can't even get yourself to buy any, I don't think you're ready for actual sex.'

'Unfair,' Adam answered. But he laughed. 'I'm just waiting for that other cashier to come back. I can't buy condoms from a hot girl. It would be pure bep.'

' "Bep"?'

'Did you even look at the Klingon dictionary I gave you? "Bep" means "agony",' Adam explained. 'And, speaking of bep, couldn't you spare me some, and just give me some of your stash? That way we could leave right now. Or I'll give you money, and you buy me some from the hot cashier. I'm sure you're used to it. I mean, Sienna Devereux walked away from Brad

Moreau for you. And from what I heard from your friend Tyler, it's not like you were hurting for female attention back in Michigan.'

Jason felt his neck and ears turn hot. 'Sienna and I haven't, uh, been together like that,' he admitted.

'Dude! You've put me in a full-on state of shock and awe,' Adam burst out. 'Why not? How could you be in the vicinity of Sienna Devereux for this long without sealing the deal?'

'You're right. Maybe I should have thrown her up against a wall while we were breaking into the lab at her dad's company,' Jason suggested. 'Or, wait, the vault her sister's psycho stalker was holding her hostage in would have been a romantic location. Or the backseat of the vampire hunter's Eldorado. I'm sure he would have let us call a time-out and held off trying to shoot us with his crossbow.'

'You've got a point. These have been strange and dangerous times,' Adam agreed. 'But come on. There wasn't *one* right time? The last few weeks have been pretty tame by DeVere Heights standards.'

Jason decided not to mention that tonight – with his parents and Dani away – could be it, even though that knowledge had been coming to a boil inside him ever since Sienna had told Brad that they might not make his party.

'True. But think about this. Sienna's previous boyfriend was *enhanced*,' he told Adam. 'You've seen what the vampires can do playing football or volleyball. It kind of makes you wonder how good they are at . . . *other* things.'

'Oh, man. I hadn't thought of that – the vampire super-powers and all,' Adam said. 'Wow. I'm glad Brianna's not from V Central.'

Jason grabbed a box of condoms.

'What are you doing?' Adam demanded.

Jason didn't answer. He just strode toward the cute girl behind the counter. When he plunked the box down in front of her, he looked over his shoulder. Adam was further back in the aisle, staring intently at something on the bottom shelf.

'These are for that guy cowering in the feminine hygiene section,' Jason told the cashier, loudly enough for everyone in the store to hear him.

The girl giggled. Adam turned and walked out of the store.

'For that, you are going to suffer a death that will make Willem Dafoe's in *Platoon* look quick and merciful,' Adam announced when Jason joined him outside.

'That movie came out before I was born,' Jason told his friend.

'DVDs have been invented,' Adam reminded him

for the millionth time as he held out his hand for the condoms.

Jason slapped the small paper bag into Adam's hand. 'Good luck,' he said, silently wishing himself the same thing. Tonight really could be *the* night with Sienna.

Jason stared at the blue and red comforter on his bed. It was total guy. Everything in the room was. All the old swimming trophies on his bookshelf. The Active Right Guard Sport deodorant on his dresser. He could at least get rid of that. He opened the top drawer, knocked the deodorant inside, and slammed the drawer shut. That helped . . . almost not at all. His bedroom was still in the negative on the romance-o-meter. Should he take down the poster of—?

The doorbell rang, saving him from turning into a complete nutball. Another few minutes and he'd have been repainting the walls and ripping up the carpet. As he headed to the stairs he heard Danielle saying, 'The place is yours. Kristy and Maria and I are hitting Granita for pizza before we go to Brad's. You be careful. Last time Jason tried to cook something fancy, we almost had to call the fire department.'

'Not true,' Jason called, taking the stairs two at a time.

'Uh-huh. So true,' Dani countered, as she started out the front door. 'He needs supervision in the kitchen,' she warned Sienna. Then she closed the door behind herself, leaving Sienna and Jason alone.

'So you need supervision, huh?' Sienna asked. She walked slowly over to Jason, her long, dark hair falling down her back in a sleek curtain. '*Close* supervision?' she asked, her throaty voice teasing and suggestive at the same time.

'Oh, yeah,' Jason answered. 'Very close.'

Sienna wrapped her arms around his neck. 'I can do that.' And she kissed him, sliding her body tight against his.

'Wait,' she said, stepping away from him. 'What about this fancy food Dani was talking about? Do we need to check on it?'

'It's pretty much on auto-pilot for a while. No worries. I set the timer and everything,' Jason answered.

'I can't believe you're cooking for me,' Sienna told him.

'There's no end to my talents,' Jason laughed. He slipped his fingers under the thin straps of her yellow sundress and started backing toward the couch. He hit the arm of the sofa two steps later. Sienna gave him one of her trademark slow smiles, then put her hands on his chest – and pushed. Not with her full-on vampire strength, but hard enough to send him sprawling onto his back on the sofa cushions – with Sienna on top of him.

Jason slid one hand behind her neck, and pulled her head down to his. Sienna's tongue flicked across his lower lip, a touch that sent shockwaves of sensation slamming through his body.

Forget the beach and the surfing and all that, he thought. This *is the moment I want to hold onto.* He could live in this moment pretty much forever.

Sienna deepened their kiss, her silky hair swirling around both their faces. It smelled like the ocean. The ocean . . . and smoke.

Wait. *Smoke.*

Jason sat up so fast, he almost dumped Sienna onto the floor.

'What?' she demanded.

The smoke detector answered for him, with long, ear-splitting shrieks. Jason bolted for the kitchen, Sienna right behind him. As soon as he whipped open the door, smoke billowed out. He grabbed a dishtowel from the stove door handle, dashed back into the hallway, and started frantically using it to fan the detector. 'You keep doing this,' he told Sienna, handing over the towel. 'I'll get some windows open.'

'Turn the stove off too,' she suggested.

Jason did that first, dialing the oven down to zero. He didn't even take a peek at his chicken breasts. From the smell, they were already inedible. He raced from window to window, yanking them open as wide as possible. He opened the back door too, then went to check on Sienna. She still hadn't managed to get the smoke detector to stop screaming.

'The thing is supposed to go off at the first whiff of smoke,' he said. 'Whiff.' He jumped up and knocked the plastic cover off, then took out the batteries. The screams subsided. 'Come on. Let's go sit by the pool until the air in here is breathable again.'

Jason ushered Sienna outside and plopped down in a lawn chair. 'Yep, we have the house all to ourselves – the part that hasn't burned down, anyway. Sorry.'

'I was supposed to be supervising,' Sienna reminded him as she sat down on the lounge chair next to him. 'Dani warned me what would happen.'

'So, what do you want to do? We could order in. Or I'll take you anywhere you want to go,' Jason offered.

'With your parents and Dani out, I vote we stay in,' Sienna replied. 'We hardly ever have a place to ourselves.'

'My parents do need to get a life, don't they?' Jason said with a grin. 'Where should we call for food?'

'We're not calling anywhere. This is the best thing

that could have happened. Now we can cook together,' Sienna answered. 'It'll be fun.'

Jason doubted it would be quite as much fun as what they'd been doing on the couch a couple of minutes ago. But they would definitely have a good time. When they were together, they always did. Well, when they weren't right in the middle of life-threatening danger. Although even that wasn't a dead loss with Sienna around.

Sienna checked the oven temperature. 'Three-fifty.' She gave a satisfied nod. Then she set the timer for forty-five minutes. She hadn't allowed Jason to use the stove or even the timer since what they'd started calling *'la fatalité'*.

'Forty-five minutes to make a dessert?' Jason said incredulously.

'It's worth it,' Sienna told him. 'And it'll give us time to clean up this mess.' She walked over to the sink where the charred remains of the first dinner were soaking. 'What did you say this was again?'

'Chicken breasts stuffed with perfection,' Jason answered. 'It was going to be awesome, with feta cheese, and those sun-dried tomatoes you like, and spinach, which I put in for you even though I find it kind of slimy and disgusting.'

'Next time we cook together, we'll make that,' Sienna promised. 'And we'll even leave out the spinach. Now, you start trying to scrub the "perfection" off that pan while I clear the table.' She headed for the dining room. Jason found a Brillo pad under the sink and got to work.

Twenty-five minutes later, the pan had been washed, dried and put away. The dishwasher had been loaded. The sink scrubbed. The floor had even been swept and mopped. Jason and Sienna stood beside the gleaming dining-room table. 'Twenty minutes until dessert,' she said. 'You're going to love the chocolate truffle cake.'

'I can't believe you never told me you could cook,' Jason said.

'All the Devereuxs can cook,' Sienna told him. 'It's a French thing.'

'I don't think I can wait a whole twenty minutes for dessert.'

'You're going to have—' Sienna's words turned into a laugh as Jason wrapped his hands around her waist and swung her up onto the table.

'No.' He shook his head. 'I can't. There's no way I can wait.' He gently lowered her back on the shining wood and climbed up next to her. 'How can I wait when it tastes so good?' He licked a line from her earlobe all the

21

way down her neck. Sienna's laughter turned into a sigh of pleasure that made him crazy.

Jason slid the closest strap on her sundress down, kissed her bare shoulder and . . . heard footsteps! He jerked his head up. *Footsteps!*

He scrambled off the table and swung Sienna down after him, just as his parents walked into the dining room.

'Something smells amazing,' his mother said.

'What are you doing home?' Jason burst out, before he realized that it didn't sound entirely welcoming.

'I couldn't sit there one more second with those arrogant—' Mr Freeman took a deep breath and started again. 'Let's just say that the dinner meeting was unproductive.'

'Doesn't sound like you got any dessert,' Sienna said, throwing Jason a sly smile.

'He hardly got any dinner!' Mrs Freeman answered.

'You two should eat the cake we have in the oven,' Sienna told Jason's parents. 'Just take it out when the timer goes off. It's really good warm.'

'Yeah, dessert's no good if you let it wait,' Jason muttered.

'What about you two?' Jason's mom asked.

'We wanted to head over to Brad's party for a while,' Sienna answered.

Jason raised his eyebrows. Sienna gave him a small, rueful headshake. It was easy for him to interpret. Clearly, they weren't going to get any privacy at the Freeman house that night, so they might as well hit the party.

'You know, one of the last parties before everyone starts going away for the summer, then college,' Sienna added.

'Don't even mention college,' Mr Freeman said. 'This one's mother isn't ready for him to fly the nest.'

'Well, right now, I'm only going a few houses away,' Jason said. 'Enjoy the dessert.'

Somebody should, he thought.

Three

Jason and Sienna turned her Spider over to the valet. Sometimes Jason still had a hard time wrapping his head around the fact that just your basic DeVere Heights high school parties had valet parking. He wondered if there'd always be a little part of him that remained a guy from one of the flyover states.

Mingled cheers and groans came from one side of the Moreaus' Spanish-style mansion as the two of them headed up to the house, hand-in-hand.

'Want to go see whatever that's about?' Sienna asked Jason.

'Why not?' he replied and they veered toward the sound, circling around to the side of the house where Brad had recently convinced his parents to install a regulation-size b-ball court.

'Should have known,' Sienna said, as they spotted Brad and Van Dyke in what looked like a to-the-death game of one-on-one, the crowd about evenly divided between who they were cheering for. 'Those guys. On

25

the first day of kindergarten, Brad was so determined to prove he could go down the slide more times than Van Dyke, he made himself puke. They've been going at it ever since.'

'Are they even going to survive at different schools next year?' Jason watched as Van Dyke casually took a three-point shot from the back of the court – and got nothing but net.

'They'll have to text each other their swimming times and test scores just to function,' Sienna predicted. The guy next to Jason – a junior – let out an amazed cry as Brad raced down the court and hurled the ball at the backboard when he was a little more than halfway down. He leapt into the air, flying up in time to smash the ball down into the net on the rebound.

Sienna frowned. 'Not subtle,' she said softly. It was true that neither Brad nor Van Dyke were giving exactly regular human performances on the court. More like Michael Jordan versus Shaq kind of stuff, only without being six and a half feet tall.

When Van Dyke actually dunked the ball by jumping up to the hoop and swinging from it, Sienna let go of Jason's hand.

'Enough.' Sienna pushed her way courtside, Jason right beside her. 'Brad, you're out of Absolut!' she called.

'Time!' Brad yelled to Van Dyke.

'You couldn't wait until I whipped Van Dyke's butt to tell me that?' Brad asked Sienna.

'She's doing you a favor,' Van Dyke shot back, winking at a ga-ga soon-to-be-senior girl. 'She could tell you needed to catch your breath.'

Sienna moved in close to Brad. 'What I could tell is that you and your friend over there were showing off more than your basketball skills,' she said, quietly enough so that only Brad and Jason could hear. 'Take it down a notch, OK, before people notice that those moves you're throwing down are just too good!'

Brad shoved his fingers through his sweat-soaked hair. 'Got it.' He turned toward the crowd. 'This guy's no challenge for me. Why don't we get a real game going? Who else wants to play?' he asked, shooting Van Dyke a pointed look. Van Dyke gave a small nod back: he'd got the message.

'Want to play?' Sienna asked Jason.

'I think I want to see what Dani's up to,' Jason replied.

'Next year she'll be going to parties all alone without a big brother to protect her,' Sienna reminded him.

'I know. That's why I want to make sure she's learnt how not to be stupid while I'm still around,' he answered. 'And I might see if Adam made it.'

'I think I'll look around for Belle and Erin.' Sienna gave him a long kiss. 'That's to make sure you don't forget me until we find each other.'

'As if.' Jason wandered around to the lagoon-shaped pool in the back of the house. Aaron Harberts, one of the guys on the swim team who wasn't vampirically enhanced, floated in the center, resting on a puffy plastic lounge chair, with a drink in both of the cup holders. A game of Marco Polo where everybody seemed to have their eyes closed – and to be doing a lot of friendly groping – was going on around him.

'Freeman, do you know where I can get a pig?' Harberts called out, wandering over to Jason.

'A pig?' Jason repeated. 'A live pig?'

'No. Dead.' Harberts sounded a little offended. 'But a whole one. I want to roast it. Brad said I could dig a pit over by the fruit trees. They're barbecuing hot dogs and stuff at the bonfire down on the beach. But a roast pig. Wouldn't that taste good right about now?' he asked.

There's a bonfire, a barbecue and bikini-clad chiquitas – the whole deal, Jason thought. *Just the way Brad promised there would be at that first party he invited me to my first week at school. Who needs a pig?*

'How much and what have you ingested?' Jason asked. Then he looked at the blissed-out expression on his friend's face and guessed that a vampire had been feeding on Harberts's blood. Being fed on by a vampire always led to a woozy, euphoric state, and Harberts was definitely in that place.

'I don't know,' Harberts said cheerily. 'But do you know about the pig?'

'Sorry. Nope,' Jason told him.

'That's OK,' Harberts answered with a beatific grin. 'I love you, man. You know that, right?'

'I do,' Jason assured him. Yeah, Harberts had definitely made a blood donation. He'd never told Jason he loved him before. Jason gave his friend a wave, then turned toward the French doors leading into the house. He followed the hard *click-clack* sound to the pool room. His little sister was a complete pool shark and he thought she might be there. But she was giving the suckers a break that night.

Jason joined a darts game featuring the desecrated yearbook photos of some of the most-hated DeVere teachers before checking out the kitchen, where he finally got himself some dessert – although not the one he'd wanted. Dani was holding court in one corner, leading a discussion of how she and the girls surrounding her were going to make this year's Homecoming legendary. It was clear that Dani was going to be one of *the* seniors when the new school year started in the fall. Not that Jason had ever expected anything less.

She's going to do fine without me, he decided. Weirdly, the thought made him feel a tiny bit sad. He grabbed himself a beer from the ice-filled garbage can and wandered into the living room. Adam sat by himself on one end of the half-moon-shaped burgundy sofa, knocking and slapping the glass coffee table rhythmically with his hand. Jason dropped down beside him. 'You really know how to party!'

'I'm working on my new script,' Adam explained. 'Butthead,' he added with a smile. 'Brianna helped me figure out the part I was stuck on. She reminded me of the way they used Morse code in *Independence Day* and suggested I use it in my script. Of course, I'll use it in a much more inventive way. That movie sucked.'

'Of course,' Jason said, mock-solemn as Adam started up his slapping and knocking again. 'So that's what that is?' he asked, nodding at Adam's hand. 'Morse code? I don't know how it works.'

'Yeah. It's basically a binary system, but not exactly, because the length of the pauses between the two sounds are part of the code,' Adam explained.

'I'm . . . not following you,' Jason said.

'There are two sounds in Morse, a long one and a short one. I'm using the slap for long and the knock for short. Each letter in the alphabet is represented by a sequence of slaps and knocks. For example, here's SOS.' Adam knocked on the table three times, slapped three times, then knocked three times again. 'It totally solves the scene I was stuck on. My girlfriend is a genius.'

'Your girlfriend, huh?' Jason asked.

'Well, OK, she's not *technically* my girlfriend, I guess. Whatever it takes to make someone technically your girlfriend,' Adam admitted. 'But obviously I want her to be. I've never had the kind of conversations with anybody that I've had with Brianna. Seriously, I know you think I was exaggerating, but she's a genius. And she gets all my movie references. I said she's a genius, right? And her hair smells really good. I don't know what it smells of, exactly, but it's good. And she makes me laugh. Usually, I'm the guy who makes other people laugh, right?'

'Even when you're not trying,' Jason agreed.

Adam kept right on talking. 'But Brianna cracks me up all the time. And she's *happy*. She's just this happy person. And—'

'I hate to interrupt this conversation,' a girl said from behind them.

Jason turned around and saw Brianna leaning over the sofa's high back, grinning down at them. 'Especially because it was all about me,' she added.

Adam flushed as Brianna walked around and sat down on the arm of the sofa next to him. *I'd probably have turned red if Sienna had heard me gushing about her a couple days after we met,* Jason thought.

At least Brianna was being cool about it. She turned to Jason, giving Adam a chance to recover himself. 'Where can I get one of those?' she asked, nodding at his beer. 'I know there's a massive bar over by the fire-place, but it seems to be mostly for mixed drinks.'

'In the kitchen,' Jason told her. 'Down that hall to the right. There's a big garbage can full of them by the door.'

Brianna laughed. 'I'm glad that some things stay the same. I was starting to feel like I'd wandered into an episode of *My Super Sweet Sixteen* or something. Not that anyone here is that obnoxious. Just that' – she lowered her voice – 'rich.'

'You know I'm not, right?' Adam managed to say.

'Dang! You mean you're not going to finance my first film if I sleep with you?' Brianna teased, standing up. 'I'm going to get that beer and see what other trouble I can get into. I'll be back.'

'That was humiliating,' Adam muttered as soon as Brianna was out of earshot.

'Don't worry about it,' Jason told him. 'Come on, what girl doesn't want to hear that a guy she likes thinks she's great?'

32

'You think she likes me?' Adam asked.

'She's here. She was at the beach this afternoon hanging with you,' Jason pointed out.

'But do you think she—?'

'Zach's coming over to talk to us,' Jason interrupted. The event was interruption-worthy. Zach Lafrenière didn't usually approach people. People usually came to him. Charisma, Jason's mom would call it. Mojo, Dani would say. Whatever you called it, it was part of what had got Zach on the DeVere Heights Vampire Council when he was still in high school. The youngest member ever.

'Greetings.' Zach set a bottle of wine and three goblets on the coffee table and sat down on the love seat across from Jason and Adam. A couple of people glanced their way. Jason got the feeling they'd like to come over, but Zach was putting out the vibe that he wanted privacy. He pulled a corkscrew out of one of the front pockets of his white linen shirt and opened the wine, then began to pour.

Under the soft party lights, the deep-red wine looked liked it had been made from liquefied rubies. It was almost transfixing.

'You need to try this. It's from my family vineyard. You can't buy it commercially,' Zach told them. There was something different about him. It took Jason a

33

moment to realize that he wasn't wearing his shades. Zach almost always kept his sunglasses on. It was as if he liked having a barrier between him and the world. But tonight he looked from Jason to Adam with his eyes unshielded. They were such a dark brown it was difficult to tell the irises from the pupils.

'It's made completely organically,' Zach continued. 'The plough is even pulled by a winch, so the heavy machinery doesn't pack down the earth.' He handed Jason one of the goblets, then passed one to Adam. The stem of the glass felt faintly warm under Jason's fingers.

'To friendship.' Zach clinked Jason's glass, then Adam's.

I guess even Zach isn't immune from a little end-of-high-school sentimentality, Jason thought.

'You've both been good friends to us,' Zach added.

Now Jason got it. This wasn't just about the end of senior year. This was about appreciation. This was about Zach wanting them to know that he appreciated their help with vampire crises past, and wished them well in the future.

Jason met Zach's gaze and gave a small nod, then took a sip of the wine. It was rich and not too sweet. 'It's good,' Jason said, hoping Zach would get that he was talking about more than the wine. 'Awesome.'

'Truly,' Adam added.

Jason figured that this was about as much of a 'moment' as any of them could take. 'So where are you heading in the fall?' he asked Zach.

'D.C.'

Did that mean a college in the D.C. area? Or . . .? Jason waited for more info, but Zach just took another sip of wine. The guy was back to his usual enigmatic self. He never gave away much. Tonight's exchange with the wine had probably been one of their longer conversations.

'I'm going to—' Jason began.

'CalTech,' Zach finished for him.

Jason and Adam exchanged a look. Zach always seemed to know everything. He probably knew where the two of them were going to be going to college before either of them had even sent in their applications. It was just part of what made Zach Lafrenière Zach Lafrenière.

Jason sat in silence for a while, thinking about what a wild ride it had been since he'd found out the dangerous secret that all the most popular kids at DeVere Heights High shared.

'Eat a pickle,' Van Dyke demanded, yanking Jason away from his thoughts. 'You too, Turnball.' He thrust a pickle jar toward them.

'I'm not eating a pickle,' Jason answered. 'I'm drinking wine, and I just had a beer.'

'Me too,' Adam said.

'I need somebody to eat these pickles,' Van Dyke yelled to the room at large. 'I'm making a batch of witch doctors and I need the juice.'

'Witch doctors?' Jason asked.

'Every kind of alcohol available mixed with the juice of the pickle,' Adam explained.

Zach got to his feet. 'This will require supervision. I don't want to have to drive anyone to the hospital.' He followed Van Dyke over to the bar where a crowd was already forming.

'I think the party has just made the jump to warp speed,' Adam commented.

A few hours later, the party had wound down to whatever was the lowest speed. Not that Brad and Van Dyke had noticed this. They were back on the basketball court, and back in the competitive zone again, as captains of the teams in a three-on-three. Jason, supposedly on Brad's team, had not seen much of the ball. And since Brad didn't look like passing the ball to him – or anyone else – any time this year, Jason was enjoying the warm breeze, the stars, the quiet happiness of being at the tail end of the party with just his closest friends.

Jason noticed that Adam had finally finished 'saying' goodbye to Brianna, so he ducked off the court – probably unnoticed – and headed over to his friend.

'That lipstick's a good color on you,' Jason joked.

Adam wiped his mouth with a grin.

'So I'm guessing you and Bree had a good time,' Sienna commented as she, Maggie and Belle – the other supposed team members – came over to join them.

'Yeah,' Adam said, blushing a little. 'She had to take off, though. She's helping a friend on a shoot at four a.m. tomorrow.'

'I got a chance to talk to her, and I've decided to give her my stamp of approval,' Belle told him. 'I'm proud of you.'

'Way to go, Van Dyke!' Maggie shouted as Van Dyke dunked the ball and swung from the rim.

Jason noticed that they'd really kicked the play into high gear now that Brianna had left. She had been the last human – well, the last *uninitiated* human – at the party.

'Are those two ever going to give it up?' Sienna asked, watching Brad grab the basketball. 'Do they really care so much who is the Supreme Sports Champion of DeVere High?'

'I guess so,' Belle said as Brad bounded toward the

opposite basket, dribbling the ball, then leapt into the air, did a triple flip, and slammed the ball home on his way back to the ground.

'Traveling!' Jason called out, rolling his hands in a circle. 'I did not see any dribbling going on during your final approach to the basket.'

'Yeah, no points for that one. The ball goes back to Van Dyke,' Maggie agreed.

'How was it traveling if my feet weren't on the ground?' Brad protested. 'I didn't take any steps.'

'Oh, shit!' Adam muttered.

Jason followed his gaze and saw Brianna a few feet away, staring at the basketball court.

'Oh, shit,' Jason repeated. Had she seen the vampires acting like . . . vampires?

Four

Jason felt Sienna tense beside him. He knew she was thinking exactly the same thing he was. Had Brianna seen enough to realize that Brad couldn't possibly be human?

'Wow!' Brianna said, her voice coming out choked. 'Does that guy do gymnastics?'

Belle let out a burst of hysterical laughter.

Adam said, 'Yeah, you know these rich kids. Their parents start them with the lessons almost at birth. Me, I'm lucky my dad came up with enough cash for a Happy Meal once in a while.'

'Poor deprived Malibu child,' Maggie cooed.

'It's true about Brad, though,' Jason added. 'He won his first gymnastics trophy when he was ... What was it, Brad? Four?' he called.

'Three and a half,' Brad answered, strolling over to the group, Van Dyke at his side.

'Most Improved Tiny Tumbler,' Van Dyke told Brianna. 'His mom still has the trophy.'

'No, Most Improved was you,' Brad reminded him. 'I got Terrific Tiny Tumbler. Van Dyke got his award for finally mastering the somersault. It took him a whole year, but he stuck with it.'

'I can still hardly do a somersault,' Brianna confessed. 'I'm not exactly the athletic type. Miniature golf is the only sport I excel in. That's why I'm making Adam take me on Saturday.'

'Did you leave something in the house?' Brad asked, sounding like a concerned host, and not at all like he was freaked and wanted her gone.

'Yeah. My jacket. I'm pretty sure I left it in the kitchen,' Brianna said.

'I'll go with you and check,' Adam told her, and they headed off. As soon as they were out of sight, everybody dropped their fake smiles.

'Do you think she bought the gymnastics thing?' Van Dyke's voice was low and urgent.

'I think so,' Sienna answered. 'She's the one who came up with it.'

'I thought everyone was gone. Everybody . . . you know.' Brad shook his head, clearly annoyed with himself.

'We all did,' Van Dyke said. 'I was screwing around as much as you. Anyway, no harm, no foul, right?'

'Right,' Maggie answered.

'You ready to head off?' Jason asked Sienna. The party definitely felt done now.

She nodded.

'Your parents didn't by any chance have a late-night appointment that would leave your house empty, did they?' he asked as they headed to her car.

'We're out of luck for tonight,' she answered, wrapping her arm around his waist. 'But dessert is definitely on the menu sometime soon.'

'You're lucky I'm such a good friend,' Jason told Adam quietly as they slowly trailed Brianna and Sienna to the third hole of the Sunshine Castle Miniature Golf course on Saturday afternoon. 'There are very few people I would play putt-putt golf for.'

'I'm with you, bro. If I wanted to induce a bout of narcolepsy, this is where I'd come,' Adam answered. 'Except, today, Brianna's with me and she loves this place. And I owe her one because she promised to go see a screening of *A Clockwork Orange* with me tonight, even though she hates violent movies. Speaking of the blood and gore, wanna watch *Reservoir Dogs* with me after school on Monday? I don't suppose you've seen it, since it didn't come out yesterday, but I know you'll dig it. And we need some male bonding time.'

'Sure,' Jason said. 'But you have to provide snacks.

Lots of snacks. Because now you owe *me*.' He nodded his head in the direction of a smiling lavender and yellow dragon off in the distance at the thirteenth hole. 'This place is a candy-colored nightmare.'

'We're up, guys,' Sienna called, waving them forward. 'Jason, do you think you could help me line up my shot?' she asked, in complete flirt mode.

'What was I complaining about again?' Jason asked Adam.

'Dude, I don't know,' Adam answered as they hurried to join the girls.

'Thanks for doing this,' Jason said in Sienna's ear as he wrapped his arms around her and placed his hands over hers on the golf club. 'I know it's not your thing.'

'Who says it's not?' she whispered back, giving Jason a flirtatious smile.

Then it was Jason's shot. He focused on trying to get his orange golf ball over the little bridge and through the spinning blades of the windmill.

'Yes! The Force is certainly with *you* today, Jason,' Brianna cried. 'I think you sent that ball into warp speed!'

Adam laughed. 'I think you mean *light*speed,' he said.

'D'oh!' Brianna smacked her forehead with her hand.

'What are you guys talking about?' Sienna asked.

'"Warp speed" is *Star Trek*. But the "Force" is *Star*

Wars,' Adam explained. 'Therefore, nobody using the Force could ever, under any circumstances, send anything into warp speed – without the universe of cinema imploding.'

Jason sank the ball and Bree clapped.

'One under par,' Adam announced. 'You keep this up, you might just win.'

'Do we eat crap food here or go out to a real place?' Jason asked when they'd finished the eighteenth hole. He'd come in with the lowest score, and the others had decided that, since he'd had the pleasure of beating them, he could buy them lunch.

'Oooh, delicious, delicious crap food please,' Brianna cried, clasping her hands together in front of her.

'This is my kind of girl,' Jason said.

'Mine too,' Adam agreed as they walked to the outdoor food court between the mini-golf and the bumper boats. 'Except for that.' He gestured to the slogan on Brianna's T-shirt, which read 'Independent Filmmakers Do It Alone'.

Brianna and Sienna exchanged a you-know-boys look and laughed.

'Well, you're an independent filmmaker too, Adam,' Brianna told him. 'So what happens when two

43

independent filmmakers get together? Do they still do it alone? Or does some kind of collaboration take place?'

'I'm very interested in collaboration,' Adam said weakly. He was clearly almost too overwhelmed by the collaboration idea for speech.

'We'll let them discuss and save a table while we go select an assortment of crap,' Sienna suggested to Jason. 'Any requests?'

'I like the greasy-salty kind especially,' Brianna said.

'They're very cute together,' Sienna commented as she and Jason got in line at the kiosk that seemed to have the highest grease and salt quotient.

'As cute as us?' Jason asked.

'No one is as cute as us,' Sienna countered.

Jason grinned. 'Did you notice Adam's reaction when he caught Brianna mixing up *Star Wars* and *Star Trek*?' he asked. 'He laughed. *Laughed!* If I'd done that, I would have been forced to watch every *Star Wars* and *Star Trek* movie before Adam would allow me to resume our friendship. And, only then, after I passed a quiz,' Jason said.

'Adam can be a little extreme,' Sienna commented.

'He's a film geek. It's his nature,' Jason said. 'The weird thing is, Brianna's a film geek too. By their standards, that was a rookie mistake to make.'

'No one can know every movie fact by heart,' Sienna answered. 'Not even Adam.'

'We're not talking just any movie fact. We're talking—'

Sienna cracked up.

'What?' Jason asked.

'Adam's rubbing off on you,' Sienna told him. 'You're becoming a geek, too!'

'No way,' Jason shot back.

'You were a breath away from giving me a lecture on movie facts. Admit it.' Sienna gave him a gentle poke in the stomach. 'I don't know if I can start college with a geek boyfriend.'

'I was just trying to explain why it was weird that Bree made that goof.' A sudden thought made Jason grin. 'Maybe Adam's taste is a little too *popular* for Bree. Maybe she only likes "films". Not movies. You know, I bet she only watches things with subtitles, or interesting lighting effects, or whatever. Maybe she hasn't even seen all the *Star Wars* movies!' he exclaimed.

'You don't have to sound so happy about it,' Sienna told him.

'I just love the idea of their first fight being about *Adam's* bad taste in movies. It's funny to me. All I hear from him is how he can't believe I haven't seen this or that movie. Now Brianna will be telling him she can't believe he actually likes, I don't know, *The Matrix*. Although she has seen *Independence Day*, but maybe that was a fluke. I'm hoping.'

Sienna shook her head at him. 'You're evil.'

'No, I'm not,' Jason protested. 'I don't want them to break up over it or anything. I just like the idea of Adam being on the other side of an Adam-style movie tirade.'

'Evil,' Sienna repeated, laughing.

'How was the mini-golf?' Dani asked when Jason walked into the kitchen.

'I won,' he told her.

She made an exaggerated I'm-impressed face.

'What's the deal here, Mom?' Jason asked. His mother was sitting at the table, flipping through a copy of O magazine. 'No cookies, no brownies, no baked goodies of any kind? I thought you were on a campaign to remind me how good life at home is, so that I'm sure to come back from college every weekend.'

'Mom got good news. It made her forget all about you and your nest-leaving,' Danielle explained.

Jason sat down in the empty chair between his mother and his sister. 'What kind of news?'

'I finally heard from your Aunt Bianca,' Mrs

Freeman exclaimed, beaming. 'You know how worried I've been. I haven't heard from her in months. She hasn't returned a single call.'

'What did she say?' Jason asked, careful not to look at his sister. His mother was almost psychic about reading her kids' expressions. If he glanced at Dani, he was afraid his mother might figure out that they had a secret and try to figure out what it was. And it was something that neither of them ever wanted her to know: her sister, their aunt Bianca, was a vampire. She'd been turned into a vampire by her vampire husband Stefan before he'd died. She'd even inherited his place on the Vampire High Council.

But Stefan hadn't known that Bianca's human genetic make-up meant that she couldn't tolerate becoming a vampire. She had succumbed to transformation sickness, and had been slipping deeper and deeper into insanity. The last time Jason had seen her, back in February, she was already seriously unstable. Who knew what she would be like by now?

'She said that she'd been having some health problems, but she'd found an excellent treatment,' Mrs Freeman told him.

'And apparently she said she'll probably be in California soon,' Dani added, shooting Jason a quick glance.

Jason couldn't quite tell if she was worried or excited. Did she believe his aunt had actually found a treatment for the transformation sickness? Was it possible?

Jason doubted it. If there was a treatment, the DeVere Heights Vampire Council would know about it, and he would have heard about it from Sienna. He hadn't heard anything about his aunt from Sienna or Zach, even though the Council was supposed to be trying to keep tabs on Bianca.

'I think I'll go check the guest room. Just in case,' his mother said. 'You know how Bianca loves to pop in unannounced.' She hurried from the room.

'You think she might?' Danielle asked quietly.

'Doubtful,' Jason told her. 'If Bianca showed up in California, the DeVere Heights Vampire Council would probably take her under their protection – by which I mean "get her under their control" – before she made it to our house.' And Jason couldn't help thinking that that was a good thing. His human family just wasn't prepared to handle Bianca's vampire problems.

'Who am I going to talk to about this stuff when you're away at school? What if something, you know, *happens*?' Danielle asked.

'L.A.'s hardly far away,' Jason said. 'A call, and I'm here. And don't think I won't hear about anything I need to hear about when I'm at CalTech.'

'Don't get carried away. It's not like I need you to tell me my skirt is too short or something. Or check up on me at a party – which I know you did at Brad's, so don't deny it.'

'I'm not going to,' Jason answered. 'I'm your big brother. It's what I do.'

'I can take care of myself. I'm only one year younger. Just if anything really weird goes down . . .'

'I'm there,' Jason promised.

His cell phone began to play the Pussycat Dolls' song *I Don't Need a Man*. 'I thought you'd grown out of changing my cell ringer,' he said to Dani.

'For old times' sake,' Dani answered with a cheeky grin. 'I only have you here for a few more months.'

Jason checked the caller ID: Sienna.

'Hey, I was wondering if you could come over,' she said before he could even say hello.

'You miss me already?' he asked.

'Absolutely,' she answered, but he didn't think her voice had quite its usual playfulness.

'Anything wrong?'

'No. I just don't feel like being alone,' she said.

'On my way.' Jason hung up the phone. He could read Sienna as well as she could read him. And she was clearly not telling him everything. Something was very wrong.

Five

Jason reached Sienna's house faster than he should have legally been able to. *Her parents don't know what time you left the house*, he reminded himself when he spotted them coming out of their front door.

'Hi,' he called to them as he climbed out of his VW Karmann Cabriolet. Had Sienna called him because she was about to achieve Empty House? She hadn't said so, but maybe her parents had been in hearing range . . .

'Hello, Jason,' Mrs Devereux said. Her tone snapped Jason out of his Sienna-fuelled fantasy. It wasn't angry or unfriendly, but there was an undercurrent of strain, and her smile seemed forced.

'Do you have more luggage I can help you with?' Jason asked, registering that Mr Devereux was loading a couple of bags into the trunk.

'I've got them, thanks,' Mr Devereux said. He shut the trunk with a quiet click, then opened the passenger door for his wife.

Sienna hurried outside. 'I found your cell,' she told her father, handing it to him.

'Thanks, sweetheart.' Mr Devereux kissed her on the cheek. 'We'll call when we get there. Goodbye, Jason. Sorry to rush off.'

He got behind the wheel of the car. Jason and Sienna watched as it glided down the driveway and into the street.

'What's going on?' Jason asked.

'That's just it. I don't know,' Sienna admitted, her eyes on the spot where the car had disappeared from view. She turned to him. 'Come on, let's go inside.'

Jason followed her into the Devereuxs' elegant living room. 'My father got a call about forty-five minutes ago,' Sienna explained as they sat together on the sofa, 'and all of a sudden, he and my mom were rushing around, packing. All they would tell me is that they needed to go to Chicago on some Council business, and that they shouldn't be gone too long. Not that they could tell me when they'd be back. It was really weird. My parents usually give me loads of information. You know, phone numbers for everyplace they'll be, even though they both have cells, and everything. But not this time . . .' Sienna leant her head against Jason's shoulder. 'I didn't mean to be all dramatic on the phone.'

'You weren't,' Jason reassured her.

'It's just that them being so secretive makes the whole thing a little scary. A couple of years ago they had to go out of town for a big gathering. There was a threat that the head of one of the French families was going to be assassinated. My parents didn't tell me a lot, but they told me the basics,' Sienna continued. 'This time, all they would say was that Zach was staying in town in case any problems came up.'

'Have you talked to him yet?' Jason asked. Zach was absolutely the person he'd want to get the facts from. 'He's in the Council. If anyone would know the real deal, he would.'

'Tried. But he didn't answer,' Sienna said. 'I called everybody else though. Everyone's parents are heading to Chicago. Even Brad's. They're cutting their anniversary cruise short. They wouldn't do that for something minor. So help me brainstorm. What do you think could be up?' She gave a rueful laugh. 'This is how you wanted to spend your Saturday night, right? Sitting around with me, coming up with conspiracy theories.'

'I love coming up with conspiracy theories,' Jason told her. 'It's one of the few times my highly-developed paranoia is an asset.'

'Thanks.' She let out a sigh that seemed to release a

little tension from her body. 'I really didn't want to be alone with all these crazy thoughts running around in my brain. I know my parents wouldn't have left me here by myself if they thought I was in any danger.'

'That's totally true. Maybe there was some kind of accounting scandal. You know, somebody got caught buying five-thousand-dollar shower curtains with Council money or something.' Jason ran his fingers through Sienna's hair.

'Probably. Anything to do with money can make my dad's head go volcanic,' Sienna agreed, sounding a bit more hopeful.

'Or maybe a non-vampire somehow wormed his or her way to the very top of the Council and a tell-all book is about to hit the stores,' Jason suggested.

Sienna smiled a little, but her eyes had a faraway look. He hadn't been able to completely take her mind off the situation. Maybe if he kissed her . . .

What was he thinking? He was here as the supportive boyfriend. He wasn't supposed to be trying to score.

Sienna tilted her face up so she was looking into his eyes. The distracted look was gone. 'Come here,' she said, using one hand to pull his head down to hers. And then, what was there to do but kiss her? And kiss her. And kiss her. And . . . kiss . . . her . . .

Their lips didn't break apart even as Sienna twisted her body and straddled him. He ran his hands under the flowy embroidered top she had on, all the way up her bare back. Completely bare. Some part of his brain registered that she wasn't wearing a bra.

Then Sienna's hands were under his T-shirt, sliding it up, sliding it off, their kiss ending as she pulled back to look at him. She glided the fingers of one hand from his chest to his belly button. His heart slammed into his ribs as her hand moved on down, past the waistband of his jeans – and then they both froze as someone pounded on the front door.

Sienna scrambled off his lap and swept her hair away from her face. Jason pulled on his T-shirt, realized it was on inside out, pulled it off, and put it back on the right way.

'Coming!' Sienna called, rushing for the door. Jason stayed where he was. He needed a minute to compose himself. Yeah, that was a good word for it: 'compose'.

There wasn't much time for composure before Sienna led Zach, Brad and Van Dyke into the living room. Brad and Van Dyke seemed too worked up to notice that they might have been interrupting something between Jason and Sienna. But Zach noticed everything. Jason knew he'd drawn the correct conclusion, even though his expression didn't change.

'Belle, Maggie and Erin are on their way,' Zach announced, taking a seat. 'There are things you all have to know.'

'So you're finally going to tell us what's going on?' Brad burst out.

'Yeah, and I only want to do it once,' Zach answered.

'Anybody want drinks while we wait?' Sienna asked. She rushed out of the room without waiting for an answer. Jason didn't follow her. He figured maybe she needed a little composing time too. When she returned, her hair was a little smoother, and her face wasn't as shiny. She carried a tray of sodas and beers.

'I see Maggie's car pulling up. She was collecting the other two. I'll go let everybody in,' Van Dyke said. A few moments later, the entire group was assembled in the living room.

Brad looked over at Zach. 'The floor is yours,' he said.

'I wanted to tell you why the meeting has been called in Chicago,' Zach told them. 'Not everybody thought you needed to know, but I do. I'm filling in everyone who was left behind in the Heights. This is big . . .'

'Well, what is it?' Belle demanded impatiently.

Jason saw that she looked frightened. *After what happened to Dominic, why wouldn't she be?* he thought.

Belle's boyfriend had been killed by the same vampire hunter who had shot Jason with the crossbow and tried to kill Sienna. Jason figured she probably went into any strange situation expecting the worst.

'Some disturbing things have been happening in New York for a while,' Zach continued. 'Vampires started disappearing, for a night or maybe a weekend. When they returned, they were disorientated. They couldn't remember what had happened to them, and they were physically weak and exhausted. It was almost like they'd been on drinking binges.'

'But a vampire would have to drink a *phenomenal* amount to get *that* effect,' Van Dyke protested. 'I had about eight witch doctors at Brad's party and I was fine.'

'I wouldn't say that,' Brad joked lamely.

'Drinking doesn't seem like a plausible explanation,' Zach agreed. 'But the council hasn't been able to come up with any explanations that *are* plausible, that's the problem . . .'

Jason waited for it. He could tell there was more.

'Lately, in the last month or so, vampires have started disappearing in other parts of the country,' Zach went on.

'Same deal? No memory of what happened?' Erin asked, leaning forward.

Zach gave a brief head shake. 'They didn't come back at all.'

'Shit,' Van Dyke muttered.

'Vampires from all over the country are gathering in Chicago to join forces, combine information and try to figure out what's going on. It's surprising that there isn't more intel already, considering how well-connected we are,' Zach said.

'Have there been any disappearances around here?' Jason queried.

'Not yet,' Zach told him. 'Trust me, the DeVere Heights Council would not have left Malibu if they thought there was any danger here.'

'But *you* do,' Jason pointed out. 'Otherwise, why—'

'I'm just taking precautions,' Zach said, raising a hand to quell any panic from the others. 'That's all.'

'What is it? Is it vampire hunters? Could a group of vampire hunters be working together all over the country?' Belle asked anxiously. Sienna and Erin both moved closer to her.

'Unlikely,' Zach replied. He hesitated, then looked Belle in the eye. 'If you remember, the hunter who came here was happy to leave the bodies behind.'

'And he hunted alone,' Van Dyke added.

'But I suppose it's possible,' Zach finished.

They all sat in silence for a few moments. Jason grabbed a soda just to have something to do.

'Should we arrange a buddy system or something?' Brad suggested finally.

'I don't think we need to go that far,' Zach answered. 'As I said, there haven't been any disappearances in our area.'

'Can I ask a newbie-ish question?' Jason didn't wait for permission. 'You said vampires are disappearing all over. Are there vampires everyplace? In every city in the country?'

'No place is like Malibu, dude,' Van Dyke answered. 'We own this place.'

'Practically,' Brad agreed with a smile.

'Our kind live all over the country. Not in every city, but in many,' Zach explained. 'But the DeVere Heights vampires are from purer bloodlines. That means we're more powerful, physically and politically, than most other American vampires.'

'Got it,' Jason said.

'I want to go back to that buddy system idea,' Belle said, looking around the room. 'I know we can all kick ass and everything, but I really don't want to be alone.'

'You don't have to be,' Sienna said immediately. 'You're spending the night.'

'Sleepover!' Erin called.

'Absolutely. All my girls are staying,' Sienna answered.

Which meant the house was not going to be empty again for a while. Not that Jason was going to complain. He didn't want Belle – or Sienna – to be alone, either.

'And tomorrow afternoon, once you girls roll out of bed, barbecue at my place,' Van Dyke said. 'We may as well all hang together. Just us.' He shot a look at Jason. 'And friends of us, of course.'

'Does that include Adam?' Jason asked.

'Adam definitely qualifies,' Van Dyke decreed. 'He can even bring the hot chick. Who I know has a name,' he told Maggie and the other girls, 'but I don't happen to remember it right now.'

'Brianna,' Sienna informed him.

'Brianna can also come. As long as Brad keeps his gymnastics to a minimum,' Van Dyke added.

'You were—' Brad began, then seemed to give up.

'This will be so fun!' Belle exclaimed. 'We haven't had a slumber party in forever. You can loan me a T-shirt or something to sleep in, right?' she asked Sienna. 'I don't want to bother going home.'

'All of you can borrow whatever you need. None of you are going home. The party starts now,' Sienna told her girlfriends.

'And if there's something you absolutely can't get along without, I'll be your errand boy,' Jason volunteered. 'There's no reason for a mere human to be afraid.'

'Do you have any Cherry Garcia?' Erin asked Sienna. She shook her head.

'Jason, will you go buy us some Cherry Garcia?' Erin begged.

'Sure.' He stood up.

'And some vinegar Pringles?' Belle asked.

'Gross, but sure,' Jason told her.

Brad and Van Dyke snickered. 'Whipped,' Van Dyke mumbled under his breath.

'I want those coconut macadamia cookies. I can't remember what they're called. But Van Dyke knows what the package looks like.' Maggie smiled at her boyfriend. 'I guess he'll have to go with you.'

Brad laughed.

'I don't know what you're laughing for – you're driving,' Van Dyke told Brad.

'Thank you,' Sienna mouthed as Jason and the other guys were pelted with more requests.

'Anytime,' Jason mouthed back.

Six

Jason ran down the steep steps leading to the beach just as the sun was weaving the first threads of pink and gold across the dark cloth of the ocean. It was pretty much only him and his board out there, although he could see one hardcore surfer already in the water, waiting for his ride.

For some reason he'd woken up insanely early for a Sunday morning, and he hadn't been able to fall back asleep. So he'd decided to give it up and get in some work on his frontside roundhouse cutback. He hadn't mastered the move, not by a long shot, and it would take all his focus.

He swam out to the line-up, the spot where the waves started to break, the water chilly even through his wetsuit. The Pacific never got very warm here. But neither did Lake Michigan, and Lake Michigan didn't have waves, so he wasn't complaining.

Jason straddled his board and waited until he saw a wave coming in that he liked. A nice tall one. The roundhouse needed speed, and for speed he needed to start high on the top of the wave. He flattened himself out on his belly and paddled for the shore as fast as he could. He felt the back of his board lift as the sweet wave rose up beneath him.

He popped to his feet, then started down the wave's face. Then before the wave flattened out too much, he started his turn. He leant back a little, but kept his board flat. If he let the board tip, he'd lose momentum. *Wait for it, wait for it*, Jason coached himself. *Now!* He pressed down on his heels and lifted the balls of his feet – and went spinning out. The wave crashed over him, and Jason came up coughing.

He'd broken the number one rule of surfing. He hadn't kept the majority of his body weight over the midpoint of the board. Well, nothing to do but try again.

For the next hour, Jason worked on his turn until his entire body felt battered, and he'd managed to perform the move correctly three times in a row. He'd even managed to touch the water with his inside hand on the last try. That was true style.

Jason decided to quit on that moment of triumph. As he paddled to shore, he spotted Adam on the beach. 'What are you doing here?' Jason asked as he climbed out of the water with his board.

'Thought you might be here,' Adam said. 'I went by your house and saw your car was gone. I'm jonesing for a Rooty Tooty Fresh 'n' Fruity. Shall we hit IHOP?'

'Well, I've already eaten a double helping of the ocean floor,' Jason admitted. 'But I could probably squeeze in a pancake. Hey, did you see my last turn?'

'Yeah. You almost took another spill. Nice recovery,' Adam answered.

'Leaning over and touching the water like that is *style*,' Jason corrected as he toweled off. 'It's flair. It's finesse.'

Adam shrugged. 'Well, it looked like you were about to fall on your butt.'

'Did you talk to Bree about Van Dyke's barbecue?' Jason asked Adam as they started for the steps in the side of the cliff.

'We'll be there,' Adam said. 'I've even got the OK to borrow my dad's car, so I can pick her up. She's at her friend's place in Topanga Canyon, so the Vespa wasn't really an option.'

'Van Dyke is going to be most impressed,' Jason told him.

'Well, I live to impress Van Dyke,' Adam shot back.

'Thanks, this looks great!' Jason said, as Van Dyke

handed him a plate of grilled steak, corn on the cob and baked beans, later that day.

'Jason's easily impressed by cooking skills,' Sienna laughed from the deck chair next to his. 'He's still working on Egg Boiling 101.'

Van Dyke grabbed another deck chair and dragged it up next to theirs. 'I'm not surprised. He's backward in many areas. I was just getting him up to speed as a member of the relay team, and now school is almost over.' He shook his head sadly.

I'm going to miss this clown, Jason thought. He didn't hang out with Van Dyke except as part of the bigger group, but Van Dyke always made any event more entertaining. 'What are you doing this summer?' Jason couldn't believe he'd never asked.

'No big plans. Enjoy the Malibu summer,' Van Dyke said with a shrug. 'Get ready to leave for Harvard.'

Jason raised his eyebrows. 'Harvard? You going to swim for them?'

'Pre-law.'

Jason frowned. 'Wow! I'm impressed. I didn't even know you had an interest in law.'

'Had young Mr Freeman paid attention to anything other than the lovely Ms Devereux all year, he might have acquired a few interesting facts about his other class-mates,' Van Dyke said with a grin, giving Jason a friendly slap on the shoulder. Jason was pretty sure it would leave a bruise.

'I've—' Jason began to protest.

I know. You've had a few other—' Van Dyke began, but he was interrupted by the ring of his cell. 'Talk to me,' he said, flipping it open. He listened for a moment, his expression turning serious. 'I'm leaving now.' He snapped the phone shut. 'That was Maggie.'

'Where is she?' Sienna asked. 'She said she was only going home to change her clothes.'

'While she was in the house someone slashed her tires,' Van Dyke said.

'What?' Belle exclaimed, an ear of corn poised halfway to her mouth.

'I didn't even know they tolerated that kind of petty crime in DeVere Heights,' Jason commented. 'I thought this was a strictly white-collar crime zone.'

Brad barked out a laugh. 'Maybe the little juniors are feeling very mature and bad ass now that the school is about to become theirs, and one of them did it.'

Van Dyke shrugged. 'I'm going to go pick her up,' he said. 'One of you watch the grill. Get whatever you want from the fridge.' He hurried away around the side of the house.

Zach tossed another steak on the fire. Erin turned the music up a little louder.

'Aren't Adam and Brianna supposed to be here too?' she asked Jason a little later.

'I saw Adam this morning and he said they would be,' Jason told her. 'And you know how Adam hates to miss free food.'

'He and Brianna probably wanted to get in a little alone time first,' Sienna said. 'They're a new couple, remember.'

As if Jason was past wanting to get in a little alone time with her!

'Does anyone know what we're doing for senior cut day?' Belle asked. 'Last year the seniors skipped school and went to the Santa Monica pier. But that's too ordinary.' She dipped a foot into the pool.

'I thought every day was senior cut day now anyway,' Brad joked.

'Not if you have Mr Tomlinson,' Sienna said. 'He announced to all his classes that if anyone is absent without a doctor's note – a doctor's, not just a parent's – he will personally write to the college where you've been accepted and tell them to reconsider because you lack the proper seriousness.'

'Ed Gerner's mom's a doctor. He'll sell you a piece of her office stationery for a hundred bucks,' Zach threw out.

'You know his mom's a cosmetic surgeon, right?'

Erin asked. 'So you guys might want to come up with a plan B.'

'Maybe we could go on a tour of the stars' homes for cut day,' Belle suggested. 'I've lived practically on top of Hollywood my whole life and I've never done that.'

'Maybe because it's so incredibly tacky?' Erin asked.

'That's why it would be fun,' Belle told her.

Everyone threw out more possibilities for cut day, until Belle announced she was frying in the sun. 'I'm going in the pool. I don't care if I don't have my bathing suit.'

Brad looked intrigued. Jason tried not to look intrigued. Belle laughed as she jumped into the pool with all her clothes on.

'I'm going in too!' Erin leapt into the pool without even taking off her jeweled flip-flops.

Jason stood up and grinned at Sienna. She grinned back and took a step toward the pool. Then her cell rang. She pulled it out of her purse and answered, then frowned as she listened.

'He definitely already left, Maggie,' Jason heard her say. 'He should be there. Call me as soon as he shows up, OK?'

'Van Dyke's not at Maggie's yet?' Jason asked as Sienna hung up. Every eye was on Sienna as she shook her head.

'Maggie lives in the Heights,' Zach said. 'Five minutes away.'

Jason nodded as everyone exchanged worried glances. They all knew that Van Dyke should have been there *and* back, already.

Seven

Belle climbed out of the pool and wrapped herself in a beach towel. The afternoon sun was hot, but Jason could see that she was shivering. She was still so on edge after Dominic's death.

'Call Van Dyke,' Jason suggested.

Sienna nodded and punched Van Dyke's speed dial number on her cell. 'His voice mail's picking up,' she told the group. 'Hey, it's Sienna,' she said into the phone. 'Maggie's wondering where you are, and so are we. Call us.' Slowly, she clicked the phone shut.

'That's it. I'm going to look for him,' Brad announced. Jason stood up. 'I'll go with you.'

'Me too,' Sienna said.

'No,' Jason told her. She stared at him. 'Some people need to be here in case he shows up,' he explained. Which was a reason, just not *the* reason. He knew Sienna could handle herself in threatening situations. He'd seen her do it. He even knew that she was stronger than he was, stronger and faster. But he didn't want her out there when who knew what was going on. The only thing they were sure of was that vampires were disappearing. Maybe whatever had happened to Van Dyke had no connection to the disappearances. But if it did, Jason was in less danger than Sienna was. So he wanted her here, with Zach and the others. This was the safest place she could be.

'Please,' he said softly.

'OK,' Sienna agreed. 'But be careful. Remember you're only human.'

Jason nodded, then he and Brad raced out to Brad's car. Brad drove to Maggie's slowly, so they could both look for any sign of Van Dyke. They didn't see his car or any indication of an accident.

Maggie burst out onto the driveway the instant they pulled up. 'Where is he?'

'We're not sure, Mags,' Brad told her. 'Maybe he decided to stop on the way for something? More ice or paper towels?' He gave a helpless shrug.

'What if that's not what's happened?' she snapped.

'We don't know what's happened,' Jason said firmly. 'Let's head back to his house. Does he always take the same route over here?'

Maggie rattled off the same streets they'd used to come by. There was no sign of Van Dyke on the way back.

'Did he call?' Brad asked, when they joined the others who were now gathered in the living room of Van Dyke's house.

'No,' Zach said simply.

'So what do we do now?' Sienna asked.

Before anyone could answer, the doorbell rang.

'Maybe it's him!' Maggie exclaimed, rushing to answer it.

The others waited in silence. Nobody bothered to point out that Van Dyke wouldn't ring his own doorbell.

'It's Adam and Brianna,' Maggie announced, leading them into the living room. Her voice was strained.

Jason got it. He didn't particularly want an outsider here right now, either. They were all way too worried about Van Dyke to bother pretending they weren't vampires in front of Brianna.

'Listen, Turnball. Something came up unexpectedly that Van Dyke had to deal with,' Zach told Adam. 'I'm sorry, but I think you should take Brianna home now.'

Adam immediately seemed to take in what category of unexpected something they were dealing with. 'All right,' he answered. 'Is there anything I can do?' he asked. 'Maybe there's an errand I can run on my way back home? Or I could drop back by here and check in to see if you need anything?'

'It's under control,' Zach said pleasantly, but firmly.

'All right,' Adam repeated. 'We'll get going.'

'I hope everything's OK. Um, tell Van Dyke thanks for inviting me,' Brianna told the group. Then she turned and followed Adam out of the room.

'So what do we do?' Sienna asked again when Adam and Brianna had pulled out of the driveway.

'Is there any way to get in touch with our parents?' Erin asked.

Zach shook his head. 'The meeting is being held in an area that doesn't have cell phone service or land lines. But this is something we should be able to handle ourselves.'

'That's not an answer,' Erin said impatiently.

'It's all the answer I have for now,' Zach told her. 'There's no point in doing anything without in-formation. For now, we go on as normal. That means school tomorrow. I'll get in touch with my sources and see what I can find out.'

'That's it? We just go to school and sit on our butts?' Brad demanded, his face twisted with anger.

'For now, yes,' Zach replied, his voice even and unemotional. It was clear from his tone that the discussion was over.

'I'm at least going to drive around town and see if I spot him anywhere,' Brad said.

'I'll go with you,' Maggie insisted.

'If you do see any sign of him, call me. I don't want either of you to take any action without my approval,' Zach told them.

Brad hesitated a fraction of a second, then nodded.

'Bring Maggie back to my place when you're done, OK?' Sienna asked.

'OK,' Brad said.

Sienna glanced from Belle to Erin. 'I guess we should all go back to my house. Will you take us, Jason?'

'Of course. Come on.'

'I'm going to stay here. If he shows up, I'll call all of you,' Zach told them as they trooped to the front door.

The drive to Sienna's only took a few minutes. 'Will you three be OK or do you want me to stay?' Jason asked.

'I think I want to go back to bed,' Belle said with a wide yawn.

'We stayed up pretty late last night,' Sienna explained. 'I think we'll probably all go to sleep. You should just go home.' She leant over and gave him a kiss that landed on the corner of his mouth. 'I'll see you at school.'

Jason watched until Sienna, Erin and Belle were safely inside. He thought about staying parked in the driveway, keeping guard. But Zach wanted them to act normally, and that wasn't normal, so he started home.

As he made a left turn, he felt his shoulder twinge, although the crossbow wound there had completely healed. Psychosomatic, he decided. The disappearing vampires had gotten him thinking about vampire hunters.

It's true that Tamburo – the vampire hunter who had shot him – hadn't minded leaving bodies around, but maybe other vampire hunters had different methods, he thought. Could Tamburo have belonged to a secret society? Were there hunters spread out all over the country?

Jason pulled into his own driveway and shut off the ignition. He folded his arms on the steering wheel. Were there always going to be people trying to kill off every vampire on the planet? Were he and Sienna always going to be in danger from someone?

He rested his head on his arms. Was this going to be his life? All through college and everything after that?

If you want to be with Sienna, maybe it is, Jason thought. Was it worth it? Was *she* worth it?

He lifted up his head, the answer instantaneous: hell, yeah, she was worth it. There was no way he was ever giving her up. 'So go ahead and bring it on,' he muttered. 'Whoever you are.'

Eight

Normal, Jason thought as he headed across the DeVere High courtyard the next day. *Here I am, acting normal.*

His body jerked as a hand slid up his back. Jason whipped round to see Sienna. 'At least I didn't squeal,' he said. 'You have to admit, I didn't make a sound of any kind.'

'We're all a little jumpy today,' Sienna reassured him.

Jason checked the clock tower. Still ten minutes before first period. He sat down on the closest stone bench. Sienna took a seat next to him. The palm fronds over their heads rattled gently in the slight breeze.

'I was thinking, would it be useful to bring the police in on this?' Jason asked her. 'Van Dyke's a missing minor. They'd get right on it. Maybe they could find out something. And it's not like absolutely everything that happens in Malibu has to do with *your* people.'

'Great minds,' Sienna said. 'I asked Zach pretty much the same thing about an hour ago. He told me that his sources go deeper and wider than the police's, and that getting the police involved could make it more complicated for us to do what we need to do – whatever that turns out to be. You know how Zach is. He doesn't exactly tell you everything on his mind.'

Jason nodded. 'I guess Zach's sources haven't . . . ?'

'Nothing yet,' Sienna replied. 'We were up all night, imagining all these terrible things that could have happened to him.'

'Sounds like quite a slumber party,' Jason commented.

'It's so weird being here today, isn't it?' Sienna asked, watching groups of kids go by, talking and laughing. 'Only a few of us know anything is wrong. To everybody else this is a totally normal day. Better than normal because school is almost out. If people notice Van Dyke isn't here, they'll just think he has a bad case of senioritis and is cutting class to go out and have fun.'

Whereas in reality he could be hurt, Jason silently added. *Maybe dead.*

Sometimes Malibu didn't seem like a place where people could die. It was naturally beautiful to begin with, but it had been shined and buffed and glossed until it was almost artificial. And maybe that was the point. When you were rich enough to live in Malibu, you could almost pretend the real world didn't exist.

You could almost pretend that shiny, glossy, beautiful –
plus safe and happy – was reality.

But the same ugly things happened in Malibu that
happened in the rest of the world: illness, crime,
divorce, death, even murder. Once Jason had almost
fallen over the dead body of a murdered girl right on
a stretch of beach so pretty it should have been on a
postcard. Living here was no protection.

'I guess we should head in,' Sienna said as the crowd
around them thinned out.

'I guess,' Jason agreed. They stood up and walked
out of the sun and into one of the cool, dim walkways
that ran through the school. 'See you in English,' he
said when they reached the stone stairway he had to
take to get to his world history class. Sienna gave a little
wave as he started up the stairs.

He reached the classroom with only seconds to
spare before the second bell. Not that even the teachers
could get themselves to care about that too much at
this point. They were as ready for summer as everybody else.

Mr Munro took roll, then popped in a DVD after
handing out a sheet of questions that would be
answered during the DVD viewing. He looked as tired
as Brad and Maggie did. Jason wondered how long
they'd stayed out searching for Van Dyke last night. He

knew they hadn't found even a hint about what had happened. Sienna would have called if they had.

Jason picked up his pen and read the first question. Mr Munro was cool about putting the questions in the order the info was given in the DVDs. Basically, all you had to do was stay awake to fill out the sheet – though that was sometimes not the easiest thing first period, especially with the lights dimmed.

A folded scrap of paper landed on his desk as he waited for the answer to question number one. He opened it after shooting a quick look at Mr Munro. The note was from Adam: 'What happened yesterday?'

Like Jason was going to start writing stuff down about the vampires and passing it over to Adam, who sat almost all the way across the room from him. He shook his head at his friend.

He heard the word 'Mesopotamian'. Damn, he'd missed the factoid he needed for the worksheet. He read the second question and got ready to listen for the answer.

Another note arrived from Adam: 'Did it have to do with Vs?' Jason crumpled it and focused on the photographs slowly flashing across the TV screen. He hoped Adam would interpret the message correctly as 'not now'.

Maybe he should have sent the message in Morse

code, because Adam didn't seem to pick up on the paper crumpling. Another note arrived less than a minute later that read: 'Let me help.'

Jason tore off a scrap of paper from the bottom of the worksheet. 'Later' he wrote on it. As he folded it, he heard the words 'cult of Anu'. Crap, he'd missed the second answer.

Screw it, he thought as he sent the note off across the room to Adam. *It's not like CalTech is going to find out that I didn't pay attention to the DVD and come tear up my acceptance letter*. At least, he hoped not.

'You two have P.E. this period, don't you?' Coach Middleton asked, catching up with Jason and Brad in the hall after world history.

'Yep,' Jason answered.

'Well, whatever they have you doing in there today, don't do it. I want you to get your swim team lockers cleaned out. I'm going to start working with the new guys over the summer and I need the space,' the coach told them. 'Don't get all sappy and nostalgic on me. You have fifty minutes. That's more than enough time. Tell Van Dyke to get his crap out of there too. Where is he anyway? He's supposed to have P.E. first period.'

'Uh, I saw him yesterday and he wasn't feeling that great. Maybe he decided to stay home,' Jason said.

'Seniors,' Coach Middleton snorted. 'Well, you call him on his cell and tell him to get his ass over here and get his locker cleaned out. I'm talking spotless or he'll be spending the summer swimming laps.' He veered off into one of the teachers' lounges.

'I guess we can pack Van Dyke's stuff up for him,' Jason suggested. He shot a look at Brad, wondering how he was doing.

'I know his locker combination,' Brad answered without emotion as they continued on.

Once they were inside the locker room, they found cardboard boxes waiting for them. Jason's locker was a row over from Brad's. They worked mostly in silence, separated by a wall of metal. Jason threw out a few comments, but Brad answered in monosyllables.

It didn't take Jason long to load up his gear. He didn't keep a ton of stuff at school. Goggles. Shampoo. Flip-flops. A couple of T-shirts and some shorts. A couple of swimsuits and a towel. Combined, it didn't even fill up half of one of the boxes.

Jason slammed his locker – he wanted to give Brad a head's up that he was finished – and circled around to see how Brad was doing. He had his gear boxed up too. He was sitting in front of Van Dyke's closed locker – the one right next to his – staring at it. Jason had the urge to back away, feeling like he'd walked in on something really private. But it was too late. Brad looked up and saw him standing there.

'Want some help?' Jason asked, trying to make the best of the situation.

Brad shrugged. But Jason's words got him moving. He dialed the combination into the lock and pulled it off, then opened the locker door. But he didn't start taking stuff out. Jason wondered if that would feel like giving up to Brad, like admitting that Van Dyke wouldn't be coming back to do it himself.

Jason was just about to make an excuse to give Brad some space, when Brad slammed the locker door shut. He pulled back his fist and rammed it into his own locker, leaving a crater. 'Whoever has Van Dyke better pray Zach finds them before I do,' Brad burst out, the muscles in his neck tense. He slammed the locker door again and strode away.

Zach was definitely more cool-headed. But Jason wasn't at all sure that that meant his punishment of whoever had Van Dyke would be any less severe.

He considered his options, then decided to clean out Van Dyke's locker himself. Zach didn't want Van Dyke's disappearance to become an issue, and it would become one with the coach if the locker wasn't dealt with.

Jason opened Van Dyke's locker door and moved a

cardboard box in front of it. *When Van Dyke gets back, I'm going to have to give him some serious grief about the number of hair and skin products he has in here*, Jason thought, hoping he would get that opportunity.

Jason loaded half a dozen fancy little bottles into Van Dyke's box, each one designed to keep hair or skin free from the ravages of chlorine.

'Need any help?' came Adam's voice suddenly.

Jason glanced over his shoulder, surprised to see his best friend. 'What are you doing in here? You don't have P.E. now. And I know you never choose to hang out in the locker room of your own free will.'

Adam held up a bathroom pass. 'It's later. And I wanted to make sure that we aren't in the middle of an emergency I need to know about.'

'The short version is that Van Dyke went missing from his own barbecue,' Jason explained. 'He went to pick up Maggie, and never got there. Nobody's heard from him since.'

'You guys don't want to get my dad involved? You do have a close personal connection to the Chief of Police,' Adam reminded him.

'We're not sure exactly what, uh, elements are involved here,' Jason said. 'Zach wants to keep it quiet until he can find out more.'

'OK.' Adam dug around in his pocket, then pulled

out a pill and stuck it in his mouth. 'My dad's on this vitamin kick,' he explained, in response to Jason's puzzled look. 'He's somehow rationalized eating a diet that's ninety per cent junk food as long as he takes this massive assortment of vitamins, and now he has me taking them too. The up side – I get to have potato chips for breakfast.'

'I wouldn't mind that plan.'

'So, anyway, there's nothing I can do?' Adam asked.

'Well, you can carry one of these boxes over to the door. I'll throw them in my car after school,' Jason said, more because he wanted to give Adam some way to help out than because he actually needed help. 'Other than that, our big assignment from Zach is to act normal.'

'Act normal,' Adam repeated, grabbing the closest box. 'I'll do my best.'

'Well, we made it through the day,' Sienna said as she and Brad caught up to Jason in the hall after last class. 'We came to school like it was any other day.'

'It felt about ten times as long, though,' Brad commented.

'Yeah,' Jason agreed.

'I talked to Zach in chem,' Sienna told them. 'He wants us to meet up at my place for a strategy session.

Belle and I are going to do a quick food run on the way there. Two nights of slumber partying emptied the kitchen.'

'Good. I want to meet,' Brad said.

'I'm going to grab the junk from my locker and dump it at home, then I'll be over,' Jason told her. He gave her a quick kiss goodbye.

'Yeah, I'll come with you. I'll get my stuff and Van Dyke's,' Brad said. They walked down the corridor in silence. The school was already mostly empty. This late in the year there were no activities to keep anybody around.

Brad stopped short about six feet from the double doors leading into the gym. 'Do you see that?'

Jason followed his gaze. Brad was staring at the ground.

'I don't see anything,' Jason said.

Brad took a couple of steps forward and crouched down. 'Right there. It's blood.'

Jason knelt next to him. Now he could see a small smear of dark red.

'It's fresh,' Brad told him.

'So someone stubbed their toe,' Jason suggested, straightening up.

'There's too much. There's a lot of it. I can smell it. You can't smell it?' Brad darted forward. 'There's some more.' He pointed to another smear along the bottom of the wall a few feet closer to the gym.

Brad rushed along the trail of almost imperceptible – at least to Jason – drops and stains of blood. It led around the gym to the locker room. Brad held one arm out, cautioning Jason, and pointed to a thin streak of blood on the long metal door handle. 'Watch yourself. We don't know what's going to be in here.'

Slowly Brad opened the door. Jason strained to catch any sounds from inside. He could hear the shower running.

Brad moved toward the sound, fast and silent as a panther. Jason followed as quietly as he could. When Brad rounded the entrance to the showers, he stopped dead and let out a sound like he'd been punched in the gut. Jason looked around him and sucked in his breath with a hiss.

Van Dyke was huddled on the tiled floor, shirtless but still wearing his pants, the shower water streaming down onto him. Blood and dirt mingled in the water and swirled away down the plug. The water was obviously warm because steam filled the room, and yet Van Dyke was shivering violently. Brad raced to his side, turning off the water, while Jason ran to grab a towel from the stuff he'd cleared out of his locker.

Jason returned and helped Brad to wrap the towel

around Van Dyke's shoulders. Jason could see that his feet were bare and bleeding, one of his fingernails was halfway ripped off and his pants were torn. Despite the shower, some grime still streaked his chest and there was a perfectly round wound on his abdomen. A section of his scalp had been shaved and there was a neat row of stitches across it.

'Who did this to you?' Brad cried. 'Van Dyke, who in the hell did this to you?'

Who could *have done this?* Jason wondered. *Who could have been strong enough to do* all this *to a vampire?*

Nine

'Who did this to you?' Brad shouted again.

Van Dyke didn't answer. He just groaned weakly and pulled the towel more tightly around himself.

Brad sucked in a deep breath. When he spoke again, his voice was gentle. 'I'm going to take care of you, buddy,' Brad told Van Dyke. Calmly, he pulled out his cell and punched in a number.

'Who are you calling?' Jason demanded.

'School nurse,' Brad answered.

'Isn't this a little out of her league? We need an ambulance. EMTs,' Jason protested.

'Can you come to the boys' locker room? There's been an accident. Nothing too serious. Some minor cuts. Thanks,' Brad said into the phone.

Has he gone into shock? Jason wondered, staring at Brad.

Brad took him by the arm. 'This is what he *needs*.'

Finally, it clicked in Jason's head. He got it. Van Dyke was dangerously weak. What he needed was blood.

Brad had called the nurse so Van Dyke could feed on her. 'Sorry.' Jason shook his head. 'I wasn't thinking.'

'Why don't you go wait over by the lockers? I'll wait with Michael,' Brad said. Jason realized it was the first time he'd ever heard Brad call Van Dyke by his first name.

'Sure.' Jason automatically headed over to his own locker and sat down on the wooden bench in front of it. He knew all about the realities of vampire blood-drinking. But there was a part of him that was still deeply uncomfortable with the fact, even though he knew, knew from actual experience, that it was extremely pleasurable when a vampire fed on a human, and that the vampires never took enough blood to do any harm. Only a rogue vampire *drained* the donor when he drank.

About five minutes later, Jason heard the nurse hurry into the locker room. Heard Brad direct her to the showers. Then, about five minutes after that, he saw Brad and Van Dyke walk her back out into the main part of the locker room, and saw the dazed and happy expression on her face as they easily convinced her that Van Dyke was absolutely fine and his parents didn't need to be contacted.

As soon as she was gone, Van Dyke's pleasant expression hardened. 'We need to get everyone together,' he declared. '*Now!*'

* * *

Jason called Sienna as he strode across the parking lot to the VW. 'Change of plans. We're meeting at Van Dyke's place in an hour. He's back. He's going to tell us everything when we all get there.'

Sienna hung up almost immediately so she could pass on the news. Jason hit Adam's speed dial number.

'What's going on?' Adam asked as soon as he picked up.

'Just wanted to tell you I can't do *Reservoir Dogs* tonight,' Jason said.

'Oh. That's . . . OK. I figured it was off, with everything else that's going down,' Adam answered.

'Yeah, I figured you'd figured, but I wanted to make sure. Also, Van Dyke is back.'

'He is? Where was he? What happened to him?' Adam asked in a rush.

'I don't really know yet. I'm not even sure how much he knows. He was hurt pretty bad,' Jason said. 'We're meeting up at his place in an hour and he's going to fill us in as much as he can.'

'I'll be there.' Adam hung up before Jason could say that maybe that wasn't a good idea.

Except it actually *was* a good idea. Adam had come through for the vampires in lots of ways this past year. Zach had even pretty much said so at Brad's party.

They'd probably be glad to have him around tonight. In Jason's opinion, they were in a we-need-all-the-help-we-can-get situation.

'Start from the beginning. We need to understand as much about the situation as we can,' Zach told Van Dyke when everyone in the group was gathered. Everybody seemed fine with Adam being there. It had only been awkward on the weekend because he'd had Brianna with him.

Van Dyke wiped his face with his fingers. 'I'll try. But I'm telling you right now I don't remember everything.' He sucked in a deep breath. 'So, the beginning: I get a call from Maggie.' He reached out and took her hand. 'I start driving over there. On the way, there's an accident blocking the road. I can see a body on the street.'

Jason heard Belle give a little gasp.

'I pulled over and ran to check on the guy. I wasn't sure if he was still alive. I had my cell out. I was about to call 911. But when I leant down to check his pulse, he sat up and zapped me with some kind of stun gun,' Van Dyke explained.

Brad looked like he badly wanted to punch something again. Jason felt the same way.

'When you get hit with one of those, your whole

nervous system gets disabled. Human or vampire,' Van Dyke continued. 'So I'm on the ground. I can't move. And five guys – I think five – pour out of the van. I forgot to say that one of the vehicles in the accident was a van,' Van Dyke added, turning to Zach. 'The guys had me in the back in seconds and we were out of there.'

'One of them must have driven your car off,' Brad said. 'There was no sign of it when we followed your route to Maggie's house.'

'They really had the whole thing planned out,' Jason added. 'Not just staging the accident, but slashing Maggie's tires. They must know you're her boyfriend and figured that she'd call you for a ride. They knew exactly which streets you'd take to get to her place, too.' *They aren't going to be easy to stop*, he thought.

'They have to have been watching us closely to know all that. I don't like it,' Belle said.

'That's the kind of information we need about them. That kind of detail,' Zach told them, his voice cold.

Zach's not going to be easy to stop, either, Jason acknowledged. He looked around the room. At Brad's clenched fists. Maggie's tight jaw. Erin's ramrod straight posture. Sienna's blazing eyes. None of them would be easy to stop. They were all pissed off. Even Zach in his own icy way. And Belle, scared as she was.

One of their own had been hurt and someone was going to pay.

'What do you remember about where you were held?' Zach asked Van Dyke.

'My cell was small,' he answered slowly.

'Cell!' Belle exclaimed, outraged.

'It was . . . maybe . . . nine by six,' Van Dyke continued. 'A cot. A bucket. Damp. Smelly, obviously. It's weird, because other parts of the place were really hi-tech. They brought me into operating rooms a couple of times.'

Jason saw Sienna's face pale. His hand drifted to the spot on his head that had been shaved on Van Dyke's. When he realized what he'd done, he jammed his hand in his pocket.

'Were the people who captured you human?' Brad asked.

'Yeah. But they had some hi-tech equipment. They strapped me on a gurney to move me and the straps were made of nothing I've ever seen before. Like something from a space shuttle. I couldn't make even a tiny tear in them. Sometimes they half knocked me out with gas. Every time they wanted me not to use my strength, they gassed me.' Van Dyke stared blankly into space for a moment. It seemed like he was focusing on a memory. Then he gave his head a brisk shake. 'Like I said, I wasn't always conscious, but I know they drew a lot of blood from me, and they took some spinal fluid. And they kept sticking me with these long needles. Not injecting me. Pulling stuff out.'

'It sounds like they were doing biopsies of your organs,' Adam said. 'They were doing a real workup on you.'

'Is that what happened to his head? A brain biopsy?' Erin asked.

'Maybe,' Adam replied.

'How did you get out of there?' Maggie asked Van Dyke. Her eyes shimmered with tears she wasn't allowing herself to shed.

'They have another vampire,' Van Dyke told the group. 'I should have said that right up front. Christopher. I've never seen him around here before.' Again his gaze went to Zach. 'I think they've had him for a while. He doesn't look too good. But he managed to pass me a key to the handcuffs they used.'

'How did he get that?' Zach asked.

'I'm not sure,' Van Dyke answered. 'I'm not sure about anything. We didn't have the chance to talk much. Anyway, they were going to do some experiments on me – something where they had to take me outside the main location. They put the cuffs on and put me back in the van. They weren't paying as much attention to me, because they were sure I was restrained and the van was moving. So I used the key to get the cuffs off, yanked open the door and jumped.'

'Obviously, we don't have any time to waste,' Zach announced. 'One of us is still being held captive. We don't know how long he can survive, so we have to rescue him. We have to find the place where Van Dyke was held and shut it down before it's too late.'

'So you think you were held in a warehouse . . .' Zach recapped, as Brad slipped out of the room.

'The place was big, that's for sure,' Van Dyke answered. 'And my cell felt like a warehouse, cold and damp. Definitely not heated like a building that was used by a lot of people. At least, not that part of it.'

'Did you see anything that made you think you were being held by vampire hunters like Tamburo?' Jason asked. 'Any ritualistic objects? Anything with the phases of the moon as symbols?'

Van Dyke shook his head. 'All the equipment these guys had was really hi-tech,' he said, pacing back and forth across the living room. His wounds had visibly improved and he was clearly eager to go out and kick some ass. 'The stuff could have come out of your dad's labs, Sienna. It was that cutting edge. Some of the tech guys were even wearing what looked like hazmat suits. This wasn't some rinky-dink operation.'

Brad hurried back into the living room. 'I snagged this from the study,' he said, spreading a detailed map of Malibu out on the coffee table. 'I thought it could help. Let's go over everything you remember about your escape. You said you jumped out of the van. Can you show us where on the map?'

Van Dyke sat on the floor and leant over the coffee table. 'I hit the ground hard and rolled. I was going to try to stand up and start running, but I picked up momentum. It turned out there was a hill at the side of the road. A steep, scrubby hill. And I was going down it whether I wanted to or not. When I finally stopped, I got up and ran.'

'I'm thinking the school must have been closer than your house and that's why you went there,' Brad suggested.

'Yeah,' Van Dyke agreed.

'Any idea how far you ran?' Jason asked.

'It felt like a marathon. But maybe a mile. At least a mile,' Van Dyke answered.

Van Dyke studied the map. 'Here's the school.' He tapped the map. 'And I think this has got to be the hill.' He tapped it again. 'So this has to be where I jumped out of the van.' He pointed to a road.

'Now we just need to work back from there,' Sienna

said. 'How long do you think you rode in the van before the heroic leap?'

'I probably had a brain biopsy before this all happened,' Van Dyke reminded everyone.

'Best guess,' Erin urged.

'Twenty minutes,' Van Dyke told them.

'And how fast do you think the van was going?' Jason asked.

'This is starting to feel like one of those word problems from the third grade. I never liked those,' Van Dyke complained. 'When I jumped out, it felt as though we were going about forty. Let's say we were going around forty the whole time. I don't remember speeding up or slowing down a whole lot.'

'Twenty minutes, forty miles an hour,' Brad muttered. Then he drew a large circle around the place Van Dyke estimated he'd rolled down the hill. 'This is the area we're looking at,' he told the group. 'We're trying to come up with a large building, like a warehouse, somewhere near the perimeter of the circle.'

'More or less,' Van Dyke added.

'Right,' Brad agreed.

'I can't think of a large building anywhere out there. But I don't know that many large buildings that don't sell stuff,' Belle admitted apologetically.

'Maybe we can narrow it down some more,' Jason

said. 'Think about smells and sounds and anything you caught sight of from the van windows. Say whatever comes into your head. It might make one of us think of something.'

Van Dyke frowned, tapping his fingers on the map. 'This isn't a sight or sound or smell, but the road was mostly smooth,' he said.

'That eliminates the northernmost part of the circle.' Zach shaded that section with a pencil. 'The roads up there are bumpy as hell.'

'Excellent!' Maggie cried. 'What else?' she asked Van Dyke.

'I couldn't see much from the back of the van. They had me flat on my back. But I know the driver had to stop twice to open gates so that we could keep going,' Van Dyke said.

'Gates.' Sienna tapped her bottom lip. 'Did you hear any water around that time?'

'Yeah!' Van Dyke exclaimed. 'Why do you ask that?'

'Because Vera Canyon has smooth roads. They repaved them about two months ago. And there are some gated sections, and waterfalls leading into Zuma Creek,' Sienna explained.

'That could be right. I couldn't see much from the van, but I did see a lot of tree branches,' Van Dyke told her.

'Down in Vera Canyon there are places where the trees practically make a tunnel!' Erin added, her voice filled with excitement.

'OK, so we know we need to go this way to get to the warehouse or whatever building Van Dyke was held in.' Brad traced a line from the hill over to Vera Canyon. 'We still have eight or so miles to figure out.'

'I'm trying to think of other stuff,' Van Dyke said, his eyes closed. The room fell silent as everyone willed him to remember something. 'You know, there was this weird smell,' he said after a moment. 'I first noticed it not long after we'd started out. Maybe only four or five miles from the warehouse.'

'What was it like?' Maggie asked.

'It's hard to describe. I've definitely smelled it before, but it's not common,' Van Dyke answered. He took a long sniff, like he was trying to suck in the odor again. 'The circus,' he said. 'It smelled like the circus.'

'What part of the circus?' Erin asked. 'Like the popcorn and peanuts?'

'Or sawdust?' Brad suggested.

'I bet I know!' Belle exclaimed. 'I bet you were smelling the Hollywood Star ranch. That's the place where they keep all the exotic animals that are trained for the movies.' Belle turned to Maggie. 'Remember, our girl scout troop went there in the fourth grade?'

'Oh, right. That place definitely smelled. They had some big animals too. Elephants and everything – like at a circus.' Maggie pulled the map a little closer to her. 'The ranch is right about here.' She pointed to a spot that was very near part of the circle's perimeter.

'It was kind of a funky animal smell,' Van Dyke confirmed. 'That could be it.'

'I've been to the ranch, too,' Brad said. 'I'm pretty sure there's an abandoned warehouse close by. I vaguely remember seeing one.'

'Yeah. There's some kind of big building up there. I shot some footage of it once,' Adam added. 'I remember thinking it might be a good location for something. It's built into the hillside.' He pointed at the map. 'About *there*.'

Jason could feel expectation rising up in him. He looked around the group. They were feeling it too

'To me it sounds like a good location to kick some ass,' Van Dyke declared.

Ten

'Let's go,' Zach said.

Jason glanced at him in surprise. 'Go? Where?'

'To that warehouse.' Zach's voice was hard. 'And if it's the same place where Van Dyke was held, we're going to shut it down.' Zach got to his feet, joining Brad and Van Dyke, who were already up and ready to go.

'Hold on,' Jason protested. 'Don't you think we need to plan this out a little better?'

'No,' Zach replied. 'The assholes who took Van Dyke know that he's escaped. They're probably out there looking for him, right now. Looking for all of us, maybe.'

'Yeah. The sooner we get rid of them, the better,' Brad muttered. 'Then we can all stop living in fear.'

'I agree,' Jason said. 'But—'

'With the rest of the council unreachable, it's up to us to handle this,' Zach reminded him. 'So let's go handle it.'

Van Dyke cracked his neck. 'My pleasure,' he said grimly.

Jason sensed a strange undercurrent of excitement in Van Dyke's voice, and he glanced over at him. *Van Dyke looks good*, Jason thought, startled. *Vampire good*. The guy was practically glowing, his hair shiny, his cheekbones sharp enough to cut someone. Jason turned to Zach and Brad. Same thing. They'd let their regular 'human' appearance slide a bit, and he could swear they actually looked bigger than usual.

'Uh, guys?' he said. 'You want to tell me why you're going all superhuman?'

Zach stared at Jason for a moment, his brown eyes glinting, looking almost black. Then his face seemed to soften, his wiry frame taking on a more normal look. His eyes lightened, slightly. He was regular Zach again – or as regular as the guy ever got.

'We're just pumped up is all,' Brad muttered, returning his appearance to normal. Van Dyke didn't change a bit.

'I get that,' Jason said. 'Believe me, I want to find the guys that took Van Dyke as much as you do. But when you get all vampired-up, it makes me think you might forget yourselves.'

'We're wasting time,' Van Dyke growled.

'Look, I know how strong you are,' Jason told him.

'And it's OK to beat up those jerks. But it's not OK to kill them.'

'We can control ourselves,' Zach said shortly. 'Van Dyke.'

'Fine.' Slowly, Van Dyke returned his appearance to normal. 'Now, let's go.'

'You're all acting crazy,' Sienna said. 'We have no idea if there's even a warehouse there, it's dark out, and we haven't even driven by to see if Van Dyke is sure it's the right place. We should come up with a strategy.'

'The strategy is simple. We get over there, I see if it's the place, and if it is we tear it down and take care of the guys running it,' Van Dyke said angrily.

'What do you mean, take care of them?' Belle asked.

'What do you think he means?' Brad demanded. 'These people *experimented* on him.'

'And they're probably still torturing Christopher,' Van Dyke put in. 'That dude saved my life! I'm not waiting. I'm taking them out the first chance I get.'

'The three of us are more than a match for half a dozen humans,' Zach said brusquely. 'If they know what's good for them, they won't try to stop us.'

'Yeah, we can just burn the lab down and ruin all their research,' Brad said.

Sienna still looked concerned. 'So, no hurting anybody?'

'And what's with the "three"?' demanded Maggie angrily. 'We're also vampire-strong – we're coming along too!'

'Better not,' Zach pointed out drily. 'These are *humans*, remember? We can't take the risk of exposure that girls along would lead to – you know that, Maggie.'

'Anyway, they're not gonna learn their lesson unless we rough them up a little,' Van Dyke continued. 'Believe me, they deserve it.'

'Come on.' Zach headed for the door without another glance at Sienna's worried face.

Whoever experimented on Van Dyke deserves at least a punch or two, Jason thought. But if the vampires did more than that, word could get out and then there would be trouble.

But when Brad and Van Dyke started after Zach, Jason went along with them. If his friends got too hot-headed, maybe he'd be able to stop them somehow.

Zach glanced over and caught his eye. For a brief moment, Jason got the distinct feeling that he wasn't welcome in this little posse. But he held Zach's gaze and, eventually, Zach nodded.

As Jason reached the door, Sienna grabbed his hand.

'Be careful,' she said, her voice tense. 'I don't like this. I wish I could come with you.'

'Don't worry,' he said. 'I'll be extra-careful. And I'll try to make sure everyone else is, too.'

Over her shoulder, he caught a glimpse of Adam staring at him open-mouthed. His best friend clearly thought that Jason had lost his mind, tagging along with a bunch of vampires on an illegal search-and-destroy mission.

Jason pulled the door closed behind him, hoping that Adam was wrong.

These vampires are freaking me out, Jason thought wryly as Brad drove through the dark Malibu night. He'd been hanging around the toothy types for so long now that he usually didn't even think of them as being different from him. But tonight there was a strange energy in the car, and it definitely wasn't normal.

Nobody had said a word since they left Van Dyke's house. But the air throbbed with intensity. The three vampires were so filled with anger that Jason could feel it in his own body. The road they were on climbed up the side of a hill, twisting and turning back on itself over and over as it ascended. There were no houses, and the inky blackness seemed to press in around the headlights.

'We're almost at the top,' Zach said, his voice loud in the silence. 'Park out of sight.'

Brad nodded and pulled to the side of the narrow road. A small stand of trees blocked their view over the edge of the hill, and also blocked the car from the sight of anyone lower down on the hillside. As the guys climbed out of the car, Jason realized that his heart was beating fast. Were they in the right place? Would they really be able to find Van Dyke's captors and rescue the other vampire?

'The building we're aiming for is sort of built into the hillside, like Adam said,' Brad reminded them. 'We can check it out from behind the trees, see if there's anyone there.'

They crept over to the trees and peered down into the darkness. Jason could just make out the dark out-line of a large, low building. Only one light was on, a pale yellow security bulb over the doorway.

'It does look like a warehouse,' Jason murmured. 'But it also looks pretty empty. I think it's abandoned.'

'What do you think, Van Dyke?' Zach asked. 'Does anything look familiar?'

Van Dyke squinted into the darkness, then slowly shook his head. 'I don't know. I honestly can't remember a thing about the outside of the place.'

We should creep down the hill, get a closer look, Jason thought. *Maybe something would spark Van Dyke's memory.* But before he could even suggest it, Brad was heading for the open hillside.

'There's one way to find out if it's the right place,' he called over his shoulder.

'Yeah. Let's go.' Van Dyke took off after him, and Zach followed. Jason watched them, surprised. 'I guess we're not being stealthy,' he muttered as he went after his friends.

The hillside wasn't as steep as it looked from above, and it only took them a minute or two to reach the driveway leading to the old warehouse. A van was parked out front, but otherwise the drive was empty.

'It's quiet,' Brad commented.

'That doesn't mean there's nobody home,' Jason said.

Zach took a step forward.

Suddenly a white light snapped on with a metallic clanging sound. Jason winced as the brightness stabbed into his eyeballs. A second later, another light clanged on. The dark hillside was as bright as daylight – and Jason felt as if two fake suns were aimed right at him. Spots swam in front of his eyes.

'What the hell?' Brad complained, shading his own eyes.

'I see six of them,' Zach said quietly, staring into the lights.

Jason squinted at the building. Zach was right – there were six dark shapes silhouetted against the brightness. Six *large* dark shapes.

'This is private property!' a gruff voice called. 'Get out!'

'For an abandoned warehouse, it's got some pretty tough security,' Jason said.

'Who's in charge here?' Zach called, stepping forward. Jason had to hand it to the guy – he wasn't squinting, or covering his eyes, and he seemed completely cool and in control. Well, why not? Jason thought. *Six humans are still no match for three vampires*.

'I said *leave*. You're trespassing,' the gruff voice replied, in a thick New York accent.

'I'll leave after I talk to the man in charge,' Zach said. 'Who's running this operation?'

There were a few chuckles from the darkened figures. 'There's no operation,' the New Yorker replied. 'This is a toy warehouse. You want to buy some *Dora the Explorer* dolls?'

'They're lying,' Van Dyke whispered. 'I recognize that guy's voice, his accent. He's definitely one of the dudes who was holding me captive.'

'Good,' Zach said. 'I was getting sick of this small talk, anyway.' Zach was already striding forward, Van

110

Dyke and Brad half a step behind him.

'Forward!' the New Yorker growled, and the six security guys rushed to meet them. Even as he got ready for a fight, Jason felt shocked. If these were the people who'd taken Van Dyke captive, that meant they knew about vampires. And they obviously knew about the vampires' strength, otherwise they wouldn't have kept Van Dyke sedated. So why were they rushing in to fight not one, but *three* vampires? And for all they knew, Jason was a vampire, too.

They're crazy, Jason thought. *They think they can win by outnumbering the vampires. They don't know what they're in for.*

In the glare of the spotlights, the humans and vampires came together, and for a few seconds Jason lost track of his friends. A bunch of darkened figures grappled together. He moved closer, looking for one of the security goons to take down. His friends could handle two humans each with no problem, but Jason was determined to help them anyway.

There was a loud grunt, and the sound of fist slamming into flesh. Somebody yelled in pain, and a big guy came flying toward Jason.

He leapt out of the way just as the huge dude hit the ground, blood spraying from his mouth.

One down, Jason thought, stepping over the security

guard. He glanced down to make sure the guy wasn't going to be getting up again any time soon – and stopped, astonished.

The guy on the ground was Van Dyke.

Eleven

Jason locked eyes with Van Dyke. 'What the hell?' he gasped.

Van Dyke frowned. 'Dunno,' he grunted, pushing himself back to his feet. 'They're strong.' Shaking it off, he rushed back into the blinding lights, where Brad and Zach were still fighting with the six human guys.

Jason ran after him. Closer up, he had a better view of the humans. They were all big dudes, but none of them had weapons. They were just fighting hand to hand with the vampires.

And they were winning.

Did we get it wrong? Jason wondered. *Are these security guys vampires, too?*

But even though they were strong, none of the security men *looked* like vampires. Not one of them had the sort of glow that Zach, Brad and Van Dyke had shown earlier.

'Van Dyke,' Jason called, running into the fray. 'Are these guys . . . like you?'

Van Dyke didn't even look at him, he was too busy trading punches with a dark-haired security dude. 'No. No way,' he grunted.

Jason tried to figure out how he could best help. His friends were being pummeled.

Brad took a forearm to the jaw that snapped his head around. Before he could recover, the guy fighting him threw a punch into Brad's gut. The vampire doubled over, gasping for breath.

On the other side of Jason, Zach was trading blows with the New Yorker, who was the biggest of the humans. Zach got in a few good punches, but the big guy didn't even seem to feel them. As Jason watched, he casually backhanded Zach across the face, then followed up with a sucker punch to the side of Zach's head.

Dazed, Zach stumbled into Jason. Jason grabbed his arm to steady him, but Zach looked pretty out of it. The New Yorker was heading right for them.

Jason stepped in front of Zach and threw up his arm just in time. The New Yorker's huge fist slammed into Jason's arm with an incredible amount of force, but Jason managed to hold strong. He ducked and ran head-first at the guy's stomach, tackling him to the ground.

Jason landed on top of him and immediately

reached back to hit the guy in the face. But the New Yorker grabbed his arm before the blow even fell. He bent Jason's wrist back until Jason cried out in pain, rolling off him.

The man immediately jumped back to his feet and rushed at Zach again.

Jason took off after him. His wrist still ached, but Zach couldn't take this guy alone. Running up behind the man, Jason snaked his arm around the guy's neck, secured his hold with his other hand, and squeezed. As the New Yorker tried to pry Jason off his back, Zach pummeled his torso with punches that would've floored a normal human.

The New Yorker bellowed in rage and spun away, moving faster than Jason thought possible for such a big guy. The sheer velocity of the movement made him lose his hold on the dude's neck. The guy grabbed Jason's arm and yanked, pulling Jason off of him and sending him flying through the air.

Slam! Jason's back hit something hard and cold, and he fell to the ground, winded.

I've got to get up before he comes after me again, Jason thought. But he couldn't move. He could barely breathe. He dragged himself to a sitting position and looked up. A black van loomed above him, the metal side dented where he had slammed into it. Jason shook his head, trying to think clearly. Maybe he could use the van as cover if the New Yorker came for him.

Jason glanced back to the fight. The New Yorker was still battling it out with Zach, both of them moving so quickly that they were a blur.

He doesn't care about me, Jason realized. *He's only interested in taking down Zach.* In fact, all six humans were busy fighting Zach, Brad and Van Dyke. None of them paid any attention to Jason at all.

They must know I'm human, he thought. He wasn't a threat to them, so they weren't bothering to go after him.

But the vampires didn't seem like much of a threat to these guys, either. Whenever the New Yorker stopped hitting Zach, one of the other dudes started in. Van Dyke was on his knees, two big guys raining punches on his head.

They have to be vampires, Jason thought. How else could the dudes be pounding on his friends this way? Maybe Van Dyke had got it wrong.

Brad let out a cry of pain, snapping Jason back to attention. Human or vampire, these guys were destroying Jason's friends. He had to help them.

Jason got to his feet and waded back into the battle. One of the guys beating on Brad had his back to Jason. Jason leapt up and shot a fast kick into his kidneys. It wasn't a fair kick, but these security guys had been fighting dirty right from the start. Jason figured he and his friends were going to have to do whatever it took to get out of here alive.

The guy hit the ground, moaning in pain. Brad shot Jason a grateful look, but he was too busy fending off the other guy to do more than that. Jason took a step toward them, but another security dude suddenly blocked his path.

'Get out of our way,' the guy muttered. He placed his hands on Jason's shoulder and shoved – hard.

For the second time in about three minutes, Jason was eating dirt. His whole ribcage felt bruised from the shock of being thrown around. At least this time he'd just landed on the ground instead of slamming into a car. Jason lay there for a moment, mentally checking himself for injuries. Once his head was clear, he dragged himself to his feet and looked around. These security dudes were too much, even for the vampires.

But would they even be able to make it to their car? Things looked bad. As Jason watched, Zach went down, the New Yorker on top of him. Van Dyke's face was covered in blood, and Brad was getting punched in the stomach, over and over, while only managing to get one or two return blows in.

This is no ordinary brawl, Jason thought. *My friends are really in danger.*

And then an engine roared to life. Jason's head snapped toward the sound, and he saw the black van's headlights come on. 'What now?' he muttered.

The engine revved loudly, then the van sped into the knot of fighters. Everybody scattered.

With a cry of surprise, the New Yorker jumped out of the way. The van squealed to a stop just inches from where Zach lay.

Jason blinked into the light. Was that . . .?

'Get in!' Sienna yelled from behind the wheel. Belle sat beside her, gesturing frantically.

'Thank God,' Jason said. In a second, he was up and running toward Zach. 'Let's go! Let's go!' he called to the vampires.

Brad turned and stumbled toward the van as Jason grabbed Zach under the arms and dragged him to his feet. The security guys were already after them again. 'Van Dyke, come on!' Jason yelled.

The double doors at the back of the van opened with a *clang!* and Adam appeared, holding out a hand to Brad. The security dudes fell back as Brad got into the van, followed by Zach. Jason had to grab Van Dyke to keep him from going after the guys again, in spite of his bloody face.

'Get in the van,' Jason ordered him.

Reluctantly, Van Dyke climbed in. Jason followed, and he and Adam jerked the doors closed as Sienna tore away.

Nobody said a word as the van made its way up the winding drive to the top of the hill. Sienna pulled to the side of the road behind Brad's car, and cut the engine. The sound of crickets filled the air, and for a moment they all sat in the darkness, listening.

'Are they coming after us?' Jason asked.

'I don't hear anything,' Zach replied.

'Well, good then. Because you have super-hearing and all,' Adam joked nervously. 'So we must be safe.'

Jason threw open the back doors of the van, and they all climbed out. Sienna came around from the driver's side and slipped her arms around him. 'You OK?' she asked quietly.

'Yeah. They weren't interested in me,' Jason told her. He turned to the vampire guys. 'You three took a pretty bad beating. Everyone all right?'

Van Dyke wiped his face with his shirt. Jason was surprised to see that, once the blood was gone, he looked absolutely fine. 'We heal fast, remember? We'll be fine.'

'It might take me an hour or so,' Zach said wryly. 'That New York dude had it in for me. I'm glad you all showed up when you did.'

'What are you doing here, anyway?' Brad asked the girls.

'Sienna and I were worried about you,' Belle explained. 'Actually, we were worried about the humans. We thought you might get carried away and hurt somebody real bad. So Adam suggested that we come along ourselves and keep an eye on things.'

Jason glanced over Sienna's dark hair to see her Spider parked about twenty feet away.

'We got down to the warehouse just as you all started fighting,' Sienna said. 'We wanted to be around in case the humans needed help. But then it turned out that you were the ones who needed help. So Belle and I decided to commandeer the van to get us all out of there – fast.'

'I tried to get the girls to climb back up the hill so they'd be safe,' Adam told Jason. 'They ignored me.'

'Good thing they did,' Jason replied.

'I'll say,' Belle agreed. 'What on earth happened?'

'I'm not sure.' Zach rubbed his neck and winced. 'Those security guys weren't normal.'

'Are you absolutely positive they were human?' Jason asked. 'Because the only time I've ever been thrown around like that was when Luke Archer was doing the throwing.' The memory of fighting a bloodlusting vampire wasn't a pleasant one. But Jason couldn't help thinking about it tonight.

'Yeah, they definitely had vampire strength . . .' Brad said slowly.

'They're human,' Van Dyke declared firmly. 'They're the same guys who held me captive. Human.'

'I agree,' Zach said. 'I just didn't get any kind of a vampire sense from them. But they had the strength, and it's superhuman strength.'

'How can that be?' Sienna asked, her voice tense.

'That's what we have to find out,' Zach said. His eyes met Van Dyke's. 'Before we make our next attempt to rescue Christopher.'

Van Dyke looked as if he wanted to argue, but Brad nodded. 'Definitely. Next time we'll be prepared.' He turned to Van Dyke. 'Dude, I'm gonna stay at your place tonight, just in case they decide to show up. We'll all meet up tomorrow and devise our rescue plan.'

Slowly, Van Dyke nodded. Jason could see that he was still itching to get back there and save the vampire he'd left behind.

'Now let's get out of here,' Belle suggested. 'It creeps me out with them just down the hill.'

'What about the van?' Sienna asked. 'Should we just leave it here?'

'No, let's take it with us,' Jason replied. 'It was parked

at the warehouse. Maybe it will give us some information about the operation they've got going down there.'

'We can put it in my garage,' Van Dyke said.

'Good idea. I'll drive it back,' Zach said, heading for the driver's side. Belle climbed in beside him as Brad and Van Dyke headed for Brad's car.

Sienna slipped her arm around Jason's waist.

'Coming, Adam?' Brad called over his shoulder.

'I came with Sienna,' Adam said obliviously.

Van Dyke turned around, clapped his beefy arm over Adam's shoulders, and steered him away from Jason and Sienna.

'Oh. OK. Um . . . I'll catch a ride with these guys,' Adam said.

'Great.' Jason grinned and waved as his best friend was dragged off.

'You sure you're OK?' Sienna asked as they walked toward her car.

'Well, I'll feel better once I see your car actually start,' Jason teased her. 'What were you thinking, driving all the way up here in that piece of junk?'

'I was thinking my boyfriend was here and he could fix it,' she teased back. Then her expression grew serious. 'Stay at my house tonight, Jason. Can you? I'd feel better.'

'I thought all the girls were sleeping over,' Jason said.

'Even so, I'd rather have you there. It's been a really weird day.' Sienna leant against the car and turned toward him, pulling him against her. 'Of course, if you don't want to . . .'

'Oh, I want to.' Jason bent to brush his lips against hers, astonished to find himself so hot and bothered in spite of having been thrown against a van twenty minutes ago. 'But I'm kind of banged up. If I come home with you, will you kiss all my bruises and make them better?'

'I'll kiss whatever you want,' Sienna purred. She slipped out of his arms and got behind the wheel.

Jason climbed in next to her, his heart racing – and not from the recent fight. He could hardly wait to be alone with Sienna. The drive back to DeVere Heights seemed to take forever.

The other girls had set up camp in the living room and were busy watching *Smallville* DVDs.

'Don't mind us,' Maggie called teasingly as Sienna pulled Jason past them toward her room.

Inside, Jason pulled her to him and kissed her passionately, moving her toward the bed. They collapsed onto the soft mattress, and Jason felt his body sink into the silky sheets.

'Wow,' he murmured. 'This is really comfortable.'

'I know,' Sienna agreed, her voice sleepy.

'It's been a long day,' Jason said. His body ached from the fight, and he couldn't keep his eyes open.

'Yeah.' Sienna sounded far away.

I'm in bed with Sienna, Jason thought happily, just before he fell sound asleep.

Twelve

'We're late,' Sienna said the next day at lunchtime.

'I'm going as fast as I can. I don't have super-fast healing skills like some people,' Jason joked, making his way slowly through the hallway toward the school cafeteria. His body was still sore from last night's fight.

Sienna slowed to match him. 'Ugh, I'm so stressed,' she sighed. 'I know we all thought coming to school and acting normal was the right thing to do. But I can't think about anything except Christopher, the vampire who helped Van Dyke. Who knows what kind of experiments they could be doing on the poor guy right now.'

'I know.' Jason took her hand and squeezed. 'I think everyone is preoccupied. Adam hasn't made a single film reference all day!'

'Wow!' Sienna said with a tiny smile.

'Don't worry. We'll make a plan today and we'll rescue Christopher as soon as possible,' Jason assured her.

When they reached the cafeteria, the other vampires were all gathered around a big table in the back. Adam was on his way over, carrying a tray with a gigantic salad and a bottle of water.

'What, are you on a diet?' Jason teased him. 'Where's the pizza and Coke?'

Adam looked startled, but Sienna chuckled. 'Ignore him, Adam. Brianna probably convinced you to start eating healthy, right?'

'Um, yeah.' Adam blushed.

'Oh, I should've guessed,' Jason said. 'You guys must be pretty serious if you're letting her dictate your diet.'

'Well, I did have a taco for breakfast,' Adam defended himself. He plopped his tray onto the vampires' table and sat down. Jason and Sienna sat next to him.

'What's going on?' Sienna asked.

'Argument,' Belle told her. 'Van Dyke wants us to gather as many vampires as possible and then charge the warehouse because there's no way they could fight so many vampires at once. Zach thinks we need to sneak in and avoid another fight.'

'I'm with Zach,' Jason said. 'One fight against the freakishly strong humans was enough. And what if they called for reinforcements after last night?'

'Good point,' said Brad.

'Besides, I don't fight,' Belle put in. 'I believe in peace.'

'You just don't want to break a nail,' Van Dyke grumbled.

'I can kick your butt, Michael. Or don't you remember the locker incident from eighth grade?' Belle said sweetly.

Van Dyke flushed red, and Jason smiled. 'You'll have to tell me about that sometime,' he murmured to Sienna.

'Focus, people,' Brad commanded them. 'If we're sneaking in, that means we have to find an entrance that the security goons aren't watching.' He grabbed a pen from the table and began sketching on a napkin. 'The place was all one storey, with the lighted doorway here . . .' He drew a rough plan of the place as he talked. 'I thought I saw a bank of windows on this side—'

'But there were bars on them,' Zach put in. 'We can't get in that way.'

Brad drew little Xs over the window on his napkin blueprint.

'Let me see that pen,' Sienna said suddenly, grabbing it from him.

'Hey!' Brad protested.

Sienna ignored him. 'Where did you get this?'

'I borrowed it from Belle in English,' Brad said.

'I took it from the van last night,' Belle added. 'Why?'

'The logo looks really familiar to me,' Sienna said thoughtfully. 'Look.' She held the pen out so they could all see the logo: an H and a C intertwined in elaborate script.

'I don't recognize it,' Zach said.

'Me neither,' Jason admitted.

'Well, I do. And if it came from the van, it could give us some more information about what we're dealing with.' Sienna stood up. 'You guys keep planning. I'm going to take this to the computer room and see what I can dig up about the logo.' She gave Jason a quick kiss and took off.

Brad sighed. 'Anyone else have a pen I can borrow?'

'Don't worry about drawing the warehouse,' Adam said. 'I think I can get the actual blueprints for us.'

Everybody stared at him in surprise.

'Brianna's mom is a realtor,' Adam explained. 'And she just happens to cover commercial real estate in that area.'

'What are you saying?' Zach asked.

'Well, I mentioned the warehouse to Brianna this morning, and she says her mother brokered a deal for it last year. So I can get Brianna to look in the files, find out who bought it, and get us a copy of the schematics for the whole place.'

Brad let out a whistle. 'That would be great.'

'You can't tell Brianna why we need them, though,' Jason pointed out. 'How are you going to convince her to help?'

'I'll make up a story,' Adam said with a shrug. 'It'll be just like writing a movie script. Leave it to me.'

'Thanks, Adam,' Zach said. 'You're a good friend.' He turned to the rest of the group. 'Let's meet up at Van Dyke's place after school. Adam will bring the schematics, and we'll figure out the best way in.'

'Hey! Maybe we could tunnel in,' Van Dyke suggested. 'Like in that film, er . . . *The Great Gatsby.*'

He means The Great *Escape*, Jason thought, waiting for Adam to correct Van Dyke. But Adam didn't say anything. Jason guessed the situation was just too serious.

'Let's wait until we've seen the plans,' Zach said.

'OK,' Van Dyke agreed. 'But then those security guys better watch out, because I'm not leaving this time – not without Christopher.'

Sienna was waiting on her doorstep when Jason pulled up in the VW that evening. She'd changed out of the short skirt she wore to school, and now she had on a pair of jeans that hugged her curves and made his pulse pound. *I can't believe we fell asleep last night*, he thought ruefully. Was he ever going to get a chance to really *be* with his girlfriend?

'Thanks for the ride,' she said, climbing in next to him. 'The Spider started, but it was making that funny clanging sound.'

'That's never good.' Jason put the VW in gear and pulled back out onto the road. 'Did you find out anything about that logo on the pen?'

'Yup. Ten minutes of internet research and I had it. HemoCorp. That's what the H and the C stand for.'

'What's HemoCorp?' Jason asked.

'It's some kind of scientific think-tank. I must've seen the logo on papers in my dad's office or something. It's a subsidiary of Medi-Life, I think.'

'The big drug company?'

'Yeah, their headquarters are around here, off Mulholland Highway,' Sienna said. 'You don't think those security guys stole the van from Medi-Life, do you?'

'I think it's more likely that they stole the *pen*,' Jason said. 'But either way, we should get rid of that van as soon as possible. Because *we* definitely stole it, and even though Adam has connections with the police, I don't think we can get away with grand theft auto.'

'Let's search the van for evidence tonight, as soon as we get to Van Dyke's,' Sienna suggested. 'Then while the guys are breaking in to the warehouse tonight, the rest of us can get rid of the van somehow.'

'Sounds like a plan,' Jason replied. 'Although if there's any breaking and entering to be done, I'm going along.'

'Jason—' Sienna began.

'I'm going,' he insisted. 'I wasn't much help last night, but you never know when a spare set of fists can come in handy. I feel like I owe it to Van Dyke to help save Christopher.'

Sienna didn't look happy, but she nodded.

Jason turned the VW into Van Dyke's driveway, and they went inside. Everybody was gathered in the living room, waiting for Adam to arrive with the schematics.

'Sienna and I are going to check out the van some more,' Jason announced. 'See if Van Dyke's captors left anything behind that might give us a little information about what we're dealing with.'

'It's in the garage,' Van Dyke said. 'I meant to search it myself today, but I couldn't handle getting back inside that thing. I feel like I might explode if I don't get to Christopher soon.'

Brad laid a hand on his shoulder. 'We'll save him. Don't worry. As soon as Turnball gets here, we'll have a plan.'

Sienna led Jason through the kitchen and into Van Dyke's attached garage. Jason frowned when he saw the large dent in the side of the black van – the dent made by his body colliding with the metal. Whatever their plan was for tonight, he hoped it didn't involve a repeat of last night's brawl.

'You take the back, I'll take the front,' Sienna suggested.

Jason nodded and opened up the double doors at the back. Since it was a cargo van, it had no seats in back, just bare black floor mats. 'Shouldn't be too hard to search,' he said. 'Although I feel like I should be wearing gloves, just so I don't leave any evidence of myself behind.'

'This isn't *CSI*,' Sienna told him. 'Besides, we were all in this van last night. If there's evidence, there's evidence. I'm more interested in what those security goons left behind.'

Jason crawled around for ten minutes, pulling up the floor mats and peering at the dusty metal underneath, but he didn't find anything more interesting than a couple of paper clips and an old can of WD-40. He climbed out the back and went around to the driver's side door. 'I got nothing,' he reported.

'The cab is pretty clean, too,' Sienna said. 'There isn't even a registration in the glove compartment. But I did find this.' She handed him a small brown bottle.

'Looks like a prescription bottle,' he said.

'But there's no label,' Sienna pointed out. 'And there are no markings on the pills inside.'

Jason took off the cap and shook a couple of pills into his hand. They were dark red with no identifying marks. 'Are you sure they're not just mutant M&Ms?' he joked.

'You want to try one and find out?' Sienna challenged.

'Nope. Let's go show everyone else.' Jason pocketed the pills and helped Sienna out of the van, helping himself to a kiss along the way.

When they got back inside, the group had moved to the kitchen, where they were all studying a set of blueprints spread out on the table.

'Hey, Adam,' Jason said, surprised to see his friend there. Usually Adam would seek him out before just sitting right down with the vampire crew. But maybe he was as anxious to get down to business as the rest of them.

'Hi.' Adam shot him a smile. 'I got the plans, but we have to get them back to Brianna by tomorrow morning so she can sneak them back into the filing cabinet before her mother notices they've gone.'

'What did you tell Brianna?' Jason asked. 'Some elaborate conspiracy story?'

'Sort of,' Adam said.

'He probably told her he was researching a movie,' Belle said, giving Adam a nudge. 'Am I right?'

Adam grinned. 'You know me too well.'

'Does the file say who the warehouse was sold to?' Sienna asked.

'No, just that it was a private investor,' Adam replied. 'There wasn't even a name, just a bank account.'

'Well, you can hack into that and find out whose it is, can't you?' Zach asked.

'I tried, my man. The account was closed right after the sale last year,' Adam said. 'It's a dead end.'

Look at him getting all cosy with the vampires, Jason thought, amused. *I don't think anyone has ever called Zach Lafrenière 'my man' before.*

'Tear yourselves away from the plans for a minute,' Sienna told her friends. 'We found something in the van.'

Jason pulled out the bottle of pills and placed them on the table. 'No markings,' he said.

'But they were in the driver's seat. I think maybe they fell out of someone's pocket when they were driving,' Sienna said.

Zach frowned as he looked at the pills. 'We need to find out what these pills are,' he said. 'Sienna, can you take them to the DeVere Center and get the lab techs to analyze them? I know it's late but, given that your father practically owns the place, they should be willing to work all night if you ask them.'

'I'm on it,' Sienna said.

'I'll go with you.' Belle got up and grabbed her purse from the counter as Sienna bent to kiss Jason.

'Be careful,' Sienna whispered.

'You too,' he told her.

As she and Belle left, Van Dyke looked worried. 'Hang on, we're not waiting for the analysis before we make our rescue attempt, are we?'

'We probably should,' Zach said. 'But I'm starting to worry that Christopher may not have time for us to wait. You said he was in bad shape already, right?'

Van Dyke nodded. 'And that was two days ago,' he added.

'I say we go tonight,' Jason put in. 'We find a way in on the blueprints, and we go pull Christopher out.'

'You're going with them?' Adam cried, surprised.

'Um, yeah.' Jason raised an eyebrow. 'Aren't you?'

Adam's mouth fell open and his face paled. 'Uh . . . well . . .'

Everybody burst out laughing.

'Chill out, Turnball, nobody expects you to get involved with this,' Brad said.

'Well, *more* involved,' Erin put in.

'No, no, if I'm supposed to go, I'll go,' Adam said, his voice a mere squeak.

'Honestly, dude, I think you'd be a liability in a fight,' Van Dyke told him. 'I'd be so busy trying to protect you that I wouldn't be able to think straight.'

'I thought the point was to do this without another fight,' Maggie chided him.

'Yeah, and besides, I know how to punch,' Adam protested. 'I've seen lots of boxing movies.'

'That settles it, you're not coming,' Zach laughed. 'You can't risk getting caught breaking and entering, anyway, Adam. Your father would kill you. You've already helped us enough.'

'OK, OK, if you insist,' Adam replied in a relieved tone. 'Anyway, look, I was thinking this air vent might be the best way to go.' He pointed out a section on the north side of the warehouse schematic. 'This says the opening is two by three. Plenty of crawling room.'

'And it will take us right into the main warehouse,' Zach said. 'Good plan.'

'Let's get ready.' Brad jumped up, followed by Van Dyke.

'Erin and I will take the van out and dump it some-where. I'm thinking long-term parking at the airport — that's what they did once on *The Sopranos*. Call if there's any trouble,' Maggie said. She hugged Van Dyke. 'Don't fight.'

'We'll see,' he said grimly.

'I'm gonna get these blueprints back to Brianna,' Adam said, rolling them up. 'Jason, walk me out?'

Jason nodded and followed Adam out to the driveway where his Vespa was parked. 'Listen, I wasn't kidding in there. Are you sure you want to go along with them?' Adam asked quietly. 'I saw that fight last night, Jason. Those guys might have *killed* you if we hadn't gotten you out of there. They meant business.'

'I know,' Jason said. 'And those are the guys holding Christopher hostage. That's why we've got to save him.'

'Agreed. But maybe you should just let the vampires handle this,' Adam argued. 'They can take the beatings and be better in an hour. You can't.'

'I appreciate the concern,' Jason said honestly. 'But they're my friends. I can't let them do this alone.'

'OK.' Adam climbed onto his Vespa. 'But Jason . . . don't say I didn't warn you.'

Thirteen

'What do you think?' Brad asked. They were hiding behind the same stand of trees as last night, and the warehouse looked just the same – except that now there was a guard standing under the pale yellow security light.

'Is that a gun?' Van Dyke asked.

'I don't think so.' Zach squinted into the darkness. 'It's definitely a weapon, though.'

'Guess we scared them last night,' Van Dyke said, 'even if we didn't hurt them.'

'I only see the one guard,' Jason put in. 'As long as he doesn't notice us, it should be fine.'

'Yeah, we've been watching for fifteen minutes. If they had anyone else patrolling, we would've seen them by now,' Zach said. 'Let's move.'

They moved stealthily down the hillside. Jason could hardly believe how silent the vampires' movements were. Watching Zach and Van Dyke ahead of him, he might almost have thought they were shadows.

When they reached the driveway, Zach stopped. He pointed to the right, where the small parking area curved around the warehouse. Between the building and the steep hillside there was only a space of about twenty feet.

Jason frowned. They had to circle around that way to get to the air vent. Unfortunately, that meant crossing directly in front of the guard.

'We have to take him out,' Brad whispered. 'There's no other way.'

'Adam says that when he's writing a screenplay, the simplest solution is usually the best,' Jason whispered.

'Meaning?' Zach asked.

'Oldest trick in the book,' Jason said. 'We throw something over to the left, the guard turns to check it out, and we run by on the right.'

'Seriously?' Even in a whisper, Jason could hear the doubt in Van Dyke's voice.

'It's worth a shot,' Jason said. 'If it doesn't work, we'll try to take him down before he raises the alarm. But that's risky.'

'I agree. I'll do it,' Zach said. He glanced around, then grabbed a sizeable tree branch lying on the ground. With a simple flick of his wrist, he sent it flying so far through the air that it crashed into the warehouse at the opposite end from where they were crouched.

The sound was loud in the silence. The guard jumped, then jogged over to check it out.

'Go, go, go!' Jason whispered frantically.

They all took off running, straight past the yellow-lit door and around the corner of the building to the right. Jason flattened himself against the wall and held his breath. Five seconds . . . ten seconds . . .

'Is he coming?' Brad's whisper was so low that Jason could barely hear him.

Zach, closest to the corner, inched along the wall until he was at the end. He listened for a moment, then shook his head. 'Let's get moving.'

They moved down the building, searching for the air vent. Finally Jason shook his head in frustration. 'We should've seen it already. We're almost to the end and the schematic showed the vent right in the middle of the north side.'

'I see it,' Brad replied suddenly.

They all turned to him in surprise.

'Look up,' he added.

Jason looked. Sure enough, there was a darker square in the dark wall – *fifteen feet up* in the dark wall.

'Huh,' Van Dyke said. 'I didn't notice that on the blueprints.'

'Whatever,' Zach replied. 'We'll just have to jump up.'

'Um, guys,' Jason told them. 'Not all of us can actually jump that high. Sorry.'

'Right,' Brad said. 'I'll give you a boost.' He shot Jason a teasing grin, and Jason rolled his eyes.

'You're just afraid to go first,' he joked, putting his foot into Brad's cupped hands. Brad's version of a boost practically catapulted Jason into the air. *Sometimes these vampires don't realize their own strength*, he thought. *Or maybe Brad's just messing with me.*

'There's a grate,' he called down as quietly as possible. 'Hold me steady.' He dug his fingers underneath the metal frame and tugged with all his strength. The grate gave way with a pop, and Jason pulled it all the way off. He handed it down to Zach, who put it on the ground silently.

Jason stuck his arms into the vent and pulled himself up and inside, crawling forward so that the vampires would have room to get in behind him. He heard Brad jump up to the edge and pull himself up, then Van Dyke. Zach brought up the rear.

Jason crawled forward as quickly as possible. It wasn't easy, as the vent was smaller than Adam had thought it would be, and Jason had to pull himself along combat-style on his stomach. He hoped he wasn't going too slowly for the vampires. They could probably combat crawl with superhuman speed, too. But nobody said anything and Jason decided not to worry about it. He'd been with these guys in bad situations before, and they'd never complained.

'We're here,' he whispered back when he saw another grate in the floor of the vent up ahead. There was some dim reddish light coming through it. Jason peered at the metal up close and realized that this grate was attached on the other side. 'Piece of cake,' he muttered, pushing it down. It popped out of the vent and began to fall into the room. Jason caught it by one corner to keep it from crashing onto the floor below. He pulled the grating up into the vent and put it on the other side of the hole.

Cautiously, Jason stuck his head down through the opening. The vent was attached to the ceiling in here, and the floor was lost in darkness below. The red light came from an 'Exit' sign hanging over a doorway in the wall to the far left. *Probably the door with the guard outside*, Jason thought.

Getting down wasn't going to be fun. The air vent was too narrow to turn around in, so Jason eased himself over to the other side of the opening on his stomach, then let his feet drop through. He scooted down until his body hung from the vent with only his arms and head still inside.

'It's a long drop,' he muttered.

'I'll lower you,' Brad said. He grabbed Jason by the wrists and leant through the opening, lowering Jason another few feet down. Jason took a deep breath, nodded at Brad, then dropped. He fell through the air for a moment, then hit the concrete floor – hard. But Jason was ready for it. He went immediately into a roll, then jumped to his feet. The fall had been jarring, but nothing was broken. Still, watching as Brad, Van Dyke and Zach jumped down and landed lightly on their feet, Jason couldn't help being a tiny bit jealous of their vampire super-abilities!

Zach glanced around. 'What a dump!' he murmured.

Jason took it in. The warehouse was mostly one big room, empty except for a few trolleys for moving stock around. The only light came from the 'Exit' sign and a few windows high up in the walls that let in some moonlight from outside. A dark doorway was cut into one wall.

'Does this look familiar?' Jason asked Van Dyke, keeping his voice low.

'No,' Van Dyke said shortly. 'But I know for sure that the guys here last night were the same guys that were holding me captive. I'd know that New Yorker's voice anywhere.'

'The place is empty, though,' Jason pointed out. 'You couldn't really hold prisoners in here. You said you were in a cell, right, Van Dyke?'

Van Dyke nodded.

'Then it can't have been in here,' Zach said. 'Let's see where that door goes.' He led the way over to the darkened doorway and stepped through. Jason and the others followed. The door led to a hallway that ran the length of the warehouse and ended in another outside door marked with an 'Exit' sign.

'It's a dead end,' Brad said, frustrated.

'No, it's not.' Jason felt a thrill of excitement run through him as he pointed to the floor five feet in front of him. 'There's a trap door.'

The other guys stared at it. 'Nice work, Freeman,' Zach said quietly. 'The cells must be underground.'

Jason stalked over and tugged on the steel handle. It didn't budge. He tried again. Nothing. 'It's bolted shut,' he said. 'We didn't bring any tools.'

'Back up,' Zach said. He grabbed the handle and jerked it straight up. The entire steel door flew up, its hinges busted. Zach put it down next to his feet.

'Oh, right, you don't need tools,' Jason said wryly.

'Stairs,' Van Dyke announced, peering into the hole. 'They look pretty rickety. Go slow.' He stepped down into the darkness, Brad following him. When it was

Jason's turn, he put his foot gently on the wooden step, feeling it give way a little bit under his weight. He got down about five steps before Zach climbed in behind him, pulling the trap door back over the opening to cover their tracks.

Jason climbed down another few steps in darkness. They had flashlights with them, but everyone had agreed they were only to be used in emergencies. Flashlights were a sure way of getting noticed in the dark.

'I hear something,' Brad's voice came softly from below.

Jason listened. 'Me too,' he whispered. 'Sort of a . . . buzzing noise.'

'Right. A hum,' Van Dyke put in. 'It's coming from the bottom.'

His voice sounded strange, but in the darkness Jason couldn't see Van Dyke's face to tell if he was all right. 'Do you . . . do you recognize that sound?' he asked.

'Yeah. I think so.' Van Dyke's voice shook.

'I can't see a thing,' Brad complained.

'I'm at the bottom,' Van Dyke replied in a loud whisper. 'There's light down here.'

Brad climbed down, then Jason. As he got lower, the ambient noise became louder. When he got to the bottom, he stopped to wait for Zach. He'd been expecting a basement cut out of the rock of the hillside, something dank and rough. But the walls here were smooth concrete. And, just like Van Dyke had said, there was light coming from further down the passageway. It flickered blue and white.

'The light's coming from round the corner,' Brad said. 'That's why it doesn't shine up here.'

'Go slowly,' Zach told them. 'If they built prisoner cells down here, there are probably guards. And the buzzing sound could be a security system.'

They inched up to the end of the concrete wall, then peered around the corner. Jason drew in a breath, shocked.

It wasn't a small hallway with a couple of rough-hewn cells. It was a wide, sanitary-looking white corridor with closed steel doors on either side, fluorescent tube lighting overhead, and polished linoleum floors. The hall stretched out so far in front of them that Jason couldn't even see the end of it. He did see another corridor intersecting with it about a hundred feet away, though. The place was huge.

'What the hell?' Van Dyke asked.

'It looks like an office building,' Brad said, confused.

'An office building out of some sort of Bond movie,' Jason replied. 'Adam should be here.'

'Does this look familiar?' Zach asked Van Dyke.

'No. They had me blindfolded a lot. But that noise . . .' Van Dyke shook his head and Jason could tell he was freaked out. He shook it off and peered around. 'This place looks big. I have no idea which way to go to find Christopher.'

'Then there's only one thing to do,' Zach said. 'Start here and look behind every door until we find him.'

'That could take hours,' Jason said. 'Should we split up?'

'Could be dangerous,' Brad replied.

'Let's stick together for now,' Zach decided. He stepped out into the white hallway and moved swiftly to the first door. He peered through the window in the door and turned back. 'That's just an office. Hopefully a lot of these doors will be like that and we can rule them out quickly.'

'Yeah, because when we find the prisoner cells, it will be obvious,' Van Dyke said grimly. 'Believe me, they weren't like this. I remember it being dark all the time.'

Jason glanced into the next door window. A desk, a filing cabinet and a white board on the wall. 'Another office.'

'This door has no window,' Brad said from ten feet further down the hall. 'And it's locked.'

'That shouldn't stop us,' Zach told him, reaching for

the door handle. Before he could even touch it, the handle jerked down and the door began to open. Zach sprang away, and they all sprinted back to the dark staircase they'd come from.

Jason threw himself against the wall, then inched out slowly until he could see down the white corridor. Two men had come out of the door and were busy locking it again. They both wore crisp white lab coats, and one of them carried a clipboard. When the door was locked, they headed down the hall without even a glance toward the hall with the staircase. Jason watched until they turned left down the other hallway.

'They're gone,' Jason reported to his friends. 'They were dressed like lab technicians.'

'Maybe they were the ones doing experiments on me,' Van Dyke growled.

'Let's find Christopher.' Brad stepped back out in the corridor and they all moved quickly to the locked steel door. With a quick jerk on the handle, Brad broke the lock and pulled the door open. Inside was an examination table and a stainless steel counter, but no vampire prisoner.

'Keep moving,' Zach said. He led them back out into the corridor. The next door was on the other side of the hallway – another empty exam room. Zach went to the next door and reached for the handle. As Jason walked over to check out the one opposite, a tinny-sounding voice crackled through the air, gradually getting louder as if it was moving towards him.

'. . . eye out for intruders,' it was saying. 'Four males, possibly dangerous.'

'That's a walkie-talkie,' Jason whispered frantically to his friends. 'They know we're here!'

As he spoke, he became aware of the sound of approaching footsteps – footsteps moving in unison, as if an army unit were marching toward him.

'In here!' Zach called, yanking open his door and frantically gesturing them inside. Jason rushed in with Brad and Van Dyke, and Zach pulled the door closed behind them.

'You're stepping on my foot,' Brad complained to Van Dyke.

'Give me a break, man, this is just like a storage closet or something. There's no room,' Van Dyke grumbled.

'Quiet!' Zach hissed. He eased the door open a tiny crack, and Jason could see a sliver of the corridor. The marching feet were practically on top of them now. Jason spotted a guy dressed in black, a nasty looking crossbow clutched in his hands. Another man followed, and another, all armed with crossbows.

'Check the warehouse,' a deep voice ordered. The

three crossbow guards kept going, headed for the staircase, while a fourth big guy stepped into Jason's line of sight and stopped. He rested his crossbow on his shoulder and pulled out a walkie-talkie. 'No sightings in the office wing, Mr Norton,' he said into the walkie, his deep voice echoing in the hallway, 'but we're checking upstairs and expect to apprehend the intruders soon.'

The walkie-talkie gave a beep and another voice crackled through. 'Keep me posted.'

'Roger.' The guard holstered his walkie-talkie, gripped his crossbow, and marched off after the others.

'We must've tripped an alarm when we opened the trap door,' Zach said. 'Dammit!'

'They have crossbows,' Jason added, the memory of Tamburo's crossbow bolt flying toward him filling his mind. 'They're prepared for vampires.'

'So they know we're here, and they know what we are,' Brad said, fear creeping into his voice.

Jason nodded, trying to ignore the growing pit of terror in his own stomach. 'You guys? They have scientists, cells and guards with crossbows . . . What the hell kind of place is this?'

Fourteen

'Whatever it is. We have to move, and fast,' Zach said. 'Those guards went upstairs to search the warehouse for us, which means they'll be back.'

'That place is so empty, it will only take them two minutes to see that we're not there,' Van Dyke agreed.

'There are only two doors on this hallway we haven't checked,' Jason said. 'Then we hit an intersection with another hall.'

'Brad and I will check the door on the right,' Zach said. 'Jason and Van Dyke, get the one on the left. Then we'll turn down the new hallway to put some distance between ourselves and those guards.'

'The lab coat guys went to the left,' Jason told him.

'Then we'll follow them,' Zach said. 'Let's move.'

He shoved open the door and they all took off at a run. Van Dyke reached the last door on the left, listened for a moment to see if there was anyone inside, then grabbed the handle and pulled. Jason threw himself into the room and took a quick look around. Stainless steel counters, an empty examination table and some lightboards on the wall.

'Nothing here. Let's go,' he said, pushing past Van Dyke into the hallway.

Across the hall, Zach and Brad were exiting another door. Zach met Jason's eye and shook his head.

Without breaking stride, Jason took off for the other hallway, the three vampires right behind him. He rounded the corner at a jog and glanced around. The fluorescent lights here had a weird lavender tinge to them, but otherwise the corridor was identical to the last one – white floors and walls and a series of unmarked steel doors.

Jason rushed forward, heading for the first door. But suddenly a high-pitched shriek split the air, pulsing in a way that made Jason's head throb. There was some-thing else in the noise, too, some kind of odd tone that made him instantly nauseous. He spun around to see Zach, Brad, and Van Dyke a few steps behind him, holding their ears in pain. All three of them were doubled over, and it was obvious that they were in much worse shape than Jason.

Super-hearing equals super-painful, Jason realized. *And that weird sound is obviously meant to hurt vampires.*

He started back toward his friends just as the

shrieking sound changed to a strange metallic clang.

Jason stopped in his tracks and looked up.

The ceiling was moving. *Collapsing.*

'Look out!' Zach yelled.

Jason leapt back just as a thick steel plate dropped from the ceiling like the blade of a guillotine. He fell onto his back, gasping in shock and relief. The thing had fallen less than an inch in front of him.

Jason scrambled to his feet and stared. Where his friends had stood two seconds ago was only a blank metal wall. For a split second, his brain couldn't compute what had just happened. Then he hurled himself at the wall, pounding on it with his fists.

'Zach! Brad!' he yelled. 'Van Dyke!'

Dimly, he heard pounding on the other side. 'Freeman!' Zach called, his voice muffled by the steel door. 'We're trapped in here. There are walls on both sides.'

'I'm still free,' Jason called. 'How can I help?'

'It's all steel,' Brad answered. 'There's no way out.'

'Run, Freeman!' Zach yelled. 'You have to find Christopher.'

The high-pitched alarm was still blaring, and Jason felt his heart pounding along with it. The guards would be here any second, obviously. Jason turned and sprinted down the hall. He couldn't get caught. He was Christopher's only hope now.

I'm everybody's *only hope now*, a voice in his head whispered. Somehow, he had to find a way to rescue Christopher – and all of his friends.

'Think, Jason,' he ordered himself. He absolutely could not afford to be found. Which meant he needed to fit in here. Which meant . . . what?

Jason reached a doorway and grabbed the handle. Locked. He raced to the next one . . . it was open! He slipped inside the room and pulled the door shut. A quick scan of the room told him it was another office. Filing cabinet, desk, chair, lab coat . . . Lab coat! As soon as Jason saw the coat draped over the back of the chair, he knew what to do. Running through a secret underground facility looking like an intruder wasn't going to work.

But walking confidently down the hallway dressed as if he worked here? Well, it was worth a shot.

He snatched the lab coat and slipped it on, glancing at the ID tag clipped to the pocket. 'Bill Baldwin, hope you don't mind,' he muttered. Then he frowned, looking more closely. In the corner of the ID tag was a small logo – an H and a C, intertwined. 'HemoCorp,' Jason said, surprised. 'Guess that pen in the van wasn't stolen, after all.'

He opened the door and stepped back out into the hallway, then walked as fast as possible away from the steel wall holding his friends, his head spinning. HemoCorp ... this place belonged to HemoCorp. What had Sienna said about that company – that it was a think-tank?

He came to another intersection of corridors. Without stopping, he turned left, his mind still on HemoCorp.

It doesn't make sense, Jason thought. *Why would a think-tank have a bunch of underground offices? Why would they have giant steel doors that drop from the ceiling? Why would they kidnap and experiment on vampires?*

'I think they're a subsidiary of Medi-Life...' Sienna's voice rang in his memory.

Jason kept walking, forcing himself to think. Medi-Life was a drug company, one of the biggest and most successful. This place was huge and secret and filled with laboratory rooms, all with an obviously expensive security system. The guys guarding it were humans who seemed to have vampire strength. And in the van they'd found a pen from HemoCorp, a part of Medi-Life.

And a bottle of pills, Jason remembered suddenly. What did those pills have to do with it all? Could this entire place be funded by Medi-Life?

All of a sudden, Jason felt a surge of fear so

overwhelming that he stopped walking. Stopped even thinking. This was bigger than Van Dyke or Christopher. It was bigger than some human guys who were freakishly strong. Zach, Brad and Van Dyke hadn't just been captured by some little operation with a vendetta against vampires. They'd been taken by a huge company with seemingly unlimited resources. A company that was experimenting on vampires . . . and Jason had no idea why. But the ideas that ran through his head weren't comforting.

'Do you know what's going on?' A voice broke into Jason's thoughts.

'I heard there was some kind of break-in.' Two women in lab coats were walking toward him, speaking in hushed voices.

Jason began walking again, trying to shake off his fears. He couldn't get caught, so he had to get past these workers without arousing suspicion. He kept his eyes on the ground and walked quickly down the hall, not even glancing in their direction.

The women passed him and disappeared around the corner, and Jason breathed a sigh of relief.

He forced himself to focus. The main thing right now was to find Christopher and get him out of here. Freaking out about who was behind it all wasn't going to help anybody. For the first time, Jason took a good look around and realized that this corridor wasn't the same as the others he'd been in. This one was narrower, darker, *older*. The lights overhead were dim, and the steel doors in the wall were solid, with no windows.

The hallway felt damp, more like a basement than like the scientific labyrinth he'd been in. *Van Dyke said his cell felt cold and damp, like a warehouse*, Jason remembered. Maybe he'd looped back around under the warehouse again.

Tap, tap, tap.

Jason frowned, listening. The sound was muffled, like a hammer tapping in an underground mine.

Bang, bang, bang.

It was louder now, a little, but Jason still couldn't tell where the sound was coming from. He glanced behind him. The narrow hallway was empty.

Tap, tap, tap.

Jason hesitated, then kept walking forward. It looked as if the hall ended about fifty feet away. The hammering sound was probably just the HemoCorp people – or the Medi-Life people – doing construction on their big underground lab. Other than this hallway, everything in the place screamed 'new'.

Tap, tap, tap. Bang, bang, bang! Tap, tap, tap.

Jason stopped. That didn't really sound like

construction hammering. It sounded like a pattern – a familiar pattern.

Tap, tap, tap. Bang, bang, bang! Tap, tap, tap.

'It can't be,' Jason gasped.

Tap, tap, tap. Bang, bang, bang! Tap, tap, tap.

It was – he was sure of it – Morse Code. Just like Adam had shown him at Brad's party. Three dots, three dashes, three dots: SOS. Somebody was asking for help!

Jason veered over to the nearest steel door. He pulled on it, but it was locked. He pressed his ear against the cold metal, and waited.

Tap, tap, tap. Bang, bang, bang! Tap, tap, tap.

The sound wasn't coming from this door. Jason moved to the next one, and listened. Then the next.

Tap, tap, tap. Bang, bang, bang! Tap, tap, tap.

This time, the banging was louder, and Jason thought he could feel the tiniest reverberation in the steel of the door. He pulled on it. Locked.

'Christopher?' he called.

Silence.

'Were you banging on the door?' Jason asked.

'There's nothing you can do to me, you know. I saw *Old Boy*, so I'm down with all the torture methods you can come up with!' a voice called from inside.

Jason gaped at the closed door. That wasn't Christopher. It couldn't be – because it was Adam.

That's impossible, Jason thought. *How did they get a hold of him?* Suddenly a bolt of fear shot through him. If these people had grabbed Adam, did that mean they were going after all of Jason's friends? Could they have Sienna, too?

'Adam!' Jason yelled. 'Are you alone in there?'

'Jason?' Adam's voice called. 'Is that you? I'm alone.'

'Hang on.' Jason grabbed the door handle again and pulled with all his strength. It didn't budge. Forcing himself to calm down, he studied the door. It was thick, and made of steel, and there was no way he could kick it down. He doubted even the vampires, with their super-strength, could knock out a door like this.

A tiny, flashing light caught Jason's eye. Set into the wall next to the door was a small sensor pad. It had two lights, red and green. And the red light was flashing.

'It can't be that easy,' Jason said. He glanced down at the ID badge on his stolen lab coat. Jason flipped the badge over. There was a magnetic strip along the back. 'Bill Baldwin, let's hope you have high-security clearance.' He pressed the magnetic strip to the sensor pad on the wall.

The light switched from red to green, and the heavy door gave out a distinctive *click*.

Before Jason could even move, Adam shoved the

door open and leapt out into the hallway. He threw his arms around Jason.

'I knew you'd come!' he cried. 'I heard people talking about intruders in the hallway, and I figured it had to be you. No one else would be crazy enough to try to infiltrate a place like this!'

Jason slapped his friend on the back and released him. 'Glad I could help,' he said, smiling. 'Although I wasn't actually here for you.' He studied Adam's face. The dude looked even paler than usual, and he was obviously shaken up, in spite of his joking behavior. 'You OK? I'm glad I was able to get you out so fast. How did they catch you?'

'I was on my way to Brianna's friend's place, and she's down in one of those winding canyons, you know? So all of a sudden, I see a tree branch down over the road. Which is weird, because it hasn't rained in months and there's no wind or anything. But whatever, the branch is blocking the road. So I get out to move it, and somebody jumps me from behind.'

Jason just stared at him. 'Huh?' he asked.

'I know,' Adam said. 'What do they want with me? Listen, how long have I been here? Is Brianna OK?'

Jason frowned. 'Wait. Why were you going to Brianna's friend's house? I thought you were heading back to her mother's office with the blueprints.'

Now Adam stared at Jason. 'What blueprints?'

'The schematics. For the warehouse,' Jason said. 'Or were you meeting Brianna at her friend's?'

'No, I was going to pick her up, remember?' Adam replied. 'For the barbecue at Van Dyke's place.'

'What?' Jason felt as if his brain was filled with cotton. He simply could not understand a thing his best friend was saying. 'The barbecue was two days ago. What are you talking about?'

'Two days!' Adam cried. 'I knew it had been a while, but I didn't think it was that long.'

'*What?*' Jason asked again.

'I mean, not like in the time-flies-when-you're-having-fun sense,' Adam corrected himself. 'Because I've totally not been having fun. But they've been decent to me – they keep feeding me and all. And nobody's taken me out to experiment on me, or torture me, or whatever. The guy in the next cell ... well, it's bad. He's just whimpering constantly, like a dog with a broken leg. He's in real pain. They came a few hours ago, I think it was, and took him away somewhere. And when they opened his door I heard him screaming like he was terrified.' Adam's expression was more serious than Jason had ever seen it. 'It's horrible, Jason. We have to do something.'

Somewhere in the back of Jason's mind, he

registered what Adam was saying. A prisoner, being experimented on, in pain: it had to be Christopher.

But Jason still couldn't quite understand what Adam was talking about when he said he'd been here for two days. Or at least, his brain couldn't understand how to compute what Adam was saying. Because it would mean . . . it would mean . . .

'Are you saying that you've been locked in here since the day of Van Dyke's barbecue?' Jason asked. 'You don't know anything that's happened since then?'

'No. I mean yes. And no,' Adam said. 'I've definitely been here since the barbecue day. Why? What's happened?'

But other thoughts were rushing through Jason's head now. Bad thoughts. Terrifying thoughts. 'Adam,' he said. 'If you've been here for two days, then who gave us the blueprints for this building? Who helped us plan how to get in? And just who the hell has been with us in Malibu, pretending to be *you*?'

seemed to calm down. 'Well, at least he's only a human.' A slow, self-satisfied grin worked its way across his face. 'Besides, if Freeman tries to cause any kind of trouble, I have just the thing to keep him in line.'

Jason's heart seemed to skip a beat. What did Norton mean by that? What did he think would keep Jason 'in line'?

Sienna. The thought was instantaneous. Norton – as Adam – had seen enough of Jason and Sienna over the past few days to realize how deep their relationship went. Did he have Sienna? Had he taken her hostage, too? Jason stared at the face on the monitor, anger fighting with terror in his mind.

'But, Abell, I want him found,' Norton-Adam was saying. '*Now.*'

'Yes, sir.'

'If he's not in custody by the time I get there, I will be very unhappy. Do you understand?' Norton-Adam's voice had taken on a deadly edge, and Jason could see that Dr Abell was frightened.

'Yes. Yes, sir. I'll—' Dr Abell began. But Norton-Adam was gone.

They all stared at the blank monitor for a moment. Then Dr Abell snapped back into command. 'You heard him! Find that boy!'

The clean-suit guys all scrambled for the door.

'He's probably going for the prisoner cells, thinking we'd put the new subjects there,' one of them said.

'Or else he's coming here, to get them out of the lab,' another put in.

'Two of you go to the cells,' Dr Abell snapped. 'I want someone on guard here, too, while I get to the security room to organize new search teams.'

'We'll stay here,' Jason said quickly. 'We can work on the wiring while you take care of security, Dr Abell.'

'Good. Work fast.' Dr Abell turned to the third clean-suit guy. 'You – get up to the warehouse and get me the head of security. He's up there with the outside teams. If we don't catch that kid, I'm not taking the blame by myself.'

The four of them piled out of the room, pulling off their helmets as they went. In a matter of seconds, Jason and Adam were alone with the vampires.

'Nice move,' Adam said.

'Thanks. But we have to work fast. They're all coming back.' Jason shoved his fear for Sienna down and rushed over to Zach's tank. He studied the outside, looking for a way to open it.

'Here.' Adam reached over and pushed a small button near Zach's feet. The top panel of glass slid to the side, leaving Zach open to the air. Almost immediately, the cloud of gas escaped into the room.

Jason was glad he had the clean suit on. If that gas could subdue vampires, there was no telling what it would do to humans. Quickly, Jason undid the restraints around the vampire's wrists.

'Hang on, Zach,' he said, reaching in to pull off the tape that held the tube in Zach's mouth. 'I think this might hurt.' He grabbed the tube and pulled it as smoothly as possible out of his friend's mouth. Even so, Zach began to gag, and bloody foam formed around his lips. Finally, the end of the tube appeared, and Jason sighed in relief.

'One down,' he muttered. 'You OK, man?'

Zach didn't answer.

'He's still out of it,' Jason said. 'Open the other tanks to let that gas out. It's what keeping them dazed.'

As Adam went over and opened Brad's tank, he glanced at Jason. 'That guy – Fake Me – he said he had something to keep you in line. What does that mean?'

'He's kidnapping vampires,' Jason said. 'And he's been hanging with me for two days. He knows about me and Sienna.'

Adam gasped. 'You think he's got Sienna?'

'If he does, he's a dead man,' Jason said. 'I don't care if he has vampire strength. If he hurts her—'

'Freeman,' Zach cut in. His voice was weak, but

clear. Jason spun around to see him sitting up in the tank. 'We have to get out of here.'

'You've still got an IV in.' Jason hurried over. 'Are you OK?'

Zach nodded. 'The gas is wearing off.'

Suddenly, the outer door to the lab banged open. Jason's eyes locked with Zach's. Zach dropped back down onto his back, grabbed the feeding tube, and stuffed it back into his mouth. Jason slid the restraints over his wrists without hooking them together.

Adam picked up a clipboard and went over to Van Dyke's tank. He hit the button to open it, and then began pretending to make notes as if nothing was weird. Jason turned to face the man who had just come through the sliding door of the airlock.

It was Adam. Or rather, Norton.

'Why are the tanks open?' Norton demanded, grabbing himself a gas mask from a compartment on the wall labeled 'EMERGENCY'.

'We were getting ready to wire the subjects,' Jason told him, trying to make his voice sound deeper than usual. He kept his body turned away from Norton, hoping the guy wouldn't think to look too closely. If he managed to see through the window in Jason's hood, Norton would recognize him for sure.

But Norton wasn't interested in him. He strode over to Zach's tank and leant in to see him. 'The great Zach Lafrenière,' he said tauntingly. 'Not so special now.'

Zach ignored him, gazing at the ceiling like he was still out of it.

'I hear yours is one of the purest bloodlines,' Norton went on. 'Just imagine how rich I'm going to get, thanks to your DNA.'

Jason studied Norton as he spoke. The guy didn't look so much like Adam anymore. His nose seemed bigger, and he had heavy jowls instead of Adam's thin face.

The drug is wearing off, Jason realized. *His vampire powers are weakening.*

'I'll make millions of dollars – billions, even,' Norton was saying. 'Just for spilling your secret to the world. Don't worry, Zach, you'll be a part of it. Well, your body will, anyway. Of course, I can't say for sure whether you'll survive long enough to see humans everywhere using your powers . . .'

If his appearance is slipping, then maybe his super-strength is slipping, too, Jason thought. *He's alone in the lab. Now's my chance. Maybe I can take him.*

He inched closer to Norton, working his way around the tank so he could reach the guy.

'Tell you what, I'll show you what it's like,' Norton

said, still taunting Zach. He reached into his pocket and pulled out a bottle. He popped the top, opened his mouth, and shook two red pills onto his tongue.

Those are the same as the pills from the van, Jason realized.

Before Jason could move, Norton began to transform. His nose shrunk. The jowls disappeared. The muscles of his face contracted until he was a carbon copy of Adam once again. 'This is a neat trick,' Norton told Zach. 'I don't know why you vampires don't use it more often. With different faces, you could get away with so much! Whatever you wanted to do, you could do. When this is all over, maybe I'll make myself look like you for a while. Might be a good way to lure your parents in to the lab.'

Jason saw a flicker of anger in Zach's eyes. He hoped his friend would be able to hold it together and not reveal that he was free. Norton's vampire skills were obviously back on. There was no chance Jason could beat him in a fight now. If the security guards at the warehouse were anything to go by, right now Jason would have a better chance taking on Floyd Mayweather and Oscar De La Hoya simultaneously than he would Norton after a dose of vampire-ness.

Still, Zach wasn't entirely restrained anymore. Maybe Jason could attack Norton and Zach could help.

But it was risky. He had no idea how weak Zach still was from the gas.

'Mr Norton!' a voice blared from the walkie-talkie strapped to Norton's belt. 'Are you there, sir?'

'Yes.' Norton turned away from Zach and spoke into the walkie. 'Is the complex shut down?'

'Yes, sir. We're on lockdown,' replied the unmistakable voice of the New Yorker. 'But our guest is here, and Dr Abell told her you were in the lab. She's on the way to you now, sir. And she's angry.'

'Dammit!' Norton barked. 'Send security to this lab, now.'

The outer door opened, and a tall figure strode over to the airlock. When the glass door slid back, Jason thought he might be hallucinating from all the gas. He had to be.

Because striding through the doorway, looking as glamorous – and as dangerous – as ever, was his Aunt Bianca.

Seventeen

Jason gaped at his aunt in astonishment. What on earth was she doing here?

Bianca's eyes flashed with anger, and she stalked over to Norton without even bothering to reach for a gas mask. 'What is the meaning of this?' she yelled, getting right in his face. 'How *dare* you use these vampires in your experiments!' She gestured around to the incubator tanks, specifically Zach's. 'That is a Lafrenière, for God's sake. I specifically told you he was off limits. In fact I told you *none* of these kids was to be used for experimentation. Release them this instant!'

Norton had backed off when Bianca first walked in, but now that she was screaming at him, he straightened up and advanced on her. 'I'm not releasing them now or ever,' he snapped. 'And you'd better start watching your tongue if you know what's good for you.'

Jason felt Zach's eyes on him, and Adam's. But he couldn't tear his gaze away from his aunt. He hadn't seen her since she'd tried to get Dani's ex-boyfriend to transform Dani into a vampire. His aunt was going insane as a result of her own transformation years ago, and in his mind Jason had pictured her getting smaller and thinner and, well, less powerful. But Bianca seemed as tall and strong as ever, her long dark hair cascading around her face and her deep-blue eyes practically glowing with fury.

'You little ingrate!' she growled, not backing off an inch as Norton approached. 'You'd still be languishing in some stupid think-tank if not for me.'

'Well, I'm not,' Norton sneered. 'And I'm through taking orders from you, Bianca. If you want a cure for your transformation sickness, you'd better learn to shut up and start doing as you're told.'

The outer door banged open and two big security guards appeared, armed with crossbows.

Bianca's eyes widened in surprise. 'I'll have you replaced in a heartbeat, Norton,' she snapped.

'Don't you get it? You have no power anymore,' Norton taunted her. 'You already gave me all your information — about vampires, about the purest bloodlines and where to find them. Your knowledge was your only value to me. And now that I have it, you're of no further use.'

Jason saw his aunt's shoulders began to sag a little.

He got the feeling that she hadn't realized any of that until now.

'In fact, if you weren't tainted by your disease, I would stick you in a tank and harvest *your* blood, too,' Norton said.

'We had a deal,' Bianca cried. 'I gave you that information in return for a cure. It was a *deal*!'

'Sure it was.' Norton chuckled. 'And now I'm changing the terms of the deal. So keep this in mind: if I decide to devote any of HemoCorp's resources to finding a cure for you, it will be because I want to, not because I have to.'

Bianca gathered herself and lifted her head. 'Those little pills are making you pretty brave, Norton,' she said. 'But my husband gave me some of the oldest and strongest vampire blood in existence when he transformed me. I'm one of the most powerful vampires you'll ever meet. I could snap you like a twig – right now!'

Norton chuckled and lazily gestured to the security guards at the door. One of them lowered his crossbow, taking aim at Bianca. 'Bianca, you really need to calm down,' Norton said reasonably. 'You know your transformation sickness makes you . . . unstable.'

'How dare you—' Bianca began.

'And besides, your nephew wouldn't live very long if

you snapped me like a twig,' Norton continued. 'Or didn't you know that Jason broke in here along with these three?' He gestured to Zach, Brad, and Van Dyke.

'Jason?' All at once, Bianca's bravado vanished and she actually seemed to shrink in front of Jason's eyes.

'He's in the complex. It's only a matter of time until we find him,' Norton said. 'If you want him to get out of here alive, you'll stop getting in my way.' He gestured to his men, and they stepped forward, placing themselves on either side of Bianca.

'Where are we going?' Bianca asked quietly.

'To the security center. I'm sure you'd like to watch as we take down your nephew.' Norton glanced over his shoulder at Jason and Adam. 'You two, get those vampires wired. I'll be back.'

Jason was too stunned to speak.

'Yes, sir, Mr Norton,' Adam called, his voice squeaking.

The airlock door slid closed behind Norton and Bianca, and a second later the outer door closed too. They were alone again.

'Jason—' Adam started.

'We've got to move,' Jason cut him off. He turned to Zach and found him already sitting back up, spitting out the feeding tube he'd shoved in his mouth. Zach flicked off the wrist restraints and started working on his ankle straps.

'You need help with that IV?' Jason asked.

'No,' Zach grunted. He grabbed the IV needle and jerked it out of his arm with a grimace. 'I'm good.'

Jason rushed over to Brad's tank, while Adam went to Van Dyke. Both vampires were awake. Jason untaped the tube from Brad's mouth and prepared to pull it out. 'Sorry,' he muttered, then he pulled.

Brad coughed and retched as the tube came out. 'Man, that sucked,' he finally sputtered.

'How long have you been conscious?' Jason asked.

'Long enough to watch Turnball turn into somebody else and back,' Brad muttered.

'We weren't really *un*conscious,' Zach explained, climbing out of his tank. 'Just zonked by that gas. As soon as you released it, the effects began to wear off.'

'Yeah. I heard everything that was happening,' Brad agreed, yanking out his IV as soon as Jason freed his wrists. 'By the time your aunt got here, I was just pretending to be woozy.'

'What the hell, dudes?' Van Dyke said, climbing from his tank with Adam's help. 'What's Bianca doing in league with that guy?'

'She's lost her mind,' Zach said grimly. 'There's no telling what she might do. But I have to say, I never thought she'd turn on other vampires.'

'Me neither,' Jason said sadly. 'I guess she thought Norton could help her overcome the madness.'

'Christopher!' Van Dyke cried, peering into the last incubator tank. 'Is he alive?'

'I don't know,' Jason said. 'But they didn't have the tank closed, so he's not being gassed anymore.'

Van Dyke reached in and pulled out Christopher's IV. 'Maybe it's just some kind of drug,' he said. 'They talked about putting us in comas.' He pulled out the feeding tube, then began yanking all the other tubes out of Christopher's body.

'Hey, go easy,' Jason said.

'No time,' Van Dyke grunted. 'We've got to get him out of here. He'll heal himself.'

'How do we get out?' Zach asked. 'Obviously the warehouse exit is being watched.'

'Yeah, but I've got a plan,' Jason said.

'You do?' Adam asked in surprise.

'Yup. Let's go.' Jason opened the sliding glass door and stepped into the airlock, pulling off the clean-suit helmet. Adam followed him.

'Turnball,' Brad said. 'That is the real you, right?'

'I certainly hope so,' Adam replied.

'Well, what are you doing here?' Brad asked.

'Long story,' Adam told him. 'And thanks for not

noticing that Evil McNasty was impersonating me for two days.'

'That's definitely the real Adam,' Brad said happily.

'He's awake!' Van Dyke suddenly called from the lab. He held Christopher under the arms and helped him sit up. 'You hurt, man?'

'I'll live,' Christopher croaked.

Jason couldn't believe it. The dude looked pale and weak and generally awful, but the fact that he was even conscious and talking was astonishing, given the state he'd been in just two minutes before.

'Is there anyone else in the cells?' Zach asked him. 'Any other prisoners?'

'Just some funny guy who was next to me,' Christopher said.

'That was me,' Adam told him.

'Then there's nobody else. Dr Abell told me I'd lived twice as long as any of the other vampires he worked on.' Christopher grimaced as Van Dyke helped him climb out of the tank. 'I think it's gonna take me a while to recover from this.'

'So what's the plan?' Zach asked Jason.

'Yeah, because Norton will be back any minute, and the guys who went to check on the prisoner cells are going to notice that I'm gone pretty soon,' Adam said. 'Any minute now, a bunch of guards are going to come rushing in here like Storm Troopers – and by the look of this place, they might even *have* Storm Troopers!'

'Well, good, because my plan is basically from *Star Wars*,' Jason replied. 'Adam, you and I are going to act like bad guys escorting our vampire prisoners to another part of the complex.'

'Nice. Episode Four, Han and Luke pretend Chewie's their prisoner,' Adam said.

'You two better have an *actual* plan,' Brad cut in.

'Look, we've all seen Norton, right?' Jason said. 'He looks like Adam.'

'Yeah. We get that,' Van Dyke replied. 'So?'

'So if he looks like Adam, Adam looks like him,' Jason said.

'Genius.' Zach nodded. 'Adam can pose as Norton and all the jerks who work here will listen to him because they'll think he's their boss.'

'Right. But I need some kind of disguise,' Jason said. 'I can't go walking all over in a clean suit. Adam, you have to lure a guard in here.'

'No problem. I bet this place is crawling with security right now.' Adam strode over to the door, pulled it open, and stepped out into the hallway, holding the door with one hand. 'You!' he yelled. 'I've got Jason Freeman in here. Call off the search, then get in here and help me.'

He stepped back inside, letting the door close.

'Did he buy it?' Jason asked.

'I don't know. I figured Norton's not the kind of guy who waits around to see if people are obeying him,' Adam said. 'If he shows up, we'll know he bought it.'

Two seconds later, the door opened and a security guard stepped in. 'I've cancelled the alert, Mr Norton. Where is . . . ?' his voice trailed off when he saw Jason and the vampires standing in front of him.

'I'm right here,' Jason said, flattening the guy with a punch to the jaw.

The dude jumped right back up, aiming his weapon at Jason, but Brad was too fast for him. He grabbed the crossbow out of the guy's hand and turned it until the point of the bolt was at his throat.

The guard froze, and Zach and Van Dyke grabbed his arms. Jason was about to clock him again, when someone got there before him.

Christopher.

The injured vampire had found a surge of desperate energy from somewhere, and had latched onto the guard like a leech, his teeth going straight for the man's neck.

Jason hesitated a moment, reminding himself that Christopher needed the boost, however tough it was to watch. After the vampire had taken four or five loud gulps, Jason shot Zach a look.

Zach nodded back as he prised Christopher off the guard, who had that blissful, drunken look of a human who had just been fed on.

'That's enough,' Zach told him. 'We have to get moving.'

'I need his uniform,' Jason said.

'You heard him,' Adam told the guard. 'Strip.'

The guard was so out of it, he obeyed Adam's command without complaint. When the guy had taken off his dark-blue jacket and pants, Brad and Zach dragged him over to the incubator tanks and made him climb inside. They taped his mouth shut with the medical tape and tied his hands and feet with the restraints.

Jason took off the clean suit and put on the guard's uniform. 'Let's go,' he said.

'You need the crossbow,' Zach said, handing it to him.

Jason took it reluctantly. He'd been shot with a crossbow. He didn't really want to touch one, ever. But Zach was right. He needed it to look like a real guard.

'Everybody look beat,' Jason instructed the vampires. 'As if you're prisoners and you're totally unable to escape from us.'

'No problem,' Christopher said, leaning on Van Dyke for support. Though he was looking a little stronger, he was still a long way off full strength. But then, he wasn't a Malibu vampire.

'They have motorized supply carts,' Jason remembered. 'If we pass one, our fake Mr Norton can commandeer it to carry the disabled prisoner.'

'Will do,' Adam promised.

Just as Jason reached for the door handle, something vibrated against his side. He jumped, startled. It took him a moment to realize it was his cell phone. He'd been so consumed by events down here in the complex that he'd practically forgotten about the world outside.

He pulled out the phone and checked the ID. 'It's Sienna,' he told the others, hitting the 'Talk' button. 'Are you OK?' he asked her.

'Yes. Are you?' The sound of her husky voice instantly made him feel better.

'We're having some trouble. This thing is bigger than we realized,' he told her.

'I know. Jason, the DeVere lab analyzed those red pills. You won't believe it—'

'They give humans vampire strength and vampire powers,' Jason said. 'I know. I've seen them in action.'

'Oh.' Sienna sounded confused.

'They work really well,' Jason told her. 'They let the

head of this operation shape shift to look like Adam. He set us all up.'

'*What?*' Sienna cried.

'Don't worry, the real Adam is here,' Jason assured her, smiling at Adam as he spoke. But Adam wasn't looking at him. He was staring at something on the inside of the door. Staring intently.

'Hang on,' Jason told Sienna. 'What's up, Adam?'

'This is a floor plan. Evacuation routes and alarm system status and all that,' Adam said. 'Look at it.'

Jason did. Zach looked over his shoulder. The thing was like a big computerized map of the complex, with temperature readings, blinking lights to indicate working alarms, and information readouts on laboratory conditions in all the rooms.

'This lab must be the nerve center,' Zach said. 'From here, you can see what's going on everywhere else and keep track of all the experiments.'

'Which is pretty damn cool,' Adam said. 'But that's not what I'm interested in. Look. This is the warehouse,' Adam pointed to it on the floor plan, 'so these must be the hallways we're in right now. They're like tunnels that burrow under the hill.'

Jason nodded.

'This place is huge,' Zach said. 'These tunnels – hallways, whatever – seem to go on forever.'

'No, they have an end,' Adam replied. 'Right here, in this building.' He pointed to one end of the floor plan, as far from their location as could be.

Jason frowned. 'A building? But the warehouse was in the middle of nowhere.'

'The tunnels go on for miles,' Zach said. 'And they go under the hills. That building, on the outside, is nowhere near the warehouse. They're just connected underground.'

'Connected *secretly*,' Adam added.

'Where is that building?' Zach asked.

But Jason had a sick feeling that he already knew the answer. 'It's on Mulholland Highway,' he said quietly. 'It's the headquarters of Medi-Life.'

Eighteen

'Oh, my God,' Adam said. 'You're right.'

'Oh, my God,' Sienna simultaneously gasped over the phone. 'Medi-Life?'

'They're behind this whole thing,' Jason told her. 'Remember the HemoCorp pen you found? Well, their logo is all over the place here. And HemoCorp is owned by Medi-Life.'

'Jason,' Sienna said. 'This is really, really bad.'

'I know. They've got so much money that this place is rigged like a maximum-security prison. It's going to be hard to get out,' Jason said.

'No, I mean it's bad because of the red pills,' Sienna explained. 'If it's Medi-Life developing this drug ... well, it means they're planning to distribute it somehow. I bet the military would pay big bucks for a pill that turned regular people into super-soldiers.'

'Not to mention what people would pay on the black market,' Jason muttered. 'Mr Norton, the big cheese, is already talking about the billions of dollars he's going to make.'

'That's not the worst of it,' Sienna went on. 'The DeVere researchers said the pills are unstable. The formula breaks down unpredictably, and the side effects on any humans taking them could be fatal.'

'Well, I wish they were fatal sooner,' Jason said. 'I'd really like it if Norton toppled over right about now.'

'Jason, you guys have to get out of there,' Sienna said.

'I'm on it!' Jason replied, then a thought struck him. 'I wonder if they're storing the drug here or someplace else . . .'

'What's going on?' Zach demanded.

Jason quickly filled him in on Sienna's discovery. 'Even if we get out of here alive, we'll be leaving these goons with stockpiles of a dangerous drug,' Jason concluded.

'But if we could get rid of it, we'd be setting their research back by months!' Adam put in.

Jason turned to Christopher. 'Did you hear anything about the pills? Where they might be keeping them?'

'No. Sorry.' Christopher shook his head.

'Jason,' Sienna said. 'The researchers here say it's easy to destroy the drug . . .'

'Excellent! But, how?' Jason asked.

He heard Sienna talking to someone on her end of the phone. 'They say it's very delicate,' she finally told him. 'The active ingredient needs to be kept at around room temperature. If you can expose the pills to warm temperatures, the active ingredient will break down, and the drugs will be ruined.'

'OK, so we just have to turn up the heat,' Jason said. 'But I still don't know how to find it.'

'I do,' Adam put in.

Jason looked at his best friend quizzically.

'Temperature readings.' Adam pointed to the computerized floor plan.

'Yes! Find someplace that's cold,' Jason told him. 'And that looks big enough to store a bunch of medicine.'

'Belle and I are going to head over to the warehouse right now,' Sienna said. 'It sounds like you guys need help.'

'No!' Jason cried. He turned away while Adam and Zach studied the floor plan. 'Don't go to the warehouse. They'll be waiting for you and they'll grab you both.'

'OK, then, where should we meet you?'

Jason thought about it. 'At the Medi-Life headquarters. This whole place is a big, secret lab. I doubt the regular people who work in the Medi-Life building know anything about it. So if we can get there, we might be able to get out. Can Belle's car take all of us?'

'Yeah, we took her parents' Escalade,' Sienna said, confusion in her voice. 'But I don't understand. You're just going to walk out the front door?'

'If the plan works, yes. A very public exit could be our only chance.' Jason took a deep breath. 'Be careful. I love you.'

'You too.' Sienna's voice shook a little. 'I'll see you soon.'

'Let's hope so,' Jason muttered as he stuck his phone back in his pocket.

'We got it,' Adam reported. 'There's a room two hall-ways from here. It's the only room on the whole corridor, and the temperature is a steady thirty degrees.'

'Refrigerated.' Jason grinned. 'Is it on our way to the Medi-Life building?'

'Yup.' Adam pulled open the door. 'Let's go.'

The hallway was empty when they stepped out, but Jason could hear voices calling to one another from somewhere nearby. 'This way – fast.' He gestured to the right, where the hall intersected another hall.

But the vampires couldn't go very fast. Christopher had to be supported by both Van Dyke and Brad in order to even walk.

'We need to find carts,' Jason told Adam.

'I'm on it.' Adam turned onto the next hall and spotted a maintenance man. 'You!' he yelled. 'Two carts, pronto. I need them for the prisoners.'

The maintenance guy jumped, then turned and raced down the hall. 'Right away, Mr Norton!' he called over his shoulder.

'Stay here and wait for the carts,' Jason told his friends. 'I'm going to find that storage room and turn up the heat.'

He jogged away from the group and turned back onto the original hallway. The room they'd seen on the floor plan was two corridors up. Jason slowed as he passed a man in a lab suit rushing the other way, then sped up again until he reached the second corridor.

This place was deserted. The corridor was short, a dead end. And sure enough, there was only one door. Jason pulled Bill Baldwin's ID out of his pocket. 'Tell me you had drug access, Bill,' he whispered. Holding his breath, he swiped the card. The door clicked open.

A rush of relief flooded Jason, and he smiled. Inside, the room was cold and dark, and Jason could sense that it was a big place. Luckily, the temperature controls were right inside the doorway, protected by a plastic covering.

'Finally, something that's easy,' Jason murmured. He

smashed the plastic with his fist, then hit the red 'Up' arrow to raise the temperature. He pushed it to the maximum: eighty degrees. Then he hit 'Enter'.

And an alarm went off.

'Damn it!' Jason looked up – red lights were flashing over the doorway, and bells were clanging through the hallway, echoing up and down the other corridors.

Jason slammed the door, then grabbed the crossbow bolt from his weapon and stabbed it into the sensor pad, scratching and tearing at it until there was no way anybody could use it to unlock the door and turn down the thermostat.

Then he ran. Back to the main corridor, down to the first intersection, and over to his friends. They had two motorized carts and were just settling Christopher onto the back of one of them.

'Something you want to tell us?' Adam asked as Jason ran up.

'Yeah. It's time to go.' Jason jumped onto the cart with Christopher and Van Dyke, spun the little wheel, and hit the gas. The thing shot off down the hall. Adam leapt behind the wheel of the second cart while Zach and Brad jumped into the back.

The maintenance man watched, baffled, as Adam sped away with a wave.

Jason reached the end of the hallway and took a

right, keeping an image of the floor plans in his mind. 'This corridor should lead us straight to the Medi-Life building,' he told the vampires, hitting the gas until they were at maximum speed.

'When?' Van Dyke asked, peering ahead. The hallway vanished into the distance, no end in sight.

'I don't know. I think it's a couple of miles,' Jason said.

He heard Adam's cart behind him, picking up speed. After a minute or two, the sounds of the alarm behind them began to fade. There were no more doors, just smooth white walls. This section was clearly just a connector to the main building, not part of the HemoCorp complex anymore.

'We might make it,' Jason said. 'This might actually work!'

Just then, two guards appeared about fifty yards ahead, standing at attention.

'Oh, no,' Adam moaned. 'A security checkpoint! Meaning, that's two guys who could potentially go Bruce Banner on our asses. Look sharp, folks.'

Jason slammed on the brakes, squealing to a stop just a few feet from the men.

Adam's cart crashed into his, pushing him further toward them.

The guards both lifted their crossbows. 'This

hallway is off limits,' one of them growled. 'Orders from Mr Norton.'

Adam jumped off his cart, walked right up to the bigger guy and swatted the crossbow out of the way. 'We've got a situation in the complex,' he said. 'Don't you hear the alarms? Get back there and check it out while I escort the test subjects to a secure area.'

The two guards stared at him for a second as the alarms blared dimly in the distance.

'Go!' Adam yelled.

They took off at a run down the long white corridor. Jason grinned at Adam, raising his eyebrows.

'I could get used to being in charge,' Adam joked, climbing back on to his cart. 'For anyone who wasn't paying attention, I was channeling James Caan from *Godfather* one, just without the hammy New York accent. But even *you* guys must have known that, right?' Adam read the look on all their faces. He sighed. 'Not the right time, I guess.'

Jason hit the gas again, and they sped on.

'I see something,' Van Dyke said a minute later.

Jason squinted into the whiteness. 'Yeah,' he agreed. There was something silver up ahead.

After another minute it became clear: silver doors. Silver *elevator* doors.

'We're here,' Adam cheered from the other cart. 'The

corridor ends at the elevators. They must lead up to the main Medi-Life building.'

They pulled the carts to a stop, and Jason jumped off and hit the 'Up' button on the elevators. The others helped Christopher off the cart, practically lifting him into the air and setting him on his feet. Jason bit his lip. The guy was in really bad shape.

Sienna and Belle are coming with a car, he thought. *Let's just hope they get here in time.*

With a soft buzz, the elevator arrived. Jason half-expected Norton to jump out of the opening doors, but nothing happened. It was just a regular elevator. They all piled in, and Jason pushed the button that said 'Lobby'.

The elevator shot up with a *whoosh* . . . and kept on going.

'How far underground are we?' Zach asked.

Adam shrugged. 'If the tunnel goes through the hills, there's no telling how deep it is. The Medi-Life building is at the top of the hill.'

Finally, the doors opened and they all stepped out into a huge marble lobby. The ceiling over the lobby was made of glass, letting in the pale light of early morning. Jason blinked, staring up at the blue California sky. Had they really been down in the HemoCorp complex all night?

'This is surreal,' Brad muttered, glancing around at the corporate lobby. Sunlight glinted off a waterfall along the back wall, the smell of fresh coffee wafted over from a fully stocked breakfast stand, and polished-looking workers were making their way in for the day.

Jason nodded. It was bizarre to come from the hi-tech, nightmarish vampire experimentation labs, up here to normality, all just by taking an elevator.

Judging from the looks they were getting, the people on their way to work found it pretty bizarre to see a bunch of exhausted teenage guys and a security guard with a crossbow, too. Jason pulled out his cell and speed-dialled Sienna.

'Where are you?' he asked when she picked up.

'About half a mile from Medi-Life,' she reported. 'We'll be there soon.'

'I need you to get to the front entrance. Just pull as close to the doors as you can,' Jason told her. 'Christopher won't be able to make it much farther than that.'

He hung up and they started across the lobby toward freedom. Jason could feel the tension melting out of his body. They were nearly out, and surely nobody would dare to stop them in a public place like this!

He glanced over at Van Dyke and Brad, supporting Christopher. 'Will he be OK?' he asked Zach.

Zach nodded. 'We'll keep him here in Malibu until he's fully healed.'

Jason looked at the bank of doors ahead, leading out to the parking lot. No sight had ever seemed so beautiful to him.

'Freeze!' yelled a deep voice. 'Stay right where you are!'

Suddenly, about eight guys with crossbows rushed the lobby, lining themselves up in front of the doors. In the center was the big New Yorker they'd fought at the warehouse. Jason and his friends stopped walking.

'You idiots,' someone said from behind them. 'Did you actually think you could escape when I have the entire place under constant surveillance?'

Jason turned to find Norton-Adam approaching them from the elevators, Bianca and Dr Abell behind him.

'You're scaring the Medi-Life employees,' Zach said smoothly. He nodded toward the scandalized people in suits who had gathered around to watch.

Norton turned to them. 'This is a security procedure drill,' he announced. 'Please go to your offices and remain there until I give further instructions.'

Murmuring in confusion, the workers all headed for

the elevators or for doors to the hallways leading off the lobby. Suddenly one of the front doors opened and a girl in a business suit rushed in, not even seeming to notice the guys with crossbows.

'Close the entrance!' Norton snapped. 'Direct new arrivals to the side door.' One of the guards rushed outside to do it.

But Jason was still watching the girl in the suit.

So was Adam. 'Brianna?' he gasped.

The girl stopped and looked up. It was definitely Brianna. Her face paled as she looked from Adam to Norton and back. But she wasn't surprised, Jason noticed. It was as if she'd known all along that there were two Adams.

'Of course!' Adam murmured. 'She set me up! She asked me to drive out to get her, and that's when I was ambushed.'

'I guess she's been working for Norton all along,' Jason said quietly.

'Take the subjects back down to the complex,' Norton ordered the guards.

Four of the guys started forward, crossbows up. Jason felt a wave of exhaustion. They'd already managed to escape so many times in the past few hours. How were they ever going to pull it off again?

Suddenly, Adam stepped in front of the guards.

'You morons!' he shouted. 'Don't listen to him. Don't you even know who you're working for? That's Adam Turnball. *I'm* Mr Norton.'

Nineteen

The guards hesitated, confused, letting their weapons drop a little.

'Do you think some *kid* would be able to make off with four vampires?' Adam asked, his voice dripping sarcasm. 'I should have you all replaced by people with brains.'

The guards looked doubtful, and one of them raised his crossbow again. But he didn't seem entirely sure which version of Adam to point it at.

'Listen to him,' Bianca cried suddenly. Jason shot a look at his aunt. She was gazing at him, a pleading expression on her face.

She's sorry, he realized. *She wants me to forgive her.* For a brief moment, she looked so much like his old, cool Aunt Bianca that a lump formed in Jason's throat. But there was no time to get emotional right now.

'*That's* Mr Norton,' Bianca said, pointing at Adam. 'He's your boss. The other one has been holding me hostage all this time. He wanted to use me as a bargaining chip to get his friends back.'

'How dare you!' Norton roared.

But Bianca's trick had worked. The guards lowered their crossbows, totally confused. They glanced back and forth between the two Nortons – or the two Adams.

'I'm sorry, sir,' said the New Yorker, addressing both of them. 'But we have no idea which is the real you.'

'I'm the real me,' Adam said, brimming with confidence now. 'Thank you for clarifying things, Bianca.' He stared the New Yorker straight in the eye. 'Now, escort the real Adam Turnball back to his cell.'

'I've had enough of this.' Norton strode forward angrily. Some of the guards aimed their weapons at him.

This is working perfectly, Jason thought, shooting his friend a grateful look. He took advantage of the guards' confusion to inch toward the doors. Zach, Brad, Van Dyke and Christopher took the hint and moved that way, too.

Norton stopped, staring aghast at his own guards pointing crossbows at him. 'The impostor is right about one thing,' he snarled. 'I should replace you all!'

'Are you calling *me* an impostor?' Adam snapped.

'Yes.' Norton turned to face him, and the two

versions of Adam glared at each other – until one of them began to change. As Jason watched, Norton's nose grew longer, his cheeks heftier. His ears went from sticking out to drooping. His eyes developed bags underneath them, and his entire body seemed to thicken. In a matter of seconds, he was a middle-aged man.

Bianca turned to Jason. 'Run!' she yelled.

Jason ran, barreling through two of the guards to open the door and hold it for his friends. Zach sped through, but Brad and Van Dyke were moving more slowly as they helped Christopher.

By the time they reached the door, the guards had all recovered from their confusion and were aiming their crossbows at the fugitives.

'No!' Norton yelled. 'We need the vampires alive. Shoot for their legs.'

A crossbow bolt flew at Brad's thigh.

Jason jumped for him, pushing him out of the way just as the metal bolt sliced through the air and hit the glass door. The door shattered, showering little cubes of safety glass across the floor.

'Run! Go! Go!' Jason yelled, pushing the four vampires ahead of him. They were all outside now.

Jason turned to find Adam. His friend had skirted the guards to the back, and he was sprinting for a door at the opposite end of the entrance from Jason.

'Jason, get out of here,' Bianca called. She was heading his way, fending off a guard who had her by the arm.

Outside, Jason heard the squeal of brakes and saw Belle's car jump the curb and skid to a stop on the sidewalk in front of the building. Brad and Van Dyke dragged Christopher toward the car.

'Aunt Bianca!' Jason called, turning back. But he'd lost sight of her in the press of guards.

'Kill the humans!' Norton commanded. 'Stop the vampires!'

The New Yorker looked right at Jason and aimed his crossbow at his chest. Jason stood for a second, paralyzed, his shoulder aching where Tamburo's crossbow bolt had almost killed him several months before.

Time seemed to slow down as the New Yorker shot his weapon.

Jason watched in sick fascination as the deadly bolt flew toward him. *It's not going to hit my shoulder this time*, he realized. *It's going to hit my heart.*

He was moving, he knew. He was diving out of the way. But it was too late. The bolt was coming for him. It was about to hit him—

And then Bianca was in front of Jason, blocking his

view of the crossbow bolt. There was a confusion of dark hair flying, a strange sound from Bianca like the air being let out of a tire, and her body slammed against his.

Then suddenly everything sped up again, and Jason was falling with Aunt Bianca on top of him. He landed on the sidewalk outside the door, and his aunt rolled to the side. A crossbow bolt was sticking out of her chest.

'Aunt Bianca!' Jason cried. He grabbed her shoulders, trying to ignore the way her head flopped to the side. 'Aunt Bianca!'

'Freeman.' Zach was at his side. 'We have to go.'

'My aunt . . .' Jason couldn't stop staring at her face. Her eyes were open, staring. Her lips were pale.

'She's gone. Leave her.' Zach pulled at his arm, but Jason shoved him away.

'Jason.' Now Adam was there, too. 'We have to go. Right now. Come on!'

Jason glanced up at his best friend. Adam's eyes looked haunted, but his face was determined.

'I can't just leave her.' But Jason was up and moving; somehow he was running, with Adam holding one arm and Zach holding the other.

In front of them, Belle's car door was open. Van Dyke and Christopher were already in the far back row. Zach shoved Jason in, and Brad pulled him across the seat so Adam and Zach could climb in behind him.

Belle peeled out, the door still open. Jason saw guards running after them, crossbows aimed. A loud, metallic *thunk* made the car shake as they bounced down off the curb and took off into the parking lot.

'I think they shot your parents' car,' Van Dyke said.

'We have insurance,' Belle muttered, hitting the gas.

In the passenger seat, Sienna turned to look at the guys, her eyes roving over all of them, and stopping on Jason.

'Everybody OK?' she asked.

Her dark eyes seemed to pour comfort into his soul, and, for the first time in hours, Jason felt safe. He nodded, as Adam gave a faint smile.

'Yeah,' Adam said. 'I can't quite believe it, but I think we're all going to live.'

Twenty

'Fireworks!' Sienna declared four days later.

Jason looked at his girlfriend in her strapless minidress and nodded. 'I'll say.' He grabbed her around the waist and pulled her down to sit on his lap on the couch.

Sienna laughed and smacked him lightly on the arm. 'No, I mean actual fireworks. Zach says they're starting in five minutes. He got a professional firm to do them, so they should be spectacular.'

'Figures.' Jason laughed, gesturing around Zach's incredible house, which was filled with about a hundred people at the moment, all of them laughing, dancing, drinking and generally having the best time of their entire lives. Graduation had been yesterday, and Zach was having the party of the century to celebrate. 'Everything here is spectacular.'

Jason spotted Danielle dancing with her friends Kristy and Billy under a gigantic disco ball that had been hung in the living room. Van Dyke and Maggie were cuddled up on a *chaise longue* in front of the ten-foot-wide fireplace, complete with roaring fire. Adam was interviewing Brad on camera, and Erin and Belle were busy flirting with a couple of senior guys from school.

Graduates, Jason corrected himself. *None of us are seniors anymore. We're high-school graduates.*

It felt strange to even think the words. Jason wondered if he'd ever get used to the feeling. He sighed. Graduation had been bittersweet, so soon after losing his aunt.

'Thinking about Bianca?' Sienna asked, taking his hand.

'You're too good at reading me,' Jason told her with a smile. 'I know I shouldn't be thinking about Aunt Bianca at a party. I should be enjoying myself, happy to be with my friends one last time before we all scatter to our colleges.'

Sienna squeezed his hand. 'It's all right to feel sad, even at a party. Bianca was family and you loved her.'

'She sacrificed herself to save me,' Jason said. 'I still can't believe she did that.'

'She loved you, too,' Sienna told him. 'But, Jason, it's really a gift that she died that way. The transformation sickness was killing her. She was facing a long, slow, agonizing death. At least, this way, she's out of her misery. And she did a noble thing and saved you.' Sienna leant closer and trailed her fingers along his cheek. 'I know I'll be grateful to her forever for that.'

Jason kissed her, letting his lips linger on hers for a moment.

'Fireworks,' Zach announced from the balcony.

'I'll say,' Sienna joked, looking up at Jason.

He grinned, then followed Zach and Sienna out to the balcony.

'Worth filming? I think not,' Adam said, coming up beside Jason and Sienna on the big balcony over-looking the Pacific.

'I didn't think there was anything you found un-worthy of filming,' Jason said, surprised.

'My friend, look at those fireworks. They are spectacular. No camera could capture their true beauty.' Adam sighed dreamily as the first round of fireworks exploded over the water, sending a thousand stars rain-ing down from the sky while their reflections shot up from the depths of the ocean. 'Unless, you know, I had a really big special effects budget,' Adam added.

As the fireworks continued with everyone gasping at each new explosion, Jason felt a hand on his shoulder. Zach drew him away from the crowd.

'Freeman, I wanted you to know there was a DeVere Heights Vampire Council meeting this afternoon,' he said quietly. 'We got the help of the High Council on this one, and we've managed to recover Bianca's body from the Medi-Life building. I know your mother will want to give her a proper funeral.'

'Yes,' Jason said. 'Thank you.'

'Also, we're going to take care of everything,' Zach went on. 'We don't want you or your parents to have to deal with any of it. The official police report will list Bianca's death as a result of experimental drug testing done by Medi-Life. We've had the entire complex searched, and we've exposed some of the facts to the media, enough to make life very uncomfortable for Charles Norton. In fact, HemoCorp has already been disbanded and we've begun a wrongful death lawsuit against Medi-Life.'

'So it's over?' Jason asked. 'We don't have to worry about them anymore?'

'Believe me, we'll litigate Medi-Life into non-existence,' Zach said. 'That's the kind of thing the Vampire High Council does best.'

'I appreciate it,' Jason told him. 'I'm glad I'll have something to tell my mom.'

Zach nodded. 'Christopher's heading back to New York in the morning. He's going to tell the Vampire Council there how Bianca really died – with honor. It will go a long way toward restoring her legacy.'

Jason had got a glimpse of Christopher earlier. He'd come down to the party for a half hour or so before heading back upstairs to bed.

'Christopher's really OK, huh? He looked good when I saw him before.' Jason smiled. 'Only four days of healing – pretty impressive.'

'Well, he *is* a vampire,' Zach said.

Jason raised an eyebrow at the haughty tone in Zach's voice, but then he noticed the smile playing around his friend's mouth.

'How could I forget?' Jason murmured with a grin, as Zach walked away.

When Jason returned to Sienna and Adam, he found his best friend complaining loudly over the booming of the fireworks. 'I'm doomed. Just doomed to be single forever. How can I ever trust a girl again?' he was saying. 'The way Brianna set me up ... She was like Kathleen Turner in *Body Heat*.'

'Wow, really? Your girlfriend asked you to kill her husband for her? That's hardcore!' a girl standing nearby exclaimed.

Adam whirled around to look at her. She was short and cute, with a dark-red pixie haircut and a T-shirt with a picture of Snoopy on it.

'You don't go to DeVere High,' Adam said.

'Nope,' she replied.

'You've actually seen *Body Heat*,' he went on.

'Sure. It's an incredible movie,' she replied.

'Who directed it?' Adam asked.

'What is this, a quiz?' the girl demanded.

'Yes.' Adam tried to look stern, and Jason had to turn away to hide his smile. Sienna pressed her head against his shoulder to muffle her giggles.

'Lawrence Kasdan,' the girl said. 'Duh.'

'I think I love you,' Adam replied. 'Want to go inside and get a drink?'

As they headed for the swanky bar set up in Zach's kitchen, Jason and Sienna burst out laughing. 'So much for Adam being doomed to singlehood,' she said.

The fireworks had ended, and everybody was drifting back to the party. But Jason found himself wanting to stay out here, with the roar of the surf in his ears, and Sienna in his arms.

Maggie and Van Dyke stood nearby, gazing out at the ocean. And Brad, Erin and Belle had perched themselves on the stone wall surrounding the balcony. It seemed that nobody else wanted to leave, either. Jason smiled. Here he was, hanging out with a bunch of vampires.

How was he ever going to go back to having a normal social life after this?

Zach appeared from inside, a bottle of champagne

in his hand. He looked around at the group and raised the bottle. 'A toast to surviving our senior year,' he said. He grinned at Jason. 'With a little help from our friends.'

The vampires all applauded. Zach handed the bottle to Jason, and Jason held it up. 'And one more toast . . . to friendship.'

'That was a great party,' Sienna said a few hours later, resting her head against the back of the VW's passenger seat.

'As always,' Jason agreed.

'I think it was better than usual,' Sienna said. 'Maybe because it was the last one.'

The VW gave a loud groan and sputtered to a stop in the middle of the road. 'What the hell?' Jason said. He turned the key – nothing. The car was totally dead.

Sienna burst out laughing. 'Now you know what it's like! You'll never be able to make fun of my car again!'

'I will too,' Jason muttered.

He tried the car two more times, but it was no good.

'We can just walk home from here. It's less than a mile,' Sienna pointed out.

'I can't leave the car in the middle of the street.'

'We'll push it to the side,' Sienna said. 'I do have super-strength, you know. I could push this thing one-handed.'

231

'You trying to intimidate me?' Jason teased, as they got out and pushed the car to the curb.

'Is it working?' Sienna teased back. 'Some guys like a girl who's a little intimidating.'

Jason put on his best 'hick from Michigan' expression. 'Well, I don't know how you Malibu girls flirt, but us boys from the flyovers like to say what they mean.'

'And what *do* you mean?' Sienna asked, stepping closer to him.

Jason breathed in the incredible scent of her. 'I mean I love you, super-strength and all,' he murmured.

'And I love you.' Sienna brushed her lips against his. 'You know, my parents are off visiting Paige this weekend. The house is empty.'

'An empty house,' Jason mused. 'And no vampire crisis happening to distract us. I wasn't sure that would ever happen.'

'Some things are worth waiting for,' Sienna told him.

And Sienna is one of them, Jason thought, watching her walk on down the dark street, her long hair gleaming in the starlight.

'Are you coming?' she called.

'Oh, yeah,' he said, jogging after her. 'Wherever you're going, Sienna Devereux, I'm going too.'

Seductive and supernatural . . .

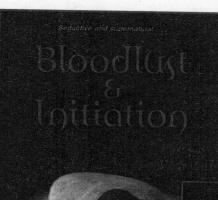

Seductive and supernatural...

Sienna's dark hair was glossier than he'd ever
seen it, her skin was clear and creamy, almost
luminous, and her lips glowed a deep rose red
that he didn't think came from lipstick.
She was stunning, spectacular, impossibly beautiful!
Jason realized he was staring. 'What is it?' he asked.
'Sienna, you can tell me anything.'
And then Sienna smiled, slowly revealing a pair of very
white, very sharp, and very real fangs.

Jason has just moved to Malibu – home to rich kids
and fabulous parties. He's flattered to be included –
and very flattered by the interest of the stunning
Sienna. But Sienna and her friends hide a dark secret
. . . and Jason is risking his life by falling for her.

BLOODLUST and INITIATION: Two passionate,
romantic novels with a sinister, suspenseful twist.

978 1 862 30896 1

Seductive and supernatural . . .

He'd seen her look this gorgeous once before, when she
had first told him that she was a vampire.
She'd let him see her true beauty then and it was just
as mesmerizing now. Her black hair glimmered in the
dim light, her skin was pure golden perfection and,
all of a sudden, Jason felt like the biggest idiot in the
world. Why had he ever let himself think that Sienna
would want to be with him? She was one of them.
He wasn't. End of story. Then she turned. Her dark eyes
met his across the sea of faces, and she smiled.
A sizzle raced through Jason's body and all his doubt
disappeared. It didn't matter what she was or what he
wasn't. They were made for each other.

Jason's life in Malibu is looking up, especially now
Sienna, the most beautiful girl in town, seems to be
interested in him. Jason is learning to live with
Sienna's dark secret - that she and her friends are
vampires - but is she more trouble than she's worth?

*RITUAL and LEGACY: Two passionate, romantic novels
with a sinister, suspenseful twist.*

978 1 862 30897 8

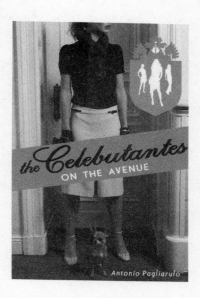

the Celebutantes
ON THE AVENUE

Antonio Pagliarulo

The Hamilton triplets - Madison, Park and Lexington - are accustomed to living in the public eye. Heiresses to a billion-dollar media empire, they have been raised in New York's most elite social circles and, at sixteen, know first hand the demands of being celebutantes. It isn't always about designer labels and lavish parties. There are people to impress, appearances to make, and paparazzi to outrun. Not to mention high school to finish.

But when fashion editor Zahara Bell is found dead in a one-of-a-kind frock from Lex's unreleased clothing line, and then the priceless Avenue diamond goes missing, getting to class is as far from the triplets' minds as their first pair of Manolos. One of the girls is a suspect, and the sisters find themselves in the middle of a scandal that could sink their reputations and their father's companies for good. And the press is ready, willing and able to lend a hand.

The Hamilton sisters need to stick closer together than ever before - the killer is still out there, and if they don't solve the case, their (sometimes) good name could become dirtier than a certain hotel chain. And their threesome could turn into a twosome quicker than you can say Cartier . . .

ISBN: 978 1 862 30462 8

Secrets at St Jude's

New Girl

By Carmen Reid

Ohmigod! Gina's mum has finally flipped and is sending her to Scotland to some crusty old *boarding school* called St Jude's – just because Gina spent all her money on clothes and got a few bad grades! It's so *unfair!*

Now the Californian mall-rat has to swap her sophisticated life of pool parties and well-groomed boys for ... hockey *in the rain*, school dinners and stuffy housemistresses. And what's with her three kooky dorm-buddies ... could they ever be her *friends?* And just how does a St Jude's girl get out to meet the gorgeous guys invited to the school's summer ball?

978 0 552 55706 1